Also By Douglas Bell

For the Love of Cake Series
Love Cake, the sequel to Cake Walk

Threads of Purpose

Douglas Bell Website

Cake Walk - 2nd Edition

A Novel

Douglas Bell

Bumbershoot Press

Praise for the Second Edition of Cake Walk (2026)

This book is a must read not only for its relevancy but also from the unique perspective from which it is written. A true and realistic voice of an ally for the trans community. This book takes you on a rollercoaster ride that I would sign up for again and again! – *Quote from Fresh New Voice*

Praise for the First Edition of Cake Walk (2022)

Our company book club read this in honor of Pride Month and I am so glad that chose this book! The story is wonderful, touching and eye-opening. There are so many interesting nuances in this book and the author does an excellent job of drawing you in right from the start. I quickly became invested in the characters and really loved how things came together in the end. And while the book shines a light on a lot of important and current challenges/issues people deal with from racism to spirituality, it is also simply a wonderful story about a man who is on a journey to find happiness and his authentic self. – *Amazon Reviewer*

Cakewalk is a riveting read that explores the nuances of the human experience and the many ways we all possess blindspots to the trauma we inflict on each other. I can't sing the praises of this book enough. – **Amazon Reviewer**

This book gave me a whole new perspective on the struggles that both black people and LGBTQ+ people face on the daily; to see it laid out so bare is heart wrenching to read. It takes both of those hardships and meshes them nigh perfectly into the main character, turning it into a compelling and at some points tense narrative. I also like the end notes with how the book got its name, to the authors Buddhist perspective about putting aside any prejudice, labels or beliefs and accepting yourself just as you are. 10/10, would recommend to others. – *Amazon Reviewer*

Bell describes a very nuanced struggle that as a cis man don't understand. The growth of a queer relationship, between two people and also their friends and family. Bell shows empathy in both the highs and lows as Bryan and Nadia navigate life together. I could tell that Bell did his research in the community and I learned helpful things that also make me more aware and can be a better ally in the community. – **Goodreads Reviewer**

I loved Nadia for her "I don't take crap" mindset and for sticking up for herself. I endeavour to be as strong and brave within my life journey.
A great story about choices, and the harsh reality of hiding who you are, and the repercussions of these choices. I thoroughly enjoyed this. – *Goodreads Reviewer*

I am grateful to BookSirens and Bumbershoot Press for giving me an advanced reader's copy of the new fiction book, Cakewalk. I also want to thank its author Douglas Bell for writing this book about these difficult subjects in society today: racism, sexism, homophobia, and LGBTQIA+ issues. – *Goodreads Reviewer*

Bumbershoot
Press

Dedicated to
the men who love trans women and wonder if the world will still love them
back—
it will.
But only when you stop hiding.
This is your invitation to let go of shame,
to honor her with your truth,
and to trust that becoming fully yourself
is the most radical act of love there is.

Thank you for reading *Cake Walk.*

To my knowledge, *Cake Walk* remains the only novel on the market told from the perspective of a trans-amorous man. That matters. Because men like Bryan often live in silence—carrying love in one hand and fear in the other, without community or language to hold their truth. That invisibility becomes a quiet kind of harm.

And I understand that harm. I know what it's like to feel unseen. If that's you too—I see you. Because I am you.

The original version of *Cake Walk* was published in 2022. At the time, I set out to tell Nadia's story through Bryan's eyes—to be a good ally to the trans community, especially to trans women, because of an emotional connection I carry to someone like Nadia. But the deeper truth is this: *Bryan's story is my story.*

I want to sincerely apologize for missing the mark in that original version. I made Bryan cold, defensive—even mean. I thought that stark contrast would emphasize his transformation. But in hindsight, I realize that made it hard for readers to connect with him—let alone root for him. That was my mistake, and I own it.

This revised edition gave me the opportunity to make it right. I worked hard to bring more empathy and emotional truth to Bryan. In this version, his love for his son Lance is undeniable. He prioritizes honesty with the people in his life. And perhaps most importantly, he begins to show himself the same patience he's learning to offer others. I believe this makes him more relatable—and more deserving of the reader's hope—**on his journey to developing self-acceptance.**

Through deep reflection and years of spiritual practice—including meditation—I've come to understand how shame distorts us, how silence isolates us, and how growth begins in the stillness when we finally allow ourselves to feel.

In rewriting *Cake Walk*, I didn't aim to perfect Bryan—I wanted to humanize him. I wanted his evolution to feel real, flawed, and ultimately, aspirational.

One of the most important realizations I've had is this: trans-amorous men like Bryan must be embraced *within* the LGBTQIA+ community—not simply tolerated as "allies," but welcomed as part of the community itself. That's why a particular plot point in this novel had to happen. It was necessary to push Bryan off the sidelines and into the fight—for himself, for love, and for all those whose identities are misunderstood, erased, or feared. That moment had to happen. Because silence is no longer an option.

If this is your first time reading my work, I invite you to continue with *Love Cake*—a novel about community, chosen family, and the radical power of living in truth. And if you're looking for a story that inspires personal transformation, stay tuned for *Threads of Purpose*, my upcoming novel about creativity, courage, and healing.

Thank you for giving this book a chance—and for giving all the Bryans in the world the space to be seen, understood, and loved.

With gratitude,

Douglas Bell

www.douglasbellbooks.com

FB / IG / YouTube: **@douglasbellauthor**

Twitter: **@douglasbellblog**

CAKEWALK

by

Douglas Bell

2nd Edition

Content Warnings:

Cake Walk contains material that might prove to be explicit sexual content and contains potentially triggering subject matter including racism, homophobia, transphobia, and hate speech.

1

Bryan arrived well before his mother. He opened the door of the sun-splashed restaurant and dipped his head beneath a fern that was growing over the doorway. Once inside, he passed a hand over his hair and straightened the already-perfect knot of his peacock-blue tie, his elbow grazing his mama's gift, which was hidden in his sports jacket outer pocket. He slipped his phone from a trouser pocket, turning it off without even glancing at his messages. No distractions, no incriminating texts. He simply wanted to be his mama's golden boy for a few hours—although he was in the latter half of his forties and Black. Perhaps topaz or brass? These days, fool's gold seemed more apt.

For years, he had taken his mama out every two weeks for lunch, but it had been many months since they had gone on a special date, just the two of them. He'd told his mama that he had too many spinning plates to keep aloft with finishing a project at work and spending time with his kids, but the truth was, his new lover, Nadia, was keeping him occupied. Before his absence registered as too suspicious, he sent his mama flowers with the invitation for today. Normally, he would love to gush to his mother about a new girlfriend, but Nadia was too new, and too different from the few girls he'd introduced his mama to. For a moment, Bryan tried to imagine what it would be like to invite Nadia to lunch with his mama. Would she pass as a woman? And if she did, would his mama still have a problem with her being white? Bryan had learned to hide his true desires because her punishment for disobedience was swift and lacked judgment. He remembered being a teenager and getting whipped with a belt for seemingly frivolous trespasses, such as the way he ate his food. An image of her disapproving face flashed into his mind, and for a moment, he saw a younger version of himself finishing his mashed potatoes before having touched his chicken or green beans. He winced in pain at the memory. Looking back, he wondered how she determined what was meant to be punished and what wasn't. This exact unpredictability confirmed his decision to hold off on telling his mother the truth.

A dish clattered, startling Bryan and reminding him why he was there. Bryan glanced around the empty hostess booth, his eyes taking in the scene. He had picked this restaurant based on newspaper reviews gushing over the food and decor. His mama would be delighted by the greenhouse windows and copious plants dangling from reclaimed box beams and erupting from exposed brick walls, its whimsy cut with velvet couches in vibrant hues and faux-animal-skin rugs. The menu was French-Tex barbeque with cumin potatoes au gratin; collards drizzled with genuine olive oil and brie queso. He hoped it would all be enough to make up for his absence. The last thing he needed was a guilt trip with his collard greens.

He was also looking forward to this meal as a pre-celebration of sorts. Before he'd logged off his work computer for the day, he saw the job posting for the Vice President of Polymers and Specialty Chemicals go live. He had been waiting for the position to open up for months, since his co-worker Jerry alluded to the fact that the current VP would be stepping down soon. Getting this promotion would mean finally being recognized for his hard work. It would also mean a significant pay increase. The smell of garlic and cheese wafting through the air combined with the image of a fat paycheck was making Bryan begin to salivate. While he did well for himself in his current position, the added financial security of this promotion would allow him to comfortably send his two kids to college and handle any unexpected setbacks. He also knew it would make his mother proud. She was always so worried about Bryan and his sister fitting in. She had convinced Bryan that the cost of expressing his individuality was too high. According to her, Black people needed the approval of the white male community if they wanted to be successful in corporate America. So Bryan learned to fit in. If he got this job, he'd be the highest-ranking Black person in his industry.

Until it was decided, he needed to keep his head down. Several people had hinted that he was being considered as a strong diversity candidate, which meant being watched extra carefully. No mistakes of any kind. His unmarried state already put him at a disadvantage. He didn't want to imagine what would happen if any of the senior executives found out about Nadia. Being single is probably a better look than dating a white transwoman, he thought.

Before he could let his thoughts about Nadia spiral out of control, his mama bustled through the doorway in the chic St. John separates that Bryan had bought her the previous Christmas, her dark, straightened hair twisted into its usual neat chignon. Her attention riveted on Bryan as soon as she spotted him; she didn't duck, and the fern grazed her head. "Oh!" she said, momentarily goosed before retaining her composure. She pulled the offending leaf through her loose fist. "Ah, Asplenium nidus." She glanced at Bryan, both officious and warm. "Bird's-nest fern. And next to it is a slightly shriveled Asplenium scolopendrium. Hart's tongue, my favorite."

Bryan grinned and enfolded his mama in a hug. She was bright as ever, though she felt noticeably frailer in his arms today. "Smarty-pants."

"I can't help knowing what I know," she shot back, visibly pleased by his compliment. "But this jungle is reminding me how hungry I am." She craned her head towards the empty hostess stand. "Where is—"

Just then, a person wearing a slim-cut blazer and cigarette pants swooped into the entryway. "Hicks, party of two?" breathily emerged from subtly glossed lips. The rest of the face was made up so that not a hint of stubble was visible, the chestnut-brown bob lacquered to a high shine.

Bryan's heart jumped into his throat, and he cast a glance at his mama's raised eyebrows. Oh boy, he thought, Mama, don't say anything rude. He wanted to both swear and hit his head against the wall. Is this how she'd look at Nadia, he wondered. Why hadn't he checked out the place first before bringing his mama here? He knew how badly she reacted to anyone she perceived as being what she called "homosexual." He wasn't entirely sure why she was homophobic, but he was pretty sure it had something to do with her believing that everyone needed to conform to certain societal expectations. He didn't have the heart to tell his mother that the "proper society" she was raised in during the 1940s was not considered "proper" anymore.

Mama took a faltering step back just as Bryan took one forward. "Yes, that's us."

The young person looked Bryan up and down before addressing his mama. "Aren't you a lucky duck, having lunch with this handsome man," the host drawled, sliding two menus off the stack before turning on black patent platform heels and swishing into the main room.

Mama gripped Bryan's arm. "Is that a man wearing lip gloss or something else entirely?" she hissed. Bryan felt his heartbeat still in his throat and tried to swallow. All Bryan did was raise his brows as if he were shocked in an attempt to mask his panic. Following behind the host, Bryan couldn't help but notice that the blazer emphasized the nicely tailored trousers, showcasing her slim, boyish figure. Yes, focus on fashion, Bryan thought. You just need to get through this meal.

Bryan raised his gaze, looking straight ahead. Unless his mama could literally see through him, she didn't have a clue where he was looking, but her sixth sense was keen. She had always warned him that mothers always know the inner workings of their children.

They arrived at a table perfectly situated to appreciate the sunshine without being blinded or overheated by it. The host pulled out a chair for his mama, batting his mascaraed eyelashes at Bryan. "Your extremely fortunate server, Elana, will be with you in a moment." Mama gave Bryan a withering stare. She brushed the man's manicured hands off her chair as if they were flies. Frowning, she jerked her chair closer to the table herself. Out of the corner of his eye, Bryan saw the host's chest slump before saying in a voice bright with propriety, "Enjoy your meal. Remember to leave room for our famous Black Forest!"

Bryan smiled at the hostess to counter his mama's bad manners. Mama opened her napkin with a flick of her wrist and spread it over her lap disgruntledly, but that action seemed to help her to shuck off her sourness. Just enjoy lunch, he thought, knowing he did not have the spine to call her out on her rudeness. Instead of wasting his breath, he decided to leave a big tip to show he was not like his mother. "Tell me about the children," she said, perusing the menu with interest.

Bryan was about to launch into the most flattering anecdotes about his two kids, but before he spoke a word, his mother fixed him with a gimlet-eyed stare. "Speaking of children. You know, being a parent takes a lot of courage."

"That's true, Mama," Bryan said, happy to be agreeable.

"For instance," Mama said, still fiddling with her napkin. "Did I tell you about the Hancocks next door? It turns out their son, who always seemed so nice, but quiet—you know, for a teenager. Polite." Her gaze had been flitting around the room, but now landed softly on him. "Well, now, he told his parents he's—" she lowered her voice conspiratorially— "homosexual."

"And?" Bryan tried not to sound terse. His heart rate beat faster. His jaw tightened; he hated when she used that word.

"Oh, his parents kicked him out." Mama's eyes once again roved over the restaurant. "I'm sure they'll invite him back once he realizes the error of his ways." Her brow furrowed. "Parents must sometimes draw lines—hard lines, you know. And . . . let the chips fall where they may. I don't blame them one bit. Their son doing those things puts a target on their backs too."

Bryan couldn't help shuddering. He felt sweat beginning to collect on his palms and wiped it on his pants. "Mama, that is terrible," he said, unable to talk about the kids. Bryan's mind began racing. Between the comments about the hosts and the comment about the Hancock's son, his mama seemed awfully focused on the gayness today. Had she seen him and Nadia somewhere? He had been so careful to only see Nadia at her apartment, but had they slipped up and run an errand together? Bryan tried to subtly focus on his breathing to calm himself down. She was too busy looking at the menu to realize that Bryan was doing breathing exercises at the table. He began to feel his heart rate slow down a bit and reminded himself that Mama's snobbery was rooted in her desperation to keep her Black son safe, and the more Bryan was "like everyone else, but better," the less afraid she had to be. Any time he had wanted to pierce his ear or temporarily color his hair, say, bright blue for a Halloween costume, she repeated the same phrase: "Only white people can do those things without any consequences." He'd heard his mama say this so often it was tangled in his DNA.

A Latina in a neat navy dress appeared and introduced herself as Elana. Bryan almost breathed an audible sigh of relief that she was what his mother needed to feel comfortable. Bryan hated that she had so little room for different people. He ordered for himself and his mama, more food than they'd be able to eat in one sitting but wanting to spoil his mama with choices. Mama excused herself to use the restroom, and Bryan slid the box from his overcoat pocket and placed it on the table in front of his mama's place setting.

Missing Nadia, he turned his phone back on and checked it to see if she'd texted. Even a heart emoji would ease the soreness in his own heart after hearing his mama's harsh words about her neighbors.

As the phone's glowing screen flashed on, his mama reappeared and sat down. Bryan quickly typed his passcode and dropped the phone in his lap face-up.

"Oh!" Mama exclaimed with genuine pleasure, plucking the rectangular box with her perfectly manicured fingers. "Is this package for little ol' me?"

"Yes." Bryan beamed his sweetest smile at his mother. "I'm sorry for having been a bit MIA lately. I've missed you, Mama, and I love you."

"This is so sweet." Mama's face looked like a lighted Christmas tree. "Oh, my handsome son." She went to work on the satin ribbon and slid a pearly fingernail under the tape so as not to rip the exquisitely flowered wrapping paper.

Bryan glanced down at the phone in his lap. There was a long text from Nadia: *I found the gift. You're so sweet. I added a little something to it that we can play with later. I wrapped it back perfectly so I can act surprised.* She ended the text with a deep red heart and smiling devil emojis.

Bryan blinked, not comprehending. The sun reached higher in the sky, bleaching the opposite wall of clear glass panels milky white, as if light had been tossed from a bucket and stuck to the wall.

Mama opened the lid of the box. Inside was the expensive scarf. Bryan gasped, and quickly drank water to prevent himself from saying anything incriminating. To Bryan's horror, instead of lying flat in a neat rectangle, the patterned silk was looped in a faux-gold ring with textured notches around the inner rim. A cock ring.

Bryan lost his breath, his mind scrambling. In his mind's eye, a battering ram blasted through the soldered glass panels, now blanched and opaque, shattering them. Everything he knew was ruined. He would be thrown through the spiky hole in the wall, glittering splinters under his skin, his bloody hands emoji-heart red.

Mama turned the ring over, inspecting it. "I have heard of these . . . holders," she said, slightly more faintly than normal. "But they're for those who don't know how to tie a scarf like a Frenchwoman." She unknotted the scarf and tugged it out of the ring, which thankfully hadn't come with a tag or any marking to indicate its intended purpose, and Bryan was grateful for this small favor from the universe. He couldn't believe that Nadia had thought that was for her and added the cock ring to the box. He would have to tell her later how she had unintentionally gifted his mother a cock ring. She would probably joke, "This is why you need to let me take her out to dinner first." He wasn't sure when, if ever, Nadia and his mama would be in the same room long enough to share a meal.

Mama wound the silky fabric around her neck and knotted it expertly. "See, perfect." She gingerly picked up the ring and placed it back in the box as if it were dried excrement. "Thank you, son."

Bryan gathered his breath and forced a placid smile on his face. "You're welcome, Mama. It's beautiful on you. Wear it in good health."

"I plan to, thank you," she said. The host sashayed by, seating another group of diners. Mama's eyes narrowed. "I must say," she said in a tone that was only categorized as merry-go-round cheerful. "The food promises to be delicious, and the ambiance is certainly wonderful. However, I am never setting foot in this restaurant again. And I'll tell my friends not to patronize this place either."

Before Bryan could intercede and gently dampen her dramatics, his mama waved her hands to indicate their lush surroundings. "Imagine, taking all this care with the decor and then hiring . . . that." Her eye contact was severe and unwavering. "I'd toss Miss Such and Such out of my house faster than he-she could fasten those ridiculous shoes." She dabbed her lips with her napkin and fixed Bryan with a radiant smile. "Now, tell me everything about you."

2

They had met at an upscale adult bookstore. After his divorce was finalized in 1992, Bryan found himself completely lost. He had done everything his Mama had told him to do: get married, have kids, work at a good job that allowed for prestige and a good salary. He still had the job, but with the word divorce on his record and only having partial custody of his kids, a black void began to envelop him. Unsure of what he even wanted out of love, he found himself perusing magazines and watching videos in adult bookstores to assuage his baser needs. Initially, he began with watching men have sex with women.

One day, when he was in the store, he saw a video cover featuring an attractive, tall, thin white woman. He browsed until his eyes met the sign at the center of the shelf that said, "Gay". He sulked into the back of the store, his eyes scanning for who could be watching him. She was a cross-dresser. *I'm not gay*, Bryan had thought, *what am I doing here?* He left the store empty handed that day and took a shower upon getting home.

As the internet's expanse of porn began to grow in the mid-1990s, he found himself exploring realms, privately, he had never considered before. He was suddenly clicking on crossdressing porn and found himself more sexually satisfied than he had been in his marriage. Eventually, he got tired of watching the same internet videos over and over again. His boredom eventually outweighed his curiosity, and he went to a different bookstore that was an hour away from where he lived and worked so as not to risk anyone recognizing him.

This time, he told himself, *It's only gay if I'm acting on it.* He sidled in, eyes down, to the alternative section hidden behind a red curtain that reminded him of his unstable days as a magician. That store quickly became his go-to place. He felt safe there.

By the time the mid-2000s rolled around, he was beginning to find more variety in the tapes he rented. With the new millennium approaching, Bryan's desires for watching cross-dressing porn had transformed into a new interest: transwomen. His attraction to transwomen felt much deeper than a fetish; he saw something different in them, but he did not know how to express what he did not understand.

One evening in April of 2015, he walked in, and there was a new woman at the till. She was white, with long hair, the color of honey. He stared at her. "Let me know if you need help finding anything," she said. Bryan flipped through the videos and snuck glances at her. Her face was beautiful. It wasn't until she stood to reach a harness on a high shelf that she revealed her willowy height — six-foot-four to his six-two—that he knew the answer to his unspoken curiosity. He felt she might be trans. *Why do I want to talk to her so badly?* Bryan contemplated asking for help just so he could talk to her more, but decided against it. *I can talk to her at the register,* he thought.

Nervously, he chose a video featuring a tall blond trans woman pictured from behind, wearing lace panties and a bra, and shyly brought it up to the front. *What the hell am I doing? Why am I feeling butterflies for someone I've never met?* Bryan handed off the tape, wiping off some moisture on the edge closest to him with his sleeve. Bryan discreetly wiped his hands on his pants, hoping the woman didn't notice any lingering moisture on the tape. The woman at the till looked for several seconds at the video box cover before deliberately meeting Bryan's eyes. Bryan's stomach was still fluttering as he met her intoxicating light green eyes that seemed both sly and sweet. "That's a good one. You'll enjoy it," she said, putting out her hand. It was slender and very soft-looking, graceful in its movement. "I'm Nadia," she said and handed him her card. He memorized her number, fantasized about her that night, but didn't dare call. He went back the next night, and they flirted more openly. On his third visit, he pretended to be unable to find the sequel to a tape he had at home. They spent 10-15 minutes talking about the franchise, and contemplating how on earth they made it look like they were actually a plane in the films. On his fourth visit, Bryan took a risk; he brought Nadia a bouquet of long-stemmed red roses. Nadia gushed as she smelled the roses.

"I need to tell you that I'm trans," Nadia said confidently.

"Oh, okay...Thanks for telling me," Bryan responded happily. *Thank you*, he thought. A tension had been released, giving them the freedom to talk about their interests, favorite movies, and TV shows that had nothing to do with porn. He drove home, smiling from ear to ear, knowing he had a friendship with a real transwoman.

It wasn't until his fifth visit that Nadia took the bull by the horns. "My shift is over in ten minutes," she said, fluttering her lashes. "Why don't you take me out for something to eat?" Grateful for her forwardness, he did. He knew it probably would have taken him another five flirty conversations to get up the courage to do anything about his attraction to her.

The first time they had sex was surprisingly natural and utterly astounding — both of these feelings worried him deep inside. By sleeping with her, he unknowingly inserted himself into the LGBTQIA alphabet. *What letter was he?* He didn't see himself anywhere in that lexicon. What he hadn't counted on was that after sex with Nadia, he'd dropped himself forever after into a void between two worlds, the known and her. He had played this in his mind so he wouldn't be scared if the opportunity to date a transwoman presented itself.

3

A few days later, Bryan was anxiously tapping his steering wheel, scanning the crowded parking lot like a sentinel as his mind raced back and forth about lunch with his mama. He hoped the servers and staff who waited on them felt the tip made up for her disrespect. As usual, his ex-wife was late. Bryan had been living west of downtown since their divorce ten years ago. Still, Lawanda insisted on this particular gas station, a truck stop all the way on the east side, as the pick-up/drop-off location for their children. Armies of eighteen-wheelers screeched and roared. This was Texas, a driving state. Cars pulled in and discharged all kinds of people stretching after many hours behind the wheel, their dogs bounding toward the skinny strip of grass.

Pungent wafts of diesel seeped through the vents, which was blasting air conditioning. The ugly castles of oil refineries and chemical plants pumped clouds of muck into the sky. This reality was partly his fault, Bryan knew. As an engineer for Big Oil, his work revolved around clean numbers and graphs, but he was part of the machine that made those pestilential clouds.

His children were both quiet. Lance, a ninth grader and a carbon copy of his mother, was sitting in the backseat engrossed in *The Great Gatsby*, his backpack clamped under his arm. In the passenger seat, Lindsey peered at her phone. Already seventeen, she had been born with Bryan's smile, though lately, that expression was a rare sighting. In a black ball cap labeled Beacon Security, an older white man paced back and forth along a curb, one hand resting on his holstered gun. He stared at Bryan, slowly switching a toothpick from one side of his mouth to the other. Sitting in an unmoving car while Black was considered loitering. Bryan drove a recent model Jaguar. This car made him simultaneously safer, insulated by status, and more vulnerable, since white people were often suspicious of seeing a Black man behind the wheel of a luxury car.

Bryan suppressed a yawn. The vacation-like stress of constant togetherness, the pressure to do as much as possible together, meant he was often exhausted after the weekends with his children. Normal visitation weekends were filled with some homework, mixed with having fun with activities that both Lindsey and Lance might enjoy. Occasionally, he would perform sleight of hand magic tricks to entertain them; there was a time he had tried to make it as a magician for a couple of years during college.

Bryan's phone dinged. Lance craned forward, wrapping his arm around his father's neck from the backseat. "Is that Mama?"

Bryan glanced at the screen.

Nadia had texted. *Hi sexy*.

"Someone from work," Bryan said, dropping the phone face down in his lap, making sure Lance did not see the name. He believed his kids should not be aware of intimate partners until the relationship was serious. He patted Lance's arm hanging around his neck. Lance's hugs were always welcomed.

"Oh," his son said.

Lance released the hug, and Bryan's mind traveled back to Nadia as they waited. He'd forgiven her for what she'd done with the scarf he'd bought for his mama. After all, he purchased presents like that for Nadia to be creative and spontaneous. He had hidden the box clumsily, right in his jacket pocket around their five-month anniversary. In fact, he bought another similar scarf, added the notched ring, wrapped the box, and presented it to Nadia. If she had noticed it was a slightly different pattern, she hadn't said anything.

He couldn't believe they'd been dating long enough to regularly exchange gifts. He thought back to the first time they met and suddenly felt warm from shame mixed with arousal. He cautiously picked up his phone and tapped out: *I wish I was with you already*. He sent it and erased the entire chain, as he did after every five or so of his and Nadia's texts.

"You said you're texting someone from work?" his daughter asked, raising an eyebrow.

"Ooh, is it Uncle Jerry?" Lance asked eagerly.

"We haven't seen him in a while," Lindsey commented.

Before Bryan could respond, a call from his mama interrupted them. He hit Accept. "Hello, my handsome son," she trilled.

Bryan died inside a little bit every time he thought of what his mama's re-action would be if she knew of his proclivities. His mama was convinced—and told him often, to the point of irritation—there are only so many seats at the table of your life and if someone who is not good for you is sitting there then you keep yourself from meeting the right person. In his mother's eyes, Lawanda left because the universe was making room for a better partner. The partner who would make Bryan a better version of himself. That was how his mama soothed his pain after the divorce. If Nadia was sent to fill the empty seat at the table, then his mama was going to have to make extra space at the table for her. Bryan always colored inside the lines and never deviated from what people expected from him. After their lunch the week before, he was even more nervous about her ever finding out about Nadia. He forced a smile into his voice. "Hey, Mama."

"Are you and the children coming over this evening?"

"Next week. I'm waiting on Lawanda right now."

"Hmph," she replied.

He could imagine his mama rolling her eyes. There was no love lost between the two women, which was a moot point these days, but it had been a big issue throughout the short marriage. "Hug Lance and Lindsey for me. I love them so much. I want more grand-babies, but that requires you finding—"

"I will," Bryan answered dutifully. He knew his mama wanted him to find a wife because she needed to show the world she was a good mother. She hadn't thought Lawanda was good enough for him, though at least she was Black. His mama hung by his side when Lawanda was caught cheating, so he could at least give her credit for that.

A black Chevy Impala with dark-tinted windows, low-profile tires, and expensive rims stopped a few feet away, perpendicular to Bryan's car, blocking his exit if he needed one. Out popped Lawanda from the passenger side in distressed jeans and knee-high boots. The driver's-side window lowered. The face was unfamiliar, and the man's threatening scowl, heavily tattooed shoulder, and a cigarette dangling from his lips told a story much different than Bryan's. He felt an odd combination of pride, foolishness, and guilt sitting in his newish Jag.

Bryan got out of his car and carefully crossed his elbows on the dark blue top of the Jag. He tried to keep his tone light and conciliatory. "Hi, Lawanda. Who's your new friend? The kids haven't met him and—"

He was expecting his ex-wife to scowl, but when she turned her face to him, it sparkled. It was a false shine, as if a pail of glitter had been poured over her head. "How do you know he's new? Just because he's young and fresh . . . unlike your tired old ass?"

Bryan almost gulped. He was incredibly vain about his backside.

"Mama, can we go get my hair done?" Lindsey asked, wrapping her earbuds around her phone and stepping out of the Jag.

Lawanda jerked the back door of the black car open. "No."

"Why not? I need to get my braids redone."

"Your father had an entire weekend, plenty of time to take you." She stretched her lips into an aspartame smile and directed it toward Bryan. "But he was busy doing whatever he does with y'all before he brings you back to me, nappy and half-starved."

"You've got to be kidding me!" Bryan sputtered.

Lindsey sucked in her cheeks, and he regretted not keeping his mouth shut. "Lindsey, I love you," he said.

Lindsey hugged Bryan loosely, while Lance held him tightly. "I will call you later in the week," Bryan said.

"Promise," Lance replied

"You know it," Bryan said. As Lance exited the car, Bryan noticed something rectangular and colorful sticking out of a partially zipped pocket of his back-pack. *Is that a make up palette?* he questioned. *Maybe he grabbed Lindsey's bag by accident?*

As Lindsey ducked into Lawanda's back seat, Lawanda patted the top of her daughter's head. "Mama will get your braids redone later this week."

"Where are we going, Mama?" Lance asked shakily as he, too, lowered himself into the back seat.

"I'm dropping you off at Big Momma's," Lawanda said to Bryan's immense relief. If his ex-mother-in-law was in charge, Bryan felt better about letting his children go.

With one hand on the front passenger door, Lawanda pivoted to face Bryan. "You really should find a girlfriend. Everybody else has moved on," she said. With that, she popped back in the car and slammed the door.

Whatever, Bryan thought. *You've got a new man every month,* he wanted to respond.

The car screeched out of the parking lot. Bryan's phone dinged—a text from Nadia: *Have you left yet?* Bryan collapsed in the driver's seat. He texted back: *On my way. Can't wait.*

***

Two hours later than planned, Bryan turned onto the street that led to Nadia's neighborhood. As his Jag glided up the road, the lingua franca changed from English with some Spanish to primarily Spanish. Her apartment complex was technically gated, but the gate was always broken. An exact description of their city, he thought, cruising through the entrance, the corrugated metal falling off its hinge and gaping wide enough for anything smaller than an eighteen-wheeler to maneuver through. Luckily, it was safe. The first time he had come over, Nadia had told him how lucky she felt living where she did. "My neighbors' hearts are as unlatched as the gate," she had said earnestly, which had charmed him.

Every time Bryan turned onto Nadia's street, he tried to imagine how his mother would respond if she ever found out. He could practically see her face contort in disgust, her upper lip furling the way it did whenever the words, "I'm not angry, just disappointed," used to come out of her mouth when he was a child. He shook his head as if he could shake out the image. *Being her son has to count for something, doesn't it?* Bryan thought

As much as he wanted his mother to approve of both Nadia and his life in general, Bryan wasn't ready to tell anyone in his life about Nadia yet. He carefully avoided the possibility of anyone he knew noticing them by only spending time at Nadia's house. Even if he attempted to discreetly bring her to his place, he was put off by the constant presence of a doorman, not to mention twenty-five floors of nosy neighbors. For a blissful few months, she abided by his silently telegraphed preference. Lately, however, she had expressed displeasure about their dates being limited to sitting at her home, her tone at first halting, progressing to wistful, and lately edged with the beginnings of impatience. His chest tighten thinking about her displeasure.

After counting the hours until he could see her, Bryan finally arrived at Nadia's landing, where a calico kitten rubbed against his leg. Nadia opened her door and reached around him to scoop up the cat. Cuddling him to her chest, she crooned, "Oh, hello, Brad Kitt, I've missed you."

Bryan turned his lips up. "Brad Kitt? Seriously?"

"Look how handsome he is. And he's not late, like some other male mammals I know."

He enjoyed the way she ribbed him. After being married to someone who had started out witty but soon defaulted to passive aggression, or just plain aggression, Bryan was relieved to be with a woman who expressed her displeasure but didn't blame him for things that weren't his fault.

The cat jumped down, and Nadia waved to someone in the building next door. *"¡Hola! ¿Cómo está usted?"* Bryan followed her gaze to an older woman in a red dress who called out cheerily. *"Estoy muy bien."*

Nadia's apartment was clean but not tidy. Unpaired shoes littered the yellow carpet and worn clothes had been flung over the couch. Bryan understood that after a long workday, she wanted to get comfortable as quickly as possible. Her apartment was small; the kitchen and living area were basically one room. If it was even a little messy, it resembled the carnage of a Category 5 hurricane.

He'd once complained, mildly, about the state of her living space, and she'd put a finger to his lips. "Didn't you read *Harry Potter*? Don't say evil things aloud," and he'd been so delighted by the reference he didn't ask if she meant "hurricane" or "messy apartment."

He went in for a kiss, but after a quick peck, she wriggled out of his arms and poured him a glass of water. "Your ex-wife strikes again."

Bryan downed the cool liquid in one gulp. It did little to douse the taste of exhaustion in the back of his throat. "What do you want me to do? Just leave the kids at the gas station?" Nadia flinched, and Bryan softened his tone. "I'm sorry, I didn't mean to snap at you like that. I hate that you were waiting on me," he said.

"I'm not mad at you. And, no, I don't want you to leave your children at a gas station." Nadia kissed him more deeply this time. "Come sit down. I cooked. It got cold, so I zapped it."

Nadia had set up a card table in the corner of the small kitchen with four non-matching chairs. Bryan sat down in the least creaky one. "Thank you. Is this meat loaf?" He smiled, grateful that she always took the time to make him a nice meal.

"Yes, meat loaf with a bourbon glaze. I adapted my mama's recipe using the bourbon that was left from when the girls came over." She giggled.

"Mmm, comfort food."

"Yeah. I'm thirty, and I feel like I'm twelve again whenever I cook like my mother. We bonded big-time over our love of mixing and stirring." She snapped a photo with her phone and a second. "One for Insta, one for Mama."

There were a few minutes of silence between them as he dug into the meal, and she washed some dishes. The meat loaf tasted more special than he'd assumed.

Nadia walked toward the living area, flicking on more lights, illuminating the layer of cooking magazines littering the living room table. The autumn days were darkening earlier.

Nadia pummeled a couch cushion to plump it. "What was she like when you met? I've never asked before."

"Who? Lawanda?"

"You have another ex-wife?" She yanked the chain of a side-table lamp. Besides two narrow windows covered with translucent fabric, flanking the front door, the square window in the kitchen provided the only natural light.

As much as Bryan liked being here, there were times when he longed for his expansive high-rise with floor-to-ceiling windows and skylights, his full bookshelves, copiously indexed by subject.

She sat down next to him. "You've never really talked about what drew you to her."

Bryan swallowed and patted his mouth with a napkin. "She was fun. Funny, too. I had a new job, a new car. More money than any of my friends from my neighborhood. But I was still a skinny, awkward kid who didn't know how to talk to girls."

Nadia squeezed his bicep. "You're not skinny anymore."

"Lawanda was the first girl to want me in a long time. You have to realize that I did not have a girlfriend during the last four years of college. I just rushed in, you know, with the obvious results." Bryan almost expressed how relieved he was that Nadia could never get pregnant, but he didn't want Nadia to think that was the basis of his attraction to her. It was a big part of it for sure. Now that he was in his forties, if he had more kids and a relationship ended, then he would be paying child support into his late sixties. "Marriage seemed the right thing to do. It all happened so fast. I mean, we met pretty soon after I got my engineering degree. I partied a little bit after graduation. I was in my mid-twenties, but green as grass."

"Huh," Nadia said, stroking his arm. "I like you better the color of dark chocolate." She kissed him, but before their kiss unfolded, she jumped up. "Speaking of, close your eyes."

Bryan heard her take something out of the fridge. He opened his eyes and beheld a round chocolate cake, the frosting so shiny he could see his reflection. "Oh, baby, that looks incredible."

Nadia focused her phone above the plate. "Okay, sit back. Place your fork behind the dessert, yes . . . better, now move your hand out of the way."

Finally, he was allowed to take a bite. "Mmm. Perfectly balanced between sweet and bitter. So smooth." He scooped up another forkful. "Is there cognac in this? Are you trying to get me drunk so you can have your way with me?"

She smiled as she met his eyes, which made his stomach flip over, full as it was. "Oh, yes."

Rinsing the dessert dishes, Bryan gazed mindlessly out her kitchen window, overlooking a dumpster overflowing with trash. Nothing like the view of the city skyline from his high-rise, he thought.

"Hey, I forgot to tell you," Bryan said over his shoulder. "I'm meeting my old college friend, Reggie, for a drink tomorrow night." Bryan had dodged meeting up with his old friend since he'd started dating Nadia. By now, he was out of excuses. Plus, he missed Reggie.

Nadia was covering the cake with foil. "I'd like to meet Reggie," she said, placing the cake in the fridge. "Oh, and I really want us to go to this fun place, Club High Five, with my friends too."

Bryan wiped his wet hands on a dish towel. "When the time is right, I promise I will introduce you to my kids, my friends, and my Mama," he said, sidestepping her bid about the dance club. In a perfect world, Bryan preferred their relationship to evolve more publicly, but he couldn't imagine when that would feel safe or natural. For now, he craned his neck, and Nadia bent her head down. Meeting halfway, they kissed. When he pulled away, Nadia's face was contorted with agony.

"Honey! What's wrong?"

She steadied herself on the table. "Ouch."

Tripping over a shoe, Bryan steered Nadia toward the living area, where she had hung an old flat-screen TV and abstract reprints from Walmart. "Come sit down. I'll rub your tummy. Gentle circles, right?" Her stomach was frequently queasy from estrogen injections.

Nadia stretched out on the lumpy couch. "The headache is even worse. Start there, please." Bryan cradled her head in his lap and stroked her temples.

Nadia tucked her legs into her chest and massaged her own calves, hurting, he knew, from long hours on her feet at the bookstore. "One day, when I'm rich, I'm going to buy myself a new couch." She sighed. "Sometimes, I really wish I'd gone to college. Maybe I wouldn't be in this dead-end job, living month to month and dealing with creeps asking me to"—she air-quoted— "demo the new dildos."

Bryan kissed her forehead. Early on, he had learned not to ask Nadia about her workday, since it was far from an innocuous question. Besides the normal drudgery and boredom of retail, her days were filled with monitoring the behavior of unsavory types. These customers regularly swiped handfuls of lacy thongs and disappeared to the far corners with magazines they hadn't bought or propositioned her from every approach possible, from the absurd to the menacing.

Nadia tilted up her chin. "My grades were decent, and, of course, my parents wanted me to go to college. But I wanted to become more of myself, and so I bought these instead and all my other surgeries," she said, pointing to her augmented chest. She had admitted that she had always felt like a girl and was lucky that her parents supported her transition early on. They had allowed her to use her college fund to pay for her surgeries.

Nadia's eyes grazed his. "Are you happy with me? Like, happy being with me?"

Bryan felt his heart jump into his throat and his pulse quicken. He tried his best to relax his muscles, as she was always very attuned to changes in the emotional climate of the room. *If we could stay in our own little bubble, I'd be the happiest man on* earth, he thought. She had never asked this question before, but he knew there was only one right answer. He tried to take a deep breath without drawing attention to it, hoping his struggles with how he would be perceived by his family and friends were not apparent. Instead, he dipped his head to nuzzle her, gathering her lips into his own in a fervent kiss. He whispered what he hoped would suffice: "Mmm, baby, of course, I am."

"Well, then, I want to start going out on real dates. Let's have a picnic at Discovery Green. I want to walk and hold hands under the moonlight. I want a real relationship with you."

"I hear you," Bryan replied.

4

Bryan felt buoyant, especially considering it was a Monday and he was driving home from Nadia's at five thirty in the morning, which gave him space to think. He enjoyed being in her presence more every time they interacted. Her soft skin and gentle touch made leaving her bed especially hard. Images of her face slightly creased from the pillow overnight floated into his mind. This morning, he had made a point of kissing her eyelids before he left, and she had responded with a sleepy yet angelic smile. He hadn't felt this same level of intimacy and longing with Lawanda, or anyone else for that matter. The quality of his other dates with other romantic interests was the opposite: those had all followed the law of diminishing returns. This was different. Nadia was different.

The streets were dark, though not ominous, due to birdsong breaking through the quiet. Bryan drove slowly, savoring the city's calm before frenetic noise and raucous morning traffic.

Nadia's apartment wasn't far from his luxury high-rise next to The Galleria, but in some ways, it was a galaxy away. He eased into his building entrance, surprised by the number of people jogging and walking their dogs. He chose never to be out this early in the morning in any neighborhood without a car.

While he felt relatively comfortable in this zip code, he still stood out in a community mostly populated by white men and women who subsisted on their daily Starbucks and wore Lululemon. On the day he had moved in, a middle-aged white woman in his complex had called the police. She didn't know Bryan, but he guessed she knew enough to fear him because of what he might be—a criminal, a thug. She might be even more fearful of what he was—someone who belonged there. Bryan had been lucky the cops were more impressed—or cowed—by the resplendence of his hi-rise than by the color of his skin.

He greeted the doorman with a hearty good morning, intentionally making eye contact as always so his face remained familiar. Middle-aged well-to-do whites and perhaps a dozen people of color, mostly Asians, owned hi-rise condominiums here. Bryan had rarely seen another Black person in the building who wasn't cleaning some part of it.

Once he entered his tenth-floor high-rise, the smell of eucalyptus from the diffuser tickled his nose. Before checking his mail or making coffee, he walked straight to his closet to hang his clothes. Bryan extracted his favorite designer suit to wear to work that day. Nadia liked to poke fun at the fact that even his casual clothes were expensive and beautifully maintained. She didn't even know about his secret closet where he housed suits purchased directly from the runway. He valued these clothes as if they were great works of art by Van Gogh, Monet, or Degas. Before he started dating Nadia and when he did not have the kids, he had spent most Sundays ironing these admired pieces.

His dad, a blue-collar man, never attended social functions without newly shined shoes topped with a suit or, at least, a jacket. His father had taught him the power of dressing well, an attempt to favorably alter how others, especially whites, perceived him before he spoke. Bryan remembered the iron grip on his skinny eight-year-old shoulders. "Remember, son, the world might not give you a chance to be heard."

Bryan's parents had divorced after two decades of marriage. Never a saint, his father had become increasingly difficult to live with. The divorce increased his father's drinking and hastened his decline. He died of cancer a handful of years ago with all of his rigid ideas intact about being a man, women's roles, and sexual desire. Bryan worked hard to show him that his masculinity was unshakeable and his desire for women was unquestionable. He remembered how he used to try to impress his father with his masculinity when he was a teenager. Bryan had spent summer breaks helping him with painting jobs and would smile and lightly flirt with some of the girls who lived in the houses they painted. Even though Bryan acted like he wanted their approval, it was his father's approval he was yearning for. Whenever his father overheard him say something particularly smooth and Bryan garnered a "That's my boy" from his father, Bryan had felt like he was doing something right. This memory made Bryan sigh. There was no way Bryan would have dared to consider dating a transgender woman if his father were still alive. He didn't want to think about his mother, but he hoped she wouldn't disown him.

Bryan arranged the cushions ergonomically in the corner of his living room dedicated to his meditation practice. "It's like a suit for your mind, Daddy," he said aloud to his dead father, who certainly thought Buddhism was both foolish and for white folks.

Bryan lit a candle and set the timer for thirty minutes. He had found meditation only a few months before meeting Nadia. Much like meeting Nadia, he came across meditation through happenstance. He had read about the power of meditation to calm your anxieties, and the Houston Zen Center was having beginner classes. He meditated when he thought about it, but it never turned into a daily ritual.

Unfortunately, sitting in the lotus position, thoughts of sex the night before kept intruding, both arousing and shaming him. An article he'd once read bubbled to the forefront of his brain. It had listed celebrities and politicians caught in compromising situations with same-sex or transgender partners. Their lives had been ruined. An image of him and Nadia being seen in public by his mother, or worse, his boss, flashed into his mind and he could suddenly see the two of them on the cover of a tabloid. Getting caught was not an option: he needed his job, he had child support to pay, and more importantly, he needed to be seen as straight to achieve his professional goals. He sneaked a look at the timer. Only eight minutes had passed. No voice from the universe today. He stood, deciding to stop meditating. The quiet time was only making space for what he was avoiding: himself. He reached for his suit.

***

He arrived at his office at seven thirty. While his hours began earlier than a typical nine-to-five job, his company paid him well and his coworkers were overall intelligent and pleasant. The work itself was challenging but not creative enough to be satisfying. His office was small and unimpressive, with two nubby orange guest chairs. Not at all like the corner offices the senior managers occupied. If he had that job it would be both challenging and satisfying, with an executive pay grade of 94. He started his computer to only see a flurry of emails. At least he was blessed with a large window that gave him a view of a meandering path, half-hidden by slender pines.

Bryan heard Jerry talking down the hall. He and Jerry had worked together for nearly twenty years now, as they were both hired right out of college. There were only a handful of Black people working at the company, so the Black folks knew each other. Bryan and Jerry had developed a close relationship because they had worked on several projects together over the years. While they initially bonded over sharing the ridiculously racist things that they had heard throughout their workday, their friendship eventually evolved to trading stories over drinks after work. As Bryan's kids got older and birthday parties and barbecues began to take up more of his spare time, meeting Jerry for drinks quickly turned into balloon animal competitions between the two of them. Shortly after Jerry became a regular in his kids' lives, Bryan began climbing the corporate ladder, quickly outpacing Jerry in position and pay. They still talked, but Bryan began to focus more on making it big than on maintaining his friendship with Jerry. After Bryan and Lawanda divorced, Jerry saw less of Bryan's kids and Bryan saw less of Jerry outside of work. Jerry still regularly made a point to stop by Bryan's office though, keeping their work friendship intact despite the fact that Bryan was several pay grades above him now.

Jerry popped his head in Bryan's doorway, as he did at least once a day. The first time Bryan had asked him to please knock, Jerry quickly told him, in typically dramatic fashion, that he was allergic to even the idea of that formality.

Bryan released a sigh of resignation. He hated that his driven nature probably made Jerry feel unappreciated because deep down he really liked Jerry- he just liked the idea of being promoted a tad more. As Bryan glanced up at Jerry with a smile, he couldn't help but remember the eagerness Lance had expressed when he thought Bryan was texting Jerry the other day and felt a twinge of parental guilt. Jerry would often say he saw parts of himself in Lance and Lance seemed to talk more with Jerry than he did with his own father when the three of them were together.

"What's up, Jerry?" Bryan said, swiveling around in his chair. Bryan knew he had a lot of work to do and glanced at his watch as Jerry sauntered into his office. Jerry sat down on a short filing cabinet, swinging a leg back and forth. Jerry sat wherever he wanted, and Bryan wondered where he got the confidence to do so. He was sure it rubbed some people the wrong way, but Bryan knew that Jerry didn't have the same people-pleasing tendencies he did. Bryan would never dream of taking up space like that, and silently admired Jerry's casual confidence. He grinned, thinking about how Jerry was ridiculed once by a group of steelworkers for crossing a construction site wearing a pink hard hat and silk scarf. Jerry had flippantly readjusted his scarf without saying a word and the titters had ceased.

Of course, Jerry had not presented himself that way at the company from the beginning. He had started out straitlaced and added one small "real" detail at a time. Bryan's phone dinged. *Probably a text from Nadia,* he thought. In a flash, Bryan turned his phone over on his desk and rearranged some papers in what he hoped was one fluid, natural, and unsuspicious movement.

Jerry glanced at the overturned phone, and his eyes narrowed. Bryan held his breath. Luckily, Jerry's expression shifted, and in an affectionately mocking tone, he said, "I declare, you never disappoint." He looked Bryan up and down. "Your clothing is impeccable." Jerry's short and stout frame was enrobed in loose fitting slacks and dress shirt that covered his belly just enough to be tucked into his pants. Bryan smiled, proud of the care he took in his appearance despite knowing his fastidiousness could call his masculinity into question. "It's all in the ironing and quality fabric."

"I'm sure Angela appreciates your ironing," Jerry sniggered. Bryan's steadfast reluctance to share anything about his dating life irked his coworker. Jerry was always searching for ways to pry.

Bryan shrugged. Angela was an attractive Black woman who worked in accounting that he'd had an ongoing flirtation with for the past few months. "She's nice." Bryan said, wondering if his flirtation with Angela was discussed by others. He needed to be perceived as an eligible divorcé.

"I came to work to rest," Jerry said, moving from his perch on the filing cabinet and into one of Bryan's ridiculous orange chairs. "I think I've only slept five hours this whole weekend." He wagged his brows at Bryan. "Did I tell you I'm seeing somebody new?"

"Really?" Bryan said sarcastically. As much as he liked to rib Jerry for some of his weekend shenanigans, it was enjoyable hearing funny stories about Jerry's love life, such as the one about when he fell for a guy who bragged that he worked for the CIA as a spy. Bryan knew most women had one close gay friend—he guessed guys could too. After all, having a gay friend didn't inherently make someone gay.

Bryan hoped his being straight never made Jerry feel uncomfortable. Jerry had asked Bryan several times to go to the PRIDE parade with him and a few of his friends, but Bryan never felt he belonged. He knew he wasn't homophobic in a mean way, but he was a little afraid of getting hit on by a guy. What if he gave off a gay vibe? He knew he liked Nadia for her feminine features, and aside from seeing her genitalia, he had always been the dominant one. The concept of handling her penis hadn't come up yet and he was comfortable with their physical relationship staying as it was for the time being. He also had not spent a lot of time around same-sex couples and was scared of saying the wrong thing. He didn't want to accidentally offend anyone at their celebration of identity.

Jerry slouched further down in the chair. "He's tall, a little darker than you, and handsome. Yes sir-reeee." He paused to let Bryan comment, but Bryan had taken up his pen as a cue to hurry the story along. "Anyway," Jerry continued. "He took me to this new spot, *High Five*. It used to be the *Red Necktie*."

Bryan stiffened when he realized that was the same club Nadia was talking about.

"What, do you know it?" Jerry teased.

"No," Bryan answered curtly. He felt his face getting hot as he swallowed the white lie.

"That place was teeming with cute guys. I could barely focus on my man." Jerry started fanning himself.

"I really need to get back to work," Bryan said.

"You should come with us. I know you straight guys enjoy the attention. They would just love you."

Bryan shifted his eyes to his computer screen. "Thanks for the invite, but I wouldn't want people to get the wrong idea." He paused for a second. "Can straight people even go to gay clubs? Like is that even allowed?"

"It's okay," Jerry said, "we wouldn't want anyone to think you're straight." He raised an eyebrow. "You do know the expression 'the lady doth protest too much,' right?"

"What?!" Bryan exclaimed, suddenly feeling flustered. He swallowed, feeling a knot forming in his throat. He could feel his armpits beginning to get damp, and he had only put deodorant on a few hours ago.

"I'm just playing with you." Jerry looked thoughtful for a few seconds, noting Bryan's tightened jaw, before craning his neck to peek at Bryan's monitor. "You heard about the email?"

"What email?" Bryan avoided gossip at work. The barrage of questions and loaded comments from Jerry was stressing Bryan out, and Bryan could feel his pulse quickening with every word out of Jerry's mouth. He needed to get Jerry out of his office so that he could calm down and collect his thoughts.

Jerry opened his mouth to start speaking, and Bryan quickly cut him off. "You know some of us have to work around here. For instance, we had forty scaffold builders quit and go to our competitor for a twenty-five-cent-an-hour raise. And ten thousand feet of shop-fabricated pipes were each short by three inches at the Louisiana facility."

Jerry waved his hand. "Yes, yes, I know all that. But more importantly, Human Resources found some plant operators sharing offensive gay jokes on Facebook. I think it was a night-shift crew." Jerry bounced out of his seat. "The audacity is what gets me," he said, standing by the door.

Bryan's fingers trembled on the keyboard. *God, why am I so flustered today? he thought.* He tried his best to steady his hands. "That's terrible," he eeked out, his voice sounding mouse-like. "I'm sure HR will figure it out like last time," he said, attempting to lower his voice. He wondered if he was sounding as cartoonish to Jerry as he was to himself. He glanced at his watch and realized he had a meeting in ten minutes. *I can't deal with this right now. I have too much to do to get distracted by Jerry right now,* he thought.

In reality, Bryan didn't have much faith in the human resources department at his company. A few years earlier, he and Jerry had briefly bonded more substantively when a noose was found hanging from a steel girder inside one of the chemical plants. At the time, Jerry's sexual preferences were his business and Bryan listened to his stories without providing much input. The noose incident had forced them both to face reality- they were both just two Black men trying to survive the games white guys played to make them quit. Surprising to Bryan, it had been a white woman who had put the noose up. She had been summarily fired, though Jerry had wondered aloud to Bryan if one, a white man would have been more readily excused, and two, if the company fired her so quickly out of fear of consequences rather than a genuine desire to protect or respect the Black people in the building. Bryan had dismissed Jerry at the time, calling him paranoid, but he still thought about it.

Jerry stood up, his hands balled into fists. "I don't get you. You are the highest-ranking Black at this company. Nothing will get better unless somebody like you says something. They listen to you. You're one of the 'good' ones," Jerry said sarcastically.

"What's that supposed to mean?" Bryan could feel his heart rate continuing to increase. He was ninety percent sure that he was sweating through his shirt.

"You know what I'm talking about. This isn't the first time jokes like this have surfaced here. We need to file a grievance with the Equal Employment Opportunity Commission." Jerry shook his head at Bryan, "I don't know what's happening to you. We used to keep these guys in check. Since you got this role, you've always found a reason to let these guys off the hook. You don't want to be a troublemaker, right?"

"C'mon, man. You got me all wrong," Bryan said, standing. "Things are different now, man. I can't go directly at these guys as if I were still a grade 84 or lower. Trust me. I need to handle these guys with finesse."

Jerry continued to pace. "That's a cop out. I need you to get involved. I need you to be an advocate for us, all of us. What are you scared of? Not being accepted? Being Black? You wish you were white?"

Not white, just accepted by whites, Bryan thought. He did everything he could to fit the mold of the successful black man- he was easy to talk to, was frequently referred to as "trustworthy," and was promoted often. But he was not one of them. "Now you're going too far," he said, clenching his teeth. He could feel his anxiety beginning to transform into anger.

"How about I go a little further. You want to be like them so badly you hide your head in the sand. What else are you hiding? We are the way we are in every part of our lives."

"I'm not like you," Bryan practically growled.

"Not like me. You mean because you're not gay? Tell me something I don't know. You can tell me the T," he urged. A slight smile broke underneath his words.

In this moment, Bryan wished with all his heart he could tell Jerry everything about Nadia, the girl who had his heart, his mama's homophobia, and his shame attached to being some letter of the LGBTQ alphabet. He had never tried to put himself in Jerry's shoes before, and was starting to wonder if maybe they would fit too tightly. He squirmed in his discomfort.

"I know you're straight because you don't even know basic gay slang," Jerry continued. "You know, the T, the truth."

"I don't have anything to hide. You're right. I am straight," Bryan retorted. If he told Jerry, the dam would be broken, and Bryan was terrified of the destruction in the path of the tumultuous rush. There were moments when Bryan found himself at such a profound loss because he truly had no one to talk to; his situation was different than Jerry's. He fixed his gaze on the far wall. The whiteboard was covered with black marks depicting the steps to weld pipe. "I pick my battles. You should try it sometimes." Bryan noticed Jerry was periodically looking out the window. "What are you looking at?

"There's something in those trees," he said, pointing outside. "Like a huge nest? Anyway, if you get the VP role—"

Bryan interrupted. "I'll be surprised if I get an interview. Amy is more qualified than any of us."

"You know her husband was promoted to CFO of a plastics company," Jerry said. "They are looking to start a family."

"So?"

"You know them. They're going to pass her up just like they would me. Or if they do offer her the job, she'll pass because she needs to stay home with the kids." Jerry squinted out the window again. Like every executive in the company, who were currently all white men, Bryan had earned his engineering degree from a large state public institution, whereas Jerry had attended an all-Black college. While the execs never vocalized it in front of Bryan or Jerry's face, they made it clear that they thought his education was second-rate. Bryan thought their opinions were narrow-minded, and he knew how smart Jerry was, but this was how the world worked.

"There aren't enough of you 'straight' guys fighting against this type of discrimination." Jerry continued, shaking his head.

"You're right. I have to run to a meeting, but let's touch base about it later," Bryan said weakly. Hand on the doorknob, he said, "I've got to run to a meeting. I'll ask around about what they are doing about those messages and as much as Bryan enjoyed his friendship with Jerry, he didn't have the mental bandwidth to figure out how to handle human rights issues in his workplace.

Bryan was hesitant to ask for any punishment for those workers. It was outside his purview, firmly in HR territory, and they were a territorial bunch. Complaining to the leadership about a hostile environment was only going to jeopardize his chances of getting promoted, hopefully to a grade 94 at some point in his career. The company's profitability was down and now was not the time to add any external issues to the conversation. Bryan's direct boss had recently been fired due to not getting all his projects completed. The best bet was to just keep his head down and stay out of trouble. Which meant no gay clubs. He could easily shuck off Jerry. How much longer could he keep denying Nadia what she wanted? Deserved, he thought.

5

Larry's Steakhouse boasted two tall mahogany doors, so heavy that many people had to use two hands to open just one door. It was a comfortable dark on the inside, with an old bar top imported from a farmhouse in Italy. The restaurant had an extensive cocktail drink menu that the bar manager changed often, and the bartenders were talented and charismatic. Bryan saw Reggie sitting at the bar, high ball glass in hand. They had met a few weeks into Bryan's second semester at college, when Bryan had torn himself away from solving equations and made his way to the campus gym. He'd been pulled into a game of pickup basketball by Reggie. When Bryan effortlessly evaded a blocker's face and dunked the ball, his friendship with Reggie was sealed. If not for Reggie, Bryan would have been lonely in college. Many of Bryan's white friends from high school attended the same public Texas institution with him but those relationships had drifted away for reasons he had never understood while they were there.

Reggie greeted him with arms wide: "Big Bryan, what's up, bro-ham? It's been too long."

How long is it going to take him to ask me who I'm dating, Bryan thought.

Reggie seemed shorter, Bryan thought, giving him the special handshake all Black men give each other. "Man, it's good to see you too. You look good." In truth, his friend had put on weight. He was always a big guy, strong from lifting weights, but he had lost his former definition. His skin was loose around his cheeks, and he had bags under his eyes, the effects of a nasty recent divorce and thirteen-hour days at a law firm.

As if no time had passed since they'd last seen each other six months ago, Reggie grinned at him. "So, Big B. How many rivers did we pollute today?"

Bryan chuckled. "I don't know, how many hours did you overbill?"

Reggie slapped Bryan on the back. "Aw, these guys don't read the contracts and then expect me to save them. Litigation ain't free." A shadow passed over his face, but he rubbed it away. "Hey, what're you drinking?"

Bryan thought of the hundreds of times Reggie had asked him that question throughout college. Reggie was a year older and had a big personality, and even though Bryan studied more and partied less than Reggie's crowd, he had always made sure Bryan felt included.

Reggie scanned the room. "I'll take another double Grey Goose on the rocks," he told the bartender, then addressed Bryan: "Some hotties, here tonight, Big B. By the way, I can't stay too long, I've got a date later. Man, I wish dating was as easy as it was in college. All we had to do was make a few baskets"—Reggie twinkled—"and a-tisket, a-tasket." He cracked up at his own silliness, and Bryan smiled, remembering. The campus gym was the perfect spot for the few Black girls on campus to check potential suitors.

"Reg, you still seeing that same girl from a few months ago?"

"You mean half a year ago? Naw."

Bryan thought he sensed a hint of resentment as Reggie took a small sip of the remainder of his drink. He deserved it- he had been telling Reggie he was too busy to see him for the past three months. "What happened?"

"I don't know, man, you know me."

"Yeah, I know you. She slept with you, and now there's no challenge, right?" Bryan said, laughing.

Reggie chuckled. "No fair using our long history against me." He gave Bryan a once-over. "You look good, brother. I don't know how you keep the weight in check."

Bryan shrugged. "Good genes, player." Bryan gestured respectfully to the bartender, a young guy in a tight T-shirt, and handed him a business card.

The bartender received the card with a bit of apprehension. A moment later, he said, "Not a problem. Will do."

"What did you give him?"

"A new thing I started. I've got a special drink that I ask for now that's printed on the card."

"What are you now? The Black James Bond? What's it called?"

Bryan grinned, thinking how good it felt to play the role of successful heterosexual man. "Hick's Brew."

Reggie laughed. "Okay, Mr. Bryan Hicks. We have come a long way since college."

"We have, indeed," Bryan agreed. "Is everything going, okay? How are your kids?" Reggie had two kids a bit younger than Lindsey and Lance.

"Yeah, man, I'm good, and the kids, I assume, are okay," Reggie replied, taking their drinks from the bartender, "I don't really see them as much as I'd like to. Did I tell you Katrina got remarried?"

Reggie's ex, Katrina, had caught him a few years ago with a twenty-four-year-old flight attendant, and Bryan knew their divorce had been drawn out and ugly. "Oh, man, no, you didn't."

"Yeah, to a neurosurgeon." Reggie took a long sip of his drink. "They moved to a new home in Three Oaks. Her new husband is a dick. Can you believe she married a white guy? I don't like the way he looks at me."

Bryan bounced his legs against the bar chair. Reggie was one of those Black men who got pissed off whenever he saw a white guy with a Black woman. He hadn't been thrilled when Bryan briefly dated a white girl, Sarah, in college. "Katrina married a white dude?" Bryan shook his head. "You gotta be kidding me."

Reggie threw back the rest of his drink. "Her husband makes double my salary. She's driving a new Range Rover, and he bought her a second home on Martha's Vineyard, the whitest place on earth." Reggie slammed the highball glass on the bar. "I know I was a dick to her, and I know what goes around comes around, but, man, seeing my kids once every other weekend is rough. I've been replaced by a white man."

"Look, man, figure it out with Katrina. Swallow your pride, apologize." Bryan said.

"Yeah." Reggie traced some moisture on the bar with his empty glass. "Bartender, can I have another? And two rib eyes, medium rare. You're hungry, right, B?"

"Sure," Bryan said. He hadn't planned on eating, but he realized he was hungry. "Lindsey is still dating the same guy who wears his pants down to his knees," Bryan said to change the subject. "I hope he doesn't try to keep her here; she needs to go away and experience college."

"Some days, I wonder if the Black college experience was what we needed. College was hard on us," Reggie said, eyeballing a dark-skinned woman wearing a yellow sleeveless dress. "Man, look at that beautiful sister. We just had a few Black girls to choose from at college. Like Katrina."

"Do you remember when a white girl had been attacked on campus, and she said that a Black man did it?" Bryan asked.

"Who can forget?" Reggie took his second drink from the bartender. "The campus police lined us all against the wall in the gym," he said. "They were looking for a dark-skinned brother between five foot and six two, one-sixty to one-eighty pounds. Hell, we all matched that description. I don't know if they actually caught anyone. But they had all of us terrified."

"I was headed to my chemistry class when three campus police stopped me. They pinned me against the nearest building wall and started riffling through my bag." Bryan took a sip. "Their treatment was bullshit." He remembered them spreading his feet apart, forcing him into the brick wall to brace himself, a group of white kids staring as the cops patted him down. He rubbed his palms together, trying to erase the tactile memory of the rough bricks.

Since he'd attended private secondary school, Bryan had gotten comfortable around white people, but this experience reminded him he was Black and therefore at the mercy of a system that blamed him first, no matter how high his average was in physics. "The nineties were a tough time for us."

Reggie was drinking way too fast. "Nineties? Shit. It's happening today. All kinds of hate crimes are on the rise."

Reggie pulled out his phone. "But, man, we had some good times, too. Can you believe Big Blue reached out to me on Facebook?"

Reggie passed his phone. Big Blue was smiling hugely in a family photo, though he, too, was puffy. A more happily worn-out version of Reggie. Bryan had never known Big Blue's real name. His nickname came from being six five with skin so dark it looked indigo. "What did Mr. Soul Night say?" Bryan said.

"Big Blue, he's doing fine," Reggie answered. "Man, you remember his big ass was break dancing on the dance floor."

Bryan started smiling. "Oh, man, I do remember that. Each time the DJ put Chuck D, Flavor Flav, and Public Enemy on, Big Blue would get out there. The girls would go crazy when he started dancing. Public Enemy was my group back then."

Soul night was every Thursday night. The university had allowed the Black students to gather in the Student Union. Black kids from nearby colleges hung out together for what they'd christened Soul Night. Soul Night was more significant than just kids listening to the latest rap songs. It felt like liberation for him and Reggie and their friends to be free to live in a Black world for three hours a week.

Bryan hadn't thought of it at the time, but now Soul Night made him think of all those car trips that Black kids would take back then to get from their smaller colleges to his big one out in the country. How did those Black kids avoid being stopped while driving Black along those country roads? Or had there been some who were stopped? Bryan thought of Sandra Bland, who'd been driving from one place to another, and had been frightened to death, one way or another.

"Yeah, Public Enemy, their hit song was 'Fight the Power.'" Reggie pumped the fist, not holding his drink. "You met Sarah one of those nights. The only white girl there, with that white girl booty."

"Yeah, Sarah was . . ." Bryan was going to say, "my first love," which was true, but he didn't want to get into that with Reggie tonight, "My girl," he said instead.

"When she left, I had to scrape you off the floor." Reggie chucked him lightly.

When Sarah quit college and moved back home to Maine, Bryan stopped going to class and even Soul Night. His grades had dropped for a semester. Thank God Reggie had taken care of him. He hadn't approved of Bryan dating Sarah but hadn't held it against him either.

The steakhouse's noise reduced significantly as patrons watched a commercial reminding residents about the importance of coming out to vote on the transgender bathroom bill.

Reggie pointed at the TV. "What do you think about that?"

"Well...," Bryan said, keeping his voice level. "What do you think?" Bryan answered with a question because he was unsure of where Reggie stood.

"I know we have the first openly lesbian mayor in the country. I think she's doing a great job, but this bathroom bill is a step too far."

Bryan didn't say anything, but his foot tapped faster on the bar chair's footrest. "I don't know man," Bryan said, not wanting to stir the pot, "The trans community isn't hurting anybody. There is no evidence of anyone being hurt by anyone in that community simply wanting to relieve themselves."

"Not yet," Reggie countered.

A waiter set down their food and they dropped the subject.

The excellent meat tasted like glue in Bryan's mouth. Reggie was a product of the mainstream Black community, and now probably wasn't the time to try to open his mind. Bryan swallowed. "Who are you going out with tonight?"

"Bad petite chick, dark skin, mid-thirties . . . I don't know. I love my sisters, but I look at how Katrina left me."

"I hear you," Bryan said. "Lawanda was a nightmare."

Another ad about the HERO bill came on again. They both stared at the television.

"I don't know about this whole trans thing," Reggie said. "It's hard for me to believe that a guy...a straight guy would be interested in a trans woman," he said, laughing, "They seriously want me to believe this guy is going to get a real man to look at her."

Bryan scratched the back of his neck. "Look, man, there's somebody for everybody. Okay, so it's not your thing. I get it."

Reggie took another sip. "Any guy chatting up a woman in a wig needs to admit that he's as gay as they come."

Bryan quietly sighed. *Was he always this narrow-minded?* Bryan wondered. He knew Reggie's comment was ignorant, but he did not know how to defend himself and Nadia without outing himself. He felt a wave of shame settling into his gut, as if the steak were adhering to his intestines. Bryan kept his eyes focused on his drink.

"What have you been doing? Playing video games? You been dating? You need to be out, player. People start to wonder."

Here we go, he thought. Bryan's face felt warm. He wanted to ask, "Reggie, what are you implying?" But Bryan wasn't sure if he would be able to handle the answer. If Reggie thought he was less of a man because he was attracted to trans women, Bryan would lose his oldest friend and he couldn't handle that right now. Bryan took a deep breath before responding.

"Naw, man. I'm dating." He checked his phone as a distraction, hoping this answer would suffice.

"I don't know why you're playing all private. Back in the day, before you met Lawanda, it was me and you talking to the ladies at the club. What gives?"

Bryan's mind drifted to Nadia's silhouette, outlined by the streetlamp shining blurrily through the fabric tacked up over the kitchen window. She was the tall blond woman he had dreamed about even as a young boy. The ones he saw on television, ogled in magazines, noticed on his college campus, and flirted with at work. He moved her hair to the front of her shoulders, revealing her pale back, her ladylike waist. He kissed where the red slash of her bra strap had dug in. He snapped out of his daydream.

"Okay, okay." Bryan raised his hands up, palms out. "I've got a steady girl-friend. But it's new, man." He couldn't help smiling. "Her name is Nadia."

"Nadia. Oh, I know she's white. You got a picture. Is she blond?"

Bryan grinned. "Yeah."

"I'm surprised you're just now mentioning her. Did she just get out of jail?"

Bryan chuckled.

"Missing teeth?"

"Ha."

"I just want to see," Reggie said, reaching for Bryan's phone.

Bryan realized he was acting like someone with something to hide. He found a selfie of Nadia and reluctantly flashed it at his friend.

Reggie snatched the phone. "Oh, shit! She's hot. You still think white guys will accept you if you have a white girl on your arm, huh?"

"Whatever," Bryan replied, quickly, quietly taking offense because that was not true. He didn't understand why Reggie was only a year older than him, yet still held the same antiquated views that Bryan's mama did. Bryan took his phone back from Reggie's hand before he could start scrolling through all the photos. The last thing he needed was for Reggie to find an erotic photo of Nadia. They were always taken from the back, but who knew if anything else was visible, even as a shadow. "Okay, you saw her."

"Man, I don't understand why you're hiding this chick from everyone." Reggie slapped him on his shoulder. "White girls are not my thang. She looks good. Damn, player. Is there something you're not telling me about her?"

Bryan's heart began to beat faster. For a moment, he imagined himself telling Reggie the truth, and saw Reggie leaving him alone at the bar in his mind's eye. He nodded his head "no" to shake away the image.

"Naw, man. Thanks, I appreciate it," Bryan said. There is a time and place for everything and now was not the time or the place, he thought.

Reggie pivoted to grab his jacket off the back of the bar chair. "You guys sound serious. I want to meet her."

Bryan nodded.

Reggie grinned, and the weak overhead light caught his white teeth and his jacket zipper, both gleaming through the semi-dark interior as Reggie stood to leave. "This girl needs to be privy to all your dark secrets that only a college friend knows." He patted Bryan's chest. "I'll bring that girl I was telling you about; the four of us can get together. Sorry, I gotta bounce before the check man, I'll pay for our double date."

"Soon, man," Bryan responded. He let out a sigh of relief as Reggie exited. Once Bryan paid the bill, he made his way out to his car and found himself glancing at the time.

It wasn't too late to call Lance. Bryan liked to check in on his kids periodically when they were at Lawanda's. "Hey, son, I called to say I love you."

"I love you too," Lance said. Bryan heard Lindsey's voice in the background and listened as his two kids argued over who should talk to him first.

Lindsey must have won the fight, because her voice came over the line. "Hey, daddy. What are you doing?" she asked

"Just finished having a drink with a friend," he said, "Did you get your homework done?"

"I did. We were up all night last night," Lindsey said.

"Well, good, honey. I love you," Bryan said.

They hung up. I know Reggie would like Nadia, he thought, starting his car, realizing he had to figure this out.

6

On Thursday night, Bryan found himself at Nadia's again and ready to be more open with her. "Do you smell that delicious meat cooking?" she asked as he stood in the threshold of her apartment.

Bryan nodded eagerly. He was practically salivating. Entering Nadia's apartment made all the tension in his body leave.

"Sorry to disappoint, it's next door at Señora Vasquez's," Nadia said, shutting the door after Bryan and going to the kitchen. She pulled out two plates. "Reminds me of my mom, though she didn't use those yummy spices. Lots of love, though."

"You're lucky," Bryan replied. "My mom was the breadwinner, so cooking was on the back burner, so to speak."

After dinner, they cuddled on the too-small couch. Nadia was having another bout of nausea from her injections, and Bryan kissed her nose. "Are you feeling better?"

"Yes, thank you." Nadia took a sip of water. "Hey, I was thinking about what you said on Sunday. Aside from your kids' mother, you really never dated a Black girl?"

"No. Not really." He paused. "I went to catholic prep school, so I was around more white people. The kids and the teachers—hell, even the janitors—were white or Hispanic." Bryan remembered feeling terrified to even talk to some of the girls in his class. His mama used to tell him that if he dated a white girl, both white guys might hurt him and some Black people will have a problem with it. "It's funny you asked me that question. Just the other day, I was thinking about an incident when I was a kid." Nadia twisted her body toward him.

"Me and my two friends were playing in this field near my house, and we saw white limbs flailing around in a car. We, of course, went closer to see what was going on."

"I bet you did," Nadia said, glancing at his phone on the coffee table, "Lawanda is calling. Finish your story. She can leave a message."

He waited to see if a message came through, but none did.

Nadia patted his thigh. "Go on."

"Oh, right. The girl was on her back. She tried to cover herself as quickly as possible after she saw me." Bryan placed his hands on his chest to demonstrate. "I was not moving until I got to see her. I remember she was young with blond hair and her face, neck, and chest were white with red freckles. I thought she was an angel. Like you."

"Had you ever seen a naked woman before?"

"No. The guy started frantically waving us away like we were stray cats or something." He chuckled. Bryan had seen his first *Playboy* in that field as a ten-year-old, which was a white woman's lips around what looked like a thumb, which he now knew was not a thumb. "White girls were off-limits, but they were everywhere to be desired."

"I've been thinking about this lately. Is your mother going to be okay with me?" She sounded both flat and hopeful.

"You mean because you're trans?"

"No, doofus, because I'm white. I've heard some Black mothers don't like their sons bringing white girls home."

Bryan bit his bottom lip, leaning closer to Nadia. "My mama has no problem with race, but she doesn't like Black men dating women from other races." Bryan attempted to be casual, but he did not want to lie. It pained Bryan to admit his mother's opinion. "I don't want you worrying about that."

"Okay," Nadia said, sounding unconvinced.

He kissed her cheek, hoping to derail her questions and her concerns.

Nadia pulled back. "Wait, have you or have you not told your mother about us?"

"No. I haven't yet." Bryan paused, "But I will. There's no rush. And when she meets you, everything will be fine." He looked into her green eyes to assure her everything was okay.

"I told you that I want to meet your family," Nadia responded.

"In due time," Bryan said. "My mama is a complicated woman. I need to couch this a certain way with her. I don't want to surprise her with this."

"Okay," she said, with a slight smile. She seemed relieved. "Do you want to spend the night?"

"You know I do," Bryan said. Nadia reached for her phone and took a few quick selfies of them. "Can you put your phone down for a second and kiss me?" Bryan asked impatiently.

"Your lips are soft like rose petals," she said, touching his lips with her index finger.

"That's the best compliment I've ever received." He didn't mention how many times kids had made fun of his big lips. "I had to grow into these lips."

Bryan tugged her top off her shoulder, but Nadia brushed his hands off. "I'm not comfortable being naked in the living room. I worry people can see through those windows by the front door."

Bryan caressed her face. "Nadia, do you know how beautiful you are?" He took her hand and led her to the dark kitchen, its window higher on the wall. Throwing her shirt to the floor, Nadia undid her bra, her breasts pale in the darkness. She slowly unbuttoned her pants and slid them down inch by inch. "Oh, girl," Bryan requested. "Stop teasing me." She tilted her head. "Okay." She took his wrist and guided his hand to the front of her panties, something she hadn't done before. He felt a tingle of excitement, which was quickly followed by panic. He pulled his hand back and placed his palm on her hip, gently turning her to face the kitchen counter. She acquiesced, but he heard a small sigh escape from her mouth. *Desire, disappointment, or both?* Bryan wondered.

They became one under the filtered light from the streetlamp outside the kitchen window. Afterward, he lay on the cool kitchen floor, breathing hard. When his strength returned, he propped himself against the low cabinet and wiped his forehead theatrically. Nadia only gave him the briefest half smile and stood up, silently rifling through her drawers for a towel.

Bryan's mind raced with a million excuses as to why she hadn't been completely satisfied, but he knew better than to say them aloud. Bryan preferred to believe that there can't be fireworks every time. For him, sex was still good even when it was okay. Her displeasure made her seem a million miles away. Towel in hand, she turned back around to face Bryan, her face fixed into a slight scowl. "What's wrong, honey?"

"Nothing," she said, wiping lube from her buttocks with the tea towel. He noticed her eyes were glistening, and stood up to comfort her. He gently placed his hands on her shoulders, and she stared back at him, small tears forming in the corners of her eyes. Her eyes locked on his and he could feel her sadness crashing into his shame, the whole gamut of emotions settling in his stomach, which felt suddenly heavy. "Everything," she said, wiping a tear. "I need to know that you want all of me, not just parts of me," she said, placing her hands over his and gently removing them from her shoulders. She walked into the living room and curled up on the couch, looking like a wounded animal. Bryan hoped that she knew he felt as awful as she did. He didn't know how to tell her that they were both going through different types of hell and that he'd hoped they could help each other. He suddenly wondered if maybe they were dragging each other down.

Bryan followed Nadia and sat down on the opposite side of the couch. He had never shared this much with her before, but he knew that he would lose her if he didn't. "When I first got divorced, I tried." He lightly touched her hand. She curled her fingers into a fist. "I met this trans girl, and we went back to her place."

"You never told me this," Nadia said, sounding surprised. She sat up and wiped off some tears. "Where did you meet her?"

"Well," he said, pausing, "Well, I called her from the back pages of the Greensheet magazine ads."

"She was a sex worker," Nadia said.

He nodded embarrassedly, scared she might judge him.

"Interesting," Nadia responded. "So, what happened?" "We kissed. Things got hot and heavy pretty quickly. She wanted me to go down on her after she gave me oral sex for a few minutes," Bryan confessed.

Nadia faced him squarely. "Did you?"

"No," Bryan said sheepishly. "I just couldn't." The memory of them sitting on the couch flashed in his mind. "I couldn't look at *it*. I kissed her neck while she stroked herself to completion."

"You still can't look at it," Nadia pushed.

"I have never talked to anyone about this. I wasn't ready for her. I thought I was. I had never seen it before in real life. Only in videos," Bryan said, facing Nadia. "Right at that moment, I don't know but it looked much different in real life and that's when I got scared."

"What do you mean?" Nadia said, leaning away.

"Suddenly, I realized that I was with a trans woman. That's when I froze," Bryan said, taking a deep sigh.

"Froze."

"Yeah, I just kinda of froze up. I guess I got scared. I felt I was doing something wrong. I had flashes of my father calling me gay slurs."

"Well, that was in the past and today is a new day," Nadia said. "I need a man who isn't scared to be his true self. Do you see me as different?"

Bryan felt hot. "No, I don't see you as different. I see you as a woman like any other woman," Bryan said. His stomach did a flip as the words came out of his mouth and he wished she would change the subject.

"Good. Because I am. And I deserve the same amount of respect you give to other women. Right?"

"Yes."

"I had never seen *it* before in real life. Well, I mean other than mine. I never saw myself putting my mouth on *it*. That felt gay to me."

"It," Nadia responded forcefully. "Interesting, you keep saying 'it.'"

"I don't know what else to say," Bryan said, his stomach doing another somersault out of nervousness. He was unwilling to admit the label "it" was another form of denial or dissociation, not wanting to dig himself into a deeper hole.

"You call this," Nadia said, spreading out and looking between her legs, "by its real name."

Bryan looked confused, raising his eyebrows, maintaining eye contact with Nadia.

"Girl-dick," Nadia said, locking her eyes on his, "Yes, good old red-blooded American girl-dick. Acceptance can only start when you face the problem."

"I can't say that," Bryan said, shaking his head. His face was getting hotter and his body suddenly felt like lead. He needed air, but he wasn't sure if he could get up off the couch. This was so new to him. He'd never had to be vulnerable in his other relationships. Hell, Lawanda would have laughed him out of bed if he shared half of what he shared with Nadia with her. *Does saying girl-dick out loud mean I like it?* Bryan wondered.

"Well, at some point, you'll need to. Second, I don't think it makes you gay. That's my opinion. You are simply pleasing your woman," she said. There was silence. She took his hand, placing his hand on her girl-dick again.

Bryan took a deep breath. *I can't believe it. I'm holding her girl-dick,* he thought. She rubbed his cheek. He grinned because at this moment, holding acceptance for the first time did not feel like resignation, but rather like an opportunity.

"See, you're okay," she said, smiling. "Does that feel gay?"

"Maybe a little. But, I'm not gay because I'm attracted to guys. I'm attracted to you," Bryan explained.

"So, what if you are queer?" Nadia countered. "I need you to relax. Don't be so serious."

What is queer? Bryan wondered. But I'm not that or gay, he thought, his hand still resting on her girl-dick. He could feel her girl-dick warming up. Something was happening. Nadia smiled modestly. Bryan's gaze moved downward and he glimpsed the outline of her girl-dick as it became engorged. Beet red. He looked back up just as quickly as he had glanced down. "That is girl-dick," Bryan said, feeling overwhelmed. He suddenly felt as though his hand wasn't attached to his body, that it was someone else's hand that was stroking Nadia. The queasiness he had felt was replaced by a sudden hollowness in his stomach, and he felt that he was slipping away from himself. It felt good, almost meditative, as he continued stroking her. He realized it wasn't as terrifying as he had thought it would be, but the thought of her eventual orgasm suddenly snapped him back to reality.

"I said it. Can we take a break?" Bryan breathlessly asked.

"I'm so proud of you," Nadia said, "Okay."

Bryan slowly removed his hand, her sarcasm stinging. She tried to stand up, but he grabbed her arm. "I've never admitted to anyone that I'm attracted to trans women. This is a big deal for me. I don't have anyone to talk to about this." He looked up at her. Her girl-dick was only a few inches away from his face, staring at him. He smiled back at it. She helped him up.

"You think you're the only guy hiding in that closet? Most guys who date us are in the closet. It's 2015, it's time to get over it."

"I'm sorry, it's not that easy for me," Bryan sighed.

"Honestly, men are funny. You want us to suck your dicks, but you can't return the favor. A lot of you guys are selfish. I need more foreplay," she said. Her face was smiling but her tone was serious.

She began getting dressed. "I understand all of this is new for you. In the beginning, I didn't want to pressure you into something that you weren't ready for. But now, you need to start showing me that you want to be with all of me. You're lucky. Another woman wouldn't be as patient when she's not satisfied."

Bryan started getting a better sense of how unhappy she was.

"Honestly, I think men are too coddled by their mamas," Nadia complained. "This whole patriarchal system makes you the center. We are forced to cater to all your needs: your nourishment, your health, even your maturity."

"Nadia, I really like you. I will do better. I promise." He was surprised by the force and directness of his own statement. He realized she was not playing, and realized that he wasn't either. Some time in the past month or so, Nadia had become more than just someone fun to hang out with and fulfill his sexual urges with. Their conversation was allowing for a much deeper connection. What kind of connection he didn't yet know, but in the past month, something had shifted and multiplied without his being aware of it.

"Hmm." She plopped on the couch a few yards away. "TV?"

"Sure," Bryan said. "I don't think I'm meditating early tomorrow morning."

"I don't know why you spend so much time meditating, anyway. It's not helping you be a better lover."

Ouch. And yet, there was truth in her judgment. Even when he forced himself to sit on his cushion for thirty minutes, his mind jumped from thought to thought like a caffeinated cricket. "Come on, honey," he said, holding out his hand in order to bypass an argument. "Let's watch TV in bed. Whatever you want. *Chopped*, right?"

Stretching to her full length and draping her legs over the end of the couch, Nadia yawned so wide it seemed fake. She emitted indifference, a lioness swatting at flies. Bryan felt his desire rise again, but she was obviously not in the mood. "You go ahead and go to bed. I'll be there soon."

She needed her space, he thought. Maybe he did too. Forced to face accepting all of her made contemplating about all the things he was closed off to in the beginning felt overwhelming. He pulled the covers over his head, searching for answers to how they had become so disconnected.

7

Thinking about Nadia kept him up all night. Bryan did not know how to process what had happened earlier. Instead, he kept replaying their earlier conversation in his head on repeat. *I should have been more comforting,* he thought. He had never wanted to hurt Nadia, but now he was wondering if that was inevitable. He sat up in his bed, realizing eventually that he had to be the man Nadia wanted him to be or lose her. All of this made meditating even harder every time he closed his eyes, he saw her tear streaked face, her wounded eyes penetrating his soul. How can I show her that I'm sorry?

The next day, Bryan sent Nadia a bouquet of red roses and a romantic card to the bookstore, stating that things would be different. He had no kids and a Friday off from work. Bryan decided to visit his mother and stepfather, Robert. They lived nearby in a wealthy, primarily Jewish neighborhood, called Bellaire, near the professional football stadium. Bryan involuntarily straightened his back as he turned onto their leafy street.

He hadn't grown up in this home, but he wished that he had. It was a large white farmhouse with black trim, surrounded by a manicured front yard. Easing the car to a stop on the circular driveway, he saw his mama motion to him from the doorway, her beautiful smile in full force.

"How is my handsome son?" she asked as she greeted him at the door.

"Hi, Mama."

She was dressed as if she had somewhere to go, in a knit jacket and knife-pleated black slacks, and, as usual, resembled a young Cicely Tyson. His mama was the first Black female executive to run a local television station. She also generated income from rental properties and a carwash. As one of the few Black women who hobnobbed with white, old-money families, she was often invited to luncheons and galas. Bryan was proud of her and awed by her accomplishments.

Mama positioned herself for a kiss on the cheek. "Come in."

Bryan stepped inside to see Robert sitting in his recliner in the adjacent living room. Robert was athletic as a young man, but now spent most of his days shuffling from his recliner to his kitchen chair. CNN blared news of Dylann Roof, who killed nine black worshipers inside a Charleston church, and Bryan grimaced. Robert, noticing Bryan, lowered the volume and said, "If it's not the cops, it's some pissed off white person we have to worry about. White people say they're scared of us. We should be the ones scared!"

Bryan nodded in agreement. The ticker on the bottom of the screen then switched to the upcoming bathroom bill, and Bryan tensed. He followed his mama into the kitchen. She fixed him with a penetrating stare. "I'm definitely voting against that nonsense, even if it is part of the Houston Equal Rights Ordinance, which is overall good for the city." She pursed her lips, and lines around her mouth deepened. Bryan wished he could tell her what discrimination did to her face. Perhaps vanity would stop her. "Third gender. Pfft. What will people think of next? Anyway, something has been bothering me since our lunch date."

"Yes?" Bryan said. His heart was pumping as if he'd started sprinting. He knew he had gotten off too easy that day. *Was it the restaurant itself? Or had his mama figured out that she had really gotten a cock ring, not a scarf?*

"It is not so much about what you did. It's as much about what you didn't do when that host-person flirted with you."

Oh, thank God it's not the cock ring, he thought. "Mama, he wasn't flirting. He was being friendly. What did you want me to do, anyway? Speak to him rudely?"

"I'm not stupid. I know when a man is flirting," Mama said. "It makes my stomach turn. Did you know that man? I saw you paying attention to him."

"No, Mama. I didn't know that man. I was just being polite. Please stop making something out of nothing." He cleared his throat.

"I hope he knew, without a shadow of a doubt, that you're normal."

Normal, Bryan thought, *here we go with this gay stuff.*

Thankfully, Robert chose that moment to enter the kitchen. He briefly clasped Bryan's shoulder before sitting down and unfolding his napkin.

Mama handed Bryan the plates and silverware, and he distributed them around the table. "I ran into Mary's oldest daughter yesterday. She asked about you. She's a pretty girl: smooth, dark skin, tall with a cute little figure, and she's an engineer, too." She dropped a heaping spoonful of sweet potatoes on Bryan's plate. "Why don't you call her?"

Bryan snuck another roll. There was no food like his mama's, seasoned with love and her particular brand of spice, which, perhaps confusingly, included her transphobia. How could he extract the sweet from the bitter?

"Son?" Her tone was sharp.

"I hear you, Mama. I know I've not mentioned it, but I'm sorta going out with someone."

"Is this another Lawanda? I can't do a Lawanda again. I tried to save you, you know." She pointed her wooden spoon at him.

"Here we go," Bryan groaned.

"For the life of me, I didn't know what you saw in her." She raised a thin eyebrow. "Was it that good?"

"Seriously, Mama?" Bryan blushed. "Daddy liked her," he said sarcastically.

Her mouth turned down. "Your daddy liked anyone who breathed."

Bryan hesitated. This fussing was nothing compared to what she might say if he ever brought someone like Sarah home. Or Nadia. He exhaled loudly. "Mama, let that go."

His mama was not done. "And with a name like Lawanda. All these Black children with these hard-to-pronounce names. It's already tough enough to get a job with white folks doing the hiring. This is why you and your sister have common names. Bryan and Rebecca. Normal names people can live with."

"Is 'normal' another word for 'white'?" Bryan teased.

She didn't crack a smile. "Boy, don't play with me. You like pleasing other people too much. And I worry about your choice in women somedays. I think your picker is off." Shaking a finger at him, she said, "Your downfall will come one day because of your lack of backbone.

"Mama, don't say that. My picker is just fine," Bryan countered. He could feel defensiveness rising in his chest, but held it back. He wanted to have a good time with his mama and not spend the whole time arguing.

"I hope you've learned some lessons. Try meeting different kinds of women and see what you get. You might actually like what God has in store for you." Mama took up the oversized fork and speared ham onto his plate. "What are you smiling about?"

"Nothing," he said with his mouth full. If his mama only knew God's plan, this was not the conversation they would be having.

Robert interjected. "Did you guys know the government is going to give every Black person ten million dollars for slave reparations? You just have to send a thousand dollars to get it."

Mama raised her voice and shook her head at Robert. "That's a scam." Bryan and his mama smiled at each other. They did have a bond, but Bryan didn't know how to be his real self and be close to his mama at the same time. Even as a kid, he tried to always show his mama the most polished version of himself because he feared disappointing her. He had never felt comfortable enough to be his true self with her, whoever that was. He wasn't even sure if he'd ever shown his true self to anyone before. Maybe Nadia, but he was even nervous he might disappoint her if he showed her his flaws.

"Last week," Mama whispered conspiratorially, "He got an email for buying supplements to make Black people lose weight. It only works on Black people. He almost bought it!"

Bryan rolled his eyes and was rewarded by his mama's tinkling giggle.

"How are the kids?" Mama asked.

"Lindsey is fine, but Lance," Bryan paused. He didn't know how to explain his forebodings about Lance.

"Don't worry. Lance is a sweet child."

"He is. He's so tense. I wished he could go more with the flow, like Lindsey. How's Rebecca?"

"Good." Mama wiped her lips delicately. "Her therapy practice seems to be going well." She handed him the ham plate. "But I wish she'd come home. Their money can go so much further here than in New York."

Bryan and Rebecca had never been close, even as kids. "She's happy in the Big Apple, though, Mama."

His mama nodded yes.

There was a comfortable silence while Bryan cleaned his plate. Mama placed something down beside his water glass. It was a photo of him as a kid with a big afro, red plaid pants, and a white shirt, standing next to Doug Henning, the famous magician.

"Do you remember this?" Mama said.

"Doug Henning was my inspiration."

"You were maybe five or six." She replaced the photo in a drawer.

Bryan remembered his short stint as a magician. He performed during his college years, and had almost considered pursuing it full-time.

"I can't believe you actually considered doing that as a career. That's what I get for sending you to private school. Hanging out with those privileged white kids got you thinking you can do like them. Look, you did the right thing getting your engineering degree. You want me to be proud of you, right?"

Bryan nodded. *That's all I've ever wanted, Mama*, he thought. Bryan placed his dirty plate on the counter. He squirted Dawn into the sink filled with water. He sometimes missed the world of magic.

"Plus, have you ever seen a Black magician?" Mama started again.

Bryan said nothing. *Really? Can I just do something without judgment once?* Bryan thought.

"Exactly," she said, leaving the kitchen.

He finished washing and drying the dishes and went to the living room to say his goodbyes. *Cool Hand Luke* was on TV. His mama put her hand over her heart. "Paul Newman. Now, that is a handsome white man." *Oh, Mama, such mixed messages*, he wanted to say but held his tongue. She was oblivious to her own hypocrisy.

***

Bryan drove away from Mama's house and, while stopped at a light, his mind drifted off to their conversation. The light changed to green, and a guy behind him honked loudly. Bryan waved his hand to apologize, pressing the accelerator so hard that his tires screeched.

Maybe Mama was right and his picker was off. *No, that can't be true*, he thought. It felt too good when he was in Nadia's company. He loved that she was straightforward and transparent. As he drove, images of Nadia flooded his mind. He saw himself holding girl-dick for the first time, then saying girl-dick out loud. *Was that gay? Is it a gay act to hold another person's dick if you have one yourself? Or can you be straight and just do things that might be considered gay from time to time? But, it felt good*, he thought. He smiled. The stream of questions flooding his mind became a crack in the unconscious dam that encased him since this journey started. He hoped Nadia knew his hesitation was not from being repelled by her womanhood. Bryan's thoughts then shifted to more practical matters. Admitting a leaning toward girl-dick was not going to make it easier to date in public and introduce her to his mama or Reggie or anyone at work. In fact, to protect himself and all he had and hoped to achieve, he had to keep her far, far away. Just then, Reggie text: *Do you and your girl want to meet us for dinner tonight?*

Bryan turned his phone off, feeling overburdened with anxiety, no longer questioning how he could make things up to Nadia.

8

"What a day," Nadia said, throwing her keys onto the kitchen table. It was Saturday, the busiest day for retail. She ran to the restroom. Bryan glimpsed her unfolded credit card bills underneath the keys, both cards maxed out and past due.

The streaming sound of peeing revealed how comfortable she was around him, reminding him about how other women he dated made him go to the store for milk whenever they had to relieve themselves, not wanting him to see that side of them.

"Phew! I almost didn't make it," she blurted out.

"Girl, you're going to get a bladder infection if you keep doing that," Bryan said jokingly. A moment later, Bryan realized that it was her limited access to restrooms that was the culprit driving this crisis and wished he could take back his previous statement.

When Nadia emerged, Bryan approached her with outstretched arms. They hadn't really connected since their tense exchange about sex. She leaned in, only allowing their cheeks to touch, which only intensified Bryan's panicky unease. He had his struggles, but he did not want to lose her. He offered the one physical touch that was always welcome. "Honey, let me rub your shoulders."

She tilted her head to the side, considering his offer. Finally, she sat on the couch and piled her hair into a makeshift bun to expose the nape of her neck. She turned on the television.

Bryan was silent, letting his hands do the talking. He squeezed and rubbed, willing the bunched-up shoulder muscles, as well as her impatience with him, to soften. After a few minutes, he asked tentatively, "Are we okay?"

"Yeah," Nadia mumbled. "But it's technically not fair to ask me while you're doing your magic hands–thing."

Bryan grinned. She was back. "Magic hands, huh?"

"Speaking of hands, I reached into a bag to grab a movie that a customer was returning, and the idiot had filled the bag with lube. People are so disgusting. I've got to find another job."

"Yuck," Bryan said, shivering in disgust. "I hope it *was* lube."

"It's hard for me, a trans woman, to find a decent job. Hard for all of us in the trans community."

"I can't imagine how difficult this can be, day in and day out. You deserve better," he said compassionately.

Nadia was proud and determined, and Bryan appreciated that about her, but he wanted to help. "Let's look around. Maybe something else is out there."

Nadia cradled her head in her hands. "Nobody will hire me. I'm lucky to have this job. So many trans women end up doing sex work to feed themselves."

Bryan's shoulders slumped, accepting he was complicit in promoting this reality, he did not mean any harm.

"We're trying to survive the best we can." Her voice was jagged with emotion. "I'm so tired."

"What about your parents?"

"I try not to ask often. They help when they can. 2008 was hard on their 401(k)s, and they haven't completely recovered."

"It's tough," Bryan said, stroking her hair. "Changing the subject, you have a birthday soon. I'd like to cook you a special meal."

Nadia stretched her legs, dangling them over the armrest. She tried to make her voice cheerful. "Yep, in three weeks, I'll be thirty, a glorified cashier at a sex shop." She snuggled her head in his lap. "To your point, I wanted to go to Mattio 54, but I will gladly accept a home-cooked meal at your place if you'd prefer to stay in."

Her reply caught Bryan off guard. Mattio 54 was the hippest new restaurant, and everybody who wanted to be seen was there. He made his voice echoic. "Oh, I was thinking of cooking for you over here." He traced the knobs of her spine. "In our love grotto."

Nadia didn't move her head from his lap, but she shifted so she could look up at him. "We have been dating a while now, and I've never been to your house. Are you trying to keep me a secret? Are you afraid of something?"

"No," he said, pausing, "I've got a bunch of nosy neighbors."

"Today is a new day," she commented.

An ad for *RuPaul's Drag Race* came on and caught Bryan's attention and he raised his eyebrows in surprise as he saw a drag queen sitting in a chair, putting on blush. *The make up in Lance's bag*, he thought. *Was it really for a school play?*

"What's wrong?" Nadia asked, sitting up.

"Nothing," Bryan sighed. *It could be makeup he's keeping for a friend*, he thought. *Don't religious parents forbid their daughters from wearing makeup? Yeah, he must be keeping it for one of his friends.* He picked up the remote.

She snatched the remote from him and slid it under her butt.

Bryan tried to wrestle it from her but soon found himself in a headlock. "Are you sure you want to do this? Or do you want to talk?" She was serious and seriously annoyed.

He answered, but his voice was muffled because his face was smashed into her stomach. "I can't hear you," she said in singsong.

He tapped her shoulder like a WWE wrestler. She released him.

"We can talk," he said, breathing heavily. His face was noticeably redder. "I'm listening."

"Are you cooking my birthday dinner at your house or not?" she said, not smiling.

Bryan took a deep breath through his nose. "Yes."

"Well, good," she said, smiling, "I need to ask you something else."

Bryan, still feeling locked in her grip, waited for her response.

"On Sunday, I'm meeting the girls for brunch at The Yellow Brick Road. I want you to come."

"Is that the gay restaurant and lounge on Summit?"

"You know it is," Nadia said crisply.

"I don't want to go. I told you that." He hoped that massaging the back of her neck again would mollify her, but she wriggled away and stood up. He remembered she was three inches taller than him barefoot, which verified her dominance as he stood beside her. *I love how tall she is*, he thought. In a flash, she went into her bedroom and slammed the door.

Damn. Bryan both hated and liked that she made him fight for her. He knocked on her door. His fears of being outed were going to make this gorgeous woman walk right out of his life. More than just sexy, she was smart, strong, and everything his mother described he needed in his life, he thought. He suddenly realized that going wasn't optional, and he would have to take certain precautions not to be seen by anyone he knew.

"Nadia, talk to me," he said, ear pressed against the bedroom door. Maybe he'd wear a hat with the brim pulled down low. He needed an invisibility cloak that would render him unseen to everyone except his lover and her friends. "Please. Honey, I want to meet your friends."

He didn't want to lose her. *How can I convince her that I want her?* In a flash, he had an idea. He ran to the kitchen. He found the paper towel roll under the sink and pulled off a sheet. He had learned from an older magician how to make flowers out of a paper napkin, so he hurriedly made a rose. It was sloppier than he wished but still cool. With his makeshift gift clutched in his fist, he knelt at her bedroom door and gently pushed the paper flower through the bottom gap. "What time are we meeting your friends?" He watched the rose slowly disappear as she pulled it through to her side. He heard the door unlock and crack enough to reveal her soft green eyes.

The paper flower rested against her cheek as she said, "Thank you for agreeing to meet my friends. Nadia twirled the rose in her fingers. "By the way, when am I meeting Reggie?"

"After we meet your friends," he replied. She was happy and so was he. He would deal with the Reggie place once he survived brunch.

9

Bryan sighed. Taking a seat on his meditation cushion, he found his breath. He counted each inhale and exhale in an attempt to center himself. *One. Two.* His eyes squinted, feeling the air enter at the tip of his nostrils and then release when he expelled his breath. *Three.* He tried to be present, but his mind jumped around. Frustration set in. *What am I doing wrong,* he thought. There were times he felt much calmer after meditating but today he was too overwhelmed. He was meeting Nadia's friends. *Do they think I'm gay? Are all men who date transwomen secretly gay?* Bryan tried to find his breath amidst the swirling chaos of fighting against himself. *Stop!* Bryan yelled at himself. He leaned into the conflicting thoughts as he had been taught to do. Eventually, his internal battle subsided and his mind drifted off into the darkness of the unknown. In his mind's eye, Black and white began to clasp together like a yin-yang symbol; he felt a sense of calm wash over him and accepted its presence. The timer chimed. He had meditated for thirty minutes. He stood up stiffly, convinced he could handle whatever came at him today.

When Bryan picked Nadia up at eleven in the morning for brunch, his earlier conviction began to fade. He was nervously quiet. He felt as though he was doing his first tandem parachute jump and was convinced his parachute would somehow get tangled mid-jump. Nadia touched his shoulder lightly and Bryan pulled back as if his skin were burning.

"Lord, you're so tight. You're gonna squeak when you walk. Are you really that nervous to break bread with a few trans girls?"

"I'm fine," Bryan said. His knuckles were practically white from his grip on the steering wheel. Nadia fell quiet, leaving Bryan to focus on the road. He silently maintained his gaze on the street for a few minutes before course-correcting. What do I have to lose? It's not like anyone who signs my paycheck will be there. And Mama's friends definitely don't brunch there, he thought. He noticed his hands were beginning to hurt from his iron grip on the steering wheel and made a conscious effort to relax them. He took one hand off the wheel and touched hers. "Hey, sexy," he said.

She smiled. "This means a lot to me. You meeting Sophia and Stacey."

"I know. But don't you think your friends might think I'm—" he craned his head around to check his blind spot and changed lanes. "I don't know . . ." he trailed off.

"Bougie?"

"I'm not bougie," Bryan said defensively. "I'm cultured."

"*Cultured.*" Nadia mimicked his articulation, adding a vaguely British accent. "You are kind of white, you know."

"I am not!"

She held his hand. "Good try, but you still sound white."

He gave a *whatever* expression.

"I'm just playing with you." She looked in the mirror, checking her makeup. "So excited to see my girls. Even though we've only known each other for a few years, boy, have we had some good times. "Once, Stacey threatened Sophia's ex-boyfriend with her stiletto heel." She cackled. "She keyed the guy's car that night, too." Nadia fell back in her seat. "Bad girls for life."

"Bad girls for life, huh?"

"You know, like the movie *Bad Boys* with fine-ass Will Smith. Bad boys, bad boys, what are you gonna do?" She bounced in her seat.

"Seriously?" He grinned, feeling his body relaxing a bit. "You don't even know all the words."

As they drove through various neighborhoods with signs written in Vietnamese, Thai, and, of course, Spanish, Bryan thought that this was the perfect city for three trans girls from different backgrounds. They sounded like such a force of nature. He realized that secretly he was excited to meet her friends.

Situated on the edge of the vibrant gay club scene, The Yellow Brick Road was housed in a white Craftsman, especially quaint in contrast to the explosion of color and energy a block away.

As they walked toward the restaurant, Bryan noticed their strides had started to match. Broad daylight was much different than being at Nadia's house in the evenings. Bryan walked as confidently as he could despite feeling a little wobbly. He wanted her friends to like him.

The cozy restaurant was decorated with mahogany-stained wainscoting and blond wood flooring. "It's like you and me, the colors in the wood," Bryan commented, briefly thinking about the symbol he'd seen while meditating that morning. A young man with Keith Urban–style highlights and sparkly lime-green nail polish greeted them warmly. The restaurant was packed with young people. *Am I the only straight guy in here*, he thought.

Bryan looked straight ahead just as he would do at the adult bookstore. They were led to a round table near the back, where Stacey and Sophia were already seated. The girls jumped up and hugged Nadia. One of them squealed, "Are those *another* pair of shoes?" Bryan couldn't help sweeping his eyes over the diners—surreptitiously, he hoped.

"Girl, is this him?" a petite white transgender girl asked, reaching her hand toward Bryan.

"You must be Stacey?" he asked, taking her hand. She was the youngest of the three women, with ivory skin and naturally long eyelashes. Her cropped brunette hair was streaked with turquoise, making her look like a punky Audrey Hepburn or the child of Tinkerbell and Peter Pan. He remembered Nadia telling him that Stacey had run away from home when she was fourteen. Nadia and Sophia had rescued her off the streets.

The taller dark-skinned Black transgender woman grabbed his arm. "My turn." This was followed by a throaty chuckle as Sophia polished and primped. Her hair was freshly set, and her nails were long and tapered and painted fuchsia. Bryan shook her hand. "I'm Sophia."

Sophia hooted. "Girl, he might be a keeper, but we gotta see what he's talking about. How long has it been now?"

"Five and a half months," Nadia said primly.

"Actually, six months," Bryan corrected. "I assume we are going to be together for at least two more weeks."

They all laughed, and Nadia shot him a look of pure adoration. Bryan was relieved that he seemed to fit right in, as if he were an old friend, too.

They sat down, and Nadia asked Sophia about her work at the Human Rights Campaign, night-school accounting classes, and her volunteering at the Women's Center. Bryan was familiar with the shelter. His mama had been involved with it when he was in high school. *Is she still involved? Does she know Sophia?* Bryan wondered. He tried to let the thought go- he was already nervous enough. There was no need to think about his mother right now.

"I'm ready for someone special in my life," Sophia declared proudly. She put her hand over Stacey's small one. "Oh, and I asked my boss, and she's going to call you about the admin job at HRC." Sophia giggled. "I know you don't need the money because your sugar daddies take care of you but if you ever get bored of them..."

Stacey gave her a playful swat. "Yes, but I also want to give back to my community. Plus, sugar daddies come and go."

Bryan tried to stop canvassing the restaurant. He was worried the girls were sensing his self-consciousness. He tried to listen intently, desperately trying not to lose the overlapping threads of their conversation. Eventually, everyone ordered their drinks and food, and Bryan began to calm down.

"Zorro spent the night last night," Stacey said, fanning herself and smiling, "That man can—"

"Stacey, girl, hold your conversation for another time. This is Bryan's first time with us. I don't want to scare him off with all those details. We are demure ladies who lunch at this table," Nadia said, reaching out for Bryan's hand. Nadia stroked the palm of his hand, sensing his uneasiness.

Bryan was intrigued. He assumed Zorro must be a boyfriend. "What kinds of guys are you girls attracted to?"

The three girls quietly mulled over the question. After a few minutes of performative hemming and hawing, they looked at each other and shrieked with laughter. In unison, they held their hands about eight inches apart. In response, Nadia spread her hands a little farther apart.

Bryan blushed. "Fair enough."

"We like good guys," Sophia said, pointing to Nadia and herself. "Some of us still need a lot of drama."

Stacey was half listening and half perusing the restaurant. She blew a kiss to a young guy with longish wheat-colored hair. "Look at that tight ass. I wouldn't kick him out of bed unless he was better on the floor." The girls chuckled.

"Damn," Stacey said. "He's got a ring. All the good ones are married."

"Even lots of the bad ones are," Nadia interjected.

"Oh, girl, you said it." Sophia said. "Last year, I was going out with this guy, and he texted me by mistake instead of his wife."

Bryan laughed. "How did you know?"

"First, the dumbass was texting his wife from my bathroom. Telling her when he would be home. He loves the kids, yada yada."

Stacey mime-heaved in disgust.

"I don't like lying," Nadia said, nibbling a tortilla chip.

Bryan knew that was her biggest pet peeve and felt a pang of guilt. While he wasn't outright lying to her about anything, he knew he wasn't exactly being completely honest with her. He hadn't told her that his mother was transphobic because he hated putting his mother in a bad light.

"I started dating this guy about two years ago." She patted Bryan's knee. "I told you about this, honey. When I found out he was married, I broke it off."

"Men are pigs," Stacey said. "Unfortunately, I love me some bacon."

Nadia took a sip of her Bloody Mary. "I know not all guys are like that, but I'm not going to share some guy just to say I have a man." She kissed Bryan on the cheek. "I'm glad we met when we both were ready for a serious relationship. We've got your kids. I'm done with games. I'm not getting any younger." Nadia sighed.

Bryan felt her ache for something serious and took a long sip of his drink. He wanted her in a serious way too. He just feared she might be a little more serious than he was in terms of meeting friends and family.

Sophia leaned in. "Who are you telling?"

"Honey," Nadia said, squeezing Bryan's thigh. "You aren't saying much."

"Just listening." He reassured her. "I'm having a good time hearing your stories. I've never been here before. I like this place."

She launched into a story from the bookstore, waving her long arms around for emphasis. Bryan wasn't paying too much attention to the words, as he'd heard this story before. He was about to tease her for gesticulating so wildly when her hand hit her fork and it clattered to the ground. He ducked underneath the table to pick it up. He heard a familiar voice. "Hey, ladies. What's the tea?" Bryan froze. *Shit! Is that Jerry?* Bryan stayed bent over, heart racing, face contorted in agony. He cursed himself silently for his stupidity. *What should I do? Can he see me under the table? Or can I just camp out under here for a while?* Bryan suddenly found himself wishing that he owned an invisibility cloak.

"Hi, Jerry." Sophia's voice was full of delight. Stacey's chair scraped back to give Jerry a hug.

"Jerry, this is my friend, Nadia, and her boyfriend, Bryan Hicks," Sophia announced.

"Wait, where is he?" Jerry asked.

Nadia peered down and peeked under the table cloth. "Bryan? Are you . . . still looking for that fork?"

Bryan raised his head and feebly made eye contact with Nadia as he emerged from the table cloth. He set the fork down on the table and sat up straight. He willed himself to look directly at Jerry but was unable to meet his eyes. Dizzy, he took a sip of water from his glass.

"H-Hi, Jerry," Bryan said. He was trying to play it cool, but his nervous stutter was giving him away. Jerry raised his eyes in response and subtly nodded his chin towards the table, as if to accuse Bryan of something. "I wasn't hiding from you or anything, that fork kind of got stuck under the table for a minute there."

Jerry put his hand on his hip. "Well, hi, there, coworker, fancy running into you here. Glad you saved the fork."

Nadia volleyed her gaze from one to the other. "You two work together? Small world."

"Yes, we do, and yes, it is," Jerry said, smiling like the cat who just caught a rat. He shook Nadia's hand. "It's so nice to meet you."

"Have a seat, Jerry?" Sophia asked.

"I can't." Jerry pointed to a handsome young Black man near the entrance. "I'm here with my boyfriend." After fluttering his goodbyes, Jerry moved off in that direction.

Nadia squeezed Bryan's shoulder lightly. "Honey, are you okay?" Her eyes creased with concern.

Bryan didn't have the breath to answer Nadia, but she didn't seem to notice. He glanced toward the restaurant entrance. Jerry winked at Bryan and reached for his lover's hand.

Bryan's accelerated heartbeat blurred to a blade, cutting him in two.

"Girls." Nadia glanced at her watch. "We have errands to run, but it was so good to see you. I miss you."

"Well, we're going to Club High Five on Friday," Stacey said, applying a fresh coat of lip gloss. "Why don't you and Bryan meet us there?"

"Why don't we, honey?" Nadia cast her gaze toward him.

Jerry and his boyfriend were long gone. Bryan's heart rate had slowed, but he didn't feel exactly fine yet, either. Still, he knew what made Nadia happy. The damage was done. Jerry had seen him. Bryan pushed out a wide smile.

"What time do you want us to meet you?" Bryan asked, signaling for the check, which earned him a knee squeeze from Nadia and a shower of thank-yous from her friends. All of which made him feel almost in control and relaxed again.

Sitting in the car, Bryan looked out the driver's window.

"Your friend, Jerry, he seems really nice," Nadia said, smiling.

"He is," Bryan replied, already dreading facing Jerry on Monday morning. He quietly sighed underneath his smile. They held hands. He started the car; he'd deal with the consequences of seeing Jerry at work. No bit of meditation could ease his anxieties.

10

Monday morning began with a heaviness in the air. Large bilious clouds blotted out the sun. As if taking a cue from the sky, traffic was heavy, which was a relief. Bryan was too anxious about seeing Jerry to even meditate. *What was he going to say? How was he going to explain his relationship with Nadia without sounding gay?* Bryan was never the type of person to procrastinate, but today he wanted to avoid Jerry for as long as possible. He decided to get a quick bite to eat in the building cafeteria despite the mountain of work he had waiting for him on his desk.

"Hola," Bryan said to the cafeteria staff.

The female staff members smiled back. "¿Cómo estás?" someone asked. Bryan responded cheerily in Spanish. He enjoyed being able to practice the little Spanish he knew when he could.

"Buenos días, señor Hicks. Es usted muy guapo," one of the other cafeteria workers said, motioning for him to strut.

He knew from a short exchange with a different cafeteria worker last week that "guapo" meant handsome and that they wanted him to model for them. They had been playing this game for years, and Bryan wondered how he hadn't learned more Spanish at this point. The other workers in the kitchen came out to watch as usual. He looked around first to see if any of his colleagues were watching, but he was the only staff member who didn't work in the cafeteria who was at work this early. Bryan stood up and placed his right hand in his pocket before strutting from the salad bar to the hamburger section. He turned on his right foot at the hamburgers and tried to emulate the model Tyson Beckford on his return. The ladies clapped and Bryan smiled as they handed him his sausage and biscuit. He enjoyed playing this game with the cafeteria staff every now and again. He felt like he could be a little silly with them, and he hoped his friendly interactions brightened their day as much as his. He suddenly remembered when Jerry and he used to have a similar, albeit slightly more professional relationship at work. He sighed. As much as he was dreading it, he owed Jerry an explanation.

He managed to avoid running into anyone he knew on his way to his office. He closed the door softly, sat at his desk, he watched the rain thump against his office window. Bryan wrung his hands constantly with the same dread that he had felt before his first prostate exam. This dread was mixed with the same nervousness he used to experience before performing magic shows. Bryan considered simply bursting into Jerry's office and revealing everything, but began returning emails instead. Once his inbox was empty, he found himself staring off into space and noticed the bird's nest that Jerry had pointed out.

Two hours later, Jerry appeared. He leaned in the frame of his office door, coffee cup in hand. He sucked his teeth, staring at Bryan with a strange mixture of gotcha and glee on his face. Jerry usually barged right in, which was irritating, but this game of chicken was worse. Bryan's elbows rested on the desk to stop them from visibly trembling, though he hoped that posture helped him to seem more powerful.

Fine, I'll go first, Bryan thought, willing to lose at the game of chicken. Leaning back against his chair, he motioned at Jerry to enter. Jerry gently shut the door behind him and half sat on Bryan's short filing cabinet. The uncomfortably long pause between them felt like a translucent wall.

"Look," Bryan said, "I don't know why I didn't tell you."

"Tell me what?" Jerry asked, his face breaking into a manic-looking grin. He slurped his coffee.

"Who I was dating," Bryan paused to choose his words carefully. "I wasn't hiding it from anyone. I just didn't talk about it."

Jerry raised an eyebrow over his cup. "It's tough not being able to come out on your own terms. Believe me, I know. But anybody dating a transgender woman is definitely not straight." Jerry slurped again, louder.

"Do you have to slurp like that?"

"Who would've ever believed you're gay," Jerry said, pausing for effect, "I mean a chaser."

"What did you say?"

"Nothing."

Bryan knew the term *chaser* referred to closeted admirers. He shifted in his seat, hating that his relationship had been reduced to a fetish. *Screw you, Jerry,* he thought. Knowing Jerry was right because he was not *out* was even more humiliating. "Whatever, man."

Jerry sat and crossed his right leg over the left. "Welcome to the club."

Bryan said nothing.

"I think guys like you are trying to cover up the fact that you really want to suck a dick." Jerry shifted in his seat. "I see it now," pausing, "The more I look I'm seeing a lot of bottom energy," he said sarcastically.

Bryan stared angrily, taking offense to being called a bottom. "Shut up!"

Jerry barked a laugh. "On behalf of the out-of-the-closet rainbow coalition, I want to insist you are, indeed, a member."

Bryan tried not to let his voice shake. "The Black straight man club is the only club I'm in." Bryan could feel his heart beating fast and his underarms getting moister by the minute.

"I don't blame you," Jerry said, his tone more conciliatory. "It's hard being a gay Black man. The gay whites discriminate against you. Believe me, some gay white men are just as racist as the straight ones."

"Huh," Bryan mumbled, trying to convey in that semi-grunt used by men for probably millennia that this was sociologically interesting but not his problem.

"And Black people, your own community, treat you badly because you're gay. I can't catch a break. Including," he said meaningfully, looking straight into Bryan's eyes, "At my job. This job," he said defiantly.

"Hey, man, Black folks have been hard on me, too."

"Shit, I don't want to hear any of your complaints. People think you're straight. I don't see your opportunities being limited."

"That's not fair, Jerry." *I am straight*, he thought.

"You know these guys will never promote a gay man—correction, an out-of-the-closet gay man—at this company, regardless of his race." Jerry let the implications of his words hang in the air.

Bryan's mouth went dry. He knew Jerry wanted him to do something about his working conditions, but Bryan wasn't sure what he could do. Would coming out as gay, if that's what he was, really help Jerry? Or would it just hurt him?

Jerry popped to his feet and brushed the front of his pants as if they were dusty chaps. "I think she's cute. You don't have to worry about me. I won't say anything to anyone," he said, walking backward out of Bryan's office. "But I do have an extra rainbow sticker you can slap on your Jaguar bumper." He stopped. "And I hope and pray that you will vote to uphold the HERO proposition to support your girl."

"Of course, but I would no matter who I was—"

"Save it," Jerry said. And he was gone.

Bryan stared into the space the other man had recently occupied. After going through life as a Black man without ever being questioned about his sexuality, just like that, he was out. Shame and fear swelled up inside him.

Unable to concentrate, he left work early and went to the gym, hoping that he'd be able to gain some semblance of control or tire himself out, at least. After finishing his workout and taking a shower, Bryan was consumed with Jerry. Why couldn't Jerry see that his attraction to Nadia was a straight attraction? His mind circled around and around.

***

Throughout the week at work, Jerry flashed him a goofy expression every time they passed each other or attended the same meeting. It was grating, to say the least. The next time Bryan saw Jerry, seeing no one was paying attention, he said, "Get that smug smile off your face. I mean it."

Jerry shook him off. "I know they are looking for a diversity candidate for the VP role," Jerry said. "The leadership needs to know just how diverse we are at this company."

Bryan opened his mouth to speak, but nothing came out.

"The rest of us don't get raises and promotions like straight guys or like you guys who haven't come out of the closet yet. The gay community needs to know when one of our own becomes an executive at a major oil corporation."

Bryan's chest tightened and he felt his fists clench. Bryan stormed away, leaving Jerry standing alone.

Back in his office, he did a few minutes of yogic breathing in front of his window to calm down when he saw a man was strolling on the walking trail, his white skin glowing fluorescently in the strong sunlight. It was one of Jerry's managers, coincidentally rumored to be gay. However, he was married to a peppy blond woman named Tiffany and had several children. He was promoted often, he thought.

Unable to control himself, Bryan pushed an entire stack of *Construction Methods* and *Engineering Standards* books off his desk. They clattered to the floor with a sound that startled him, and sure enough, a moment later, there was a knock on his door. It was another department manager. "You okay, Hicks?" the man said, eyeing the mess. His tie was knotted sloppily, and his cheeks were flushed an unhealthy red. A Black man could never get away with sloppiness like that, which made Bryan even madder.

Gathering the fallen books in his arms and returning them one by one to the shelf, Bryan shot a sheepish smile toward the doorway and gave a thumbs up. "Don't ever get divorced," he said, and the man's face whitened before he heartily gave a fake chuckle. "I won't."

After trying and failing to concentrate, he called Nadia. Each unanswered ring stretched something tighter against his windpipe. Loosening his tie, he counted to twenty and pressed her number again. This time she picked up. "Hi, honey, what's up? Busy here right now."

He sighed. "Nothing, baby, I just missed you. See you tonight." It was silly calling her at the bookstore, with its steady stream of customers. A part of him blamed her for putting him in this position with Jerry. The better side of him knew it wasn't her fault, but he continued to simmer on a low boil. She had no idea about the pressures baked into the corporate world. His reflection on the computer screen, in sleep mode, stared back at him. There was nothing he could do but log on and attempt to get some work done.

He managed to cursorily read over a few reports. His brain was not firing on all cylinders, and it was painful to continue to pretend. He decided to leave early for a second day that week and on a Thursday, not even on a Friday. He hoped management was not keeping close tabs on him at the moment. He took the stairs to the garage, hoping to avoid running into anyone, Bryan ran into a coworker he knew casually. Scrambled, Bryan couldn't remember the guy's name. The young man stopped Bryan.

"Hey, I saw you the other day. I called out to you, but I guess you didn't hear me."

Was this going to be his life from now on? Being recognized and subsequently judged and punished for where he was and who he was with? Bryan tried to relax, attempting lighthearted curiosity, but his tone came out dismissive, even accusatory. "Where did you think you saw me? Are you sure it was me?" The guy's name came to him unbidden: Josh.

Josh faltered. He was a rung or two below Bryan. "I'm pretty sure it was you."

Bryan's mind churned through different excuses explaining why he'd been hanging out in the gay part of town.

"I saw you a week or so ago on Braeswood. For sure, it was you."

Bryan let out the breath he'd been holding. "I was at my mother's. She lives in that neighborhood." He shook Josh's hand warmly.

"Traffic's a hornet's nest out there," Josh said, tilting his head toward the door.

"When is it not?" Bryan grimaced, but he was grateful for the tangle of traffic this afternoon. In his car, he'd be sealed off from the world, suspended in time before the other shoe could fall. They bid each other goodbye, and Bryan headed off to his car.

Inside the smooth leather of his Jag, everything felt more manageable, more rational. He told himself that Jerry probably wouldn't tell anyone. For one, deep down they were friends and Bryan knew Jerry didn't break promises. For another, telling on Bryan only highlighted Jerry's own sexuality. Everyone knew Jerry's proclivities, but they weren't mentioned, which kept Jerry safely employed. As for the guilt that Jerry had poked at with a hot iron, if Bryan didn't get the VP job, he was no help to disenfranchised communities. Social responsibility was great in theory. Better to get it and do well and inspire more hires like him. Bryan knew he had a responsibility to the Black community. Did he now have the gay community and the transgender community to represent too? Even if he was straight, Nadia belonged to that community. Would he be breaking her trust if he didn't fight for her community?

"No," he said out loud to himself, as if he could silence his thoughts by being louder than them. She might be in the alphabet but he didn't fit into the same alphabet. He felt confused though, despite his previous certainty. Between holding Nadia's girl dick for the first time, Jerry's comments, and his father's gay slurs floating in the back of his mind, he was feeling altogether overwhelmed. He brought his hands to his face. *If I'm not gay, then what am I?* He shook his head. The last thing he wanted was for his anxieties to drive a wedge between him and Nadia. He had to talk to her. Immediately.

11

That evening, when his exit for home came up, Bryan sped past it and made his way to the adult bookstore. The small parking lot was more than half full of customers breaking up their commutes with a little titillation. He used to do the same, but at this moment, he needed answers.

Nadia patrolled from a high central booth. From there, she could oversee the entire store. Magazines, DVDs, and other media took up three-quarters of the store, with lingerie, adult games, and sex toys positioned against a mirrored wall. A bell chimed when the glass doors parted.

"Hey, what are you doing here?" Nadia asked, beaming at him while handing cash to a customer.

"Just saying hello." He wandered away so she could finish her transaction. His chest tighten having to wait to talk.

Bryan had not been in the bookstore since they had started dating. It felt weird to have a girlfriend so intimately aware of his closeted sexual fantasies. He absentmindedly picked up a DVD with three naked women on the front and immediately put it back as though it were poker-hot. *I can't look at that*, he thought. It felt disrespectful, similar to checking out another woman in front of Nadia.

He looked in the other direction, only for a different video on display to catch his eye. A transwoman stood tall in her heels and her male costar appeared to be shyly admiring her. *Is this what I think it is?* Bryan wondered. He always ignored these types of movies but suddenly found himself drawn to the display. The guy on the cover looked masculine and happy. This made him curious about what it would be like if Nadia were to be the dominant one in their physical relationship. He tried to get a closer look at the tape without picking it up, but decided he didn't want to linger and walked away. *What if she thinks I'm less of a man if I like that? Will this be a turnoff for her?* Suddenly, every part of the store felt like a landmine that could expose his inner fantasies and risk his relationship. He did not know where to stand, so he meandered over to the sex toys, thinking that was the safest bet.

"Do you remember this?" Nadia asked. In her hands, she held the vintage video of Karen Dior that Bryan had rented the first night they met. "You were so cute that night. You looked like a scared little puppy."

Bryan remembered that night for other reasons as well. That same evening, the Baltimore protests from Freddie Gray's killing were being televised and demonized which is why he'd escaped to the adult bookstore for solace. Reminiscing about that moment darkened Bryan's mood momentarily.

Oblivious to this change in Bryan's affect, Nadia prattled on. "And here we are." She winked. "It's been a minute since we've watched it together, huh?"

A portly white man wearing a wrinkled shirt approached them and Nadia introduced him as her boss. Bryan shook off the bad feelings from his reverie and took the man's outstretched hand, once more the model of politeness and "good Black" behavior. "Pleased to meet you, sir."

The man looked him square in the eye. "Nadia is my best employee," he said. He had the kind of eyes that winked when he smiled. "Have a good night, you two," he said as he left the store.

"He seems like a nice guy," Bryan said.

"Yeah, he actually is. If he had been a creep, I would have quit." A customer approached. "Can I help you?"

"Can you tell me about this?" the woman asked, holding a sex toy. "My boyfriend is interested in this for an anniversary present."

"Well, it has a remote control. This part"—Nadia pointed— "fits around his penis and delivers a shock." She was a good salesperson, Bryan thought. Giving clear information and acknowledging the fun in this stuff, all without judgment or snickering. "You're gonna love this, too," Nadia continued. "It's the control we could only dream about."

The customer's eyes lit up with curiosity.

"Wouldn't it be fun if you could give him a quick zap whenever he thinks about or looks at another woman?" Nadia asked. Both women tee-heed in agreement.

Her suggestion caused Bryan to shrink as he felt a metaphorical hold on his balls. Still, Bryan was more impressed than cowed by Nadia's skilled customer service. He felt more constricted at his job. Even when he was certain about something after having done the math over and over and having obtained the same crystalline result, his communication was more measured and much less direct to make sure he did not overstep his authority.

"Honey, hold this," Nadia said, handing him the electric cock ring. Nadia and the customer put batteries in the remote. The ring gave Bryan a violent shock. "Oh, shit," he said, dropping the cock ring, "Aww, hell naw." The two women burst out laughing.

"I'll take it," the customer said, digging out her wallet. She left, bag in hand, with a decided spring in her step.

"This is what your day is like?" Bryan asked.

Nadia jumped down from the booth. "It pays the bills, sort of, for now. It's part of my larger plan." She approached Bryan with her hands behind her back. "That was one of the good interactions. I've told you enough stories for you to know they're not all like that." Nadia brought her hands forward, holding a large flesh-colored dildo. She poked Bryan in the side with it; he jumped back.

"What's that?" Bryan questioned.

"It's a cock, goofball. Here, hold it." She pointed it at him as if she were an Olympic fencer.

"Girl, get out of here."

"You know you want to," she said, wagging it in his face. "You are getting verrrrry sleepy," she said playfully.

He tried to bat it away as if it were a bug about to fly up his nose. "Stop. I didn't come here to hold—" he pointed— "that."

"Girl-dick. Girl-dick," she whispered. "It will make you feel better," she said, playfully kissing the head of the dildo, smiling and batting her eyes at Bryan. "Should I buy one for you? I get an employee discount."

"Uh, no, thanks."

"I'll get it so you can practice." She rubbed the cock around her chin and cheeks and peeked at him through the testicles.

"Practice what? I don't need to practice anything." *What do I need to practice?* Bryan wondered. *What is she implying?* "I'm leaving. I'm serious."

Nadia replaced the dildo on its S hook. "Okay, okay, honey. Tell me what you wanted to talk about?"

"I stopped by because I wanted to ask you something. Do . . . do you think I should tell people at work about us? Because I intend to be an executive VP or maybe a CEO one day."

Nadia frowned. "What does one have to do with the other?"

He didn't know how to explain. Telling someone now could be an obstacle to his ambitions, but it might be worse to have it come out later after he'd achieved a high position. Also, who might he tell? All he knew was that he didn't want anyone to know so that he and Nadia could continue to live high above the dirt of the city, free from judgment. "I don't know, really," he said, feeling a little rattled.

Nadia shrugged. "It's nobody's business, but you shouldn't hide it, either. For instance, I expect you to celebrate Pride with me, so somebody might ask why you're celebrating. And it's always important to tell the truth." She put her arms around his neck.

Bryan hugged her, but he looked over her shoulder to see if anyone was watching them. No one was, so he hugged her more tightly.

"A Pride bumper sticker would class up that Jag."

"I'm not putting stickers on my car," he snapped, pulling away.

Nadia crossed her arms over her chest. "If somebody asks you about me, what are you going to say?"

"There goes the most beautiful woman in the world." He was grinning so wide, all of his teeth were showing.

"See, was that so difficult?" Nadia grabbed her hair and made a temporary ponytail.

"No," Bryan said.

"Do you know why I'm with you?" Nadia asked.

Bryan raised his eyebrow. "Why?"

"Because you're trying. You're better than a lot of guys. Honey, at some point it has to stop mattering that I'm trans. People are way too focused on the wrong things. Being a man or woman is more than just genitals. It's also about how you feel about yourself."

"I don't see why I need to yell from the mountaintop about you to my employer or anybody."

"You're more successful than most other Black guys—especially gay Black guys," Nadia said, letting her hair fall around her shoulders. "There's more at stake than your own good fortune. People need to see courage in action. You're so focused on making money that you are losing the bigger picture."

"I guess. We're not a gay couple."

"We are a straight cis-trans couple," she countered, "One day our relationship will be as normal as interracial marriages are today."

Bryan nodded, overwhelmed by the entire conversation. He didn't know of any men who were open about their trans-attractions. He sighed to himself.

"You should think about telling your employer. What are you going to say if someone finds out at the company holiday party?" She followed him to the door. "Did that help?"

"Yes," he said, hugging her tightly. His chest loosen because he understood they were a straight couple, cis-trans true, but heterosexual.

"Remember, we're going to Club High Five this Friday! I already know what I'm going to wear. Oh, I almost forgot." She handed him her car keys. "Can you grab the folder from the back seat? Thanks, hon."

There was a small black bag that was open in the front seat. Bryan's curiosity got the better of him; looking inside was prescription Viagra and strawberry-flavored oral lube. *Who is this for? Does she think I need Viagra? I'm not that old,* he thought. The manila folder was half-hidden underneath her jacket. Inside was a blank application to the Culinary Institute. Was this what she meant by her larger plan?

Bryan went inside and handed Nadia the folder before kissing her goodbye. He got in his car and continued trying to wrap his head around what Jerry and Nadia were implying about honesty. Was it really lying if he just wasn't talking about his relationships at all, whether they were with cis women or not? Why would he need to tell his employer about whom he was dating? He promised himself that Jerry would be the only person who would ever know about his relationship. *They don't need to know,* he thought. *It's not like who I date affects how competent I am at work.*

His phone chimed as he was sitting in the parking lot. It was a text from Lawanda: *Kids tired. Lance has a big project for school due. His grades are slumping, so he has to do well. Kids asked if they could see you next weekend instead.*

That was perfect because he did not have to explain to Lawanda why he needed to skip this coming weekend. Bryan text: *Of course. Give them my love. Tell Lance he can do it!* Bryan felt goosebumps realizing he was going on his first real date as a couple.

12

Early Saturday morning, he lit a candle and incense. He set the timer for thirty minutes again. He closed his eyes. Soon, he counted. *One.* He was finding a rhythm and he felt his body relax. He counted four when his consciousness produced glimpses of Nadia's girl-dick. He opened his eyes, surprised by what he saw. He was also surprised that he was not scared. *Where did that come from?* Bryan thought. He closed his eyes again. He was curious. Straightening his posture, his mind slowed down as he began counting again. He was learning how to stop fighting against his thoughts and to explore them instead. He saw Nadia, bending down toward him, playfully holding the dildo close to his mouth. He reached for the dildo, and they kissed passionately. In his mind's eye, they were both holding it together as a sign of unity and acceptance. This acceptance transformed Bryan so much that he kissed the head of the dildo as Nadia kissed his neck and whispered into his ear. He felt weirdly submissive as he took the dildo into his mouth. He realized that he was allowing his thoughts to lead him when he remembered to find his breath. The timer chimed. He opened his eyes, realizing this was not meditation but rather daydreaming. He was falling in love and becoming a new person in the process. Sitting with himself in the quietness revealed there was no reason for him not to be the man she deserved. While he didn't like missing weekends with the kids, he was relieved to have another whole weekend with Nadia.

***

He arrived at Nadia's house later that night. She greeted him at the door with a kiss before disappearing into the bathroom to get ready. He could tell she was excited about going to Club Hi-Five tonight. He sat down on the couch while Nadia primped herself in the bathroom. He put his head in his hands and massaged his temples as if that could help calm his racing mind. He hadn't been able to relax all day. Even his morning meditation was a failure- he couldn't seem to breathe quite right, which was always disconcerting. His mind couldn't seem to stop replaying an image of him and Nadia being outed. The first time, he imagined his Mama caught them and when he tried to reset his train of thought, Reggie entered the picture. He understood that meditation was his opportunity to use the present moment to find your happiness, but it was difficult when his relationship with Nadia was the current anchor for his happiness. He worked hard to convince himself that he was not failing at his meditation practice.

I just have to get through the night, he thought to himself. Determined not to get caught in yet another thought spiral, he picked his head up and took out his phone to pass the time. Bryan scrolled through lighthearted selfies of him and Nadia. *We look good together,* he thought. Nadia's height established control, and he often wondered if she realized how much she could be the dominant one at times even though the roles were always reversed in the bedroom. *If she's the dominant one, then I'm the submissive. Does she realize that?* Bryan suddenly thought back to the moment in the bookstore the other day, but brushed it away as a fleeting thought. *Being curious and actually wanting to do it are two different things*, he thought to himself. He tried to pull himself out of his head by checking the time. Only ten minutes had passed, but his mental gymnastics had made it feel like ten hours.

"Girl, if you don't hurry up, we're staying home!"

"Coming!" she yelled. A minute later, she appeared before Bryan in all her splendor. "It takes time to put on makeup and get everything situated."

"I don't know how you do it. You look amazing," Bryan said emphatically.

"I'm a pro now," she bragged, smoothing out her skirt which showed off her long legs.

They arrived at Club High Five around ten fifteen. Stacey and Sophia were already waiting in the long line, which wound around the unassuming building. Tomorrow was Halloween, and it was slightly chilly at night. Bryan bounced somewhat on his toes to cover up his nervousness. Standing behind Nadia, she held his hand, Bryan held it back, he submitted to being led through the crowd; her dominant energy was on full display. *I kind of like this*, he thought.

Inside, loud music hit Bryan as if he were standing in the front row at a Who concert. The club was jam-packed with a human wall of mostly white males drinking and slinking their sweaty bodies. A redheaded man wearing sunglasses and a leather jacket with no shirt underneath approached them. When he was a foot away, he removed his shades to obviously stare at Bryan and rolled his tongue out of his mouth. Bryan's eyes widened with discomfort and he tried to avoid his gaze. Bryan was grateful to be tethered to Nadia, who tugged him deeper into the club.

Silver streamers hung low enough to touch, and the ceiling was adorned with strobe lights and disco balls. Smoke shot from tubes in the walls every time the bass dropped. A DJ mixed music in a cage that was a few feet off the ground. A young man dressed as Little Bo Peep lifted his dress to reveal a skimpy gold lamé thong. Holding Nadia's hand, acknowledging he was hers, Bryan gawked at dancers in booty shorts in cages suspended from the ceiling. People were kissing and making out like teenagers in the dark corners of the club.

One part of Bryan wanted to run out while another wanted to jump right in. *Straight guys don't belong here,* he thought. *Why was I so worried about this? So what if I run into Jerry again? He already knows about us.* Bryan felt his shoulders relax and began to stand a little taller. He knew tonight offered him a totally new experience. In the pulsating black-and-white lights, no one could easily recognize him. He didn't have to be Bryan here- he could be anyone he wanted to be.

Out of the corner of his eye, he saw Stacey stuffing bills into the top of her tight leather pants. A moment later, she climbed onto the nearest platform. She coaxed an admirer to come closer. The admirer was a slender masculine presenting man who clearly understood Stacey was in charge as he gravitated towards Stacey's crouch. Bryan watched, transfixed, as the man removed the cash with his mouth. He had never seen such honesty to a trans woman in public. The guy's vulnerability was the example Bryan craved to see in the real world, not a porn video. He was mesmerized. Excited, Bryan brought Nadia close and kissed her deeply. He put his hands on her thighs, running them up to her belt buckle.

"You'll get your chance," she yelled in Bryan's ear.

Sophia dragged Stacey off the platform and joined Nadia on the dance floor. They sashayed over to Bryan and pulled him into their circle. He shook his hips, and the girls whooped.

At Sophia's signal, the foursome wove around clusters of people dancing and drinking to make their way to a back room with seats and a stage that Bryan hadn't seen. Draped over the curtain was a sparkly banner: *Live at the Five!* Bryan had never been to a drag show. He hadn't even watched RuPaul's TV hit show before, but Bryan realized he was much calmer than he thought he'd be. The drinks, dancing, and the general happy vibes of the club helped.

"Tonight is your night." Nadia winked. "You'll no longer be a virgin."

The room was filling up quickly, but the girls pushed through. All four of them snagged front-row seats just as·the MC tossed the curtain aside and emerged in a glittering floor-length black sequined gown, a few shades darker than her skin, with a revealing plunging V-neck. Too overcome by the visual experience of the emcee's dress and full beard, Bryan missed her name.

"Where are all my trans sisters and brothers? Put your hands up," the emcee yelled.

Nadia, Stacey, and Sophia raised their hands above their heads. Bryan twisted to look behind him to see legions of trans people, all with their arms in the air. Bryan did not raise his hand, he wanted to but he was still too shy to go all in. Everybody shouted back at the emcee.

Bryan caught the eye of the emcee. "You're a cutie." She pointed to Nadia. "Is he with you?"

"Yes!" Nadia yelled, wrapping her arms around him.

"He looks nervous. Is this his first time?"

Nadia nodded yes.

"Girl, did you just pick him up tonight?" Howls and foot stomping ensued.

"Dating since April!" Nadia shouted happily.

The emcee started counting on her left hand. "So, a good amount of time. That reminds me, don't y'all hate when you ask someone how old their baby is, and they answer you in months? Like, how am I supposed to know how many years 164 months is?" The audience roared with laughter. "He's smiling. Girl, he looks happy." The emcee paused for a moment, appearing to size Bryan up. "Like a lost little puppy."

Nadia smiled, "That's how I found him."

"Girl, what are you doing here? You'd better take your man home." The emcee pretended to perform fellatio with the microphone.

"Believe me, I am," Nadia shouted.

Oh my God, he thought. Bryan covered his face with his hands. Nadia rubbed his back lovingly and smiled. As weird as it was to have all eyes on him, Bryan felt safe. And he realized it was a lot of fun being the center of attention.

"Aw, he's turning red," Stacey said in a caring tone.

"Girlfriend, God bless you. That's real love there. Can I get an 'Amen'?" the emcee said, skipping to the opposite side of the stage as if she were preaching at an evangelical church revival. The audience clapped and screamed. "Amen! Amen!"

The emcee explained to the newbies how the show worked. Nine performers lip-synched and danced, and the crowd voted for the Top Queen. She pumped her fists. "Let's get this show started!"

The first three queens were fantastic, but the fourth one, Raven, was the crowd favorite. She mouthed the lyrics of "Bad Blood" perfectly and danced with impressive confidence. After the second chorus, she flounced down to the front row and sang to Bryan. The spotlight was on him again.

Nadia nudged Bryan with her elbow. "Tip her," she whispered. Blushing, he reached into his wallet and handed Raven a twenty. She received his donation with the glamour and classiness of a movie star on the red carpet, kissed him lightly on the cheek, and winked at him as she swished away. *This is so different and fun,* he thought. *Who knew I would be such a hit at the gay club?*

The lights came on after the bearded emcee brought all the contestants out, and the audience rose to applaud, whooping and shouting "Bravo!"

The emcee announced that Raven won and she took her bow. Bryan stepped up to tip again.

After the drag show, the girls wanted drinks, which Bryan chivalrously procured for them.

After only a few sips, Nadia heard her favorite song and yanked Bryan onto the dance floor. They danced close, rubbing their bodies against each other. Emboldened by both alcohol and the attention he had been receiving, he brought her hand to his mouth. Bryan breathlessly looked up at her and sucked on her ring finger.

Nadia yelled over the music. "Let's go home!"

***

He knew his time had come. They fondled each other and made out at every red light as they sped back to Nadia's apartment. With her back pressed against her front door, Nadia scratched around with her key, desperate to find the lock but not willing to stop kissing Bryan. Finally, they tumbled inside and Nadia unglued herself from his body.

"Stay right there," she commanded. "Close your eyes." Bryan was panting like a racehorse in a stall, waiting for the gate to open. He knew he was about to enter uncharted territory, and for the first time since they had started dating, he was confident enough to explore it.

After what felt like ten minutes, she gave him permission to open his eyes. Nadia stood like a superhero. She had changed into red panties and a red bra. She towered over Bryan more than usual in knee-high black boots with a five-inch heel, and Bryan again thought of the video he had glimpsed in the bookstore the other day. He decided he was ready for whatever was about to happen and allowed himself to fully exhale since he had entered the apartment.

Nadia strutted toward Bryan as if she were walking down a runway. *My God, she should be a model,* Bryan thought to himself. He was too stunned by her beauty to even compliment her out loud. Her red lips parted, and she stared right into his soul with eyes like green ice. Time slowed down, and so did Bryan's thoughts as he felt all the blood in his brain drain downwards. He had never seen her like this before. He felt exposed and aroused at the same time. The light of her living room felt like a spotlight, but he wasn't sure if he was supposed to have prepared a performance.

"Crawl to me," Nadia demanded.

Her command startled him. Her tone indicated that this was not a request. The streetlamp outside the kitchen window lit a path to her. He lowered himself on his hands and knees. "That's right," she cooed. Guided by her voice, he began crawling, oddly comfortable on his hands and knees.

As if he was in a dream, Bryan let his hands guide him as she continued motioning him forward. He was no longer driven by logic, but a desire to please her. Disappointing Nadia was not an option tonight.

"Stop there." Bryan stopped, putting his full trust in her. He suddenly realized that this was the first time he had ever trusted someone so completely. He had never fully trusted Lawanda, and she proved him right when she cheated on him and left him

Nadia grabbed a couch cushion, fluffed it and tossed it to the floor in front of her. She pointed with her index finger where she wanted him.

He perched himself on the cushion as if he were waiting to be fed. With Nadia's round bulge level with his mouth, he placed both hands on her toned thighs. He shut his eyes and nestled his head into her warm crotch. Her confidence turned him on. Her scent aroused him. Nadia twisted his hair around her finger. "You are such a handsome man," she said, lovingly caressing his head.

This is happening, he thought. Her height demanded his submission. *Just like the video*, he thought.

He let his eyes run up and down her body as he caressed her thighs. Her legs looked like they ran miles before reaching her thong. He emitted soft moans as she continued to play with his head, lightly tugging it when she traveled to the nape of his neck. Bryan let his gaze meet hers and kissed her right thigh as he looked up at her longingly. She smiled back and exhaled sharply as Bryan slowly pulled her red panties to the side, barely exposing the base of her girl-dick rooted within the short, manicured lawn of her pubic hair. He kissed around her groin area, tasting her soft grassy mound. Following her instructions, he lowered her panties, his knuckles brushing the top of her blushing girl-dick. Beginning to breathe more rapidly, Nadia rolled her panties all the way down and off her legs. She silently watched him, biting the tip of her index finger. This was the first time he had honestly seen real girl-dick. Hers looked like his but different: pink and slim. It felt warm, much warmer than the first time. It was beautiful and majestic. It was serene like Sleeping Beauty waiting to be awakened by the tender kiss of her prince. Bryan proudly accepted he was the prince, so he closed his eyes and gently kissed it. He never felt physically submissive until tonight and realized that no matter what they were doing sexually, he secretly wanted to please her because he craved her approval. She continued to massage his head, twirling his coarse hair.

He stared at her girl dick, partly mesmerized and partly confused. "I don't know what to do," he said nervously.

"Let me help you," she replied. She brought her right hand behind the back of his head. With her left hand, she lifted her semi-hard girl dick in coordination with guiding his head closer with the right hand. Bryan, in the coordinated dance, opened his mouth; she slid her girl-dick into his mouth. "Get me hard," Nadia said lustfully.

Oh my goodness, he thought, *what is that taste?*

Nadia slowly moved herself in and out of his mouth. His mouth watered up easily as she found her rhythm. She pulled herself out of his mouth after several rounds of in and out. She lowered her hand to hold the base of his chin and caressed his bottom lip with her thumb. Nadia moved to the couch and sat down, making herself comfortable. Her girl-dick was impressively stiff.

"Come on over, Bryan," she said seductively, "You need to let your guard down and suck my girl-dick like your life depends on it," she commanded. Even though she was commanding him, he had never felt so safe before in his life. Her words turned him on, pushing him further from his comfort zone. He let go and gave in, sliding his lips around the head and gradually her shaft like a glove, relaxing his jaw. He felt her growing inside his mouth. She was warm and hard like glass.

"Do you taste strawberries?" Nadia asked.

Bryan licked her girth, "Oh, yes," he moaned, licking thoroughly enough to clean her of any strawberry residuals.

"When you think of strawberries," she said between gasps of pleasure, "You'll think about your first time," Nadia added.

She sunk her hips more deeply into the couch, spreading her legs as wide as possible. Bryan made himself comfortable between her legs, his knees on the cushion. Her legs enclosed him, protecting him from the outside, barring him or his secret from escaping. She ruffled her wild mane of hair with the hand that wasn't on the back of his head. Nadia whispered instructions in between her own moans, guiding him to a place of greater intimacy. Bryan realized he was not going to be coddled by her tonight. Nadia was no longer going to deny herself; she commanded his undivided attention on her terms.

Tonight, she was a woman in charge of her sexuality, and he was there to facilitate its actualization. She smelled of musk. The palm of her hands worked like a seashell against his ears, limiting him to the ambient noise of his sucking. Her forearms served as blinders, keeping him from distractions beyond the walls of her thighs. The taste of flesh replaced the strawberry flavor.

Nadia stopped moving her hips.

For a fraction of a second, Bryan's entire world stopped spinning on its axis. His anxieties had melted away and everything was calm. There was no confusion about who he was or who he was with- all he knew was that he and Nadia were right together. His world resumed its rotation a moment later, as her pulsations, which could score a 7.7 on the Richter scale, gradually subsided into small tremors. He rested his head against her thigh, his nose tickled by her soft mound of hair. He felt her girl-dick's warmth as it rested against his chin.

Nadia brushed the back of his head, catching her breath. "Whew," she exhaled loudly. He felt more appreciated than ever. Nadia sauntered smilingly into the bathroom. Her limp part flopped around like a stick-figure puppet, no longer hiding.

As they lay in bed later, Nadia snoring softly beside him and his body tingling, Bryan's brain turned on again. *I did it. I finally did it.* He reveled in his accomplishment, continuing to think about the look of pleasure on her face after she came. She was right; he had enjoyed it. Giving in to her made him feel better, too. He internally laughed to himself. *What was I so scared of? It's just girl dick. It's not like eating out my wife was ever that fun,* he thought, trying not to let a chuckle escape for fear of waking Nadia. He regretted that he waited so long to experience a woman in this way. Right before he drifted off, he felt her soft hands slide across his hip as she began to kiss down his chest, seeming to return the favor.

***

The next morning, Bryan stared at the ceiling fan, contemplating the previous night. He felt a weird mixture of confusion between heterosexuality and homosexuality and suddenly didn't know which world he belonged in anymore. *Can you be both straight and gay at the same time?* Bryan questioned. After all, it wasn't as though he would want to do those things to someone who looked like a man- it was Nadia's femininity that made it all the more alluring. He sighed, realizing he could not put a label on it.

He got up and made his way to the bathroom. Wiping sleep from his eyes, he glimpsed a wad of adhesive tape in the trash can. *Oh, that's how she tucks it away,* he thought. Wow! She does this all day, everyday. I don't know how she tucked all that away. That must get uncomfortable. But, Nadia was right. He would never forget his first time.

Bryan and Nadia grinned at each other as they drank their coffee at the kitchen table. The morning sun washed up against Nadia's face, brightening it to an almost unbelievable splendor.

"You were pretty sexy last night," she said throatily. "I had a good time."

"Thank you." He blushed. "And you were pretty bossy. I've never seen that side of you before. But I liked it."

"Just being myself. I can be a take-charge kind of woman when I want to be. Especially at the bookstore. Too many perverts come in there, and you can't let them push you around." Bryan held her hand in a show of support. "But you—it's a turn-on to see a man be so intentional. You wanted to please me. You knew what you wanted."

He spoke hesitatingly. "Nadia, honey. Will you . . . be my . . . woman?"

Nadia let out a dramatic breath. "You scared me for a second. I thought you were going to tell me you wanted to do drag now." She chuckled and wiped her forehead. "Whew!"

Bryan laughed. "Uh, no. It was fun to watch, though." He gave her his best puppy dog–eyes. "So, are we official now?"

She scooted her chair next to him and put her arms around him. "Yes, I will be your woman. I thought I already was. And now, a shower."

Her long legs were a blur as she left the room. Bryan could imagine his father's violent opposition to everything he was doing right now. Although he sometimes missed his father, the man had had no tolerance for things he did not understand. His dad had once broken his Prince album, *Head*, in two because he strongly disapproved of how the musical genius played with gender. Bryan considered himself lucky that he only needed to hide his cis-trans relationship from only one parent. Hopefully, if his mama ever found out, she would be more forgiving. *Who would have thought being wrong would have felt so good*, he thought. *Is it really wrong if it feels this right though?*

13

O n Tuesday morning, Nadia's car would not start, and she was nearly in tears with worry and frustration. Bryan gallantly called Triple A, waited with her while the tow truck arrived, and dropped her off at work. He told her he'd help pay for whatever needed to be fixed, which put him in excellent standing, combined with his A-plus review from their evening with her friends at the club.

"I guess I became your woman just in time, huh?" she teased, folding herself into his Jag. Her eyes were still dimmer from their usual peridot sparkle, but she was able to joke. "I know, I know. I'll put my seatbelt on before the safety police arrest me."

After dropping Nadia off, Bryan went to his polling station. *Who would vote against something called HERO, regardless of their petty grievances?*

***

At the office, Bryan logged on but wasn't able to plunge into work right away. Gazing dreamily out his window, he noticed that the bird's nest was getting sizable. *What on earth makes a nest that big?* He wondered.

He decided that he needed to refocus and decided to take a much needed bathroom break. As he was about to enter the men's room, Bryan almost collided with Jerry when the door swung open.

"Sorry," Jerry said, his eyes cast down. He tried to brush past Bryan, but Bryan's large frame blocked the door.

"Is something wrong?" Bryan braced Jerry by his shoulders, trying to get him to make eye contact.

"Nothing is wrong," Jerry said, glancing down the hall instead of at Bryan.

"Jerry," Bryan began. Jerry cut him off before Bryan could finish his thought.

"You wouldn't understand," Jerry said, pushing away from him.

"Do you need to talk?"

"No!" Jerry's voice was loud and harsh, and he finally made eye contact with Bryan. Jerry's dark eyes blazed with a mixture of fear and anger. Bryan had never seen Jerry look like this before and his eyebrows furrowed in concern. Jerry seemed to soften a bit in response to Bryan's body language.

"I'm fine," he said in a low voice, "It's personal, okay? Just drop it."

Did he just break up with his boyfriend? Maybe now's not the time to ask, Bryan thought. Bryan had known him through many breakups, and even the worst ones hadn't made Jerry this defensive and skittish. "Okay. Um, I was hoping you had the actual costs for the wastewater treatment upgrade project?"

"I can get them to you later today." The door to the bathroom opened again, and the middle manager, whom everyone thought was a closeted gay man, strolled out. *I wonder if anyone harasses him and calls him slurs,* Bryan wondered. The manager veered closer to Jerry, brushing against him rather than taking the wider berth. Jerry stiffened.

"I'm here if you need me," Bryan said.

Jerry mumbled something indecipherable and walked off. *What just happened? Maybe I should talk to Jerry later today when he's had time to cool down,* Bryan thought. He gave himself permission to worry about Jerry tomorrow and to finally plunge into his work. Jerry sent the numbers as promised, and Bryan simply confirmed receipt and kept working. *Yes, later is better,* he thought. *I've got too much to do this morning anyway.*

A few hours later, Nadia texted about the car needing a replacement valve gasket. Bryan promptly sent funds to her account and let her know he would be helping her out now that she was "his woman". She showed her appreciation with a wink emoji.

***

Afternoon coffee in hand, Bryan strode down the hallway to Jerry's office to check on him. He was about to knock on Jerry's door, but the sound of loud voices from inside stopped him. In contrast to the muffled rumblings in Jerry's office, Bryan heard the blaring sound of his own aspirations coming around the corner. It was Mike Murphy, the senior executive vice president of the chemicals division, who had to be a grade 97. He had transferred from one of the contractor companies and was frequently praised by the CEO as a "stalwart." Taller than Bryan and outweighing him by forty pounds, Mike was a good-looking guy. While there were rumors that he got regular facials and three-hundred-dollar haircuts, he was unequivocally masculine. Mike came across as healthy and easygoing, well-dressed with a full head of dark hair kept in place with a bit of gel and golden-brown skin from hours on the golf course. He looked like a corporate Ken doll. *I bet his wife picks out his clothes for him*, Bryan thought.

"Mr. Hicks. Just the man I was looking for," he said, shaking Bryan's hand. "Come by my office when you get a second."

Bryan had no idea why he was being summoned, but he knew a direct order when he heard one, even when it was couched in polite office speech. "Yes, sir, I will be right there."

At that moment, Jerry opened his door, but before either man had a chance to say anything, Bryan was practically sprinting down the hall. "Talk to you later, man," he tossed over his shoulder, hearing the thump of Jerry's door shutting. After a few minutes of dawdling near the watercooler to give Mike enough time to return to his office, Bryan ascended the stairs two at a time to the next floor. Mike's secretary, a stylish young Black woman, was on a call. She smiled warmly and waved Bryan through.

Mike was also on the phone, sitting with excellent posture in a hulking chair sized appropriately in the expansive room. He gestured for Bryan to come in.

The executive offices were designed for comfort, efficiency, and a recognizable display of power. In one corner, buttery leather chairs were clustered in a contrived, informal design, a larger version of which was positioned behind Mike's polished cherry desk. Huge windows framed the cityscape. Bryan's eyes were drawn to the large gold-framed photographs on a wood-paneled wall.

"Honey, I've got to go now." Mike hung up the phone. "Touching base with the wife and son."

Bryan felt a pang of jealousy for Mike's intact family. Having everyone under the same roof made it easy to call and check on them. He had spoken to the kids earlier that week, but phone calls never felt like enough. Luckily, he'd see Lance and Lindsey this weekend, as long as Lawanda didn't change it again.

Mike followed Bryan's gaze to the photos. "The one on the far left was taken in New Iberia."

"New Iberia?"

"Louisiana, south of Lafayette. We were there for two years before I got hired here. I was the project manager working under the director."

He's not even forty yet, Bryan thought, *I bet his father or some other relative helped him get in above the ground floor.*

"That looks cold," Bryan said, pointing to the next photo in the series. In this one, Mike was surrounded by snow.

"Fort McMurray, Alberta, Canada. The oil sands. Yes, very cold, even in springtime."

Bryan marveled at how he had managed to obtain so many fantastic assignments at such a young age. *Yep, definitely some sort of nepotism,* Bryan thought to himself.

Mike ran his fingers across his desk. Answering the unspoken question, he said, "I attended my dad's alma mater. Go Tar Heels." His cheeks reddened a bit. "When I graduated, Dad called in some favors."

Bryan nodded. At least the guy had the decency to blush at his start on third base.

"Have a seat." The younger man gestured toward three oxblood leather chairs facing his desk. Bryan chose the center one and found the cushion overly soft and had to sit on the very edge to be at eye level with Mike. If Bryan relaxed even slightly, he was forced to look up at Mike like a kid. Propped on the desk and facing Bryan was a portrait of a glamorous-looking white woman and a Black boy dressed in a sailor outfit.

Mike cleared his throat. "As I'm sure you are aware, Bryan, the company is looking to fulfill the role for VP of polymers and specialties. We want to diversify our ranks at the top level," Mike said, coming around to sit on the edge of his desk, blocking the view of the photo.

Bryan both hated being seen as one of the good Blacks and was relieved by this distinction. Getting promoted should not have to mean getting kicked out of the Black community. "Yes, I am aware of that, sir." He tried to sit up straighter, but the chair was as gooey as marshmallows. *Good trick,* he thought, *getting us to feel smaller.*

"I've been asked to mentor you, get to know you a little better. You're being considered for this role, as are a few other internal candidates."

Bryan was giddy with excitement, but he modulated his voice to a respectful murmur. "Thank you, sir." The room suddenly seemed less intimidating, as if he were sitting with a friend.

Mike shook his hand again. Two handshakes in a day were unprecedented. "I will be in touch."

Back at his desk, Bryan clicked around on the Porsche website. His future was looking pretty good right now. He intentionally kept his door closed to dissuade anyone from stopping by or interrupting. Bryan attacked his work with a new fervor. Down the hall, his colleague Amy was probably doing the same. It was a good tactic for a company to pit their top two people against one another for one promotion. As a divorced man whose ex-wife had the kids most of the time, Bryan knew he had the advantage. He hoped getting a promotion would help prove to Nadia that he could provide for her.

***

At five, Nadia texted. *We need to talk. Now. In person.*

What now, he thought. He felt his heart rate increase and his brain began spinning. What could he have possibly done to upset her between the morning and now? All he had done was send her money for her car- how could she be mad about that? And they had such a great morning together. *It can't be anything I said this morning,* he thought after replaying their conversations over in his head a few times.

Bryan canceled his workout and hurried to her house. He nervously knocked, and she cracked the door barely open to let him in. She didn't greet him, but retreated back inside without a word. Bryan slowly slipped through the door as if one wrong move could detonate a landmine at any moment.

Nadia was waiting for him on the couch. Her legs were gathered into her chest and a scowl pulled down her cheeks. He could feel a lump rising in his throat, and tried to speak. "W-what's w-wrong, honey?" His voice sounded shaky.

"Are you still dating around?" Nadia's eyes were green with jealousy, and Bryan wondered what he had done. *Did I get too handsy with the queens at the club?*

"No, you're the only person that I'm seeing."

"Don't lie to me. I will not waste my time on a player," she said threateningly. She opened her Chromebook. "Then, pray tell, what's this, Choco-B?"

He peered closer. Nadia was looking at a profile on a hookup website called BootyCall. His heart stopped at the name, which was chosen on a lark and now pronounced with disgust.

"I'm not on that dating site anymore. I promise. I forgot I even had that profile."

"Stacey found this," she said, staring at him with piercing eyes.

"What's she doing on this website?"

"She finds a lot of guys on straight websites. She was cruising, and she found your photo. I think the question is, what are you doing on this website?"

He parted his lips to speak, but she cut him off.

"You know, I don't even want to know. I just want you to take this account down."

"Yes, I will. Right away. I know you don't believe me, but I honestly had forgotten about it. You can even look at the message history," Bryan said, trying to reassure her. He racked his brain for something to restore her trust in him, to demonstrate his commitment to her. He had not logged into that account in nearly a year because he didn't want anyone else. Nadia was everything the universe promised: she controlled her anger, she fought fair, she respected him as he respected her, and she was willing to accept him as he was. *Is this going to break us up? Does she really not trust me enough?*

"Honey, I have the kids this weekend. You can meet them. I want you to meet them." *Let's start with the kids and then you can meet Reggie*, he thought. He knew his Mama would be last on the list and he could only hope that his kids wouldn't sell him out before he could tell her.

14

That coming Saturday morning, Bryan was forced to sit with the thought of Nadia meeting his children and possibly being outed was making Bryan second-guess himself. *What if my kids don't give her a chance just because she's trans? And what will they think of me? Will they stop seeing me as their father?* In an effort to control these thoughts, he picked up a small booklet called "Beginner's Guide to Meditation" by Goswani Kriyananda. As he read through it, Bryan learned that meditation was supposed to tame fear because it forced one to sit with oneself long enough to look objectively at their fears. He was starting to see more reasons to meditate regularly. He sat on the cushion, setting the timer for thirty minutes. The silence was still more uncomfortable than inviting. As he closed his eyes, his mother's face appeared in his consciousness. He traveled down the path of figuring out how to introduce Nadia to his mama. Every time he saw his mother scowl with disapproval, Bryan tried to anchor himself in his breath and erase the image. Before he knew it, the timer chimed.

Bryan picked up his kids from the usual gas station. Drizzle blanketed the windshield of his Jaguar. While he waited for Lawanda to arrive, he listened to NPR. Trump was whining about Marco Rubio and Ben Carson, who were both thankfully ahead of the Orange Buffoon, as Bryan liked to call him. Bryan shook his head in disapproval as he heard Trump blaming "Barack Hussein Obama" for artificially lowering interest rates. Local news bemoaned the rejection of Proposition 1. Almost 70 percent of residents in the city Bryan loved had voted against HERO, including his mama. In the sky, heavy-shouldered shapes traced lazy circles, darker than the smoky clouds. Vultures. *If that's not an omen, then I don't know what is,* he thought.

His kids tumbled into the car. The clicks of their seat belts reminded Bryan of Nadia making fun of him for being the safety police, and a warm glow nudged out his desolation and anger. He made his voice brighter than he felt. "Hey, guys, how do you feel about a day of take-no-prisoners bowling tomorrow?"

"Hooray!" Lance yelled. He hugged his backpack close. Lindsey gave Bryan a thumbs-up before her eyes were drawn back to her phone.

"I've invited a friend of mine, a woman friend, to join us," Bryan said, doing his best to sound casual. He hadn't ever brought up the subject of introducing someone he was dating to his kids.

"Daddy, you mean like a girlfriend?" Lance asked.

"Yes, like a girlfriend," Bryan replied. "Her name is Nadia, and I think you guys will really like her."

"Daddy has a girlfriend," Lance said.

Bryan smiled, "Today, we'll do some fun stuff with just us. You'll meet her tomorrow."

Lindsey rolled her eyes, and Lance whooped. His two kids in a nutshell. This thought was strangely comforting. Their personalities were theirs, regardless of whom or if he was dating. He didn't need to worry so much.

"How's school for you both?"

Lindsey immediately launched into enumerating her many accomplishments with the volleyball team and in her science classes. She knew what her father valued, and she predictably served it up, though happily; she liked excelling for herself as well.

"Okay, I guess," Lance mumbled. Bryan glanced in the rearview mirror at Lance, whose face was tightly drawn. He had circles under his eyes and was clutching his backpack like a life raft. *What's wrong?* he thought. Bryan wanted to ask, but felt that whatever it was a sensitive subject. Lance had left his backpack at the hi-rise a few weeks ago and seemed a bit unmoored without it. *What was in it? Shouldn't it only have homework in it? Is he hiding bad grades?* Bryan wondered. He thought that the school might have called if it was related to academics, but if they only called Lawanda there was no guarantee she would loop him in. Bryan wished he and Lawanda were able to talk more openly about the kids. Unfortunately, and maybe understandably, she took his observations only as criticism.

***

The bowling alley was noisy. Loud music blared from cheap speakers, while kids screamed, half-drunk parents laughed. The "thud, thud" of bowling balls hitting the ground reminded Bryan why he was there. The greasy smell of "kid-friendly" food wafted through the air, and he considered giving into the temptation for a moment.

Lance tugged Bryan's arm as Bryan slipped on his bowling shoes. "Dad, Dad, when is she getting here? You said one thirty, and it's one forty."

"Son, relax. She's just running a little late."

A moment later, Bryan glanced toward the entrance. A statuesque Amazonian beauty was walking toward them. Her head bobbed like a buoy in an ocean of screaming kids and average-height adults. Nadia.

When she reached the three of them, Bryan, intoxicated with uncontrollable feelings, reached for her. Nadia shook him off and flashed his children a broad, genuine smile. "Hi, you must be Lindsey and Lance."

"This is Nadia," Bryan said.

He was shaken by her rebuke. For a split second, he was hurt, but then relief washed through him. Thank goodness Nadia had the wherewithal to push him away. His kids hadn't seen him kissing anyone except their mother. He felt foolish.

Nadia held out her hand. Bryan held his breath. *Would her hands give her away? Would she pass?* He tried to distract himself by looking around at other families who were bowling.

"It's so nice to meet you two," Nadia said.

Lindsey gave Nadia a limp handshake. Before her rudeness had time to register, Lance hesitated for a moment. *Speak to her, Lance*, Bryan thought, *what's wrong with these children?* A smile gradually appeared on Lance's face. He unexpectedly wrapped his skinny arms around Nadia's middle and buried his face in her belly button.

"Easy there, son," Bryan said, pulling him away by the shoulder.

Lance was not deterred. "Ms. Nadia, you need to pick out your shoes."

After they were out of earshot, Lindsey shot Bryan an angry look. "You didn't say she was white. And how tall is she?"

"Give her a chance. I know she might not be what you expected, but she's a good person, which is really all that matters." He patted Lindsey on the back. "She's six foot four." Instinctively, he looked around. The bowling alley wasn't far from his Mama's. *Is anyone she knows here?* He thought.

Nadia walked up to them, holding a pair of red-and-black bowling shoes. Lance bent down to re-tie his neon-yellow ones. "Daddy, me, and Nadia are on the same team. Us against you and Lindsey."

"Okay, it's on. Lindsey, are you ready? Up top, girl, give your daddy a high five." Lindsey couldn't help smiling. Even though she was a teenager now, she still sometimes surprised Bryan by acting like she liked him every now and again. He could still see glimpses of her as a little girl from time to time, and the thought made him smile.

Nadia went first. The rhythm of her gait was like a visual siren's song, and he shook himself to get his mind back to a G rating. Hopefully, his kids hadn't noticed the change in his affect.

Nadia bowled a strike on both attempts. She walked back, beaming with confidence.

"You got lucky," Bryan teased, secretly impressed with her skills.

She gave Lance a high five. "I bowled all the time with my dad when I was in high school."

"Come on, Lindsey," Bryan shouted, trying to ignite her competitive spirit. "Give me a strike, baby girl. Show 'em what you got." He turned his head to Nadia. "I knew you were on the drill team, but you never mentioned bowling."

"Mama was a cheerleader, too," Lindsey replied over her shoulder. His daughter also bowled strikes on both attempts. She strutted back.

Lance was next. Bryan thought it was cute that Lance chose a ball that was too heavy. He could only knock a few pins down, but a low five from Nadia brought a smile back to Lance's face.

On his turn, Bryan knocked down six of ten pins on his first turn and finished his second with one pin remaining. He was satisfied with his results because this kept Lindsey and him from gaining too big of a lead. Bryan still scanned the crowd for anyone staring in their direction. Nadia passed easily, especially from a distance, but he did not know how to let go of his fear.

For the next hour, Nadia and Lindsey challenged each other for superiority. Lindsey never said a word to Nadia and rarely smiled, even at her father or brother. *Is this typical teenage girl stuff or does she have an issue with Nadia?* Thankfully, between Lance's enthusiasm and the adults' attempts at levity, the tension was kept to a minimum.

As the game headed into its tenth frame, the teams were tied. At the ball retriever, Nadia shot Bryan a look he couldn't decipher. In the lane, she waited a few beats longer than usual before lunging. The ball careened close to the gutter, hitting only two pins on the far-left side.

"C'mon, Ms. Nadia! You can do it," Lance shouted.

"Thanks, partner." Nadia beamed at Lance. She retrieved her ball, brought it to her chin, and took two steps forward. This time, the ball smacked loudly against the wood floor and spun wildly to the far right, hitting only three pins.

"I tried to be fancy," Nadia said to Lance. "Sorry, teammate."

Bryan's heart ballooned. Nadia was such a sweetheart, which he knew. Her parenting instincts were also spot-on, both in letting Lindsey win and in being so open with Lance. Lance responded just as sweetly. "Don't worry, Ms. Nadia. We can still win. Lindsey might miss."

"Ha," his sister said. "I never miss."

On both frames, Lindsey bowled strikes. Lindsey raised her hand for a high five.

Bryan slapped her hand. "Excellent bowling all around. And I mean everyone," he said. "Do you guys want something? Nadia and I will get some drinks and snacks." He handed his kids some money to play a claw game with while he and Nadia went in the other direction.

They cut their way through the hordes of children, only to wait in the long concession line. Bryan squeezed Nadia's hand. "Whew, I might need a beer after all that. Thank you for sacrificing your bowling score for my daughter's raging ego."

Nadia shrugged. "She's young." She got in his face. "Are you okay? You keep looking around."

"Some guys have been checking you out." He nodded his chin toward a guy in a do-rag. "Like that Ike Turner looking brother."

"You're jealous?" Nadia preened. "That's always a good thing."

When they returned with colas and nachos, Lindsey was huddled on a bench, texting, and Lance was talking to a few friends from school. Bryan and Nadia lingered outside the circle of giggling teenagers. Bryan was alarmed to see that many of the boys were wearing dark-colored wigs, skirts, ruffled blouses, and high-top shoes, though there was a red-haired kid wearing jeans and an olive-green tee standing close to Lance.

"Daddy, this is Harry," Lance said. Harry reached out his small pale hand with a shimmering smile, and Bryan shook it. Bryan missed the names of the other boys who were dressed so oddly. Meeting Lance's friends quickly confirmed which social group he was in, and Bryan sighed internally. *I hope he doesn't get picked on,* he thought. Bryan noticed that Lance's friends had seen Lindsey, but they appeared to be mutually ignoring each other.

Lance pivoted. "And this is Ms. Nadia."

"Harry, nice to meet you." Bryan watched Harry shake Nadia's hand with the same frailty. Nadia complimented the other boys on their skirts.

"You never told me Lance was queer," Nadia whispered while the boys chatted with each other.

Queer? "He isn't," Bryan said, unaware of what queer was nowadays. Bryan remembered that queer was a slur for gay men when he was growing up. *You can say that now?* He found himself a bit curious, but his defensiveness overtook his curiosity.

"Have you asked him?" Nadia replied.

She sat down next to Lance to be more at the boys' level, speaking to them. "When I was your age, I had a skirt just like the ones you boys are wearing." She leaned in closer, stroking the wig of the boy closest to her. The boy welcomed Nadia's attention. "I wore a black wig when I was in high school. After I transitioned, I went back to my blond roots and grew my hair long."

Oh my God, is she talking about her transition? Please, please don't be too loud, he thought. He looked at Lindsey to see if she was listening. She had taken her headphones off, but she seemed to be unaware of the conversation. Rocked to his core with panic, Bryan found himself speechless. He hoped the conversation sounded like white noise to his daughter.

His eyes darted around, noting the plethora of Black people inside the bowling alley. Once again, he hoped no one he or his mama knew was there.

"You and your friends remind me of my younger self," she confided. "I grew up in a small town, but in a big city, you might feel even more alone than I did."

Bryan waited until the kids were chatting among themselves again. Wrapping his hand tightly around Nadia's forearm, he tried not to hiss.

"Did you tell Lance that he reminds you of your younger self? That's crazy. You and Lance are nothing alike. He's not a girl. Let's get that straight now. I'm done talking about this." Bryan grimaced.

Nadia removed her arm from Bryan's grasp. "I'm not done talking about it. I'm trans, and he's queer. Those are different expressions of self, but we share a community, right? LGBTQIA+."

Bryan said nothing, and Nadia gave him a withering stare. Neither planned on backing down, and Bryan knew this discussion with her wasn't over.

"Well, this was lovely, but it's time for me to take off," Nadia announced. Lance gave her a big hug, which she expected this time. Lindsey waved, smirking. *Does she know?* Bryan felt about as relaxed as a hornet's nest. He could feel the bees buzzing around in his stomach and floating up to his throat. He offered to walk Nadia to her car, but she demurred. "Stay with your kids. I'll talk to you later." They hugged quickly.

On the drive home, Lance piped up, "Daddy, I like her a lot."

"I'm glad, son."

When Bryan got home, he noticed that Nadia had texted him.

I shouldn't have said anything. Kids must come out when they are ready. These queer kids need our support and protection.

Bryan texted back a heart emoji. He knew that arguing about Lance being queer, regardless of what Harry and his other friends were, shouldn't be done over text. The only terms he knew were "gay" and "lesbian". He had no idea what some of the other letters in LGBTQ+ meant.

"She was asking us questions about school. You just kinda show up to our games," Lance said.

Bryan felt like the wind had been knocked out of him. Lance had delivered the type of gut punch Bryan would expect from Lindsey, not him. He paused a moment to contemplate Lance's view. It was probably true. He tried to remember the last time his kids had told him about a school project they were doing. Had they stopped volunteering that information, or had he stopped asking? He tried to justify his actions to himself, and then to Lance, but found he had no excuse. He didn't want to make a promise he couldn't keep though, so he kept quiet and continued driving.

He quickly found himself replaying scenes from the bowling alley. He was still upset at Nadia's oversharing, but he also couldn't ignore how well she did around the kids. He wondered how much Lindsey had picked up on and if she might be questioning his sexuality. When they were stopped at a red light, he pulled the left side of her headphones away from her ear.

"Dad, what are you doing?" Lindsey was clearly exasperated, but she took off her headphones. "Nadia's okay. I don't know why you can't invite my mama out for bowling or something. But if that's what you want to do, then do you. FYI, Nadia isn't as good a bowler as she thinks."

"Lindsey, not everything is always about winning," he said, as she put her headphones back on. "There's more to life than winning."

"Says the one who wants us to get straight A's," Lindsey replied without removing her headphones.

Bryan's heart leaped into his throat. "Could you hear us talking while you're wearing headphones?"

"Yep."

Shit, he thought.

"Are we going to BiBi's for dinner?" Lindsey asked.

"Yes, we are," he said firmly. His children knew that his tone meant question time was over, and the rest of the car ride was silent.

15

The following day, Bryan squashed another attempt by Nadia to explain why he needed to open his eyes to Lance's identity. Bryan did not understand why she kept using the term "identity". Regardless, he was not open to talking about Lance being gay. He respectfully asked that she leave the subject alone. Bryan pulled into his mama's driveway with his kids in tow. The lights ringing the circular driveway glistened against the thick gray curtains of air.

Bryan checked his phone to see a text from Nadia. *Tell your mother I said hello.*

Bryan said he would and slid his phone into his pocket.

The three of them spilled out of the car. Lance ran to his grandmother, while Lindsey shuffled into the house, eyes on her phone. Mama waved her hands in front of her granddaughter and Lindsey looked up. "Young lady, you need to put that phone down for a minute and give me a big hug. I don't get to see you much. It's not going to kill you to give me your attention for an hour."

Lindsey tucked her phone into her back pocket and put her arms around her grandmother. "I'm sorry, BiBi."

Robert sat in the living room, watching the news while his mama bustled around him. "They say flood season's officially over." He tsked. "Last January through June, with the Memorial Day floods, Tropical Storm Bill, and Hurricane Patricia, were the wettest six months in the city's history."

They all ignored him. Robert lived for weather forecasts, historical and present, which was funny, as he rarely left the house.

Mama turned on the faucet to wash her hands. "I'm making this chicken recipe that was in the newspaper." *Everyone's a foodie now*, Bryan thought. When he was growing up, his mama cooked hamburgers. On Friday nights, they watched *Different Strokes* together while they ate a simple meal.

Tonight, the TV showed Hillary Clinton and Trump standing together, a jagged line between them. Mama glanced up. "That horrible man. He is no friend to Black people."

Bryan agreed. At least Black families were not torn over Trump the way white ones were.

"But we have to live as we've always done. College is already next year for my Lindsey," Mama said, proud and wistful. "I remember the day you were born."

"Yes, I want to study electrical engineering."

"Good." Mama vigorously diced an onion. "Are you still dating that same boy?"

Lindsey nodded yes.

"Don't let anyone bring you down or get in the way of your dreams. Women are being given so many opportunities in the science fields. Especially Black girls. Don't squander these years."

"Okay, BiBi. I won't."

"We put so much pressure on ourselves to be superwomen that we end up with partners who take us down from the inside."

Bryan knew his mama was referring to his father. Early on, she had chosen her career ambitions over Bryan's father's request that she not work at such a high level. Even as a kid, Bryan understood that she was trying to put the family first and that when she succeeded, they all did.

Robert turned the TV off and ambled in, sinking into his kitchen chair with a grunt. "Lindsey, when is your next volleyball game? I've been meaning to watch you," he said, eyeing the potatoes.

Lindsey smiled at her grandmother. Everyone knew Robert was never leaving the house. "Oh, there's not one for another three weeks. I'll let you know then, okay?"

"And, Lance, young man," Robert added, heaping beans on his plate. "How is school?"

"Drama is the best part of going to school." Lance's face was bright. "I'm Mowgli in the school play! You know, from *The Jungle Book*."

"Oh, how wonderful!" Mama exclaimed.

Lance had a dreamy look on his face. "BiBi, when I'm on stage, I get to be whoever I want to be, or, at least, the character I'm supposed to be."

"I thought you were just doing it to wear makeup," Lindsey added under her breath.

Lance rolled his eyes.

Bryan ignored her, and thankfully, so did his mama. "Congratulations, son, that's great! Do y'all remember the time Lance dressed in period clothing and recited some of Shakespeare's soliloquies in front of Kroger? I'm excited to see you perform." Bryan rarely missed being a magician, but this was one of those times. He wondered if some of his own stage presence might have worn off on his son.

"Opening night is the week before Thanksgiving. Will you come, Daddy and BiBi? Costumes and everything."

Bryan and his mama said "Yes!" in unison. Robert grunted in agreement.

Lance grinned. "I hope one day I'll be as good as Alaska Thunderfuck."

Bryan almost choked on the bite he was chewing. "Son, you know that isn't appropriate language at the dinner table."

"I know, but it's her name," Lance said meekly. "But Alaska . . . Alaska is really talented. She can sing and dance," he waved his hands in an elaborate flourish. "She's beautiful. You'd like her, BiBi."

"Whatever you say," Mama said, flustered. She placed a hand on her collarbone. "I don't know this person. I have no idea what young people are talking about most of the time."

Lindsey smirked. Bryan glared at her, and she looked at him with fake innocence before diving back into her salad.

"Well," Mama said, smoothing her hands down her lap. "What have you all been up to with your dad?"

Lance was putting his dishes in the sink. "Yesterday, we went bowling with Dad's girlfriend."

Mama jumped a bit in her seat. "Oh, really," she said, looking pointedly at Bryan, "I've not met her. What is she like?" She got up from the table and began busying herself with transferring leftovers into her vast collection of Tupperware.

Bryan could feel the back of his neck getting hot and the now familiar pit in his stomach returning. *If I didn't know better, I'd think I have an ulcer,* he thought.

Lindsey scraped the floor as she pushed her chair back and stood up abruptly, dish in hand. "She's white and—" Lance hit Lindsey's arm, and she shut her mouth.

"You don't say. And what else?" Mama asked, hands on her hips. "Were you going to say something else, Lindsey?"

"I guess she's okay," Lindsey finished.

Bryan rubbed the back of his neck as if that could help him cool down. He didn't dare meet his mother's eyes, but he sensed her laser-hot glare. The pit was growing, and Bryan found himself unable to form words to describe Nadia. *The kids beat me to it,* he thought, sensing that Mama felt left out.

"I like her," Lance said, stealing a cookie from the full jar Mama always kept within reach on the counter. "She's pretty, and she's really tall. They kissed at the bowling alley."

"I see," Mama said dryly. "Will you be bringing her for Thanksgiving?"

"Mama, I've not gotten that far yet," Bryan said. "And Lawanda has the kids this year, remember?" He stood up from the table and scooped up a handful of dirty dishes and glasses, glad for their clanking. "Okay, guys, that's enough. Let's all help with the dishes." He motioned to Lance to put his dirty cup into the dishwasher, and when Lance got up to do so, Bryan grabbed his son's backpack and placed it by the front door. It felt lighter than he was expecting it to. He surmised that nothing significant was inside the backpack and perhaps Lance kept the majority of his textbooks at school.

"When do I get to meet the woman my grandchildren have already spent time with?" Her voice was queenly and arched. Bryan could sense he would have several passive-aggressive comments coming his way if she didn't meet Nadia within the next month.

"Soon, Mama. Soon. I'll tell you all about her. As a matter of fact, she told me to tell you hello," Bryan said confidently. His posture relaxed, feeling a sense of connection to Nadia. When Lance came back from the kitchen, he cast his eyes around wildly until he located his backpack and then pounced on it, clutching it to his chest. This made Bryan more curious. *Maybe I should ask him what's in it,* he thought.

"Mama, I have to get the kids back to Lawanda." Any infraction to the child-support orders would land Bryan in family court again, which took time away from work. And right now, he needed to be the most present and visibly hardworking employee. Bryan and his kids headed to the door.

At the front door, Robert called out, "Bryan, be careful out there. You heard about another young brother shot by the police? They always catch us when we are alone."

Bryan had skimmed the headline, too depressed to read the details. "Yea, terrible," he said, putting on his coat.

"Bryan, he's right. Be careful," Mama said. "Especially since you have my little Lance." She gazed at her grandson lovingly. "And my beautiful Lindsey. I worry about these kids. We have a right to feel safe in our own country." Lindsey permitted herself to be hugged. Bryan gave Mama his usual kiss on the cheek. Robert was correct but he was more terrified of his mother's reaction to Nadia than some unknown threat.

16

Lindsey's volleyball game was on Thursday evening. Bryan found a seat on an aisle near an exit. Even with their custody agreement, he always made an effort to make it to his children's school events and he hadn't missed a game yet.

The high school gym was crowded. The smell of cheap popcorn wafted through the air, as balls bounced, sneakers squeaked, and parents screamed from the stands. Bryan spotted Cynthia, one of Lawanda's friends, and tried to avoid eye contact as he made his way to an empty spot on the bleachers, three rows above her. Cynthia's daughter had been scouted by some college teams and was one of Lindsey's fiercest competitors both on the court and in the classroom. Yet the two girls had remained friends, as had Cynthia and Lawanda.

The coach blew his whistle, signaling an end to the pre-game practice. Cynthia's daughter, Lindsey, and the other starters lined up at the net. Bryan's phone chimed. He glanced down at a selfie from Nadia and smiled.

Girl, you are so pretty, he texted back.

Can't wait to see you, Nadia replied.

I'm at Lindsey's volleyball game now, maybe a little later, Bryan texted back.

More parents filed in, most of them coming straight from work. Lawanda entered, and Bryan nodded hello to her. She responded with a tight-lipped smile. She found Cynthia and greeted her with a hug and a giggle before sitting down next to her. Bryan watched the two women chatting, he heard the gym doors close, a signal that the game was about to start.

As the ref launched the coin into the air to begin the game, the gym's double doors opened again, startling everyone in the stands. A tall Black man with muscular arms encased in a white dress shirt, tailored jeans, and cordovan Magnanni dress shoes strutted into the gym. Cynthia's head straightened like a hound on the trail of a new scent in the air. She tapped Lawanda on her knee to get her attention. Bryan had never seen him before either.

Is he a college recruiter? Bryan wondered. The referee announced the winner of the toss and Lindsey's team served the ball, pulling Bryan into the game. Bryan looked out onto the court to see if a girl on the floor resembled him and said a silent prayer for Lindsey if he was in fact there on business.

"Who is that fine man?" Cynthia said loudly. Bryan saw her catch herself and slouch a bit.

"Girl, you need to spend your energy on somebody else," Lawanda told her. "He's Harry's father."

"Little red-haired Harry, scrawny little white boy Harry?" Cynthia was incredulous, and Bryan was equally curious. "Girl, what are you talking about?"

"Yes, *Harry's* father," Lawanda intoned. "His husband will be here soon."

Cynthia gasped.

"I'm serious," Lawanda continued. "He ain't interested in us." She directed her attention to the court. "C'mon, girls, you can do it!"

Harry's father found an empty spot high in the bleachers and sat by himself. He seemed to be scanning the court. *He looks like he could be a college coach,* Bryan thought, intrigued by this man who was supposedly gay. *He doesn't look gay,* Bryan thought to himself.

Bryan let his eyes wander off of Harry's dad and began to scan the stands for Lance. *Where on earth is he? He has to be here because Lawanda and I are both here. It's not like she'd hire a sitter for two or three hours,* he thought.

After the second set, cheering sounds from the locker room reached a high pitch, and the volleyball cheerleaders emerged, tossing each other around. Behind them came the drill team, which much to Bryan's surprise, included Lance and Harry. *He never told me he was on the drill team,* he thought. *Is that why Lance made that comment about me not caring the way Nadia does?* He wondered.

He glanced down at Lawanda to gauge her reaction, and saw her stand up as if she was going to run down the bleachers. He saw Cynthia grab her arm and heard her whisper something. Lawanda sat back down, but he could tell by her posture that she was tight as a wire. Bryan glanced at Harry's father, who was clapping enthusiastically. Bryan's hands lay heavily on his knees. *What is he doing? Doesn't he know kids are going to make fun of him for stuff like this?* Bryan knew he would never have dreamed of doing something so risky at Lance's age. He remembered getting bullied after a talent show when he was in high school because he messed up a magic trick in his act and it took him months to feel comfortable enough to perform again after that. He tried to remember that his son was much different than he was when he was growing up, but he still worried about Lance getting made fun of. He wished he could protect him from any pushback he would get from his classmates on Monday.

Bryan's fears were made worse by the snippets of conversation he could hear from parents around him.

"Who lets their son do that?" someone nearby whispered.

"At least they're not wearing skirts," someone else said.

"But they still have glitter on them. Is that sparkly eye shadow on the red head, or is he just that pale?" a third person chimed in.

Bryan did not know what to do if somebody said something to him about Lance being on the drill team. He sat pensively. *If this is what parents are saying, I can only imagine how brutal the kids will be,* Bryan thought.

The game resumed after the second set and the whispers around Bryan were quickly replaced by cheering and screaming for the team. Lindsey made a couple of good saves, but her team was losing badly. After the fourth set, the drill team came onto the court again. Lance and Harry, wearing matching tight maroon shorts and tank tops, posed, bookending the animated girls dancing to a chart-topper. Both boys beamed. As the lyrics picked up, both boys started dancing in joyful rhythms and gyrated in impeccable sync with their female counterparts. The crowd clapped, swaying back and forth with the beat. Harry's father stood up and whooped.

Lawanda seemed to be sitting up as straight as she possibly could. With her pocketbook on her shoulder, she looked like she was about to book it out of the gym at any moment. Bryan, on the other hand, slouched in his seat, feeling hollow. How was he supposed to help his son? *Is this my fault? Is there some sort of gene that made him this way? Was this mama's sixth sense, or had she passed on a faulty genetic code?* Meanwhile, his son and his son's best friend were executing complicated and suggestive moves on the volleyball court like professionals.

"Your son can move," Cynthia said to Lawanda, "I'm enjoying this. Go, Lance! Go, Lance!"

Lawanda twisted her head around to Bryan. "Bring my children home after the game. I'm going home." She tugged her sweater down. "You need to talk to your son."

Cynthia called out to her friend's back. "Girl, what are you doing?"

Bryan watched Lindsey, noticing Lawanda leaving the gym. Lindsey's face fell, the sadness casting across her face like a shadow.

The song ended, and Lance and Harry ran off the court, shaking their pom-poms. The last set ended with Lindsey's team losing by only a few points.

Bryan ran down the bleachers and caught his daughter in a big hug. "You played so well, honey. I know the loss is disappointing, but I'm proud of you."

"Lance always ruins everything," Lindsey wailed. "I thought my mama came to see me play, not watch Lance. I hate this."

"Lindsey, look at me. Don't be like that with your brother," Bryan said, crouching down to her height. "Secondly, your mother loves you. She had to leave quickly. She saw you play most of the game, so we are going to find the good in that."

Lance ran up to them, and Bryan noticed that while he had changed out of his uniform, he still had makeup on his face. Bryan cringed, but tried to overcorrect it with a tight-lipped smile. "Daddy, what do you think about our routine?"

"I liked it. I don't know where you learned to move like that," Bryan said, hugging him. *I don't even know where to start with this conversation*, he thought.

"Lindsey, are you okay? I'm sorry we lost," Lance said.

Lindsey mustered up a more cheerful facade. "It's okay," she said and rejoined her teammates. A minute later, his phone chimed. It was Lindsey telling him her boyfriend was bringing her home later.

Be home by 10, Bryan texted back.

Harry and his father approached.

"Hi, I'm Joe Caldwell. Harry's dad."

A young athletic white man jogged up. "Hey, guys, I'm sorry I'm so late. I can't believe I missed Harry's dance!" He tousled Harry's hair and leaned over the top of his son's head to kiss Joe on the lips.

Bryan looked to the side briefly and scratched the back of his neck. He was uncomfortable seeing two men kiss, but he didn't want to come across as rude.

"It's okay," Joe said. "Harry did well, and Lance did, too. Hey, Bryan, meet my husband, Steve."

"Bryan is Lance's dad," he said to Steve. Steve had tousled oak-colored hair and a handsome, clean-shaven face. He was the same height as Joe and wore similar clothes—well-cut trousers and a Caribbean-blue button-down. *He doesn't look gay either,* Bryan thought to himself.

"Nice to meet you, Steve," Bryan said, extending his hand. Bryan wondered which of the two was the stay-at-home trophy husband. Either one was a contender because they were both so perfect-looking. Both men were exceptionally polished. Bryan found himself feeling a little jealous. Their air of confidence seemed to happen naturally, whereas he worked hard to achieve his swagger.

"You, too," Steve said. "Hey, why don't you and Lance have dinner with us? We're going for pizza."

Bryan hesitated. Having dinner with two happily married gay men who looked like models wasn't exactly going to boost his ego, but he also had his son to consider. He glanced down at Lance, and when he saw how excited he was, he realized this was an opportunity to make his son happy. "Sure, thanks. Sounds great."

***

Bryan watched Joe and Steve enter the pizza parlor before him, and saw Joe kiss Steve as he held the door open for his husband. He smiled to himself, admiring their courage. *Why can't I be like that with Nadia?*

"I missed you today," Steve said to Joe as they waited for the hostess to count out their menus.

The hostess smiled at them. An older white man—his name tag labeled him as the restaurant manager—glanced disapprovingly at their party and told the hostess to place them at table nine. The hostess walked them past many empty booths to one in the very back of the restaurant, near the restrooms. After some discussion, Joe ordered an extra-large pizza with everything on one half and only cheese on the other. Lance and Harry started talking about things in school known only by the two of them, leaving Bryan to talk to Steve and Joe.

Bryan started the conversation by asking Joe and Steve how they met. They told him they'd met nearly a decade earlier at a wine bar in Phoenix, where they both happened to be working. There had been an instant attraction. The next day, they had gone on a three-hour dinner date. "We always say we had our first kiss after our second glass of wine," Steve said, as Joe kissed the side of his head.

Their story was not only exciting, but romantic. Bryan realized he had never considered that deep intimacy between two men was possible until this conversation. He always perceived two men to be too sexual to actually stop and get to know each other. They were clearly a happy family. The more they talked, the more they seemed just like every day, ordinary people, only better-looking. Bryan watched them with envy. Spending time with them also confirmed (at least in his mind) that he was not gay.

As Joe and Steve began going on a tangent about household chores, Bryan's phone chimed. He held the phone under the table to see who was texting him. It was another naked selfie from Nadia. Bryan's heart pounded with desire.

Girl, you need to stop. I'm at dinner with Harry's parents, Bryan texted back.

"Everything okay?" Joe asked. "Do you need to go?"

But I need some attention. And clearly I caught yours, she responded with a winky face.

"No. Just texting my girlfriend."

Joe was obviously the disciplinarian in the family. Every time Harry pushed a boundary, he fell right back in line each time Joe gave him a look. Bryan also learned that Joe was well traveled, had studied for a year in France, and had his BA from Yale. He was an executive director for a nonprofit, so Bryan assumed he was the breadwinner. Steve was a children's book illustrator. He had played baseball in college and was now, he confessed, "a little too into ultimate frisbee," playing every Sunday in the park.

The couple agreed this was the most comfortable city they had ever lived in together. The gay community and people had been so welcoming, and it was a great place to raise Harry. They also shared they had adopted Harry about eight years ago. Harry had not only rounded out their family but helped both sets of grandparents focus on a grandchild and not on their gay relationship. They talked and laughed for nearly an hour, which quickly bored their kids.

"Dad, can we try that gumball machine?" Lance asked, pointing to the old-fashioned gumball machine at the front of the restaurant. Bryan nodded, and Bryan and Joe offered up quarters to their sons.

Right as the boys walked away, a middle-aged Black guy walked over to their booth. "Hello, sir, can we help you?" Bryan asked, steeling himself for the expected gay slurs.

"That's fine. You boys want to be here. I've got nothing against you, homos," the man growled. "But you, a Black man, had to go and get yourself a white boy," the gentleman said, shaking his head and staring at Steve. "When are we going to start taking care of our own, keeping our money in our communities, and stop giving all our resources to them? They enslave us, rape our women, separate our families."

Harry and Lance, out of quarters and mouths full of gum, slipped back to their seats at the table.

"Thank you, sir, for your opinion," Joe said calmly.

The man slumped away.

"There's always somebody who has a problem with us," Steve explained. "It's like . . . Wheel of Random Hatred, instead of Fortune."

Joe chuckled. He spread his arms grandly and, in a voice approximating a chipper game show host, proclaimed, "Step right up, folks. Let's spin the wheel. This fair eve, the jackpot spat out, wait for it . . . the person who has a problem with interracial relationships."

Bryan smiled. His envy of their devotion reminded him of his intimacy issues with Nadia. He hoped one day he wouldn't be so afraid of what others thought. *How did Joe and Steve manage to not care about what anyone else thought?* The families parted with warm handshakes, promising to see each other soon. Bryan had barely turned on the car before Lance said, "Daddy, I got mad when that man was mean to Harry's parents. If I could beat that guy up, I would."

"Son, you know that violence rarely changes people's minds."

"What if someone called me a bad name like that?"

"No one would ever call you gay," Bryan said automatically, not looking at his son.

"What if somebody did?"

"I don't want you fighting. It's just a label. Words can never hurt us," Bryan said. Bryan felt bad lying to his son. He knew he would be hurt if he were called gay. He wanted to be strong for his son and tell him he could be whoever he wanted to be, but he knew that wasn't true. Lance could be whoever he wanted to be as long as other people wanted him to be that way. *Oh God, what would I have done if someone had said that to me and Nadia?* Before Bryan could even attempt to answer his own question, his brain slammed shut again. *No one else can find out about his relationship with Nadia,* he thought.

"What if someone called you the N-word?" Lance asked.

"That's no different."

"You can't allow yourself to be hurt. It's their problem not yours," Bryan said. He was jumbled and out of his depth, and he felt like a fraud because he knew he couldn't take his own advice. "It's time to get you back to your mother's house." He started the car and turned on the radio to drown out his thoughts.

"Thanks, Daddy. Mama never gets dinner with Harry's parents. She doesn't like them at all. I had a good time tonight."

"I did, too." Bryan said, "Hey, since you're interested in sports these days, want to watch a basketball game together next week?"

"No, Daddy. You know the only part of sports I like is the halftime routines."

Bryan smiled. "Me too."

While slowly driving to the apartment block in the back of the complex, Bryan avoided eye contact with the young men who were drinking beer and smoking in the parking lot. He did not know how to relate to these men, and he felt guilty because he knew he was afforded opportunities most Black people didn't have.

Lawanda was behind the screen door, wearing a sheer red robe that tied at the waist and stopped above the knee. Bryan remembered that she wore it on their wedding night, which created a disorienting time warp. The light coming from the TV behind her created a shadow where her thighs met. She put her hand on Lance's head and steered him into the apartment.

"Go brush your teeth and get ready for bed."

She doesn't have any underwear underneath her robe, Bryan noticed. What is she doing? Is she trying to seduce me? he wondered.

Lawanda's voice cut through the air. "So, did you talk to him?"

"I did."

"Would you like to come in?" Lawanda asked, pushing her lips out into a pout.

Realizing he was no longer attracted to anyone who wasn't Nadia, he found his voice. "No," he said firmly.

Backing away, he called, "Good night, son," as heartily as he could into the space beyond the doorway. As he walked away, he realized that Lawanda's lingerie stunt probably meant that the kids had told Lawanda he had a girlfriend.

Pulling out his phone, he texted Nadia that he was coming over.

As he was driving to Nadia, he knew in his heart he could never be out like Joe and Steve were. He didn't know how he would ever be comfortable enough to treat Nadia the way they treated each other in public. Nor was he sure how he would have handled being the target of that man's words at the restaurant. Bryan hung his head, a feeling of loneliness enveloping him. Would he forever be alone because he was too scared to face the world? Steve and Joe were so happy, so confident in their masculinity and sexuality. He didn't think that either of them was less of a man than he was, yet he did not know how to fight back against his own fear that he would lose everything if the world knew about him and Nadia. He did not know how to accept people disliking him if they knew the truth. He only knew how to blend in, which meant acting as much like a straight white man as best you could. That's what his mama had taught him to do, and up until this point, this strategy had made Bryan very successful. No more hiding, Bryan decided to tell his mama at their next lunch.

17

After an uneventful week, Bryan was once again taking the stairs up to Mike's office on Friday morning. Jerry's voice hissed in Bryan's head: *You are crazy if you believe Mike is looking out for your best interests.* At the thought of Jerry, Bryan suddenly realized it'd been a few days since he'd last seen him. He had gotten so wrapped up in his latest project that he had completely forgotten about their most recent exchange and realized Jerry still hadn't responded to Bryan's emails or calls. Bryan weirdly hadn't run into him either. Bryan made a mental note to ask Mike if he knew about Jerry's whereabouts if the opportunity arose.

Platinum sunlight gleamed through the windows of Mike's office, seemingly dissolving the glass. The younger man clasped Bryan's hand warmly. "How are you? You look well."

"Yes, sir." Bryan's eyes drifted, as usual, to Mike's family photos.

"I understand you are divorced. They say behind every great man....Well, you know the adage I'm sure," Mike said, smiling, "A little bit of advice. The staff does better when they see someone who they can relate to."

Bryan listened.

"Personally, it doesn't matter to me, but in the best interest of the company, I expect you to be like one of the guys. We don't want to mess with the morale of your peers and subordinates. Especially the working class guys out at the plants."

"Sir?" Bryan asked. He understood exactly what Mike meant: pretend your personal life is surrounded by a wife, kids, and a white picket fence so that conservative white guys who are feeling left behind or cut out from advancement by either the Blacks, the gays, or the women can at least look at you with respect. "I don't understand what you mean," Bryan said, playing dumb. Clearly, this was not the meeting to ask about Jerry.

"You figure it out. But realize that people are watching you and how you conduct yourself," Mike paused for dramatic effect. "After all, you are the new VP of polymers and specialties."

Bryan sat forward in his chair, euphoria boiling in his belly. "I got the job?"

Mike stood, flashing a diamond-bright smile, and extended his hand toward Bryan, who jumped out of his chair and pumped it.

"Thank you, sir, thank you. I will not let you down."

"I know you won't. You'll start in the new year, okay? We'll announce it at the first leadership meeting in December."

Bryan was so excited that he let himself relax enough to sink into the marshmallow chair. *Oh thank God I got the job*, he thought. *I finally made it.*

"Why don't you come for dinner to celebrate and meet my family?" Mike continued to heap treasures upon Bryan's head, weighing down his pockets with gold. "I'll have my secretary call you to set something up for after the new year."

***

That evening, as he was driving through the city toward Lance and Lindsey's school, Bryan noticed workers lining the trees with lights to make way for the holiday season.

As Bryan entered the theater, people milled in the aisles or chatted to their seatmates. Many of the dads worked at the refinery and were still wearing their flame-retardant uniforms. Bryan knew these were the types of guys Mike was referring to. Bryan had to gain their respect if he was going to be successful as the new VP. He glanced around, and sure enough, his mama was waving at him as if she were Nantucket royalty, in navy pants and a matching double-breasted jacket. "I didn't know you were coming," Bryan said.

"I have to support my grandkids when I can," she replied, "Do you think I'm overdressed?"

Bryan gestured to his burgundy suit. "If you are, then I am, too."

She smiled her high-wattage smile. "Like mother, like son."

"You always told me to dress for success." He was thrilled to lay his excellent news at her feet, as he had with every success since he was a child. "Guess what happened today?" Bryan said, barely giving her a chance to respond. "I just found out—I was made VP."

Her eyes widened. "Oh, my handsome son." She put her hand to her heart. "I am so proud of you. I cannot even tell you how much your success means to me."

Her smile made him feel as affixed to the world as a diamond in its clawed setting. Bryan beamed in response. *Hopefully this will soften the blow if she ever finds out about Nadia,* he thought to himself.

"Like mother, like son," he repeated. He decided he would tell Nadia the good news at her upcoming birthday dinner.

Mama gave him a big hug. "Come by soon, and I'll make something really special. And you can pick up your mail that's been accumulating. And one other thing. When you come over, I want you to fix the lock on the hall bathroom."

"Not a problem," he said.

She nudged him. "Tell me again how you can become a VP but you can't change your address for your high school and college alumni correspondence?"

"Thanks, Mama. I'll come get that stuff. I'm sorry it's in your way."

"I like everything in its place. You know me," she said. Her eyes darted around. "Goodness, there are a lot of white people here," she said, patting her hair. "The school must be trying to promote diversity if Lance got the lead role."

You know Lance earned the lead role, he thought.

She twisted her head around. "I don't see Lawanda."

"I don't either, but I don't keep up with her comings and goings."

"So, where is she?" Mama asked. The lights in the theater began to dim.

"Who?" Bryan asked, whispering back. He glanced at his Rolex, its hands glowing in the dark. Three minutes. *She lasted longer than I expected*, he thought. *Here comes the guilt trip.*

"Your girlfriend."

"At home," Bryan responded.

"Tell me again why this girl doesn't want children?"

"You know, she does have a name," Bryan said, dodging the original question.

"Well, good," Mama replied. "What is it?"

"It's Nadia Brooks," Bryan said proudly. He realized a nearby couple was listening in on their conversation and lowered his voice. "Mama, do we have to talk about this now?"

"Yes, we do," Mama whispered harshly.

"She can't have kids."

"Is that what she told you?" Mama said condescendingly, "That's what Lawanda told you too." She was whispering but still seemed too loud. "Men are silly. They will believe anything. You know men have a role also in who can get pregnant." She grabbed a piece of Bryan's flesh, just above his right elbow.

"Ow," he yelped. Several people turned around, giving them the eye that communicated, *Shut up.* In this environment, both Bryan and his mama knew that as Black people, they should avoid being seen or heard. Both fell silent for a moment.

He rubbed his arm, hoping to make the soreness go away.

Bryan took a long deep breath before beginning again, "She may want kids. I don't know, Mama. At this moment, she can't have kids because she's a transgender woman." He struggled to maintain eye contact. This was not the plan. She needs to know, he thought.

Mama's face went blank. "Are we talking about the same white girl you introduced to the kids?"

"Yes, Mama," he said, trying to keep his voice down.

"What do you mean she's a transgender? I don't know what that is." His mama flopped around in her seat unable to get comfortable with this truth. "There are women and men. That's it. I don't know what a transgender is."

Bryan started breathing rapidly. He couldn't believe what he just said. *What did I just do? I might have just unleashed the hounds of hell on myself,* he thought, knowing this was not his plan to tell her this way. "Mama, she's not a transgender. She is a transgender woman. It's an adjective, not a noun. Okay." He loosened his tie. The theater felt claustrophobic. The all-too familiar queasy feeling in his stomach returned, and he debated escaping to the bathroom before the show started.

His mama turned around in her seat to face him head on. "You mean like I see on the news. Men dressing up like women," she said, her face flushed with anger. "Boy, don't play with me. I know you're not gay. Don't do this to me. Tell me about your new job and then hit me with this. What in the hell is wrong with you?"

"It's the truth. She is trans and I would like for you to meet her," Bryan said, facing her, scared of her anger yet knowing that the only way to meet it was head on.

"Private school did this to you," she mumbled under her breath. "I ain't never heard of a Black man dating a 'whatever you just said'."

"Mama, stop," Bryan pleaded. The tension was palpable. Bryan's heart was racing, and he was sure he had sweat through his shirt in only two minutes.

The house lights went dark, saving Bryan from his mama's disapproval for the time being. The principal, a middle-aged white woman with a friendly, competent air, greeted the audience. Mama physically leaned away from Bryan.

"Let's just watch Lance, Mama."

The curtain rose, and Bryan saw that Lance had slipped into Mowgli's character easily. His expressions and understanding of his lines made him a definite standout. He wasn't just pretending to be Mowgli- he was embodying the character in the way only a true performer could. Bryan saw images of Lance having a successful acting career and felt pride radiating throughout his being. *That's my boy*, he wanted to brag to the other parents.

In the end, all thirty-five kids received a standing ovation. Lance stood in line with his peers as they all bowed out. For a moment, everyone shared the light until Lance stepped forward with his right hand over his left shoulder and his chin raised, which gave off a haughty air. He stopped at the edge of the stage, allowing his presence to marinate. The clapping died down. Bryan looked at his mama.

"What's he doing?" Mama asked.

"I have no idea."

Lance slowly bent forward and held his bow long enough for the audience to quiet even further. Straightening his body, he popped up his right arm, threw his left hand out wide, and knocked the back of his heels together, like Dorothy in *The Wizard of Oz*. It was grandiose and definitely effeminate. The audience was clearly befuddled, and Bryan smiled, seeing the moment as a brief moment of child-like behavior that was quickly disappearing as Lance was becoming a teenager. But as Bryan began to hear the white people in the audience whispering in harsh tones, he felt the goodwill drain from the room. He suddenly felt fearful for his son, even more so than he had felt at the volleyball game. Bryan scanned the theater, looking for anyone who might try to cause Lance harm.

Breaking the silence, they rose to their feet, clapping vigorously and yelling, "We love you, Lance!" Bryan yelled.

"That's your son out there. I see where he gets it from," Mama said as she applauded.

Bryan smiled, ignoring her last statement. *Oh Mama, do you really love him any less because of this?* Bryan wondered. The rest of the audience rose to their feet. Lance rejoined his castmates, and they all took a final bow. The audience clapped and yelled, even more enthusiastically than before.

Finally, the crowd began to disperse.

"Let me explain something to you," Mama said as the people around them left their seats. "You don't need to bring this person around me because I don't want to meet her. Lance is a kid. He's trying to figure things out. He has room to make mistakes. You are a grown man and should know better," she said tersely.

Bryan said nothing. There was nothing to say as people milled about.

"Stop all this foolishness. Gay, my ass. Find yourself a wife. Be the man I raised. This other bullshit you got going on, I don't need to see it, hear about it or know about it," she said, quickly smiling as Lindsey approached.

"Hey, baby girl," she said lovingly, "I think you are the only normal child in my life. Well, you and your Aunt Rebecca."

Lindsey flashed a confused look, standing with her boyfriend in tow. "Hi, Dad. Hi Bibi." She gave her grandmother a hug.

"Who's that?" Mama asked, lips pursed, visibly agitated.

"My boyfriend."

Mama and Lindsey's boyfriend briefly exchanged pleasantries and she gave Lindsey another hug.

"Lance was great, but then he ruined it with his weird bow," Lindsey said.

As if on cue, Lance skipped out from backstage, still in costume.

"You were great. I loved it," Mama said, enveloping Lance in her arms. "You certainly know how to end a show."

"Thank you, BiBi."

Bryan rubbed his son's head. Lindsey rejoined her boyfriend just as Lawanda came into view. She looked perturbed and she didn't compliment Lance on his performance. "C'mon, son, Time to go."

"Hi, Lawanda," Mama said. Before Lawanda could answer, Mama kissed the top of her grandson's head. "You were marvelous."

"Okay, I'll see you in about two weeks," Bryan said, giving Lance a big hug.

Bryan sighed as Lance bounced away. How could he help him? And would Lance even tell him if he needed help? Lance was different from most of the other kids, and Bryan heard his mama's words echoing in his head: *Black kids can't afford to be different.* He checked his phone and noticed it was getting late. He texted Nadia: *Honey, I'm tired. Can I see you tomorrow?*

Everything okay? Nadia asked.

Yes. Just tired. Long day. I need to clean up for tomorrow, Bryan responded.

***

Bryan needed space to think with everything going on: the new job, his mother's crazy ass opinion, and Nadia. There were so many questionable pieces, and he was starting to believe they could not possibly fit together. Like mother, like son; Bryan was more concerned about how Lance's actions impacted him than he was about Lance's feelings. His stomach turned with a twinge of guilt about being perceived as acting like his mother.

He drove home with thoughts of Lance tumbling through his mind. On one hand, Bryan was proud of his son's performance- he had put on a professional level performance the other night, and Bryan could see acting materializing into a viable career choice for him. On the other hand, Lance's effeminate bow scared Bryan. *Where did he get the courage to be so different? Certainly not from me,* Bryan thought to himself. He thought back to when he was Lance's age and how he wanted to be a magician. Between his mama's disapproval and his own fear of rejection, he had decided to give it up after he graduated high school. He was too terrified to face a heckling crowd. In his mind's eye, Bryan saw a younger version of himself and Lance standing side by side. They physically looked similar, but Lance exuded a confidence that Bryan never possessed. He imagined how his son would respond to rude audience members, and saw him strutting off the stage with a sway in his hips, looking unbothered.

When he got home, Bryan decided to try meditating to clear his head. He realized that he needed to choose how he wanted to show up for his son. After 5 minutes of silence and the same mental images of himself and Lance reappearing, he decided to switch gears. He picked up the *Beginner's Guide to Meditation* and began to read, hoping that maybe he would stumble upon the answer. He read that meditation could reveal the pathway to the wonders of the unknown. He read that the unknown is where love exists, which intrigued him. Putting the book down, he went to his bed and laid down, looking up at the ceiling. *What a way to end the week*, he thought.

18

I t was Saturday night, Nadia's birthday. Today was the day she would finally see how he lived, and he was both excited and nervous to show her around his hi-rise. He bustled around his apartment, cleaning everything in sight and ensuring all clutter was removed. That morning, as he was hanging up his hunter-green windowpane jacket, Bryan unwound a long blond hair that was looped around one of the buttons. He chuckled to himself. He and Nadia were indeed fully entwined, and in that moment, he realized just how right the relationship felt. They were past the honeymoon phase yet still wanted to spend a lot of time together. While he had some doubts about his ability to truly go public with Nadia, he knew that they had something special. *Why can't people just see the love we have as something special? If she wasn't trans, it wouldn't matter.*

That evening, when Nadia buzzed into his hi-rise complex, he met her at the visitor parking lot. Stepping out of her twelve-year-old Ford, Nadia rocked a cute, printed mini romper that he'd bought her. Open-toed heels showed off her manicured red toes. She carried an overnight bag and purse. Nadia surveyed the parking garage, counting off all the expensive cars parked: Mercedes, Porsches, Bentleys, and Bryan's Jaguar. A silver Mercedes parked nearby. A middle-aged gentleman with gray edges and a sophisticated tall blond thirty-something woman, all legs and flawless makeup, exited the car. The woman smiled and interlocked her arm with the man's arm. For a split second, Bryan blocked out all the negativity, seeing his world in a way that he never considered or thought was possible, until now: Nadia was that woman.

"Thank you, Charles," Bryan said to the doorman as they entered the building.

"Yes, sir," Charles replied. "Ma'am," tipping his hat to Nadia.

"You look good," Nadia said.

They hugged. "Happy birthday," Bryan spoke into her ear.

"I work so much, I never really go to The Galleria anymore. All these trendy restaurants," she gushed. "Everybody seems so relaxed, and their dogs are so well-behaved."

Just as they were walking across its marbled expanse, a large Doberman pinscher, still leashed by its owner, came in from the street. The owner was white, a grim looking older man who lived on the second floor. The dog veered toward them, and Nadia bent down to rub his head.

"Look at this good boy," she said in a baby voice, rubbing the dog's head. "He's beautiful," she said to the owner, who glared at her. "Bryan, come here. He won't bite. Will you, boy?"

Bryan backed away. "Girl, let's go. Now." Once they were safely in the elevator, Bryan explained, "Don't go petting random dogs. You didn't even ask the owner first."

"He practically ran up to me, begging to be pet," Nadia countered.

"How do you know he didn't want to bite you?" Bryan asked with a hint of both defensiveness and curiosity.

"I could just tell," she said. There was a moment of silence as tension seeped out of their bodies and into the elevator. Nadia broke the silence.

"Are you scared of dogs?" Nadia asked, looking into Bryan's eyes.

Bryan sighed, "I know it's not a popular opinion, but yes." Bryan paused. He hadn't admitted that to anyone before. He felt he needed additional context, and added, "I've never really met a dog like that that's liked me." He paused for a moment, and Nadia gave him a blank, confused stare. "He's probably trained to eat Black people," he said, forcing a weak chuckle.

Nadia seemed to think about his statement. "I never considered that. That isn't my experience with dogs, but I guess everyone has different experiences. But I don't want you paranoid about them. That's not a healthy way to live." She paused, and Bryan felt her words sinking in. *Is this what vulnerability and connection is supposed to feel like?* Bryan wondered.

"It's okay that you're scared, but you don't want the people who own dogs around here to think you are rude," Nadia said, breaking Bryan out of his train of thought.

"I don't like that particular guy anyway. Didn't you see the look he gave you?"

"I'm not paying any attention to that. And you shouldn't, either."

They were alone in the elevator, and they interlocked their arms like the distinguished gentleman and his lady downstairs. Bryan laughed softly. "Ever wonder why you never see Black people on the local news getting mauled by a dog? We don't go around touching dogs we don't know."

She laughed.

The elevator opened to a plush hallway lined with ornate mirrors and delicate tables topped with vases full of elaborately arranged silk flowers. Nadia hesitated at his door. He tugged her hand into the entry and happily watched her mouth fall open as she glimpsed the gigantic window filled with the view of downtown Houston.

Mouth still agape, she braved a second step, sweeping her gaze over the two thousand square foot space, multiple floor-to-ceiling windows, and elegant decor. "Wow, this place is amazing. And, what's that smell?"

Bryan's chest puffed up at her praise. "Eucalyptus."

She swiveled on her high heels to take in the giant Buddha statue nestled in an oval alcove in the wall.

"This is really nice," Nadia said, poking her hand in and rubbing the Buddha's head like she had caressed the Doberman's.

Bryan suddenly realized that he had bought the Buddha to fill up more of his spacious apartment when he first moved in, not because of a particular belief system. Yet now he was learning more about meditation and reading Buddhist texts. *It's almost like deep down I knew I needed to go in this direction*, he thought to himself.

"This place needs a woman's touch," he said jokingly.

She blew out a raspberry. "Hardly."

Kicking off her shoes, she toured the living room in her stocking feet. Her attention was arrested by one of his favorite pieces, a framed photograph the size of a small child, depicting a gold-colored liquid from an unseen source pouring over a naked woman.

"Mmm," Nadia purred. "Look at her expression."

Bryan stood behind his girlfriend. "Can you see that she's being covered in honey?"

"I thought that was honey. I wonder if it is warm," Nadia said, gently touching the glass.

Again, he laughed to himself that she had to touch everything. He asked, "Would you like a glass of wine, birthday girl?"

"Yes, thank you, kind sir." She pointed to another painting. "Is that Napoleon?" She peered closer, her breath fogging the glass. "You have got to be kidding me! Is that Kanye West dressed as Napoleon riding a horse!"

"Cool, right? The artist's name is Kehinde Wiley. He paints famous Black people in classical settings. Dinner will be ready soon. Just relax. I will get your wine," he said.

She oohed and aahed over his open-concept kitchen, running her hand across the granite countertops luxuriously.

"My boyfriend has the professional-grade kitchen of my dreams. How convenient," she said with a sly smile. She twirled in the generous space. "And to think that I can create masterpieces in my piece-of-shit oven. Imagine what I could make here."

She kissed him, and Bryan returned her kiss with passion. Nadia broke away for a moment to speak. "The meal you make for me has to be five thousand times better, since you have better equipment." She squeezed him through his trousers, cackling at her own joke.

"I will do my best," Bryan said, head bowed. He led her back to the living room and picked up a silk scarf from the coffee table. "I want you to feel your gift before you see it. Will you let me cover your eyes with this?"

She nodded and set down the drink in her hand. He wrapped the fabric around her eyes and put a large rectangular box in her hands. Nadia shook the box theatrically. Still blindfolded, she tore the box open and sunk her hands into the folds of thick satin. "Ooh," she crooned. "It feels wonderful, very luxe. I want to see it!" She pushed the scarf onto her hair like a headband and squealed when she saw the dress. It was scarlet, floor-length, and sleeveless with a deep V-neck. Nadia put the gown up to her body, admiring her reflection in the large window. Bryan presented her with another present containing a pair of red-bottomed black pumps.

"Loubs!" she half gasped, half screamed.

"Go put it all on."

A few minutes later, she appeared from the back bedroom. "Your bedroom is huge." She slid her hands down her waist to feel the softness of the material accentuating her figure and spun around with gleeful abandon.

"This feels so good," Nadia said.

He beamed with pride, happy she liked his presents. "You look so good I would swoop you up like biscuits and gravy. Speaking of food, let's eat," Bryan said, directing her to the kitchen and pulling out a chair for her. His mahogany dining table was set with white candles and his best dinner and flatware.

Nadia unfolded her napkin as Bryan placed a plate of whole branzino over white and red potatoes in front of her. Nervously, he prattled, "My recipe is to rub the whole fish, inside and outside, with good olive oil before stuffing the inside with lemon slices, a few garlic cloves, capers, and cherry tomato halves. Then I put the potatoes in first with two bay leaves for twenty minutes before adding the fish for another twenty minutes . . ." he trailed off as he realized she wasn't verbally acknowledging what he was saying.

"Is something wrong?" he asked, still looking at the fish. *Oh God, does she think a toddler could make this? Is it not fancy enough?*

"I hope you like it," he said, then let himself meet her gaze. She let go of a big smile.

"Now, I feel like a birthday girl," she said. They clinked wine glasses. "Speaking of fancy food, I have a bit of good news to share." She smiled broadly. "I got a new job!"

"That's great, honey!"

"You aren't going to believe this story. A few weeks ago, I was helping these two ladies at the store. They own Two Moons Bakery," Nadia said, circling the lip of her wineglass with her index finger.

"Two Moons?"

Nadia rolled her eyes. "They're a lesbian couple. Don't you know anything about symbols? Anyway, they were looking for a third." She giggled into her wine. "I mean, they wanted to find someone who was passionate about food but hadn't had the opportunities they had to train. They said they had imagined someone younger and nonwhite, but a broke thirty-year-old trans woman had a certain ring to it, too."

Bryan rubbed her arm. "I'm so proud of you."

"It pays more than that bookstore I've been at forever, and I'll be taught things I desperately want to learn."

"You are welcome to cook here anytime," Bryan offered.

This was an ideal time to ask about her application for the Culinary Institute. But she hadn't shared it with him, and he didn't want to muddy her excitement about her job at the bakery in case she hadn't gotten in.

"I want to share some news too," he said.

"I can't wait to hear it."

"You are looking at the new VP of polymers and specialties."

"That's wonderful news! I'm so proud of you," she said, giving him a big hug. He nuzzled in for a kiss. They kissed in the glow of the good feelings, looking into each other's eyes.

"Look at us," she said with a twinkle in her eyes. "We're becoming quite the power couple." She couldn't stop smiling as she sipped her wine, and Bryan found it hard to stop smiling himself.

"Yes, we are," he said. "Now let's eat so that we have enough strength to save the world."

They silently ate for a few moments, exchanging loving looks in between bites. As Bryan was shoveling a potato in his mouth, he saw Nadia tilt her head somewhat as if something had just occurred to her, and she put her fork down.

"Speaking of being a couple, when am I meeting your mother? Now that we are official," she looked directly at Bryan, and he felt as if she was looking into his soul. "She knows I'm trans, and she's okay with it, right?"

Bryan was caught off guard. The romantic music playing in his head juddered to a stop. "Yeah, she knows. She knows you're a white trans woman," Bryan said. He took another bite of his fish, hoping Nadia would forget the second part of her question. She gave him a look and he feigned confusion. *Please don't ask again*, he thought.

"Okay, and is she okay with it?" Nadia asked, her eyes pleading for a "Yes".

Oh no, don't do this to me. You'll be mad if I lie and you'll be mad at the truth, he thought. He wrestled with this for a moment as he pushed potatoes around his plate, and decided that if she was going to be mad either way, it would be better for her to be mad at the truth. He popped a cherry tomato into his mouth and swallowed it, trying to delay the inevitable. He didn't want to upset her on her birthday. But he also knew lying to her, especially on her birthday, wasn't going to help him. Even after he swallowed his food, he could still feel a lump in his throat as he faced her.

"She's not okay with it," he said, allowing his face to fall. He wasn't a very emotional person, but he found himself wanting to cry. Instead, he tried to swallow both his tears and the lump in his throat.

Nadia held a puzzled look. "She's not happy about what, exactly?" she asked, throwing her fork down on the plate with a clatter. "With me being white? Or trans? Which is it?"

Bryan pulled back. The lump in his throat was now accompanied by a lump in his stomach. He gently set his fork down, trying to stay calm. *Just breathe*, he reminded himself, *she's not mad at you. You can't control Mama.*

"I guess both. She said she doesn't want to meet you. We didn't exactly leave off on the best note," he said. Nadia seemed to soften, and rubbed his arm with her hand.

Bryan put his head in his hands as she continued rubbing his right arm. "She called me gay," he said. He picked his head up out of his hands and met Nadia's expression. She was wearing a mixture of pity and concern on her lips and her eyes were filled with tenderness. Bryan realized he was safe again, and continued on. "This is just so confusing for me right now. I'm tired of people calling me gay. I have no issues with gay guys, but I just don't see myself as gay. If I was gay, I would like straight up men."

Nadia stretched out her arms for a hug. "Honey, this is not easy. It's not easy for her. For you. She needs time to process."

Bryan hugged her back. He allowed his pain to fully show.

"She just needs to meet me when she's ready. She will see," she said optimistically. "From what you've told me, she is such a strong and driven woman. As a woman, I want to hear stories about being one of the first African American television executives. I feel like I could learn a lot from her."

"I don't know if she'll ever be ready," Bryan said with a sigh. He felt like he was going to cry again and pushed his hands against his nose to prevent the tears. His mother has been there for him through so many difficult times, but Nadia was the only woman he was currently able to be vulnerable with. *How do I know which woman to please?* Bryan thought, feeling that he wouldn't ever be able to please them both at the same time.

"Hey, how about you show me the rest of your house?" Nadia said, standing up and taking him by the hand.

Bryan relaxed with her touch. In this moment, she was the only one who he needed to worry about pleasing.

"Let me show you my library," Bryan said. This was his favorite room. Its walls were lined with copious built-in bookshelves, replete with first editions and leather-bound classics. His library was where he was able to show visitors that he was an erudite individual. "Can I share a secret sexual fantasy with you?" Bryan asked.

Nadia smiled, raising an eyebrow.

"I watched a porn movie, and the transwoman was getting a blowjob in a library," he said.

She started giggling. "I've created a monster. I'm loving this," she said, "You are really getting into this. I think I've gotten a blowjob every time we're together since the club."

She was right. He decided it was okay to watch a guy go down on a trans woman. "I want to try it. C'mon, let me give you the most mind-blowing blowjob in my library. You have to pretend like people are around so you have to remain quiet, so the librarian doesn't hear you," Bryan said, looking seriously. She winked, and they began to live out his fantasy. It was every bit as amazing as he had imagined it would be, and Nadia agreed.

19

Bryan had his girl. Life could be a lot worse. The next morning, Bryan suggested a Sunday matinee, and they quickly decided on *The Danish Girl*. She was the perfect date, wearing tight white jeans, suede booties, and a yellow leather jacket that he had bought for her. They thoroughly enjoyed the movie and found themselves discussing it as they got into Bryan's car.

As Bryan put the car into drive, he realized they were right around the corner from his mother's house. *We're really happy*, he thought. *Maybe we can withstand what the world throws at us.*

"Honey, I need to stop at my mama's quickly just to pick up some of my mail. She's already annoyed enough that I've used her address as my mail garbage dump."

Nadia said nothing, and Bryan took this as a silent acceptance. He started to play out how he would Bryan just go in and get his mail, maybe make small talk if necessary. He didn't want to argue, and he didn't want to leave Nadia waiting too long. There were seven cars parked around the ring of Mama's driveway. *Oh good, she has company. She'll be on her best behavior in front of her friends*, he thought.

"Please stay in the car, " he said to Nadia. She simply looked at him in response. "I'll be as fast as I can," he said. He gave Nadia a quick peck.

As Bryan rang the doorbell, he could hear that his mama's entire crew was there, most likely drinking mimosas and white wine. Mama opened the door, dressed in a purple floral silk blouse. There were some light snacks out and it was clear that his mama was holding court, as she often liked to do. These charismatic Black women had gone through a lot together: the civil rights movements, kids, marriages, and divorces. This was the fellowship that bolstered Mama's independence. She stared at him, giving a long pause, saying nothing.

"Ladies, look who's here. My brilliant son," she said, giving Bryan a big hug and kiss. Robert was nowhere to be seen. Bryan wondered where Robert hid when Mama had these parties.

"Hello, ladies," he said, flashing a big smile. He wanted to make Mama look good, so he turned on the charm despite their misalignment.

"He's the new VP of polymers and specialties," his mama said, basking in the chorus of jealous appreciation for a few minutes. "C'mon, son, I have your mail in the back room." Mama's desk was covered with neat piles of paper. She shuffled through a stack and extracted envelopes with Bryan's name on them. Her pleasant expression changed to mean once she was away from everyone. "Are you still running around town playing gay with him?"

"Mama, she's not a 'him'. She is a girl, and whether you want to accept that or not is on you," he said, trying to keep his tone even and respectful. "Please. I only want to get my mail. I don't want to argue," Bryan said nervously.

Mama's doorbell rang. They both looked at each other and rushed out of the room, Bryan trying to beat his mother to the door. Unfortunately one of her friends beat Bryan to the door.

"Brenda, a white lady is asking to come in," one of Mama's friends called to them. Bryan's mother practically threw his mail at him with a huff and directed him to put it in a plastic bag. She quickly passed Bryan in the hallway and went to the front door, her heels clacking importantly.

"Yes, how can I help you?" Bryan heard Mama say.

"I'm Nadia Brooks."

Heart in his throat, Bryan tied up the bag and rushed towards the door.

"I'm Bryan's girlfriend. I know this is not the best way for us to meet formally. I was sitting in the car, but I decided to come in and introduce myself. We just came from the movies, and I had a large cola," she said, holding a strained look. "I really need to use the restroom. May I please use your bathroom?"

Bryan caught Nadia's eye from over his mother's head. *What are you doing,* he mouthed. She ignored him, and he leaned against the kitchen wall, wishing he could blend in like a chameleon. Fortunately, the wall also served as a way to brace himself given that he felt he was about to fall over. He felt lightheaded as he saw his mama's body tense with a moment of hesitation at Nadia's request. *Is she going to turn her away?* he wondered. It felt like two minutes had passed since Nadia had asked the question before he heard his mother speak.

"Of course," Mama said with a forced smile. She stepped out of the way. "It's down the hall, first door on the right." Mama watched Nadia hurry down the hall. "The kids said she was tall. Perfect. Just perfect," Mama murmured.

Mama pulled Bryan by his sleeve near the sink where Ms. Williams was rinsing dishes. One glance at his mother's face, and her friend shut off the tap and left the kitchen, still clutching the glass she'd been washing. "I told you that I did not want him in my house."

"Mama, I can't believe you are like this. She has done nothing to you," he said, pleading. "All she wants to do is use the bathroom."

"You just had to do this today, didn't you? You wanted to humiliate me in front of my friends."

"No, Mama, I just wanted to get my mail because I was nearby. And she just wanted to use the bathroom," Bryan whispered loudly. "I am not trying to do anything."

"Keep your voice down. Embarrassing me like this." Mama banged her hands on the kitchen counter. "What are they going to say about my successful son dating a white man?"

Bryan sighed. "Is this who you really are?" Bryan said angrily, "I'm so disappointed in seeing this side of you."

"You're disappointed in me," she countered, laughing, "Maybe your father was right."

"Right about what?" Bryan boiled over, remembering his father calling him gay slurs many times when he was disappointed or mad. "Right about what?" He breathed loudly through his nose.

"Maybe you should have moved to San Francisco to be with your kind so I wouldn't have to see it here. You could at least have the decency to do this away from Houston so you don't ruin our family's reputation."

What is she talking about? San Francisco? When did we have this conversation? he screamed to himself. "All I'm asking is for you to give her a chance," he said.

"A daughter-in-law that I can be proud of. That is too much to ask of you."

"Why does everything have to be about you?" Bryan replied.

"What did I do to deserve this? This is my fault for sending you to private school."

"Mama, that private school excuse is played out. You need to give that a rest."

"*He* sure has been in there a long time," Mama commented, folding a dish towel. "You said the other night, that person is trans," pointing towards the bathroom. "So what's his deal?"

"Yes, she's trans. Stop making such a big deal about it, and stop calling her 'him'. I don't understand your question." What had previously felt like a lump in his stomach now felt like a red hot poker. Confronting his Mama like this was no longer making him nervous so much as it was making him angry with her narrow views.

"I don't care how pretty you think she is," Mama said, practically yelling, "Was he born a girl? That is a yes or no?"

"Good Lord! Oh God in heaven. Excuse me. Oh my. Oh my!" Ms. Williams exclaimed.

Bryan and his mother rushed out in time to witness Ms. Williams stumbling into the living room, frantic and wild-eyed. She sank into the nearest chair, flopping around, wailing like Esther from *Sanford and Son.*

A blur of blond hair rushed down the hallway and the front door slammed. *Nadia?* he thought, *Damn, she's fast.*

"Lord, take me, please just take me, Lord have mercy!" Ms. Jackson and Ms. Willis fanned her furiously with old *Jet* magazines from a wicker basket, crooning, "Calm down, Dorothy. Breathe."

Mama's hair practically stood on end. She addressed her friends. "What happened to her?" As no answer was forthcoming, she turned to Bryan. "That woman hasn't been to church in twenty years. She's asking for Jesus's help now. Bryan, what's going on? Where's....?"

"Mama, you need to give her a chance," he said, cutting her off. He took his mail and left.

Nadia was sitting in the car, crying, and Bryan found himself at a complete loss for words. He wanted to both comfort her and scream at her. How could she put him in this position? Why had she done it? And why couldn't his mother see that Nadia was a human being first and a transwoman second? He sped off, his thoughts matching his speedometer. He slowed down once they were a safe enough distance away. "What happened? What just happened?" he asked, banging on the steering wheel. "Shit! Shit! Shit!" He couldn't yell at his mother anymore, and directed his anger toward Nadia.

"I-I had to pee! Th-that lady walked in on me," she said between sobs. "I thought I locked the door."

"You couldn't hold it? Look at what you've done," Bryan kept yelling. Nadia had no idea the bathroom lock was broken. Not only had he forgotten to fix it, he had forgotten to warn her about it. Shit. *Why didn't I fix it when Mama asked? Why did I put it off for so long?*

"I had to pee!" she exclaimed, crying harder still, digging in her purse for a tissue. "I have never been so embarrassed."

"I asked you to do one thing. Stay in the fucking car! Stay in the fucking car!"

"Stop yelling at me!"

"Why didn't you pee at the movie theater? God, look at what you've done, dammit!" His lips, teeth, jaw—his entire head had seized up as if locked in a vise. The red hot poker jabbed at him again, and he felt like he needed to keep breathing fire.

Nadia's face was slick with tears and snot.

"I don't feel safe in public restrooms," she said, weeping uncontrollably. "How about I just pee on your precious leather seats next time?"

Bryan only thought of his mother's eyes, empty, void of pride, and dazed. To his irrevocable surprise, she'd been angrier than he'd ever seen her at anyone, including even his father as he sped away.

Red-and-blue lights peppered his rearview mirror. His panicked heartbeats echoed the pattern of the flashing lights. He stopped the car.

Nadia looked out of the rear windshield, wiping her tears from her eyes, which only further smeared her mascara across her face.

"Please stop crying," he said, placing his hands on the steering wheel.

"What are you doing?" she said.

He tried to keep his voice level. "This is what I was always taught to do."

She began digging in the glove compartment. "I'm getting your insurance papers."

"Stop moving around. You're going to get us shot."

Nadia sat back against her seat, folding her arms. He laid his head on the steering wheel, frustrated that she was ignoring the dangerous optics of a white woman crying in a Black man's car. Her being trans was the last thing on his mind.

"Please, please stop crying," he begged. Bryan noticed a few homeowners looking out their windows, their comfortable existence disrupted by the flashing lights. *At least they feel safer now that they see the flashing lights.* Bryan had learned over the years that this truth was the only truth that really mattered. White people's stares and false assumptions were worse than the stop itself. He lifted his head and glanced in the rearview mirror. The officer was approaching, his hand covering his gun holster. With permission, he lowered his window. Bryan looked at the officer, but not in the eye. His father had taught him that making direct eye contact was disrespectful.

"Do you know why I stopped you?" the officer asked. *Because I'm Black and driving a nice car,* Bryan thought to himself. Bryan simply nodded no in response.

"You were going fifty-five in a thirty, which is excessive speed. And she's not wearing her seatbelt," the officer said, shifting his attention to Nadia, "Hello, ma'am, how are you today? Are you okay?"

Nadia's eyes were still wet from crying, her mascara running down her face. "Yes, everything is fine," she muttered.

"Ma'am, can you step out of the vehicle? I'm only making sure you're okay," the officer said with care.

"Do it," Bryan pleaded.

She reluctantly untangled her legs and stood before the officer, a full head taller than him. The officer leaned into the walkie on his shoulder.

"I've got a possible 10–16, 10–12." He made a move to reach for her wrists, but abruptly changed his mind. He took a step back, studying her arms, hands, and shoulders for any marks or bruises. A flicker of something passed over his face, but his expression remained stony. "Get back in the car," he said with derision.

Why did he stop calling her ma'am? Bryan wondered.

Nadia flopped into her seat and slammed the car door. The officer came around to the driver's side and peered at Bryan. "Where are you *guys* going?"

"Home," Bryan replied.

"What are you doing in this neighborhood?"

"We were visiting my mother."

"I need to see your license and proof of insurance." Perusing the paperwork Bryan handed to him, he looked in the backseat. "Is this your car?"

"Yes, sir."

"So, what do you do for a living?"

"I'm a manager at an oil and gas company." Bryan knew that saying he was VP sounded suspicious.

"Stay right here. We will see," the officer said, hitting the top of the car with a hint of aggression.

"What is going on?" Nadia wailed. "I just want to go home."

"This is how double standards work. He thinks I stole this car. How many times do I have to remind you to put on your seatbelt?"

"Look, I'm sorry." She crossed her arms. "You're not the only minority in this car, you know. I know how double standards work."

"You think so," Bryan said dismissively.

"That officer stopped caring about why I was crying after he clocked me."

Bryan knew the slang term meant the officer realized she was trans. "Just because he didn't ask you about your feelings." Bryan couldn't help the contempt leaking into his voice. "That's not a double standard."

Nadia pointed at him. "It's a double standard because if I were a cis woman crying, your Black ass might already be on your way to jail."

Bryan was silent, knowing she was correct.

"Bryan, I'm tired. I've always extended patience and the benefit of the doubt to you and all I'm asking for is the same from you. I'm tired of doing all the work. All of this is almost not worth it anymore," she said loudly.

"Please, keep your voice down. The cop will hear you."

"I'm practically whispering, dumbass." Now she had derision in her voice. "You think I'm yelling because I'm speaking up for my damn self. I can't help it if God made me this way. I've always seen myself as a girl." A tear rolled down her face, gouging out a road through her makeup. "Somedays you're no better than the stupid people I meet on the street. You're supposed to be the one who cares for me the most," Nadia said, sniffling. "You're no better than that cop."

"I wasn't trying to hurt you,"

She looked out the window. "You're concerned only about yourself."

I am not, Bryan wanted to respond, but he knew that would just make the fight worse. He didn't want to argue anymore. He just wanted to get through this traffic stop and get home, so he changed the subject. "I hate being stopped by cops."

"I wish people like this officer, whose job is to protect me and whose salary is paid by our taxes, brought their humanity to the fucking table. Try to see me as a human. I'm not some deviant," Nadia sobbed, wiping her face and exposing more makeup-free skin. Bryan acknowledged her experience with a nod of his head. He wanted her to know that he heard her pain.

"Since I first started driving, I get scared whenever I'm stopped. I don't want to end up like Freddie Gray or Sandra Bland. Bad things seem to happen when cops think no one is watching," Bryan said.

She acknowledged his pain with a simple sigh. "My interactions with cops have been just as strained as yours," Nadia huffed. The officer appeared at the window and handed the paperwork back.

"10–4," the officer said into his walkie. He stood up so that his face was out of view.

Bryan rested against his seat, ready to raise his window.

"Yes, it was just some flashy drug dealer pimp driving a fancy car and fighting with his tall tranny whore. Not my concern," the officer said, unaware of how loud he was talking. "You know how they are. I need to wash my hands after this stop. I'm not even giving them a ticket for not wearing a seatbelt."

"He can't talk about me like that. Is this how these guys are trained to interact with the people they're supposed to protect and serve? I'm going to get his name and badge number to report him." She had cracked her door and was swinging her legs around to get out.

He grabbed her hand. "Please, let it go. It's not worth it." *There's white privilege for you,* Bryan thought. All he wanted was for the officer to leave. *Whites were privileged enough to believe their rights should be honored,* Bryan thought. *Us Black folks just want to be left alone and not have our rights stripped away.*

"Okay, okay." She closed the car door almost tenderly.

Driving away, he wondered about their experiences and how they were both similar and different. *How can two people carrying so much trauma make it together in this world?*

20

The following morning, though sleep-deprived, Bryan tried to meditate. Instead of a peaceful presence, it was fear and anger that continued to replenish his memory banks. He kept hearing Nadia's voice repeating "I'm tired". Sitting with this pain was difficult. He forced himself to sit and try to find peace amidst his internal chaos. *This is exactly what meditation is for,* he thought. He sat, yet the thoughts kept running.

Why had Nadia gotten out of the car? Why had he been so careless to stop by Mama's with her in the car? These were the thoughts that had kept him up all night. On top of everything, Nadia's interaction with the police officer had put them in grave danger. Especially him. He replayed the whole day over again, and still couldn't get settled into his meditation. After the traffic stop, he had done the best he could to recover while maintaining his distance. He made sure Nadia got inside her home safely, but did so without a kiss goodbye or a promise to call.

He tried to shake free of his hamster wheel of thoughts, but meditating was still new to him and not yet an ingrained habit. Meditation only asked him to practice being in the present which was less weight to carry than figure out his homosexuality.

It definitely felt like a Monday. He arrived at work and pushed the elevator button, feeling like a simulacrum of a human. He was exhausted from the weekend. He wanted to call his mama and explain everything. Maybe she would change her stance if she knew everything Nadia had been through: hormone therapy, laser hair removal, voice therapy, breast augmentation, and facial-feminization surgery. All to be accepted as a woman. To pass. And Mama and her catty girlfriends had refused her this privilege, the one with which they were born.

The doors pinged open, and he stepped into a crowded elevator without a single person he knew. No one spoke, only gazing up at the floor numbers as they lit up, and mumbling, "Excuse me," as they winnowed through to get in.

The elevator halted as if the brakes were screeching to an emergency stop. It sputtered, and the lights flickered. The doors stayed tightly fused.

A minute later, all the lights went out on the panel and the elevator grinded to a stop. A few people laughed nervously but Bryan began to panic. Suddenly it felt like there wasn't enough oxygen in the elevator. He pulled at his tie to loosen it, but that didn't seem to help. He could feel beads of sweat seeping through his shirt as his heart raced. He tried to take big sips of the limited air that was available. As nervous murmurs passed through the elevator, Bryan found himself wanting to claw his way out of the elevator any which way he could. It seemed like hours before someone pushed the help button. The security personnel responded but said they couldn't find the elevator on their monitors.

A man in a cobalt colored button-down shirt noticed Bryan's ragged breathing and said, "Bryan, we're going to get you out of here soon. Just breathe. You're okay. Talk to me. Do you like Coldplay?" *Who are you and how do you know I like Coldplay?* Bryan wondered. This thought distracted him long enough to take two deep breaths. Someone knew him even if Bryan didn't know him in return. The man started to shuffle through the songs on his iPhone. The music started. Bryan envisioned being trapped in an elevator only for the world to learn who he truly was: not straight, something different, at a minimum, a fraud. The panic he had felt re-emerged and he held back his tears.

Five minutes later, a tiny crack opened in the elevator doors, enough to see the slit of someone's nostril and eye. Hands used all their might to wrench the doors apart. Bryan wasn't on the correct floor, but he didn't care. He leaped to freedom. Once outside of the jammed box, he leaned over, wheezing, gulping big gasps of air into his lungs. A woman, whom he recognized from the elevator, came up to him.

"You okay?" She put her hand on his back.

Closing his eyes and placing both hands over his ears, he shook his head violently. "No, I'm not." His voice seemed muffled or distant, as if his ears were jammed with cotton. His fears of being out as a trans amorous man took away his voice. "Thank you for your concern." He smiled weakly.

"Do you want to see a nurse?"

"No," he replied, "I'll take the stairs the rest of the way up."

She patted his arm. "Good idea."

The office was quiet. This week before Thanksgiving was one of the two or three times a year when the men remembered they had families. Mike was out too. Come to think of it, the office had been quiet since Mike and Bryan had begun their weekly ten o'clock check-ins. Deer season had started several weeks prior: white men had opportunities to get away, giving men of color a rare respite from them.

Once inside his office, Bryan clicked his door shut. Outside his window, two vultures perched on building ledges. Their hunched backs made them seem menacing and judgmental, and Bryan felt his own chest cave in. *It's like they know what I'm thinking*, he thought, locking eyes with one of them. Simulating invisibility to the best of his ability, he pulled the shades all the way down.

In the darkness of his computer screen, his reflection conjured images of his mama. He turned his monitor on, and, thankfully, the image was replaced by his email inbox, which was full of internal memos to read and decisions to make. He started by responding to emails sent by the person who would replace him in his current role.

He checked his voicemail, hoping for a message from Jerry, but he hadn't called him back. Bryan typed out a quick email, asking if all was well and to please get in touch, urging Jerry to call anytime. *Damn it, Jerry, I need to talk to you. You're the only one I know who would understand.* He needed advice to navigate these challenges. This pain was different from anything he had felt in his life. Maybe talking to Nadia could fix this. She wasn't exactly unbiased, but he needed support. He called her and the call went to voicemail. He called three more times, and all three calls went to voicemail. *Is there anything I haven't screwed up?* he wondered.

***

Determined to fix things with Nadia, he opened her Instagram feed and flipped through her latest culinary creations. No shots inside Club High Five or anyone else. There were shots of Nadia taking a selfie with the two owners of the bakery; she was wearing her white baker's uniform. The caption read, "Two Moons Bakery, Best Bread in the Neighborhood." She looked untroubled. He made up a flimsy excuse to leave work early and sped to her apartment, hoping she was home.

"What do you want?" Nadia said tersely through the door.

"Nadia, will you let me in so we can talk? Please?" Her neighbor, an older woman in a brightly patterned caftan, stepped outside her door to spy on them. Bryan couldn't decide which was the safer option, to ignore her neighbor or acknowledge her in a friendly way.

Brad Kitt brushed his kaleidoscopic fur against his leg, so Bryan picked him up.

"Give Brad to me." After he handed over the cat, she, too, noticed the neighbor. "Hola, Señora Rodriguez," she waved. Her neighbor lifted a hand in greeting and gave Bryan a curious stare.

Brad Kitt jumped out of Nadia's arms. She pivoted on her heels and strolled back into her apartment, leaving the door ajar. Not knowing whether he was invited in, Bryan didn't follow her. He watched her cute figure swaying back and forth in time to her flip-flops slapping the floor.

"You know, she has a gun," Nadia called over her shoulder.

"Who has a gun?"

Nadia stood in the front room. "Señora Rodriguez. You don't want to make her suspicious. I would come in if I were you. Plus, you're letting the AC out."

Bryan smiled at Senora Rodriguez, but she held her stone expression. He stepped gingerly over the threshold.

"Hang on for a second. I need to make sure my new boyfriend got out the window okay." Nadia disappeared into the bedroom and shouted, "Call me!"

Bryan stared widely. "That's not funny."

"And neither is the fact that you've been ignoring me until today."

Bryan opened his mouth to speak, but no words came out. Saying "I'm sorry" seemed too inadequate for the conflicts they'd had.

"We need to have a longer conversation about this," Nadia said, putting her purse strap on her shoulder. "But I'm hungry, so let's have it over food."

***

Later that night, they were eating street tacos and drinking margaritas from a popular food truck. Nadia was flipping through pictures on her phone. She had been distant all night.

Finally, Bryan asked, "What are you looking at?"

She leaned over to show him her Twitter account. "These pictures are from Transgender Remembrance Day. It was yesterday, the day we stopped by your mother's. How apt."

He was distracted by the photos Nadia was scrolling through as she tutted with remorse. He put his arm around her shoulder as he read the posts. "Who is Jasmine Collins? She was 'dead-named'? What's that mean?" Jasmine had been murdered five months earlier in Kansas City.

"That's her given name. The police didn't use her chosen name," Nadia explained. "For ten days, her friends didn't even know she was deceased because the police used her dead name."

"Awful," Bryan agreed. "There are so many trans women listed." This upset him that no one was talking about these lives. Most of the girls were Black. He honestly felt like sobbing. His impulse was to hole up with Nadia and never go out into the world again.

"Too many. If we don't talk about it, then these beautiful souls will be forgotten."

Name after name flashed by. *Is anyone looking into this? It's almost like they don't exist,* he thought. "I really want to talk about what happened yesterday," Bryan said.

She dropped her phone into her purse. "We need to talk about what happened at your mother's house?"

"You wouldn't have known this, but that lock was broken on the hall bathroom," he said. Telling her that his mama asked him to fix the lock did not seem helpful to add so he stopped talking.

Nadia shook her head. "I knew I locked that door. Now it makes sense how that woman barged in."

"That's my fault. I should have warned you."

"Thanks," she said, her face softening. "I wasn't trying to make a scene, but that woman startled me. I can't stop thinking about how I was outed."

"I'm sorry about the way my mother and her friends treated you," Bryan said. There was a throbbing between his ribs, a siren going off at the base of his spine. "I don't know what else to say."

"I feel like you are not standing up for me," Nadia explained.

"My mother and her friends, I had no idea they were like this," Bryan said, "I've never talked to my mother about these things."

"Maybe you should have because trans issues are still women's issues which are human rights issues," she said.

Bryan shook his head. *I want to, but I can't,* he wanted to say.

"It's not just my mama I'm struggling with. It's my bosses and colleagues. They would find ways to freeze me out if they found out about us. They would shred my professional life. Everything I've worked for would be jeopardized in an instant. Everything that set me apart from other Black people and got me promoted would be whisked away," he said.

"You're preaching to the choir about being left out. That's unfortunately part of my existence."

Bryan tried to give her a tight lipped smile to show his sympathy, but he knew it didn't feel right. He felt all the turmoil bubbling inside in his stomach, and tried not to let it show on his face. He tried to make his face look like stone to hide his emotion, which only made him appear cold.

"You think I'm trying to hurt your career!" Nadia exclaimed. "Gosh, all you seem to think about lately is your career and your mother. I know you think I did this on purpose, but I really did have to use the restroom. I'm sorry that I was wrong, but I really believed if she met me, maybe it would make a difference."

"You made it worse," Bryan said.

"I want you to have a relationship with your mother," she said, "I don't know if I can do this anymore. This is getting in the way of what I need emotionally."

Bryan was silent. He wanted to be strong for her. Even if she could understand, they were fundamentally different: a man had to make his own way no matter what. She had a built-in safety net with her parents. Even if they couldn't help much financially, they loved her regardless of what changes she made to her body or whom she slept with. He had no such luck. He looked away. She touched his hand.

"Do you want to come back home with me? It's your choice," she said.

"Nadia, you're so heavy-handed with me sometimes. I'm trying," he said, letting his emotions spill onto his face.

Nadia lightly rubbed a finger over his knuckle, tracing it. "I am too. This has to get easier for us," Nadia insisted.

"Let's go home so we can talk more," he pleaded.

They drove back to her house.

***

Bryan awoke the next day a little sad, it had occurred to him that he was not having Thanksgiving with his mama. And Lawanda would have the kids. "How about we invite Stacey and Sophia to my place for Thanksgiving dinner? It's our first Thanksgiving together. We can go all out. I hope it's not too late to invite them," Bryan said, feeling that breaking bread with his chosen family was just as good.

Nadia liked that idea. She paused, pulling her hair into a ponytail. "I can't wait to be a bona fide chef making my own decent salary."

"What are you talking about?" Bryan asked, feigning surprise.

Smiling from ear to ear, she handed him a piece of paper from the Culinary Institute.

"You got in! You know, I saw the application in the car that day, but I didn't ask you. I thought you wanted to tell me on your own terms." He pulled into a tight hug and kissed her forehead.

"Yes, I did," she said. "I start classes in January."

"You are going to do so well!" Bryan twirled her around. "Have you ever thought about competing in one of those shows like *Chopped* on Food Network?"

She winked. "Let me start school first." She looked thoughtful. "Though I can't stop dreaming about opening my own cupcake shop someday," she sighed.

It felt good to be back with Nadia. They'd had their first big argument and survived.

***

Getting through their first fight seemed to have made their relationship stronger. Nadia started spending the night more regularly and Bryan began finding her things at his place. He found himself needing to make sure a few of his personal things were tucked away. He stashed a book about submissive men in a drawer of his nightstand instead of leaving it out when he was done reading. Every time he picked it up, he thought about how he could never act on this fantasy. But he was curious enough to have bought the book in the first place.

As the holiday season neared, Bryan prepared to celebrate his first Thanksgiving with Nadia and her girlfriends. He cleaned fastidiously, wanting his high-rise to look nice.

Stacey was jazzed about the invite—she did not have any contact with her family. Sophia had planned to volunteer Thursday morning at the women's shelter instead of driving out of town to see her mother. It was decided that she would pick up Stacey at two, and everyone would convene at Bryan's hi-rise for a late lunch.

The day before Thanksgiving, Nadia's parents had left their home in East Texas to spend the holiday in Ohio with Nadia's last living grandparent. Otherwise, Nadia said, they would have loved to join. Bryan was thankful her parents had other plans. While he was certain it would be less eventful than Nadia's meeting with his mama, he wasn't ready to meet them yet.

Bryan ducked out of work early that Wednesday and picked Nadia up. She had a small suitcase with her. "You know it takes a lot of products, clothes, and shoes for me to look this good, right? Plus, you invited me to stay for the long weekend."

They headed to the grocery store, which was packed, but in a fun, celebratory way. Bryan pushed the cart. He enjoyed watching Nadia as she consulted her list, pursing her lips in concentration. A man who looked about his age with a light-brown goatee and hair swept to the left, shaved closely on the sides, kept sneaking glances at Bryan. It unnerved him. *What's he staring at?*

"Oh, hi, Larry," Nadia said, stepping closer to give the man a hug and turning to introduce Bryan. They chatted for only a few minutes. Larry, holding a bottle of wine and flowers, was on his way to meet his new boyfriend.

"He's really a nice guy," Nadia said.

"How do you know him?"

"We get our hormones from the same doctor." Nadia picked up a small bottle of smoked paprika. She continued walking, leaving Bryan behind. "C'mon. What are you doing?"

Bryan's confusion kept his feet glued to the floor. "Wait a minute." He pursed his lips, squinting his eyes. "He's a trans man?"

"Yes, goofball."

"I've never considered such a thing." He moved his cart out of the way to make room for a shopper reaching for spices, hoping the shopper could hear the conversation. Bryan stared off into space, befuddled by the appearance that Larry looked like any man.

"It's okay to say FTM."

"FTM?"

"Female-to-Male."

He stood there with his hands on his hips. "Wow!" he kept repeating. Nadia opened her phone and began scrolling through photos. "He's cute. These guys are transgender. The trans community has been here as long as any other community. No one even noticed us when we kept to ourselves."

Bryan peeked over her shoulder. One guy looked a lot like Reggie. "Why do you never see trans men in the media?"

"Companies make more money exploiting women of any kind," Nadia said confidently.

"I see your point."

"That's why the bathroom bill was so silly. No one even knows we are here."

***

As soon as they returned home, Nadia washed her hands and tied one of Bryan's aprons around her slim waist. Bryan watched her move like a professional, methodical and efficient, in his large kitchen, which was furnished with a Viking commercial stove, a double oven, plenty of counter space, and the latest cookery. Nadia spent the rest of the afternoon preparing everything that could be made beforehand, shooing Bryan out of the kitchen. He continued cleaning the house, singing along to nineties R & B songs playing from the surround sound, sporadically touching her waist whenever he passed her. He stopped to hold her closely while she slivered ginger, and she sang with him. Testing her, he took the chorus, prompting her to take the verses, which she also knew to the letter.

21

On Thanksgiving morning, Bryan arose before Nadia to meditate. Meditation had begun to open new doors and passages that made him question his real self, but he continued to sit, curious to see what would unfold. He was pulled by the gravity of the unknown to understand his full self. In his mind's eye, he saw himself and Nadia awake in bed. A wave of calm washed over him and he found his breath. He wanted to stay in this peaceful place. But his mind had other plans and quickly darted to his feelings about his mama. He missed his mama. This was difficult. He did not like arguing with her, and they had never fought like this before. He tried to envision sitting at the Thanksgiving table with Nadia and her friends to reclaim his sense of peace. It lasted momentarily until the image was replaced with an image of his mama and Robert eating Thanksgiving by themselves. He saw the full spread she usually prepared on the table: a ham, sweet potatoes, collards, and special family cranberry sauce. She loved going all out when cooking for the holidays. He tried to imagine himself there with them. He and his mama blinked their eyes and smiled at each other. He found his breath again. One. Settling into the present, his consciousness formed flashes of a bright white and blue light. He had never experienced these flashes of truth before- it was like his mind would go blank and reset to show him what he needed to see instead of what he wanted to see. Suddenly, he saw Nadia positioned behind him, holding him by his waist. He realized he was on his hands and knees and moaning out loud, feeling her deep within his being. He opened his eyes, both startled and aroused by the intrusive image. *Where the hell did that come from? I was trying to think about Thanksgiving dinner and finding peace*, he thought. He felt his heart racing and his breath getting rapid and shallow. He recognized he was falling out of his meditation and found his breath again, trying to reclaim the sense of peace he had felt earlier. He kept his eyes open this time, too scared to close them again. *It must be that damn book getting in my head*, he thought. He paused for a few moments, just focusing on his breath. *Or do I want to feel submissive with Nadia? And if I do, is that really a bad thing?* He decided that he was veering into overthinking territory and he stood up, needing to do something else to get out of his head.

He wandered to the bed and stroked Nadia's arm. She slowly opened her eyes. She was strikingly beautiful without makeup, and as she adjusted the covers, he caught a glimpse of her erect girl dick before it disappeared under the sheets. He smiled, thinking about how terrified he was of it at first. Now it was just part of what made her Nadia. He glanced at her face again, her unblemished skin revealing her youth. Bryan felt a pang of jealousy, which quickly dissipated when she blinked her eyes open. Bryan gazed lovingly into her eyes. She smiled knowingly.

"What?" Nadia asked, fully awake.

"How about a quickie?" Bryan said seductively, reaching for her thigh.

"We need to start cooking," Nadia said, beginning to emerge from the covers and sitting up. Bryan hovered over her, kissing her forehead, then her cheek before meeting her lips.

"You're like an addict now," she replied with a seductive smile, returning his kiss. "Okay fine, but emphasis on quick," she said.

***

Bryan couldn't stop thinking about his new submissive fantasy. After sex that morning, all he could think about was what would happen if their roles were reversed. The quickie had backfired-he had thought it would quell his curiosity, but it seemed to only bring it more to the forefront. Even though the girls were running late, Nadia was taking the food out of the oven when they arrived. The turkey, ham, dressing, five-spice marshmallow sweet potato, and brussels sprouts had been executed with precision. When he nicked a taste, he conceded that she might have cooked more deliciously than he could have, and her timing was eerily impeccable.

He was putting some light jazz on the stereo when he heard knocking on his door. Nadia quickly set down the dish she was holding and ran to the door. Bryan realized he had not seen either Sophia or Stacey since the night at Club High Five, and felt a shiver run down his spine with the memory of that night. He took the wine out of the fridge as Nadia opened the door. He had wanted to meet the girls in the lobby because a lot could happen in the span of twenty-five floors, but was glad they found his place safely.

They tumbled in, a flutter of perfume, laughter, and clattering heels. Sophia's braids were flying.

"I cannot take Stacey anywhere." Sophia mugged, feigning seriousness. "She was flirting something terrible with the valet. I was like, I'd better get this mad thing upstairs before they kick us out!'

Bryan smiled, glad that flirting was the worst thing that had happened due to his poor time management skills.

Nadia giggled, hugging each of her friends hard. "He is cute, for sure."

"Welcome," he said. He was going to add "to my home" but changed his mind. Bryan didn't want to leave Nadia out.

Sophia fanned her face. "Girl . . . this man . . . I have no words."

Stacey mouthed, "First time ever," and they all laughed. The girls admired everything they saw in his luxury hi-rise. They "oohed" and "ahhed" over the smells coming from the kitchen and thanked Bryan for the glasses of chilled sauvignon blanc he placed in their hands as they wandered from room to room.

Bryan looked around for Stacey, and realized she had disappeared. Nadia left Bryan and Sophia with instructions for setting the table. She found Stacey in the library, picking through Bryan's books.

"Girl, what are you doing?" Nadia asked, looking behind her to make sure they were alone.

"I'm looking to see where you were standing," Stacey answered. "Where was he? Did he use his cushion? In the library. That's hot."

"Oh, Bryan. Oh, Bryan. I'm. I'm—" Stacey mimicked Nadia's moaning voice.

"Oh, girl, your crazy ass," Nadia said, laughing. Bryan signaled his presence by coughing loudly.

He smiled at Nadia affectionately. He knew the girls talked, and he knew exactly what their conversation had been about. In the past, this would have made him feel nervous and insecure. But he knew from the smile on Nadia's face that told him only good things were being shared with her friends. *They know what we did in here,* he thought, feeling his smile grow bigger. He was proud that he was able to satisfy her.

Nadia pulled Stacey back into the front room.

"What were you two doing?" Sophia asked.

"Nothing," they said in unison.

"Here's to my chosen family," Sophia said, her eyes wet.

Nadia drew her friend close. "Oh, honey, we love you."

"Amen. Mine, too. My parents' loss," Stacey said. Something was different about Stacey, but Bryan couldn't pin down what it was.

"Girl, you did it," Nadia said, putting her hands on her hips and smiling. "Let me see them."

Stacey straightened her back and thrust out her chest. "I love them. Not too big, not too small. I'm starting to feel more and more like the woman who has always been inside of me."

"Girl, you're not going to believe why we're late," Sophia said, taking a sip of her drink. "Stacey was in bed with her lover and lost the key to the lock."

Stacey tossed her head. "How do you think I got these nice titties?" She placed her hands under her breasts to show off their curvature. "That bottom boy paid for them. He loves feeling them lying against his back."

"The man's little butt cheeks were red, and he moaned about his legs cramping up," Sophia said, laughing. "This girl had his ankles restrained to the two corners of the bed and behind his head." Sophia simulated where his feet were placed. "Yes, girl, she had this white boy naked and folded up like a *C* clamp with his legs spread wide. His ankles have probably never been closer to his own ears in his life. Nadia, this was a sight to see." Sophia was still laughing to herself. "All he could do was mumble because he had a ball gag in his mouth."

"Ha," Nadia laughed. "Speaking of mouths, come to the table. The food is hot!"

Sophia and Stacey meandered to the dining room.

"How long had he been in that position?" Bryan asked. They all stood around the ornately set table.

Stacey smiled sweetly. "Not that long, maybe a few hours. But don't worry, he was fine." She sat down and topped off her wineglass with the bottle on the table.

"After y'all released him, what did he say?"

"Thank you, mistress," Stacey said, hi-fiving Sophia who had also taken a seat.

Bryan felt himself getting aroused and turned around to adjust himself. *Not now*, he thought, *save it for later.* He decided to help Nadia bring the platters and bowls to the table and tried to think about anything other than sex.

Stacey and Sophia exclaimed over the delicious spread laid before them. Once Nadia sat down, they all dug in.

Stacey said, "Mmm, yum." She swallowed and took a glug of water. "Nadia, girl. You keep outdoing yourself. You're going to blow your instructors out of the water. And Bryan, you're generous to have us over for this meal. Thank you. I knew you were cool since the drag show at Club High Five."

Sophia chimed in. "We are an open community, and we know how to have fun. We're not all stuck-up, like a lot of straight people. This is who we are," Sophia said, stretching her arms out as if to embrace the world beyond the walls of his hi-rise.

"Maybe that's because a lot of straight people don't have any models for living outside the box," Bryan replied.

Sophia widened her eyes. "And you think we have any in or out of the box?" She cast her eyes to the ceiling as if she were waiting for an idea to drop down. "Okay, I know how to explain this. Who was your hero?"

"Wesley Snipes," he blurted, without having to think. "That was my man. And before him, Sidney Poitier and Sammy Davis Jr."

"Get this," Sophia's tone was arched. "I don't ever remember seeing any women who looked like me until I saw *Midnight in the Garden of Good and Evil*."

"Oh right, The Lady Chablis. That was a pretty good film," Nadia said.

"Seeing someone who looks like you on a big screen is powerful. Add them doing cool or heroic things, and it's inspiring, affirming." Sophia shook her head. "Why can't I have that?"

Bryan was embarrassed that he hadn't thought of this before.

"I remember Elmer Fudd seeing Brünnhilde," Stacey interjected.

The girls chuckled, but Bryan was confused. "What?"

"Brünnhilde was Bugs Bunny dressed like a girl in a cute skirt and sports bra. Since I was a kid, I always wanted to be like her," Stacey said, relaxing in her seat. "Elmer wanted her."

Nadia giggled. "Did he stick to her like glue?"

"Bryan, that reminds me. You're not off the hook." Sophia leaned on her elbows and interlaced her fingers. "Being trans is difficult. Do you know what we go through every day, especially if you're not passing?"

Stacey added, "We expect you to protect our girl when she's with you. That includes at your mother's house and with the police."

Bryan agreed. "I hear you," he said. *Thankfully we won't be at my mother's house together any time soon,* he thought.

Sophia played with one of her braids. "Being Black and trans is even harder. I get as hard of a time from our Black men as I do from the cops." She sipped her wine thoughtfully.

"Really," Nadia said.

Bryan leaned forward.

"Yeah, girl," Sophia said, "Look I get it. Black men feel emasculated but that's no reason to take their shame out on me. And some of their mamas only make it worse because they can't be honest."

No one directed this toward him specifically, but Bryan squirmed in his seat.

"You love who you love," Sophia continued, "and some of these mamas are doing more harm than good."

"My man is different," Nadia said, giving him a gentle kiss on the lips. "I worry about white men, too. They're dangerous in a different way. Drunk on their power. Plus, nothing can touch them. I worry how much worse they'll get if *He Who Must Not Be Named* is elected. Did you see him ride the escalators to announce his bid?"

"Ugh, I know," Stacey said. Her voice was blithe. But Bryan had never seen her face as fearful as it was before she returned to her usual bravado. Bryan remembered that Stacey was only twenty-three and had been kicked out of her home as a teen. She'd definitely seen a lot in her short life, and Bryan wondered if the thought of the upcoming election scared her more than trying to find her way on the streets.

As the conversation veered into lighter topics about nails and the newest cookery Nadia had splurged on, Bryan found himself revisiting the image Stacey had conjured up when telling her story. During a brief lull in the conversation, Bryan ventured forth with his burning question. "Stacey, have you always been a top?"

Stacey picked up her glass. "Yep. I'm a girl who loves fucking men. Sexual desire is on a wide spectrum, right? Some guys have never had as intense an orgasm as they do when they're being penetrated, dominated, and controlled, like Chevalier Cliquot." She pronounced the name with a fake French accent.

"Who?" Bryan asked.

"Chevalier Cliquot was a famous sword swallower," she explained. Bryan, waiting for more explanation, sat silently.

"Get it? He hosts these exclusive blow parties." Stacey bragged that she was the only one who knew what Chevalier looked like. He wore a red leather mask to hide his identity, though he had a Daffy Duck tattoo on his calf and a strange pattern on his upper arm.

"I like Cliquot," Stacey mused, "but lately, he's been acting creepy. He drinks too much, and he can be kind of aggressive when he's not bottoming out for me."

"These cis straight men are crazy. And people say that transgender people are sexual predators." Sophia rolled her eyes.

Nadia dished out seconds to everyone. "The same people who say that are supporting a sexual predator as the Republican candidate."

"Let's take a break from talking about all that," Stacey said. She gestured grandly to the others. "Let's talk about fun stuff, someone."

Nadia got up and walked into the kitchen. Bryan followed right behind her, snatching his plate and empty glass. He carefully placed his dishes on the counter so that they didn't make much noise. He and Nadia stared at each other. *What would Nadia feel like if they were in that situation?* he thought. Bryan pulled her toward him by the hips and began kissing her passionately. She broke off the kiss and gave him a long look.

"What has gotten into you?" she said.

He did not know how to reply, so he just smiled. He walked behind her back to the dining room.

"Sophia, are you dating anyone?" Nadia asked, holding the wine bottle out to offer the last pour.

"I met somebody special. Well, at least, I thought it was real. We had our second date the other night," Sophia said. "But he didn't call." Her voice was morose.

"Hey, girl," Stacey piped up. "Don't worry. I got you. I'm going to find you somebody."

"Only if you can find me a guy like Bryan," Sophia said. She blew him a kiss, and he blushed again.

Nadia disappeared into the kitchen to retrieve her surprise dessert, a chocolate and citrus cassata. Everyone clapped, and Nadia snapped a photo of everyone sitting around the cake. After hours of talking, eating, drinking, and laughing, Bryan felt full and content. Sophia went to the bathroom before she and Stacey got on the road. Stacey fixed her shirt to make sure that a strategic amount of cleavage was showing for the valet.

"That bathroom is to die for," Sophia said. "A girl can't be too careful out there when stopping to use the restroom." While he was helping the girls with their coats, it unexpectedly occurred to Bryan to ask them, "Have you guys talked to Jerry lately? I've called and emailed him a couple times and he hasn't responded."

Sophia tilted her head. "Well, last I checked, his Facebook account says he's working in Louisiana. Maybe he's not checking his office phone or email?"

What is Jerry doing in Louisiana? Bryan wondered.

After lots of hugging and kissing and thank-yous all around, the girls left. The silence in their wake was profound. As he loaded the dishwasher in his perfectionist way, Bryan heard Nadia hop in the shower. He finished the dishes as fast as he could and went straight to the bedroom. He was still aroused from earlier, and wanted Nadia to help him with that problem. He got naked and lay on the bed, waiting for her to emerge from the shower.

22

Nadia entered the bedroom. "Everybody had a good time tonight," she said as she approached the bedroom door. When she walked through the doorframe, she did a double-take at Bryan. Her face went from shocked to seductive in seconds as she took him in. "Are you naked?"

"I'm glad they had a good time. Hey, I'm curious. Has Stacey always been a top?"

"Yep, I think so," she replied, giggling, "She takes care of her men. You seemed interested in knowing about that." She continued, "Position?"

"I can't stop thinking about it . . ." Bryan paused.

"What?"

"I want to know what it feels like." He looked at her thighs, reaching for her.

She lifted her night shirt and looked between her legs. "Are you talking about this 'it'?"

"You mean girl-dick?" He laughed.

"I'm curious," Nadia said. "Why?"

"Listening to Stacey talk about her boyfriends did something to me," Bryan said, "I adore you. I want to connect with you this way. I've never felt this way before." His heart raced. He was surprised that he found the courage to admit. *Guess that's what happens when the blood that was going to your brain is elsewhere,* he thought.

Nadia paused before exhaling fully. "Bryan, that's not who I am. I've never liked topping. I only topped because guys were using me. This was simply another form of selfishness by men who had no desire to know me. Just another fetish."

Bryan was stunned by this perspective, and his face fell. He leaned back, looking out the window.

"Their interest in dating me evaporated once they lived out their fantasy."

"That's not how I feel," Bryan consoled her. "I've been here. I'm not going anywhere." He lay next to her, facing the large window. She turned off the table lamp and cuddled him.

"I don't want to rush this. Can we just see how we feel in the morning?" She kissed his cheek. "I adore you, too."

"Okay," he said, his voice barely above a whisper.

Bryan tried with all his might for the rest of the night to put it out of his mind as best he could and not talk about his bottom fantasy.

***

Early the next morning, Bryan snuggled up next to Nadia.

"I want to know what you feel like," Bryan cooed in her ear, rubbing at her groin.

"Are you sure?" Nadia whispered.

Bryan saw his submissive behavior was unexpectedly turning her on. She was growing in his hand. He nodded. "I want this for us. You're the only person I will let do this. I promise."

"Okay."

She reached for the drawer of the side table and grabbed a small black butt plug that she used. Bryan gulped nervously. His chest heaved. She rolled a condom over the butt plug. Bryan exposed his bare ass to Nadia, compressing himself into a tight crouching-tiger yoga position. She leaned in closer. He could feel her breath. She kissed him. Bryan watched her squeeze copious amounts of lube slowly onto the rounded tip of the butt plug, as if she were dropping soft serve ice cream into a cone at Dairy Queen.

"What is that?" Bryan said, seeing that it was not their usual stuff.

"This is the good stuff. *Elbow Grease*," Nadia replied. "This might be cold," she warned. She slowly touched his opening with the butt plug.

Bryan felt her slowly spinning the wet butt plug in a clockwise motion, as if she were whipping up cotton candy. She spread the lube just on the inside of his entrance. "Can I have some more . . . Elbow Grease?"

Nadia laughed, grabbing the clear bottle. She dripped lube onto him while spinning the butt plug at the same time.

"Oh," Bryan moaned. He closed his eyes, enjoying the world that was opening up at the same time as his body. Then he saw his father laughing at him, berating him with homophobic slurs. Bryan's eyes opened. The shame was too much to bear. He lurched forward. "No. No!" Bryan shouted. He flipped around, landing on his back. "I can't do this. Only sissies and women are submissive."

"So, what are you saying? Being a woman is about being submissive? Do I look submissive to you?" Nadia demanded.

"No, I'm sorry. That's not what I meant." He put his head in his hands.

"Then what did you mean?" She crossed her arms over her chest.

"I don't know what I meant," he said, turning to face her. "I'm not a girl. Only sissies do this."

"Who said anything about you being a sissy? There is no one way to be with each other. It's okay. Being a bottom doesn't make you a girl. If it feels good, then that's all there is to it," Nadia said, getting up to clean the plug.

"I'm not like those guys. I'm so confused."

"Don't dump your confusion on me. Honey, it's okay," Nadia said, getting back into bed. 'This is gay. This isn't. Men do this. Women do that. These rigid definitions of roles make straight men weak. I think it's an excuse to avoid maturing."

He pulled the covers over their shoulders, hiding from Nadia and trying to avoid lying on the wet spot.

"I'm tired and it's early. Let's go back to sleep," Nadia said, turning away from him.

The tension grew to form a cold stone between their bodies. Bryan couldn't think of anything he could say to dislodge it. Soon Nadia fell asleep. Clouds began to form at the bedroom window, obscuring Bryan's insomniac thoughts. Being her bottom ran counter to his definition of sex. He honestly wanted to be left alone. He cared for his girlfriend deeply, but maybe this was a mistake.

Bryan drifted off and found himself awakened by the intermittent sound of rain hitting the window a few hours later. The clouds hung around his bedroom window, obscuring the view of the city. He sat up, planting his feet on the floor. He rubbed his forehead. Leaning forward, he turned to look back at Nadia. She opened her eyes.

"Hey," she said dryly.

Bryan stood up, saying nothing as he walked into the bathroom. He washed his face slowly, as if he was moving through water. His body suddenly felt cumbersome, like he was trying to move someone else's arms. He dried his face and looked into the mirror, only to see a reflection he no longer recognized. He knew what he had to do. He walked back out to the bedroom and saw Nadia sitting up in bed.

"Nadia," he paused, "I.....I...I want to break up," Bryan said hesitantly.

"What?" Nadia said. A flash of confusion crossed over her face before it was replaced with a pained expression.

Bryan felt his heart racing again. *She's not going to take this well. How do I make her understand?* He couldn't find the words to explain himself, so he stood there silently.

Nadia stood. She plucked a piece of clothing off a chair. "Tell me again what you just said." She shrugged her shirt on.

Bryan stood as tall as possible. "I want to break up," he said with more confidence. "I don't want to be with you anymore." *Nope, that's not it. God, what is this feeling? And how do I describe it to her?*

Nadia started frantically gathering the rest of her clothes. "I can't believe you," she said, her eyes red with angry tears. "After all of this. You want to break up with me."

Bryan continued to stand in silence. *You're doing the right thing*, he heard an inner voice say. Or was it his mother's voice?

"You know what. Screw you. I can't believe I wasted my time with you," she said, zipping up her boots. "I thought you were different," she said, making eye contact with him. Rivers of mascara ran down her face and Bryan felt his heart hurt for her. He didn't want to cause her pain, but couldn't she see his pain?

Bryan watched her getting ready. As torn up as he was about having hurt her, he was feeling more confident in his decision. He needed to end his own pain. He started putting on his clothes. His chest was beating so hard he thought he was going to collapse.

"You know what, I deserve better than this," she said, glaring at him. Snatching her purse, she stomped to the front room. She looked him dead in the eye, her sadness transformed into anger.

"I will get my things later," she said, flinging the door open. And with that, she was gone.

Bryan stood with his back against the front door. *What the hell did I just do?* He was lost, much like the same feeling when Lawanda abandoned him and his family for some guy. Except this time, he knew that he was fully the cause of his misery. He tried laying down in his bed, but Nadia's presence was still palpable in his bedroom. He laid on the couch, hoping he could get some reprieve, but her scent lingered there too. *Fuck*, he thought. *I have no idea how to fix this. I have no idea how to fix myself.*

23

Bryan sat up with a start upon hearing his Monday morning alarm. Everything felt backwards or inside out. His limbs felt like lead, and he was pretty sure there was an imprint of his body in the couch after having laid on it for three days straight. He looked at the clock and felt a pang of dread in realizing that he needed to start getting ready for work. He managed to muster up enough strength to make it to the bathroom and get himself cleaned up, but his face still didn't look right. Something was scratching his collarbone. Bryan tried on four different suits, but nothing felt right. His reflection in the mirror was not worthy of the Italian-made clothing hanging off his frame. *Screw it, nothing is going to look right today,* he thought. *And screw meditation. Nothing is going to help today.* He knew that sitting on the cushion would only make space for Nadia to fill up all the space in his brain.

As he took the elevator down, Nadia was standing next to him in his mind. He could already tell this was going to be a rough journey without her. *What did I do? And what is wrong with me?* The elevator door opened and he walked out robotically. *It's for the best,* he thought. *She deserves someone who knows what they want.*

He arrived at work after nine in the morning, and his parking place was taken. As he approached the lobby, he saw a few co-workers he knew, so he hung back and waited. Bryan needed to get into his office without running into a bunch of coworkers. He rushed past the security officer who was badging in, then walked past the elevator and turned right into the stairwell. He quickly walked up the stairs to his office, closed the door, and locked it. Bryan knew he was unable to pull off being gregarious and helpful. His phone buzzed, and he jumped. *Is it Nadia? Oh no, I can't check it. If it's her, I might as well go home and curl up into a ball. But what if it's not her? What if it's about one of my kids?* Using the logic that it could be something important not related to Nadia, he braced himself to look at the caller ID. It was a sales call. He exhaled with relief. He knew he couldn't face her. The pain in her green eyes had been haunting him all weekend, and he felt bad that he had chosen his pain over hers. He stared into space, not out of boredom, but out of loss. He sighed deeply.

He looked in his email inbox. An email had been sent to the entire company announcing that Bryan had been appointed as the new VP of polymers and specialties. The email explained Bryan's tenure at the company, including his experiences, and was approved by the HR department. Bryan smiled, choosing to focus on his promotion instead of Nadia. A few moments later, emails started coming into his inbox. So many people, either emails or direct messages, reached out to congratulate Bryan on his promotion. Despite a few people from the plants in Port Arthur, Louisiana, and Alabama sending positive messages, he wondered if it was going to be a struggle to get the working class on his side. A few coworkers stopped by to say hello, and that he would be a great VP. Bryan politely smiled and nodded, grateful that he had something positive to focus on. *My romantic life might be a disaster, but at least my career is taking off,* he thought.

Bryan went about his day as usual until he received a phone call from building logistics that they were going to send boxes up to his office for the upcoming move to his new office. He began tidying up his office in preparation for packing. As he was wiping down his keyboard, he realized it was three in the afternoon and that he hadn't checked his phone since that morning. He took it out of the desk drawer he stashed it in and slipped it in his pocket without checking it. *I wouldn't want that to accidentally get packed,* he thought. The movers, a group of young Black men, brought the boxes as he was cleaning his desk. Based on their small nods in response to his "Thank yous," he did not think they were aware of his promotion. Seeing these guys made Bryan aware that he needed to benefit the Black employees in this new role, but he was unsure of how to go about it without compromising his image as a company man. He gathered his bags and took the stairs again. The initial spark of recognition from his promotion had faded as he realized now had to return home to his empty high-rise. He realized it hadn't felt empty before he'd met Nadia, but now that she had existed in the space, it felt like there was a void. *It's not like she even moved in with me,* he thought to himself, *so why does it feel like this?* Bryan simply wanted to go back to a place that felt like home, and to simply sit in the dark there. He suddenly realized that it wasn't his apartment that had made him feel at home, but Nadia herself. There was no one he could call to talk about this with. Who would he call for an honest conversation? Reggie was a great friend to pick up women with, but he had little patience when it came to consoling someone after a break up. And to tell him that he lost the one person he felt "at home" with? Reggie would tell him to man up and get laid.

Avoiding eye contact with his neighbors at the mailbox had once been unthinkable, but today he barely lifted his gaze to acknowledge the presence of others. Bryan crossed paths with the distinguished gentleman and sophisticated girlfriend and felt a greater sense of loss. He still wanted what this guy had (or at least appeared to have), but it was too big a leap to believe he could have that with Nadia. Her world was one where people were authentically filled with courage and his world was built on hiding his truth so he could live the life that he wanted.

Upstairs in the safety of his high-rise, he tore open a letter from his mortgage company and the high-rise management company, both of which cited a significant increase to his monthly payments and which would be due by January 1. He folded the letter back into its envelope and placed it with the rest of the mail, hoping to forget about it. The promotion came at the right time.

He walked around his high-rise with a sense of renewed confidence. He may have lost Nadia, but he could provide for himself. He would just have to do some reorganizing and sprucing to make his high-rise feel more homey. He could find that sense of home again. He could live without her. He found himself thinking of his father, and how he needed to start over after his parents divorced. *If he could do it, I can do it,* Bryan thought. He realized that he was about to step into uncharted territory. He realized he was no longer the person he was before he met Nadia, and that thought scared him. *Who have I become?* he wondered. He didn't know how to answer that question, so he busied himself in the kitchen. He opened the refrigerator. Even though Nadia had given away the Thanksgiving leftovers to Stacey and Sophia, he saw several containers. He opened the first one he saw. It contained oxtail noodles that Nadia had cooked a few days before Thanksgiving. The thought of eating her cooking for one of the last times felt like a dagger in his heart, but he hated wasting food and knew that he didn't have the energy to cook. Bryan sighed and placed the food in the Dutch oven and covered it. While the noodles heated up, he turned on the television to put some noise in the house. The sounds of the cooking channel entered the air space and Bryan felt a pang of sadness. He and Nadia watched cooking shows each time Nadia spent the night, which had become quite often before their relationship ended. *Well, this is depressing. I'm eating her food while watching her show*, he thought. He almost shed a tear, but caught himself and changed the channel to the news.

Unfortunately, the news wasn't a sufficient distraction from her delicious food. Bryan tried to focus on the flavors instead of Nadia, but he couldn't help thinking about how excited she was to make this dish when she had found a recipe from a Trinidadian chef. She had used the recipe as a jumping off point, and created her own blend of the spices that had really infused the food. He remembered that moment in the kitchen when he tried them for the first time and told her she was a culinary genius. She had thrown her arms around him with glee and kissed him. He felt another pang of sadness, and stood up. Even though he had just eaten, he felt empty.

He looked inside the fridge and decided to finish off the red velvet cake she had made for Thanksgiving to fill the emptiness. He was happy she hadn't given all the food away. Nadia was a wonderful cook, but her passion was baking, and it showed; the slice of cake melted in his mouth and he closed his eyes. Everything about that slice of cake reminded him of Nadia. He suddenly felt warm and light with her essence, but felt the warmth fade as he opened his eyes. *It's like she's everywhere in this place,* he thought. He finished the slice of cake slowly, the emptiness in his gut slowly filling with red velvet cake. He put his dishes in the sink and sighed. *What on earth did I do? Why can't I be with her the way she deserves?* Feeling overfilled with cake and regret, he turned out the lights and went to his bedroom. Laying in bed, looking up at the ceiling, he tried to remember why he had ended things with her to assuage his regret: he could not afford to jeopardize his future.

***

The following morning before work, his phone buzzed. It was Nadia calling. He got nervous, considering he had no idea what she would want to talk about. He walked in a small circle around his kitchen, cleared his throat, and clicked Accept.

"Hi, Nadia," Bryan said weakly.

"Will you be at home this Thursday after work?" Her tone was bone-dry. "I need to get my things."

"Well, why can't you come over on the weekend?"

She was silent. "Because I'm going out of town."

Where? Where would she be going by herself? he wondered.

"Is that a yes or no?" she snapped.

"Yes." His voice sounded strained, even to his own ears.

She hung up. *What am I going to say?* Bryan wondered. *I guess I have two days to figure it out.*

***

For the next two days, life felt like a series of sleepy interactions with the world, though with an undercurrent of anxiety. He worked to get everything ready for the move, but was told that with the holidays coming up, it would take several weeks before all his personal effects made their way to his new office. He still had not heard from Jerry despite having emailed him again on Tuesday. The days moved slowly, and Bryan was learning that with more responsibility came less paperwork. Bryan had four direct reports who spent as much time at the facilities as they did in the home office. He could already tell that he might have more responsibility, but he was no longer working long hours. He found himself at home in the early evenings, alone and with no hobbies or interests to focus his energy. Cooking had become a lonely endeavor and unsustainable very quickly. He even lost the energy to go to the gym. He sighed, knowing he needed to give himself time. It had barely been a week.

On Thursday night, the clouds rolled in, snuffing out the moonlight. He shuffled through his high-rise, looking for Nadia's things. The cardigan she wore when they watched TV was behind the couch cushions. The long red gown from her birthday dinner was poking out between the somber suits in his closet. He found her shampoo in the shower, her lipstick in his bathroom drawer, and her chain bracelet on the bedroom table. Each item brought with it its own unique form of sadness. He decided to come up with a plan so that he wouldn't see her and break down, begging for her back. As much as he wanted to, he knew he needed to play it cool. Being desperate never helped anybody. He practiced in the mirror, repeating "Hi, Nadia," as dryly as possible. He didn't want to show any emotion. He thought back to his father when he got divorced. He never saw his father cry, or even look remotely upset. He needed to be strong like him. And if he was strong in his stance, then she wouldn't linger and ask questions that would make him want to break character.

On Thursday around five in the evening, Nadia texted to verify he would be home. He wanted to see her and know she was okay. Exactly at eight that night, there was a knock. He was ready. He was going to be the cool guy. He opened the door, trying to look unphased by her arrival. Her beauty and presence diminished the brightness of the hallway lights, and Bryan felt a wave of emotion hit him. He closed his eyes. *Be cool. Remember, you broke up with her for a reason.* When he opened his eyes again, he couldn't help but take in her figure. She towered over him like Enyo, the goddess of war. Her hair was pulled back tightly, and she wore sunglasses, fitted jeans, a red bomber jacket, and a cropped blouse that glorified her perfectly augmented cleavage and pale mid-drift. *Damn, she looks good,* he thought. He broke into a big smile. He couldn't help himself. *Damn, I really screwed up.* He looked up at her and realized the fight was already over before it began. She stepped into the high-rise, and any semblance of a plan went out the window.

She spoke first. "Do you have my things?"

He opened his arms for a hug, then hesitated. *Are we still friends?* he wondered as he awkwardly held his arms out. She didn't make any move to accept his embrace and he let his arms fall by his side. "Hi, Nadia." He stopped, sensing her aura had shifted and it was no longer welcoming him. *Am I even allowed to talk right now?* "It's good to see you," he blurted out.

"No, Bryan, don't," she said, putting her hand in his face, "I only want to get my bracelet, my clothes, and my mother's recipes." She brushed past him. "My mother gave me that bracelet."

He followed. "Nadia, can we talk? I never gave us a chance to talk," he said following her into the bedroom. She grabbed the clothes Bryan had neatly folded for her on the bed and quickly left the room. Bryan followed her out of the room, racking his brain for something else to say.

"I did not handle things correctly. Can you take off your sunglasses?" She grabbed her shampoo and other belongings from the bathroom and Bryan hovered outside the door. She faced him head on, her shades still on. Bryan imagined that she was glaring at him behind them even though he couldn't see her eyes. *Just say something, anything. I don't even care if you yell at me,* he thought.

He threw his hands up in frustration as she brushed past him. "It's nighttime, and it's raining outside, for God's sake!"

She stopped in her tracks and whipped her head around. She got right in his face. He felt her presence, which was what he had missed. Even though she was towering over him and angry, he preferred this to her absence. She was close enough for him to feel the breath from her nostrils on his nose. She smelled good. Like baking and some kind of flower, the way she always smelled. Like home.

"You didn't handle things correctly. You think?" She poked him in his shoulder with her index finger. She removed her sunglasses. Her eyes were blazing a dark green and looked bloodshot and puffy. *My God, has she been crying for a week?* Bryan wondered. He felt a pang of guilt mixed with his sadness. He wanted to heal her and make the pain go away, but he didn't know how to fix both of their pain at the same time. He wasn't sure if it was possible.

"You don't get to plead ignorant," she continued, "Not this time. You are selfish, and I'm not going to allow myself to be jerked around by you. I'm done." She retreated back into the bedroom and Bryan followed again.

"Please, Nadia. Let me explain. Don't go like this. I need to explain why I did what I did."

"I gave you every chance in the world to evolve with me and learn how to talk to me. But, when it came down to it, I wasn't worth it," she said, snatching her bracelet off the bedside table.

Bryan said nothing.

"You're only concerned about your job, your mama, and your image. I've never met such a superficial person in my life."

"I'm not superficial. I'm..," pausing.

Nadia started laughing. "That's all I've seen from you. You're so worried about people not seeing you as a real man. I'll tell you something. Real men can handle what the world throws at them," she said, turning toward the door. She opened the door and stepped into the hallway. "I would move on if I were you, because I have." She didn't look back once.

He followed her a few steps out the door, his world moving in sickeningly slow motion. At the elevator, she put her sunglasses back on and tightened her ponytail. The doors opened, and the elevator light illuminated her aura, pasting her shadow onto the opposing wall. She walked toward the luminosity. The door closed, extinguishing the radiance, leaving both him and the hallway darker than ever. The light in his life, the reason for his secrets, was gone. He closed the door and whispered, "I was scared. Scared." He leaned his head against the door, wondering how he could do things differently if he was given a second chance. He didn't know what to do differently, but he knew that he was changed. He couldn't keep living the way he had before he had met Nadia. It was like she had unlocked a part of him that had been dormant for so long, he wasn't sure it had even existed in the first place. *How do you move on when you don't know who you are anymore?* he wondered.

24

Over the following weeks, Bryan went about his days with the refrain of "what's done is done" playing in the back of his mind every time he began to feel regret. Nadia's shadow followed him each morning to the elevator. He did not have control of his life. Even if he had had the energy to put on one of his best suits—the burgundy single-breasted suit that he'd worn to Lance's play—it would look as dull as dirt. His dark clothes resembled oil, pooled and wasted on the ground. He had lost his swagger, and it was visible to others. Several ladies at the office even commented that his aura was diminished in some capacity. It was mostly due to his breakup with Nadia, but his isolation from his family didn't help the situation. He had briefly forgotten about his strained relationship with his mother until his sister, Rebecca, called him one day.

"You know Mama is really hurt with all of this," Rebecca said, "I think Mrs. Manning saw you and this person you've been seeing all lovey-dovey in the grocery store."

His heart sank. His greatest fear had come true: someone had seen them.

"I know that Mama's upset, and don't you think I'm not hurt by her words," Bryan complained. "I thought she raised us to value the person. Not by the labels that have been put on them or because they are different from us." He continued to pace back and forth in his living room.

"I have enough going on in my own life," she said, "I'm not going to judge you, but why would you mess up your life getting involved in that community? That's not who we are." Rebecca's voice sounded squeaky, breathless. "It's probably best if you stay away for now. She'll call Lawanda to see the kids."

The thought of his Mama being so angry and upset that she'd voluntarily call Lawanda was enough to make Bryan's toes curl inside his Italian. He felt the red hot poker again, but this time it was in his chest.

"This is bullshit," he eked out, "I don't care what y'all do anymore." Rebecca fell silent.

In a flash of anger, Bryan snarled, "You're certainly the favorite child now," and hung up.

***

Bryan had officially moved into his new office. He sleepwalked through his workdays, doing just enough to avoid being called out for slacking. He needed to get his life back, and that had to start with his Mama. A few days later, sitting at home, he dialed her number.

"Mama, can we talk?"

"For me, there is not much to talk about. It's simple. Are you gay?"

Bryan paused, a lump forming in his throat. He was glad he chose to do this over a phone call- he didn't need to see the disapproval on her face. He took a deep breath before responding.

"No, I'm not. But...."

"Why does there have to be a but? You said you were not gay," she pushed back.

"Because it's more complex and nuanced than you are giving it credit. You need to understand that Nadia is a beautiful woman and a beautiful person to me. She was sweet and kind to me, and that should be enough for you," he pleaded. "Hell, she treated me better than Lawanda."

There was complete silence at the other end of the phone for a good minute and Bryan wondered if she had hung up. He practically jumped when she started talking again.

"Son, this saddens me that you actually believe what is coming out of your mouth. That you would put me in this position. Your father did it to me, and now you're doing the same thing. You were supposed to protect me and your sister. You are no different than your father," she said, hesitating, "I promised myself I wouldn't go through this again. If this is who you are then you will be that person without me." She hung up and Bryan slammed his phone down on the coffee table.

Bryan fell back onto his couch, burying his head in his hands as he stepped further into the unknown. *What does she mean, "Just like my father?"* he wondered, holding back tears.

***

As the days moved on, the distance between Bryan and Nadia turned into a month apart. He tried to ignore the ghostlike presence of Nadia that pervaded his high-rise. He called Nadia, but she did not answer and he could not bring himself to call her again. He found himself falling asleep on the couch, only to wake up in the middle of the night. Sitting in the dark, the moonlight shone over the modern silver liquor cabinet until it sparkled. He locked it and dropped the key behind a hutch, not wanting to turn to drinking and make the same mistakes as his father. *If I'm so much like him, then maybe I need to make a conscious effort not to be him.*

Bryan now understood why his father had chosen not to engage with the world in his loneliness. He used to think his father was the strong lone wolf type. He now saw him for what he was: an emotionally unavailable alcoholic who had made Bryan feel like less of a man. Bryan couldn't help wondering if that's who he was doomed to become. He wasn't an alcoholic, but was he emotionally available for anyone? The thought made him want to drink, and he pushed it aside. He found it easier to be adrift than to sit with his thoughts. That would be akin to meditating and meditation was too difficult. Plus, who wants to stare at a wall when you are falling apart? Bryan's phone chimed. It was a text message from Reggie.

Player. Let's get you and your girl together for dinner.

Bryan texted back that he and Nadia had broken up.

Reggie texted back quickly. *Oh, shit. Player. I hope you are not sitting around moping. There are too many women out there to be sad.*

Reggie knew him, and Bryan wondered how to break the cycle of wallowing after a break up. He had never seen Reggie wallow. Reggie was a masculine, ego-driven guy who solved all his problems through sex. *Maybe he's right,* Bryan thought. Bryan was trying to solve this emotionally. This needed to be solved like a real man. Bryan texted back.

Yeah, man. I'm a VP now. Thanks, brother.

They agreed to meet up soon and Bryan went back to wallowing in his sorrows.

***

It was the holiday season, which meant the workload at the office was lighter, and his colleagues were jovial. It was helpful to be at work and focused on something else besides Nadia. One morning, he passed by a group of female coworkers and forced a small smile.

"Hey, Bryan," a petite woman in a red suit called out. "Cat got your tongue?"

"Hey," he said, flashing a quick smile before ducking into his office. He remembered the woman's name too late. Angela. He remembered that he had shamelessly flirted with her before he had met Nadia, but he hadn't gone out of his way to see her since. He would address Angela by name the next time their paths crossed and would have to make up an excuse for why he had stopped using the copy room on her floor. He sat down at his desk, straightened his tie, and stashed his phone in a drawer before logging into his computer. Breaking the habit of texting Nadia hourly had been a challenge, but keeping his phone out of sight helped eliminate the urge.

Instead, he stared out his window. It was a hazy December morning, and it was soothing to watch the clouds pile up like blankets on a bed. Despite having changed his office location, two dark spots caught his eye. Vultures again. *How many nests do they have around here? Shouldn't they be migrating? Why are they still here?* he wondered. Big and black, they were crouched on a giant tangle of twigs and grasses. He hadn't realized they were living in the nest that was adjacent to his new office. Startled by this realization, he knocked his coffee cup to the floor. Glad to have the protection of the glass, he stepped right up to the window. Looking down, he could not see anything dead or dying on the ground. The vultures seemed to be staring at him. Reluctantly, he dragged his gaze away from the menacing birds and the unmade bed of the sky.

Determined not to let another day pass without asking about Jerry, he left his office and punched the elevator button impatiently—no dashing up the stairs for him lately. Luckily, his fear of being trapped in an elevator had receded, and so did his fears of being outed at work. He had reached a level of not caring that he wished he could have reached when he was still with Nadia. *Maybe things could have been different,* he wondered. Despite this, he hoped he could look lively and dedicated, even if he felt like roadkill.

Rounding the corner, he noted that Mike had a new, young and rosy-cheeked administrative assistant. He gave her a business-like smile to make sure she knew that he was not flirting.

"Mr. Murphy is extremely busy at the moment with his direct reports," the admin said, continuing to type. "You can wait if you'd like." She pointed to a chair too small for the average-sized executive.

Doesn't she know I'm also a direct report? Bryan thought. He debated whether to inform her but decided against it. Instead, he grabbed a copy of

Oil Rigs and Assets and pretended to read it. He heard talking and laughing coming from Mike's office. The door was cracked open. Three of the voices he recognized, but two he did not. One was lower and more authoritative; the other was clearly a subordinate because it sounded squeaky. Bryan convinced himself that it was not a formal meeting of Mike's direct reports and was probably more of a complaint session. Still, he felt a pang of loneliness in having been left out.

"I hope you know what you're doing, Mike. The next thing you know, he will start promoting them over hardworking men with families." Bryan knew this voice. It was the CFO, whom Bryan considered a work friend. Bryan knew the term hardworking men meant "White men" and that the "them" he was referring to was Black people. *As if hardworking people don't come in every color,* Bryan thought to himself.

"He's. . . metrosexual. That's what they are called now. They're educated, don't hunt, and know how to dress," the subordinate sniggered.

He realized they were talking about him, and felt like he'd been punched in the gut. *Do they think I'm less manly than they are?*

"You seem to know a lot about this," Mike commented drily.

"I'm just an old white guy with one suit," the deeper voice interjected.

"My wife tells me what to wear," the CFO bragged.

The deeper-voiced executive guffawed. "My father always said guys like that had sugar in their tanks."

Mike laughed, "Now you can say gay. You can say it directly now because they are out of the closet."

Bryan's feet awkwardly began tapping the floor. It felt spongy, as if a chasm were going to open and swallow him whole. He wanted to disappear. He contemplated making an excuse to leave. He could say he'd just realized he'd forgotten to make copies that Mike needed, or that he had just wanted to ask a quick question and would send him an email instead. His assistant probably didn't know Bryan by name yet anyway. As much as the conversation was making him squirm, Bryan found himself glued to the chair with curiosity. *I need to know what they really think of me*, he thought. *If I do, then I can prove them wrong.*

"I don't want any of them working for me," the subordinate said. "He's not married, is he?"

"No, he's not. But I've already talked to him about what I expect from him. He's here to work," Mike said, "Believe me, I'd know if he was gay."

"Really. Please explain."

"My brother is gay. I don't get those vibes."

Bryan kept pretending to read the magazine, face burning.

"I hope you're right," the CFO continued.

"You know, you guys went to the same university," Mike said.

"He's a Longhorn. It must have been affirmative action," the CFO said. "My point is, we don't need any additional problems. If he's not gay, that's great. But if you're right and he's straight, I don't want him thinking that he can start dating women at the office."

Mike cleared his throat to get their attention. "It's under control. I promise there will be no surprises."

"Talk about surprises. Mike, what do you think about Trump for president?" the deeper voice inquired.

"Honestly?" Mike paused. "Can you close the door?"

Bryan sighed. He self-consciously replaced the magazine and stood, straightening his jacket so that its pinstripes lined up with the stripes on his pants. The admin didn't raise her head as he glided past her.

By the time he reached the stairwell, he was so pissed that he was not perceived as an equal. As he descended, each step had a vertiginous effect, causing him to reach for the handrail. He recalled his father's humiliation when a landscaping customer had asked him how he could afford to send his son to private school. His father had only wanted to be given the benefit of the doubt. Of course, he had also lied, unable to admit that his wife was the breadwinner. Bryan closed his office door. He slammed his hand on his desk. He had worked so hard and knew he deserved this job. Yet he still wasn't good enough, and began to wonder if he ever would be.

***

On his way home, his phone notification chimed, reminding him of his Mama's annual holiday party. His shoulders slumped. She had started throwing these parties during his third year away at college, the first Christmas after his parents' divorce. Black elites now viewed Mama's holiday party as the event of the season. Everyone cut loose, free of society's subjugation, at least for one night. During her heyday, she was known to have hosted politicians, local celebrities, and even a few big-name celebrities, like Bill Cosby—someone she now denied ever having known.

Bryan had attended every party since he moved back to his hometown until this year. His need for connection tugged at his intention to stay away, and he cut across four lanes of traffic to take the exit to his mama's.

Her house was packed with cars doubled-parked in her driveway. He spotted Ms. Williams's car, a white C-class Mercedes. Did everyone know? Or care? Maybe no one even asked about him, he thought. He could not believe that Lawanda's car was there. As he rounded a curve, he saw Robert standing outside with a few of the gentlemen guests. Bryan hunkered down and turned the wheel away from the shimmering lights. He was an outsider here, now.

Bryan hit the steering wheel with his hand. *Where do I go now?* he wondered. It felt like he had been shut out of everywhere he used to belong. He felt tears bubbling up in his eyes and willed himself to focus his attention on something else. *I can't spend all of Christmas alone*, he thought, imagining how the image of him sitting alone in his dimly lit high-rise would look like to an outsider. *Is that what Reggie sees when he tells me not to mope? What would Reggie do?* Bryan asked himself, and then proceeded to drive to a bar.

The bar was dark and crowded; Bryan had not been in this bar before, and he noticed many of the guys in the bar looked like athletes. As he walked around the bar to find a seat, he saw a few couples laughing and talking. He found a seat and ordered a cocktail similar to his Hick's Brew. Within the hour, Bryan made eye contact with a Black woman, possibly in her late twenties, with an attractive smile. Bryan spoke. She accepted his drink, giving him permission to come and sit with her. They introduced themselves and began chatting. Her smile was inviting, and she seemed interested, but she was constantly looking around. Bryan was shocked that she was unimpressed that he was a VP as she waved to a Black man approaching, who was easily six feet six. Bryan looked closer and realized he played for the Houston professional basketball team. The woman turned completely around to face the ball player as he approached. The ball player spoke to Bryan, he took the woman's hand, and they left together. Bryan studied the room a little closer and realized the bar was full of basketball and football players. *No wonder she doesn't care about me being VP*, he thought. *These guys have money and athleticism.* He was a little fish in a big pond of guys who made ten times more money than him. He finished his drink and left, questioning what women were looking for in a partner.

***

Bryan saw the kids for only a few hours the day after Christmas. Lindsey informed him that she wanted to attend a public university in Oklahoma. Bryan broached his conversation with her with support and a touch of realism. He pointed out that while she had a lot going for her, it would be challenging. While she was a very impressive student athlete who was also involved in several other extracurriculars, getting into universities in Austin or College Station was nearly impossible without astronomical SAT scores, and hers were merely average. Lance seemed distant.

"Son, is something wrong?" Bryan asked.

Lance's head dropped and his posture became very closed off.

"Son, you can talk to me," he said cautiously, not knowing what to expect.

"I wanted a book called Drama," Lance said, pausing, "but she wouldn't get it for me. She bought me some clothes, but that's not what I wanted."

Bryan took out phone, he searched for the book. He discovered it was a story about twin brothers, with one brother being openly gay and the other still trying to figure himself out. Bryan paused. *Why this book?*

"Is that it?" Bryan asked, showing Lance his phone.

Lance smiled, nodding yes.

Bryan bought it.

"Thanks, Dad." He gave Lance a hug.

"When you stay with me. You can read it at my house. Does that work?"

Lance gave him a big hug.

Lance is the sweetest child. He is only being himself and that is all any of us can ask of each other, Bryan thought, hugging him back. *How can anyone feel threatened by my son?*

On the drive home, Bryan found himself concerned about what was going on with Lance, but he wanted to be supportive. *Is he gay? Or just flamboyant?* Bryan wondered, thinking back to the bow Lance had done on stage. Bryan was too scared to ask directly. *Can men be flamboyant without being gay?* Buying LGBTQ+-centered stuff was unfamiliar, but he thought about what his mama had said about him being "just like his father" and did it because it was something his father would have never done. He wished he could tell his mama that he was different from his father, but he knew that sharing a story about buying his son a LGBTQ+ book wouldn't make her feel better about his life choices.

He stopped at a red light, and eyed the nearby Porsche dealership. *If I have my dream job, I might as well get my dream car, right?* The light turned green, and Bryan continued home, knowing the dealership would be closed on Christmas day. He promised himself that he would return to the Porsche dealership soon.

***

A few days later, Bryan stood outside the Porsche dealership entrance, intimidated by the prestige and exclusivity it represented. As a Black man, he trod lightly in unfamiliar spaces, used to being treated like he did not belong. He gingerly stepped deeper into the showroom as if the white marble floor beneath him were a tightrope suspended over a ravine. Soft music wafting from high-resolution speakers did nothing to cover his footfalls, which thunked and echoed no matter how softly he stepped. The cars felt unapproachable, like gorgeous models who only dated fantastically wealthy men. He gravitated toward a bright red Porsche Taycan coupe, circling it as closely as he could without causing suspicion or crossing any invisible boundaries.

A Porsche salesman, dressed from head to toe in black Armani, approached. "You're welcome to sit in the car," the man offered. His hair was slicked back in a tight man bun.

Bryan gingerly opened the door and got in. He couldn't help grinning as the luxurious leather molded around his hips. He touched the steering wheel like a lover, and gently ran his hands over the center console and passenger seat. *Is this real?* He wondered if moments like this were what other people would describe as "pinch me" moments. He debated pinching himself when the salesman interjected.

"You look good in this car, my friend," the salesman said. The man had a vaguely European accent, which wavered from sentence to sentence. If my father could see me now, Bryan thought. Even though Bryan was terrified of becoming his father, he still longed for his approval, even beyond the grave. Bryan tilted his body with a mean lean to the right, pretending to race. He caught himself in his silliness and straightened his posture.

"I can get into a lot of trouble in this car," he replied. He started picturing a tall blonde walking over to him to admire his Porsche and dropping a line to convince her to take a ride with him. In his imaginary scenario, he locked eyes with her once she was in the passenger seat and saw Nadia. He shook his head to get rid of the image and refocused on the steering wheel. *No, only new love interests will enter this vehicle,* he promised himself. He tried to reclaim his headspace by reminding himself that Nadia would find his Porsche superficial.

She wouldn't understand the status symbols he needed to acquire to get the approval of his colleagues at work now that he was a VP. *That's one less fight I need to have*, he thought, trying to reframe things.

The salesman smiled unctuously. "A man of your caliber and responsibilities deserves to treat himself."

"You're right." He knew the man was feeding his ego, but he flashed a big smile at him anyway. Bryan stepped out of the car and walked around it, lightly touching the sleek lines as he inspected it. The car's energy tapped into his ego. Being able to afford a new Porsche was proof that Bryan could control his destiny.

"I'll take it," he said.

"Great decision," the Porsche salesman said, "Follow me."

Bryan took a seat opposite the salesman. *I'm really doing this,* he thought. He realized his palms were becoming damp with an excited nervousness at the prospect of this purchase. Getting a new Porsche was proof that he had made it. He had the power to make things happen for himself- he was finally in control. After signing the paperwork, he smiled. He had reclaimed his life.

25

I n the old days, the adult bookstore was his nostrum, but after Nadia, he avoided that place or any others like it. That was the old Bryan he had projected to the world, the Bryan who had been curious and scared about his sexuality. Unfortunately, he was still both of those things, but he couldn't control that. He could control how people saw him, and men who had good jobs and owned fancy cars were always admired. He'd never heard of anyone who was rich getting called gay slurs. As long as he kept his true desires hidden, he would be safe.

In the spirit of hiding his fantasies, he went to his dark bedroom and turned on his laptop, allowing the only source of light to be the glow of his screen. *Maybe there are trans women out there who aren't worried about me openly dating them*, he thought. *Don't people have closeted relationships all the time?* Bryan realized he needed to find a way to subdue his urges one way or another, and clicked on a dating website specifically matching admirers with available trans women. He scrolled through a multitude of photos and bios of sexy trans women and anyone female-presenting. He stopped, seeing a thin blonde. *She would look good in my Porsche*, he thought. A dialogue box popped up.

Hi, sailor, the chat read.

Bryan enlarged the photo attached and was pleased to discover a woman with beguiling eyes. He saw a second message come through.

I'm Karen.

He took a deep breath before responding.

Hi, my name is Bryan.

***

On a beautiful Friday morning in January 2016, Bryan's phone notified him that his Uber driver was outside. He sat on the last suitcase to zip it up. He had never been to San Francisco, so he had overpacked to be safe. He knew January could be a mixed bag of weather in most parts of the country, though winter was usually lovely in Texas. In the end, he loaded two suitcases into the Uber's trunk, and the driver struggled with the third. Breathing heavily, the driver started the car. "Long trip?"

"I'm flying back on Sunday."

The driver's confusion happily resulted in a quiet trip to the airport. While waiting at the gate for his zone to be called, Bryan was unsure if his hands trembled because he hated flying or because he was nervous about meeting someone he'd only communicated with online. They had been chatting every night for the next week into the late night. Karen was in her early thirties, and she enjoyed singing karaoke and being in nature. She admitted she was not trans but liked to cross-dress and feel pretty. Bryan had said that it didn't matter if she wasn't trans; she was still sexy to him. He wasn't anticipating any problems.

At San Francisco International Airport, Bryan retrieved his bags from the conveyor belt and glanced around for Karen. A few women resembled her picture, but none of them maintained eye contact. Just as he was certain he had been hoodwinked, a thinly built white man about his height came toward him, hand outstretched.

"Hi, I'm John."

Bryan was flummoxed. "Do I know you?"

"You know me as Karen." John smiled and rotated his phone toward Bryan.

Bryan perceived his friendly smile as a sign of truthfulness. He scrolled through photos of the woman with red lipstick he had been talking to over the past month. "I see," he said, swallowing his disappointment before remembering his manners. "Nice to meet you."

John gave him a firm handshake. His hands were soft and smooth but large and veiny. "Don't worry, you'll meet Karen tonight." A smile tugged at the corner of his mouth. "This luggage is all yours?"

Bryan nodded sheepishly. He saw glimpses of Karen—her big round eyes and long eyelashes—as he kept pace with John's long strides. He hid his disappointment that he did not come as Karen, but he understood. Speeding into the city in John's cute mint-green Fiat, Bryan admired the hills and the ocean sparkling in the distance. People gamboled on tree-lined streets dotted with boutiques and outdoor cafés.

They stopped to sip coffee at a shop that managed to combine sleek and cozy in an ideal ratio. The scent of fresh-cut stargazer lilies mingled with the sweet, bitter aroma of impeccably roasted beans. It was possibly the best cup of joe he'd ever tasted.

"How long have you known Karen?" Bryan asked, lingering over his second cup as he crammed back inside the Fiat.

John's eyes crinkled. "Since my early teens, when no one was watching."

"Where did you grow up?"

John pointed left. "Look quickly, and you can see a glimpse of the Golden Gate Bridge."

Bryan saw red-orange arches, just like in the movies. "Wow. That color."

John nodded. "Four years to paint the whole thing, and then they started over. I was a teen in a small town in West Virginia." He grimaced at Bryan. "Terrifying."

Bryan glanced at John, taking him in. He had a sweet, soft-looking face. Smiling, he saw the bright side. While John wasn't what Bryan had been expecting, he was an actual person, not just a fantasy. He needed to do what made him feel safe and proper. "So, you're John most of the time?"

"Definitely in the daytime," John admitted. "It's obviously convenient to be a man in my professional life, but when I'm dressed as a woman and my war paint is on, there's no stopping me." His eyes crinkled charmingly when he smiled. "Karen got you to fly all the way from Texas. She must be doing something right."

"You got me there," Bryan blushed a little.

"Men have to conform. Trousers, suit jackets, loafers, or sneakers. The ubiquitous dark blue button-down. Where's the fun or personal expression in that? I read somewhere that most behaviors in the animal and plant kingdoms are female impersonations." John winked. "I'm simply fulfilling my natural destiny."

John lived in a two-bedroom apartment that was smaller than Nadia's. The kitchen and living room were one large room, separated by a small yellow IKEA couch and a large flat-screen TV. John dropped Bryan's bags in the bedroom. Bryan surveyed the bathroom, standing at the urinal. The area around the sink was messy, with open compacts and brushes leaking powder onto the white sinktop. Behind him were wigs in various lengths and shades of red.

When he emerged, John was in the kitchen, half-hidden by a small shelf filled with cookbooks. Bryan made himself comfortable on the sofa. The apartment was clean, but he could hear the neighbors through the walls and cars honking outside.

John handed him two beers. "Can you open mine, too?"

Bryan twisted both caps off at the same time.

"Mmm, strong. And you're handsome."

"Thank you."

"Look at you. You're blushing! It's nice that you're not all stuck up." John touched his shoulder lightly. "Yes," he said, sliding his hand down Bryan's arm. "You work out. I love a man who takes care of himself."

Bryan flexed playfully to give him a little show.

"I see you checking me out," John said, swiveling his small hips toward Bryan. "At least you know a good thing when you see it."

"It's a cute butt," Bryan said, following John into the kitchen. "I like your apartment."

"I know," John said playfully, reaching for Bryan's hand, they touched. This was new for Bryan; he had never been touched intimately by a man. *Is this gay?* he wondered. Before he could get stuck in a thought spiral, John spoke, demanding his attention.

"We'll have fun here later." John pursed his lips and vamped, and Bryan saw another glimpse of Karen, which was promising. "Let's go downtown tonight. We'll do some dancing, meet up with some of my friends,"—his head and neck waggled in a half-silly, half-suggestive way—"come back here later when you're good and soused—I mean, relaxed."

Bryan found himself laughing nervously. This was new territory. "I'm sorry, I'm a bit nervous."

"Give me a few minutes to let the magic happen," John reassured him as he headed for his bedroom. A few minutes later, he peeked around the door. "Like any woman, when I say a few minutes, I mean an hour. Feel free to turn on the TV."

Bryan was soon engrossed in the first episode of Billions. During the second episode, the bedroom door cracked.

"Close your eyes," John said in a breathy voice. "I don't want you to see me yet."

"Okay," Bryan said, covering his eyes with a hand. Sneaking a peek, he saw John run into the bathroom wearing a padded bra and nude-colored tights, which revealed a much rounder bottom than before. Bryan felt himself getting excited, finally getting to meet Karen.

John called out in a different, feminine voice. "Are you ready to meet Karen?"

"Yes, I am." Bryan sat on the edge of the sofa, eager as a child on Christmas morning. The door opened, and Karen stepped out into the hall, blonde wig and all. Bryan couldn't help but gasp. Karen was stunning. A tight-fitting shirt dipped low to reveal a hint of cleavage. Padded, of course, but nicely rounded and full. She sported white jeans and a black leather jacket. Bryan forgot to flick the TV off and almost ran towards her. "Hi, Karen, my name is Bryan. It is so nice to finally meet you."

She was slightly taller than Bryan in her high-heeled pumps; he kissed her and felt her stubble under his lips, which surprised him. Nadia's estrogen injections had softened her skin, and the hair treatments left no stubble. *Not a fan of that,* he thought.

Karen tripped on the carpet, catching herself against the front door. "Oops, new shoes."

The nighttime breeze was stronger than any wind Bryan was used to back home. When he shivered, Karen threaded her arm through his. "Poor baby, I forgot to tell you that San Francisco weather is mercurial and often merciless, especially after the sun sets." She giggled and sounded very feminine.

He squeezed her slender waist as if she were his woman. "I'm already warming up."

They dined and danced in the heart of the gay community. For the first time since he had discovered this part of himself, he was unconcerned about running into someone he knew. He realized he loved the anonymity of a new city and found himself wishing he could start over. Bryan met Karen's friends. They were all cross-dressing men with firm handshakes and were all very sweet. He was the only non-cross-dressing man in the group. Bryan could tell they were bottom lovers to the men they dated. He danced with all of them, feeling free in public, no less than he had ever dared to experience in his hometown.

Bryan and Karen walked back to her apartment around one in the morning. Karen began to lose precision over her gait, which veered into a masculine thud. Bryan also noticed that she seemed uncomfortable in her heels. *Doesn't that happen to most women though?* he wondered, trying to justify how different Karen was from Nadia. Unlike Nadia, Karen came across as superficially feminine. With strategic padding, she had full breasts and a round butt; however, her mannerisms and idiosyncrasies were not constantly feminine, which was a turn-off. The motion of Karen's arms was not buoyant but choppy and muscular. She, at times, stood much like a man with all her weight on the right foot. At this moment, he grasped how Nadia's femininity was natural. Or more consistent, at least, which, perhaps, was the key to naturalness. They caressed each other's hands on the way home, but Bryan's attraction dulled as these clues began to add up. By the time they reached Karen's apartment, he felt his heart beating faster. *I don't know if I can do this,* he thought. He asked Karen if he could grab a beer from the refrigerator. Karen nodded yes, and Bryan sighed as he retrieved a beer.

"Come sit," she said, patting the space next to her on the sofa.

Don't be rude, he thought. *Just sit strategically.*

Bryan intentionally did not sit close, so she scooted over. *This isn't me*, he thought. *I can't do it with a guy.* But Bryan knew she wanted to feel like a woman tonight and wasn't sure how to let her down easily. After all, she was letting him stay over, and if he handled this poorly, he could find himself wandering the streets of an unfamiliar city at 1 am.

A small lamp provided a shadow, which accentuated her fake cleavage. He took a big swallow of beer as he felt the tip of her wet tongue touch the inside of his ear; she placed her hand near his groin. *Just try*, he thought to himself. He raised his hand to touch her cheek, but feeling stubble again, he moved his hand to her shoulder. He closed his eyes as they kissed, and her tongue felt big. He touched her padded breast. As Karen straddled him, he saw flashes of John and saw images of him kissing John, not Karen. He pulled back.

"Stop, please stop." He turned his face to the left. He could not face her. "I can't do this. This is not me." He looked at Karen and took a deep breath.

Karen moved off his lap. "What's wrong?"

Bryan sunk his head in his hands. "I'm sorry. I'm not being fair to you."

Karen's tone was neutral. "What do you mean?"

Bryan took a deep breath. "Meeting you first as John makes it hard to see you as Karen now." He sighed again. It did not feel right for him to be attracted to a man.

She sat back against the couch. "If we were going to date, then I wanted you to know the real me. Not just one part of me."

Bryan let her know that he appreciated her honesty and that he did not want to hurt her any more than he already had.

She went into the bedroom and reemerged as John, throwing two butt pads into the bedroom. John dug around in his bra to remove the padding and grabbed a beer.

Watching this reverse transformation, Bryan knew he'd made the right choice. "I'm sorry. It's nothing against you, it's just me. This is going to sound lame, but I'm still figuring myself out. Please don't be mad at me."

"It's okay. You're actually a nice guy. Maybe we can remain friends," John said, joining him on the couch.

"I would like that," Bryan said.

They stayed up for a few more hours talking, laughing, and watching the RuPaul Drag Show. Bryan retired into the guest room, longing for Nadia as he lay in bed. He chided himself for thinking that cross-dressers and transgender women were interchangeable. The community was not some monolithic group, and being a transgender woman was not as simple as putting on war paint. Karen was beautiful as a woman, but Nadia was a beautiful woman. *Who am I?* he wondered again. Before he could answer the question, he drifted off.

In the morning, John emerged from his room with his hair sticking up, sporting a torn old sweatshirt. Bryan stood by the door with his packed bags.

"I want to thank you for letting me stay here, but I think I should get a hotel tonight."

"You don't have to." John stumbled into the kitchen and started making coffee. Bryan paused, not wanting to offend him, and instead stood in silence for a few moments as the sound of coffee percolating echoed through the apartment. John broke the silence moments later by handing Bryan a delicious cup of coffee.

"Thanks anyway," Bryan said, finishing his coffee and putting his mug in the sink.

Bryan shut the trunk of the Uber. "Thanks for everything." He hugged John and John reciprocated. "Friends?"

John's eyes crinkled in the way that was becoming familiar. "Yes, friends."

Bryan rode away, wanting to experience the transgender nightlife on his own, not with John or Karen. After arriving at his hotel and dropping off his suitcases at the hotel reception, Bryan went sightseeing. He braved the winds along Fisherman's Wharf and took a tour of Alcatraz. Vendors hawking flowers caused his heart to shrink in his chest. *Nadia would love it here,* he thought.

A little bit of research noted a bar not too far away from his hotel that catered to trans women. He made his way to the bar, hoping to meet someone who would help him forget about Nadia instead of missing her. To his baffled disappointment, all the patrons were mostly gay men, and the few exceptions were cross-dressers. *Where are the trans women and the men who love them?* he thought. He just knew there had to be a community of guys like him. He gulped his drink and headed back to his hotel room, with only Chinese takeout and a six-pack for company. This very tangible disappointment renewed his longing for Nadia even more. Drunk on beer and loneliness, he tried calling her. Nadia's phone rang once before a recorded message relayed that the phone was no longer in service. His connection to her was lost forever.

26

The following Thursday, Bryan headed to Mike's house for dinner. As he was rounding the corner to turn onto Mike's street, he heard a loud rattle in the front suspension. The downpayment on the Porsche was the right decision. He was glad to be trading his Jag in soon.

Mike's neighborhood was an exclusive, unincorporated area within the city limits. Residents could not vote for a mayor but could vote on county referendums, like the transgender bathroom bill.

Sitting in Mike's driveway at the end of a lush dead-end street dotted with eight estate-like houses, Bryan was only able to manage shallow breaths. He shut the car door carefully and buttoned the top button of his jacket.

Mike's home was a white stucco two-story colonial with three large white pillars. A circular driveway among towering oaks preceded a tangential driveway with a black Porsche, a Range Rover, and a two-seater Mercedes.

Bryan had never stood in front of twenty-foot-tall doors before, and he couldn't help feeling uncharacteristically dwarfed by their impressiveness. He rang the bell, which was answered by the loud sound of a lock moving out of its bearing. The light inside the home shone brightly. He strained to make out the silhouette of a tall, rail-thin woman with wavy dark hair. His eyes adjusted, revealing the woman at the door to be exceptionally attractive. She wore expensive black fitted pants, a black cashmere sweater, and his favorite brand of black pumps, a hint of their red soles visible in the bright light. She opened the door wider.

"You must be Bryan. Please come in. I'm Helen." Her smile was as wide as the open door, and seemed genuine.

Upon entering the foyer, Bryan tried not to stare. He didn't want to appear awestruck by Mike's supermodel wife, the double staircase, and the crystal chandelier. An enormous bronze statue of the Buddha sat placidly on a table.

"What a beautiful piece," Bryan said, "I have a similar one displayed in my place as well." He glanced sheepishly at her. "I was just thinking that I need to meditate more."

Helen's laugh tinkled like fine crystal. "Don't we all?"

Mike emerged from a wide hallway. The large entrance seemed to further enlarge his personality as well as his customary big handshake. He was wearing a white long-sleeved tee, so finespun it could have been silk, and a pair of chinos, either Brooks Brothers or bespoke.

"Good to see you, Bryan. Come in, come in, no need to stand on ceremony. We're simple folks." He winked at Helen. "Right, honey?"

He motioned at Bryan and Helen to follow him into a side room where a black baby grand piano, polished to obsidian, held court. The walls were covered with abstract American art. Several small colorful African masks hung at eye level and a six-by-three-foot canvas painting of Mike and Helen holding a small Black child hung opposite the room's entrance.

Helen gestured at a chic couch in robin's-egg blue, plumped with pillows and screened with peacock feathers. "Please sit and make yourself comfortable. What can I get you to drink?"

Bryan sat on the edge of the couch. Much like the guest chair in Mike's office, he knew he wouldn't be able to disengage from it gracefully if he allowed himself to relax into its cushions. He flashed a megawatt smile at Helen. "Wine, please, if you have it. White."

Helen opened a baroque cabinet and brought out three perfectly chilled glasses of Vouvray. "To our new VP of polymers and specialties," Mike announced. Bryan glowed with pride. They all clinked glasses.

"Cheers," Helen said warmly, looking directly into Bryan's eyes. "It's well deserved. I'm sure"

A Black boy clutching a Dr. Seuss book to his little chest ran into the room and launched himself into Helen's arms. He peeked at Bryan shyly from around her shoulder. He looked to be about four years old and was neatly dressed in navy pants, which reminded Bryan of his own private-school uniform.

Mike lifted the boy from Helen and set him down. "Bryan, this is Abe. My son." Mike's hand on the little boy's shoulder blended in with the sweater. "Abe, shake Mr. Hicks's hand."

The little man walked to Bryan with the confidence of a grown adult and shook Bryan's hand as firmly as his tiny hand could. "Hello, Mr. Hicks." Bryan gathered that this wasn't the first time he was expected to interact with Mike's colleagues.

Bryan enjoyed Abe's serious demeanor. "Hello to you. It's very nice to meet you." He addressed Abe's parents. "That's a fine man you have." Bryan smiled, feeling that it was the perfect time to talk to Mike about the issues going on at the facilities regarding race and sexuality. *Diversity is what makes us stronger*, he thought.

Mike wrapped his arm around his wife's waist. "Thank you, Bryan. We sure think so." *Jerry would never believe this,* he thought. *Come to think of it, he still hasn't gotten back to me. Maybe I should ask Mike about him tonight,* Bryan thought.

"Can I see your book, Abe?" Bryan asked, and Abe held it out to him. *If I Ran the Zoo.*

"My mother used to read Dr. Seuss to me every night," Mike reflected.

Bryan flipped a few pages, accidentally stopping on a page depicting the island of Yerka, which featured two dark-skinned figures in grass skirts with exposed round bellies. They were drawn with grotesquely contrasting big white lips and ears, the classic racist cartoonish rendering. Horrified, Bryan closed the book. "Me too," he lied, knowing his mama had been too busy making a living for the family to read to him every night. Bryan handed the book back to Abe.

Two maids in matching uniforms announced that dinner was ready and Bryan gathered from their accents that they might be of Caribbean descent. Bryan made eye contact with them. Quiet recognition of each other in the presence of white people was customary and expected. The large dining room was as sumptuous and grand as the rest of the house, lit by recessed lighting and an ultramodern chandelier. On the Swedish ash-wood table, a feast had been spread, beautifully plated and prepared. Bryan thought of Nadia. She would have loved seeing food arrayed this way—lavish ingredients counterpointed with hearty simplicity.

As soon as they were all seated, Abe jumped up and clambered into Mike's lap. Mike squeezed his son's still-chubby middle. "Let us pray."

Bryan couldn't help but notice that Abe was a very well-mannered kid for his age. He watched as Helen cut his food into small pieces and kissed him on his round brown cheek. "I love you," Helen whispered to Abe.

"You know, you baby him," Mike scolded.

"What about you, Mr. 'No Sitting on Laps at the Table'?" Helen teased.

Bryan asked about some of the glossy photographs on the wall. Mike replied, "Most of the house is Helen's vision. She modeled in college, too."

Helen waved away Mike's boast.

"Too long ago to be relevant," she said. "I was a fine arts major and wanted to go to grad school for architecture and design, but my father insisted I get my JD."

Helen shared that she had earned a law degree from the University of Kansas and passed the bar just before she and Mike got married fifteen years ago. When she shared that she had declined a job offer at a reputable law firm to move to Texas with Mike, she slid her eyes away from Bryan. "It's okay," she brightened. "I don't think I would've been happy as an attorney. My undergrad degree was in architecture. I designed most of our house—the interior, anyway."

Bryan wondered what Helen's dad thought about her not using her education. He personally wanted more for Lindsey.

Helen continued speaking, waving her wineglass around for emphasis. "And then I couldn't get pregnant. Nothing worked, so we decided to adopt. The waiting list for a white baby was so long, but there were all of these Black boys needing loving parents right away, and it was an easy choice." She sighed, placing a hand over her heart and gazing at her son who was shoveling food into his mouth.

Mike blushed. "I wasn't as sure as Helen, but my heart melted the first time I saw Abe." He cleared his throat to cover the emotional tone in his voice, and Bryan felt so close to his boss and his boss's wife he felt momentarily dizzy. *Jerry would understand if he were here,* Bryan thought. Anyone would.

Helen hesitantly admitted, "His birth name was An'twon. Which I love, but Mike wanted to change it."

Mike shrugged. "I thought Abe might be easier for everybody."

Bryan nodded. His mama would agree with Mike.

"Bryan, I will need help with his hair." Helen's tone was both light and plaintive, an attractive combination. "I've been clipping it short, but he might want to wear it differently when he's older."

Bryan spread his hands in a magnanimous gesture. "I'm happy to help. Short is good. That way, you don't have to comb it. When I was a little kid, my cousins chased me around the house with a comb. It hurt so much!"

"Okay, baby," Helen said, scooping Abe into her arms. "It's bath time. Actually, we're way past that. It's bedtime."

Abe struggled in her arms. "I am not a baby."

Helen tee-heed. "I know you're big, but you'll always be my baby."

Bryan waved at Abe. "Good night, little man."

Abe and Helen headed upstairs. The two Black women who had served them tiptoed in to clean up the meal, and Mike led Bryan down the hall to another polished wood door, which sprang away at Mike's touch.

"My library," he said. "Or, as Helen likes to say, 'man cave.'" The room had wood panels and built-in bookshelves framing a large brick fireplace. Propped on the mantle was a photo of Mike golfing with the forty-third president of the United States. Above the photo, an expensively framed print lorded over the room, featuring a naked white man on the ground with a bird on his chest. Bryan found himself captivated by it, unable to take his eyes off the grotesque scene.

Standing at the bar, Mike gestured toward the abstract print with the bottle of Blanton's in his hand. "Chagall's Tityos."

Bryan embraced the proffered tumbler glass with its generous pour of amber liquid.

"Like Prometheus," Mike continued, "Tityos was chained to a rock. Every morning vultures ate his liver, which grew back every night." He swirled the liquid in his glass. "As you know, Prometheus stole fire from the gods to give it to us. He's a symbol for human progress against oppressive forces to maintain the status quo." Bryan nodded, unsure if his boss was aware of what he was implying, then realized it could be part of his act. *Mike supporting challenges to the status quo was deemed lofty because he was a rich white man, but if a Black Lives Matter activist shared the same opinion, people like Mike would be the first to oppress them. Maybe now's a good time to talk about promoting diversity at the company,* Bryan wondered. He decided that he would feel out the conversation before dropping anything too heavy on Mike. He needed to be subtle.

The two men sipped their bourbon. "I remember reading about Prometheus but not Tityos," Bryan said. Bryan wondered if Mike had a view of the vulture nest at work, too. He stifled a yawn. His lonely holiday week without his kids, Mama, or Nadia, had worn him down more than he cared to admit. This evening had been pleasant, but it was still a performance. He laid his head against the chairback.

A second later, he flew up and out of his seat. "What is that looking down at me?"

Mike nearly spat out his drink, laughing. "A preserved vulture head. In many African cultures, it's considered to bring good luck. Vultures are perhaps the most opportunistic of all birds. It's their nature."

From its throne of books, which included The Conscience of a Conservative, The New Rules by Bill Maher, and something by Ann Coulter, the bird seemed to be staring at Bryan out of the corner of one beady eye. "You like vultures a lot, huh?"

"I do." Mike raised his arms above his head. He was such a clean-shaven guy that Bryan was surprised to see a patchwork of dark tattoos on his arm, above the elbow. Mike saw him looking and put his arms down. "My visible regrets," he chuckled. "I was a bit of a wild child in my youth. You should see the big, goofy one on my leg." He shook his head as if in fond remembrance. "You might say I lost more than a few bets." The two men were silent, both missing Helen to ease the conversation.

Bryan twisted his head around and was shocked to see two Francis Bacon prints. "Those are great reproductions." Bryan wondered if Mike knew that Bacon was gay and that those abstract paintings depicted his lover and frequent muse, George Dyer.

Helen and Abe entered the library. Abe was clean and ready for bed. Over his Star Wars pajamas, he was wearing a felt holster with a toy gun tucked into it. "There's my little monkey," Mike said affectionately, rubbing Abe's head.

Between the gun and Mike's so-called endearment, Bryan was speechless. He hoped he didn't gasp out loud.

Red blotches bloomed on Helen's face and neck. "Mike, I've told you to stop calling him that."

"My father called me that when I was growing up." Mike sounded testy, though it seemed like he was trying not to. He appealed to Bryan. "You're a Black guy, I mean . . . African American, you don't have a problem with me calling him that, do you?"

The energy in the room crackled. Bryan grasped for the safest reply. He held a long swallow, and the whiskey burned the back of his throat. "You can say Black, I'm not offended." *At least he asked me,* Bryan thought.

Helen sighed, and Bryan felt he had let her down by not finding a diplomatic way to be honest. He wanted to let Helen know she was doing the right thing but had no idea how to do so without angering his boss.

"I'm going to put Abe to bed," Helen said to her husband, her mouth tight. Bryan struggled out of the couch's embrace and thanked her. She shook his hand, her eyes bright with reined-in tears, the spots on her cheeks faded but still visible. "Bryan, it was such a pleasure to have you over. Please come again soon."

Mike stretched. "Abe has a good life, and Bryan, you're doing well."

"Ye-es," Bryan said carefully. "I think it's more that society will always see Abe as a Black man. So, it's . . . complicated." He had no idea how to condense the everyday nuances, the weight of the perpetual fear and internal struggles of Black people—police brutality, discrimination, lack of opportunities, mass incarceration of Black men—in a few sentences. Not to mention how the current situation was informed by the past two hundred–plus years. Or without enraging the person who signed his paycheck. Mike led Bryan to the front door, as it was clear the night was wrapping up. The evening had lurched sideways, which Bryan regretted. If Mike had only refrained from calling his Black child a monkey, they would have ended as well as they'd begun. *So much for talking about diversity or Jerry,* he thought. Partially blinded by the porchlight, Bryan stumbled to the darker recess of the entry. From between two of the white colonial pillars, Mike peered out at the neighborhood.

"Your promotion is a first for our company, and I will make sure you're not treated like a token."

You just did, Bryan thought, shrinking further from Mike. He closed his eyes, his mind exploding with flashes of purples and reds. He imagined his father punching Mike in the face, and his arms jerked unexpectedly, trying to push back his imaginary father. Bryan hoped his boss hadn't seen him flinch.

Mike lit a cigar. "She doesn't like me smoking in the house." He waved his cigar around, the lit end nearly grazing Bryan's arm. "One last thing, I know you are aware of the racial and sexual harassment problems inside our chemical plants." Mike spoke through a puff of smoke. "Don't get yourself caught up in all of that. Let the guys work it out for themselves. We are here to turn a profit, not solve social issues. Conformity is what makes for a well-oiled machine."

"Yes, sir," Bryan said. "Everybody needs to conform."

27

On Monday morning, Bryan sauntered through the halls with the confidence of a new VP, making his way to his new office. He wore an olive green double-breasted suit with a patterned blue tie. He had been hoping for a version of Mike's spaciousness and views, albeit on a smaller, less grand scale. His new office was located by itself along an empty hall, which was eerie and discomforting. The room was not much larger than his old office, and the window was also about the same. In a far corner, eight boxes containing his files and personal effects sat, waiting for him to unpack. A triangulated shadow from the building opposite carpeted the center of the room.

He used his multi-bladed knife to slice through the top box. He arranged laughably out-of-date pictures of Lance and Lindsey onto the shelf so he could see them from his desk. How much easier it would be if Lance was still a fourth grader and Lindsey a seventh grader.

A middle-aged woman with a curly blond bob appeared in the doorway. "Are you Mr. Hicks?" Her voice was serrated, either from smoking or unkindness.

"Yes?"

"I'm your admin. If you need anything, my desk is around the corner." She handed him a bulging folder. "These are the pre-reads for your nine o'clock."

Bryan was perplexed by her rough demeanor, but maybe she was having a bad day. He opened the folder, quickly perusing the information, and thanked her, but she was already gone.

Smelling something awful, he sniffed around his office, trying to locate the offensive scent. The culprit was his chair—baby poop–colored cloth with plastic armrests on a broken swivel. He jerked it angrily, and it careened to the other side of the room, banging into the corner closest to the door.

He imagined Jerry sauntering in and smirking.

"This view sucks. I guess you can't have it all. At least you don't have to worry about being eaten by whatever was living in that nest," imaginary Jerry said.

Bryan shuddered in remembrance. "Vultures," he said aloud to the empty room.

Imaginary Jerry spun around. "I know. They're everywhere. Even your congenial coworkers. Even someone who shares your skin color." He arched his imaginary brows. "And your proclivities." He picked up the picture of the kids. "You and Nadia could've popped out some pretty babies."

"What are you talking about?"

"Don't be so literal. More importantly, how does it feel to be the first Black man appointed to a VP position with a transgender girlfriend? You're going to be spotlighted in Ebony and Out magazines at the same time."

Bryan tried to shake the mental image of Jerry out of his head, but the scene kept playing out like a trainwreck. "They can do one of those exposés about 'the woman behind the man.' I can see it now," Jerry arranged his fingers like a frame. "Bryan Hicks: Transparency at the C-Suite. I love it. A picture of her behind you, slightly out of focus. You know . . . the good woman behind the great man."

"We split up a few months ago."

"I know, but don't worry. You're the VP of polymers and specialties. She's not the only six-foot-four trans girl out there." Jerry rubbed his chin. "Huh, now that I think about it, maybe she is?"

Bryan busied himself by setting up his new computer, but that didn't stop Jerry's persistent mirage. "Your admin looks old-school. You know, working for old white men, not your Black ass."

"Jerry, you're all wrong about Mike. Let me tell you—"

Jerry cut him off. "I know, I know, Mike has an adopted Black child, blah blah blah." He cocked his head. "I bet he did some bad shit in a past life. Actually, I know what he did and does, but I'm going to let you find out for yourself. More fun for me." He sniffed the desk chair. "Man, this thing smells like ass."

"I'm telling you, man. He's a great dad. And his wife is a loving mother. I wish Lawanda were like her." He decided not to mention the strange turn of the evening and the pathological cluelessness Mike had revealed—all of which was made that much more jarring by him being the father of a Black son.

"You're so naive. That's why you got this old-ass furniture and Sophia from The Golden Girls outside giving me the evil eye. Mike is not your friend."

Bryan awoke from his daydream. He gathered the contents of the pre-read's folder and tapped it loudly on the desk. "Be that as it may, my first meeting with the leadership team starts in a few minutes," he found himself saying aloud to an empty room.

The insinuation that his promotion was merely filling a diversity quota disconcerted Bryan. Imaginary Jerry definitely knew his weak spots, but Bryan was determined not to let him get to him. This was his chance to shine and he was happy to be a part of the executive leadership team. He beamed with pride as he delved into his pre-reads.

Always early for meetings, Bryan had a habit of stopping to check all his notes one more time before entering the conference room. Before rounding the corner, he overheard the tail-end of a conversation.

"I never watched *The Apprentice*, but there is no way I'm voting for Hillary," a man's voice sneered. It was the same deep tone from the day he overheard that conversation in Mike's office.

"Call me old-fashioned, but a woman doesn't have it in her to run a super-power," another male voice intoned. "Maybe Iceland, but not in the United States of America."

Mike's voice boomed out. "That . . . woman will tax our asses to kingdom come."

"If the Access Hollywood tape didn't sink him, he really could shoot someone on Fifth Avenue and get away with it." The CFO sounded awestruck.

Bryan sighed. *Of course, they're all Trumpers,* he thought, turning the corner.

The conference room was packed. Bryan was the last to arrive. He rechecked his watch. Ten minutes to nine. His admin had told him the meeting start time, and he was punctual as always. *Was being more than ten minutes early expected now?* Framed by the hallway window, the rest of the leadership team, all male, gathered in groups of three or four, chatting comfortably with each other. When Bryan stepped over the threshold, everyone stopped talking and stared at him.

"Nice of you to stop by, Bryan," Mike called out.

"I don't understand. Was the meeting changed for earlier?" He felt outpaced and outnumbered, the only dark face in the room.

The only reply was chuckling from the group.

Finally, Mike threaded his way through the small clumps of men in dark thousand-dollar suits. "Just joshing you, bro." He clamped a hand on Bryan's shoulder. "Everyone, you know Bryan Hicks, the new VP of polymers and specialties." Polite murmurs of acknowledgment from the group helped Bryan to feel slightly more at ease.

"So, Bryan, how's that chair we special ordered for you?" Mike asked with a laugh.

The mirthful looks of his coworkers helped Bryan relax further. This was all a bit of innocent hazing. He was the new guy, which solidified him as one of them. "Smells like feet," he deadpanned, and everyone roared. "Is every VP so lucky?"

"Ha. Not so much." Mike slapped his shoulder approvingly. "But we got you. You'll find a new chair waiting for you when you get back to your office." He claimed his place at the head of the long gray conference table. "Alright, lads, let's get the newest member of our team up to speed."

Mike launched into the company's lagging profitability and long-term outlook, detailing the projects that were behind schedule and over budget. He pointed at Bryan as the person to get these projects completed, and Bryan straightened his back with pride.

A slight man in the seat farthest from Bryan cleared his throat. "I think we should discuss . . ." he began haltingly. The animated energy turned sour.

"Is there a problem?" Mike poured himself a cup of coffee.

Bryan sensed the man was unsure how to present whatever he needed to say. The leadership team shifted in their seats.

The small man spoke up again, this time more clearly. "Another sexual harassment incident issue landed on my desk today."

"What happened now?" Mike leaned back in his chair. "The females at the plants have got to learn how to get along and brush this stuff off."

"No, sir," the man said again, reddening. "This incident occurred here at headquarters.

"It's not on the agenda, and we have too much to get through to add it to this morning's agenda," Mike said brusquely. "We'll table it."

The man spoke up again. "As the human resources VP, I'm going to insist. It just came across my desk, and it's urgent. It involves management, but on the accounting side, so we need to discuss it here and now before a lawsuit is filed against the company."

Mike waved a piece of white paper in surrender. "Fine. Proceed."

"Jerry Bailey," the HR executive said, and Bryan jolted in his chair. The man flipped through papers in front of him. "He filed a sexual harassment complaint with human resources, stating one of the managers had created a hostile environment. You'll see, starting on page three." Packets began circulating.

Mike reached out a hand for the report. "Huh. This manager is a good employee and stand-up guy. I thought he was married with a family."

Someone else spoke up. "He is. He and his wife have three kids. Or is it four, now?"

Bryan felt his brain whirring. *What happened to Jerry? Is this why he had stayed away? What can I do to help?*

Mike shut the folder with a snap. "Okay, let's draw up severance for him. Done. Bing, bang, boom," he chuckled mirthlessly. "Literally, I guess, in this case."

The HR VP interrupted the group guffaw. "And Bailey?"

Mike pointed to Bryan. "You need to let him go ASAP. This is why I don't like having them as employees."

Them? Bryan's hands balled up in his pockets. "But sir, this is—"

Mike waved his hand. "I'm done talking about it, and so are you. Let's get back to the original agenda."

"Yes, sir," Bryan said, his heart racing. He'd figure this out and protect Jerry somehow. *Wouldn't firing Jerry due to a sexual harassment claim be illegal? Surely Mike wouldn't be asking him to do something illegal as one of his first acts as a VP.* The rest of the meeting passed in a bureaucratic blur. Words and numbers, the fates of thousands of workers and billions of dollars spun around Bryan as if he were the unwilling center of a maelstrom. His light felt diminished because he was being asked to do their dirty work, not the honorable tasks that were awarded bonuses and more responsibilities. *Is this really what being a VP is?* he wondered.

***

The moment the meeting ended, Bryan flew back to his office, nearly knocking over Angela in the stairwell. "I'm so, so sorry, Angela," Bryan stammered. "Did I hurt you?"

"I'm fine," she said. "Bryan, are you okay?"

"Yes," he said. He had to find Jerry. "I'm not used to other people using this stairwell," he said, attempting to be charming.

Angela arched a pretty brow. "Maybe you should get to know some of these so-called other people." And with that flirtation hanging in the air, she brushed past Bryan and trotted up the stairs, her little round bottom bouncing under her suit skirt. *Damn, she looks good*, he thought. Seeing Angela reminded him of Jerry's jabs about them flirting. If he wasn't going to respond to his work phone, maybe he would pick up his personal phone. He vowed to call his personal number later that day.

***

There was a knock on his office door. Bryan was not in the mood, but he called out as cheerfully as he could muster. "Come in."

"Sir, your new furniture is here."

He grinned. "Thank you." He sat in the new aerodynamic chair, almost as sleek as a Porsche's seat.

"Mr. Hicks, my name is Laura," his admin said, reaching out her hand.

Why was she suddenly acting so pleasant? Had he passed some sort of test? Or was this all a bribe to fire Jerry? In any case, having a friendly relationship with his admin was going to make the workday more productive and comfortable. "It's nice to meet you, Laura."

He worked straight through dinner, consumed with worries about Jerry and trying to get a handle on the projects now under his purview. All were behind schedule and over budget. Bryan had imagined his days talking with project teams and developing solutions, not dealing with Jerry's harassment claim. However, he knew that Jerry was the wronged party. He just needed to figure out how to convince Mike that firing Jerry would ultimately backfire without antagonizing him. To do that, Bryan needed Jerry's account of the story. If Jerry was working in the fields in Louisiana, Bryan knew he had a better chance of catching him well after eight at night. When the numbers on his monitor started to blur into faint stars, Bryan shut down his computer and picked up his phone.

Eyes burning, he convinced himself that taking a peek at Nadia's Instagram would center him before his call with Jerry. He needed to know that she was doing okay. She had posted several pictures of new dishes but none of herself, which dispirited him. The placid green lakes of her eyes would have calmed him and given him courage.

Bryan dialed Jerry's personal number. He felt guilty waiting this long to call his personal number, but he had been spending so much time at work lately he had momentarily forgotten there was another way to reach him. After the phone rang four times, someone picked up the call but didn't say anything. Bryan raised the inflection in his voice. "Don't hang up!"

Jerry breathed heavily into the phone. "What?"

"Why didn't you tell me you accepted a job at the Louisiana facility?"

Jerry laughed hollowly. "You make it sound like I had a choice. What does it matter to you?"

"It does matter to me," Bryan said. "I'm going to speak with HR about bringing you back into the home office." He didn't mention anything about his order to fire Jerry. He would find a way to make Mike understand during one of their one-on-one meetings.

"What makes you think I want to come back?"

Bryan ignored the question. "Let's get to the bottom of this whole thing. Plus, it's time for you to get a promotion."

There was silence.

"You're just like them. All talk. You just happen to be Black. At least from what I can see on the outside."

"Jerry, I'm trying to help," Bryan protested.

"You haven't helped me since you passed me on the pay scale," Jerry said. "Calling my personal number. You must be desperate. What do you want?"

"You weren't returning any of my calls."

"Maybe I don't want to talk to you."

"I was worried about you."

"I don't know why. You're only calling because you're not with Nadia anymore."

"You know about that?" Bryan's voice was soft.

"I've seen her out and about when I come home on the weekends," Jerry responded airily.

The swipe at him stung. Bryan slumped back against his chair. Was Nadia alone? He thought but decided not to ask. "I want to improve things at the company," Bryan said to Jerry in a low voice.

"Oh, Mr. VP, you wouldn't believe what's going on out here. It's crazy. There is a night shift supervisor using prostitutes as firewatchers."

"Holy shit. Wait, let me get this straight. The person hired to make sure sparks don't cause fires is sleeping with the welders?"

"Yep. This place is scattered with condoms in the mornings."

How deep does the dysfunction run in this company? He wondered. "I've never heard about any of this."

"It's all contained, of course. No one on the outside has a clue. But at least I'm not being harassed."

"Why didn't you tell me you were being harassed?"

"For what? 'Cause you were going to do something? You're probably trying to talk me out of the complaint."

"Is it true?"

"You think I'm lying? Why does the victim have to prove themselves?"

"I don't. You don't. I want to know the truth."

"The first time we hooked up was about a year ago. It has been off and on since then. I broke it off right before I met my boyfriend, but the dude would not let it go."

"Did you know he was married?"

"Yeah. At first, I could separate his wife from everything, but eventually, I couldn't. Plus, I fell hard for my boyfriend and wanted us to be monogamous. But this guy couldn't take no for an answer. He followed me to my car, showed up at the bars to beg me to come back. He even promised me a promotion. I didn't feel comfortable at work anymore."

"When can you come back in? We can sit down with HR and Mike."

"I guess I could come in a few weeks," Jerry spoke slowly. "But this is taking on the behemoth. Are you sure you're ready? To stop acting like a little mouse and be a man?"

"Yes," Bryan said as definitively as he could. "I promised to make a difference. I'm going to keep my word." *Mike will be fair once he knows the whole story,* he thought. *After all, he claims to want to help the oppressed.*

"I don't know how you live with yourself," Jerry said.

"What do you mean?" Bryan asked, fretting over what Jerry was going to say next.

"You see me going through all of this, and you have no intention of telling these guys who you really are. I know you haven't told them about being in our community," Jerry blasted.

"I don't know why you are bringing this up. We're not even together anymore," Bryan replied.

"It's not fair that you get promoted and I get pushed out. You need to tell these guys the truth because you are one of them now," Jerry said, "I need your help. They need to see when you hurt one of us, you have to deal with all of us. If you don't tell them, I will."

"Is that a threat?"

"No, it's fair," Jerry said.

His phone chimed. Two missed calls and voicemails from Reggie. "Jerry, I have to go," Bryan said, needing to get off the phone. His heart raced. *Would Jerry really out him?* He reluctantly answered Reggie's call. Maybe a sort of über masculine diatribe about women was just what the doctor ordered.

"Player!" Reggie's voice was slurred and jubilant, edged with desperation. "Get your ass down here." Ice cubes clinked in a glass. "You would not believe the array of fine, fine ass pu—"

Bryan interrupted him. "I can't. It's almost eleven. Don't you have to work tomorrow?" Suddenly, he realized he was not in the mood for this kind of talk. Propping up his masculinity for several hours was tiring on a good day.

Reggie actually giggled. He was so far gone. Bryan considered going to the bar just to drive his friend home.

"I'm fine, they're fine. We're all fine," Reggie intoned. "Hey, that reminds me, I got involved with a program at my company to present at high school career days about being a lawyer. I saw your kids and mine and lied to a bunch of teenagers about—"

"You saw my kids?" Bryan hadn't seen his kids since their brief encounter after Christmas. Lawanda kept making excuses about their having activities, and Bryan hadn't had the strength to argue. "How were they?"

"Lindsey's still hanging all over her loser of a boyfriend," Reggie sneered.

Bryan was about to ask about Lance, but he heard murmuring on Reggie's end. "I'm sorry, player. I was speaking to this chick who sat her sweet ass next to me." Murmuring again. "Have you seen Lance lately?"

"I saw him a few weeks ago."

"I almost didn't recognize him. The boy was wearing a wig and makeup! Looked like a little girl."

Bryan was speechless. His empty stomach dropped like a stone. "Maybe something was going on at school?"

"You need to look into this, man. He was walking with another boy. A little red-haired boy, and he had makeup on, too." There was a short pause. "Player, I gotta go. There are some sistas in here."

***

At home, Bryan undressed, lovingly hanging up his First Day as VP suit and relegating his nicest bespoke shirt to the To Be Dry-Cleaned section of his vast closet. He glanced at the kitchen table, his eyes grazing the book he had purchased for Lance for Christmas. He was concerned that Lance was willing to be so transparent at school. Bryan knew he could never be that transparent at work. *Why does Lance feel that's okay?* he wondered. Lance's Christmas gift was laying on the table. He knew he had to dissuade Lance from going down this path. *It's almost like I don't know my own son,* he thought. To Bryan, Lance was still a young boy, but Bryan had to wonder: how did Lance see himself? And would the world accept the way he wanted to be seen? Bryan found himself upset that Lance chose not to hide his truth. Where had he gotten the confidence to do that? Was it the fact that he had a community with Harry and his other friends?

28

B ryan labored over Jerry's situation and threat so much that his anxieties ramped up again. He decided to meditate to calm his nerves, determined to reignite his non-existent meditation practice. He set the timer for thirty minutes. He lit a candle and arranged himself on his cushion, knees cracking from not having been in his meditation pose for so long. He placed the tips of his right fingers just inside, lightly touching the left fingertips as his thumbs pressed together, forming a triangle with his fingers. His posture was straight. Daylight pierced the clouds, scattering them like broken china. He tried to rein in his chattering thoughts, but his to-do list and other worries kept intruding. It was his sister's birthday today, and he needed to call her, which made him emotionally uneasy and soon manifested into physical discomfort. *You can do this*, he reminded himself. He found his breath. Squinting his eyes, he counted an in and out breath as complete. Soon, his consciousness allowed the unknown to penetrate his fears. A moment of peace filled his spirit. He had not felt this type of solace before, and found it exhilarating. Unfortunately, the moment quickly passed and was replaced yet again by his racing thoughts. After only ten minutes, which felt as long as an hour, he began to itch and fidget. He blew out the candle. *What was that?* He thought. The sense of peace was tangible.

Coffee was more satisfying than meditation. As he wandered through his place, coffee in hand, his space came into sharper view. Perhaps his senses, dulled by heartbreak and loneliness, were finally reawakening. He noticed the shoes and clothing uncharacteristically spread around like the room of an adolescent teenage boy. This was the perfect time to dust and straighten up. Maybe cleaning was just as illuminating as seated sitting meditation.

He threw his dress shirts in the washer, always set to cold water. He liked to be frugal when it made sense. He gathered all the dress slacks that needed to be sent to the cleaners. He wriggled his hands into his vinyl gloves to clean the bathrooms, vacuum, and dust all the furniture.

He dusted some photos of his kids that depicted the good days, the days when they all lived under the same roof. He picked up an old photo of Lance, marveling at how talented he had become over the years. *I need to look up Alaska Thunderfuck,* he thought. He placed Lance's picture down and picked up a picture of Lindsey, almost as tall as her fifth-grade teacher. He did not have a favorite, but she was the child that knew how to play the game. He wanted her to be the opposite of Lawanda. He was fighting every day for her to achieve that dream—or his vision for her.

Setting up the ironing board and gathering the dress shirts from the dryer, he wielded the iron as if it were an authentic samurai sword. He attacked every wrinkle like it was the enemy. Eventually, his clothes and home were made whole again, and it was high noon.

His sister's phone rang several times. He debated if he should leave a message, but on the last ring, he heard someone pick up. There was silence.

"Hello? Hello?" *Is anyone there? he wondered.*

"Bryan," Rebecca whispered hoarsely.

He heard a door close. "Rebecca, what are you doing?"

"Mama is here."

"She is?"

"Yes, she's staying here for a few weeks to recuperate. What do you want?"

"I wanted to wish you a happy birthday. Recuperate from what?"

She sighed. "Mama is hurting. You know why. Please stay away until you get yourself together. You've done enough damage." She hung up.

Bryan's heart crumpled. His phone chimed, notifying him that his brand-new Porsche was ready for pickup.

He checked his watch. There was just enough time to dress carefully in his freshly ironed, most sumptuous clothes and wind his way back to the Porsche dealership.

***

The entrance was not as intimidating the second time; neither was the same piano music tinkling over the marble. The salesman was busy filling out paperwork.

"I'm glad to see you again, sir. Feel free to look around and let me know if you need anything."

Bryan lingered over the red supercharged Porsche coupe from before, but soon another beauty beckoned, and another. Each car was more gorgeous than the last, an embarrassment of riches akin to perusing Playboy. Unlike a magazine, however, he was able to run his hands over each model's striking features.

An hour later, he placed a Mont Blanc pen emblazoned with the Porsche signature beside a piece of paper that represented a significant drain on his savings account. His body was tingling with euphoria.

***

Later that night, he christened the new vehicle with a drive through the gay club scene. Windows down, he honked at a few girls in their twenties in leather pants and knee-high boots. They called him over, but he only waved at them. He was just getting started. He gave the soft leather wheel a complete turn, and the car leaped, as if it, too, was excited to explore the rainbow side of town.

Bryan snaked his way through the crowds, his face masked by the car's tinted windows. Some attractive transgender girls were clustered outside a bar called *Cousins*, which was lit up like a Christmas tree. Bryan knew that was the bar trans women typically frequented the most, and he slowed down as he drove by it. *I could never go in there*, he thought.

He stopped the car at a red light. Heart racing, he revived the engine.

A girl with long, shiny hair sauntered into the street and struck a defiant pose in front of his car, inviting him to make himself known. The headlights silhouetted her body, accentuating her long legs. She sashayed to the driver's-side window. Once there, she paused, allowing him to enjoy the view. He gripped the steering wheel tighter. She unexpectedly bent down, playing with her hair in the reflection of the tinted window. He looked away, thinking she could see his face. She knocked on the window. He revved the engine again. She uncapped a tube of lip gloss as shiny red as the Porsche, licking her top lip. She began to lavishly apply the gloss, then puckered her lips for effect. The light changed to green, but Bryan was too entranced to move. Cars honked angrily and sped around him like a rushing current encircling an island. Draping her body over a good portion of the windshield, she kissed the glass sumptuously before dashing back to the sidewalk. Bryan received more honks and middle fingers as the light turned red. He inched forward, dazed by the encounter, waiting for the light to turn green again. The large smear of red gloss on the windshield was like a crushed rose.

Bryan arrived home and handed the keys to the valet, who nodded and said his line as if it were fed to him on a cue card. "That car was made for you, sir." The Porsche was exactly what he needed to kickstart his romantic life again.

29

The purchase of the car garnered a lot of attention for Bryan at work. The next day, Mike slapped him on the back. "You and Dennis Rodman and the fancy cars, huh, buddy?"

The next time Bryan ran into Angela, she commented on the Porsche, too. "I guess you don't need to race through the stairwell anymore if you have a car like that." She and Bryan seemed to have more meetings together lately.

Perhaps, Bryan thought, she'd gotten a recent promotion. There was no denying she was a ten on any scale. "I would be honored to take you for a ride in it or squire you to the restaurant of your choosing," Bryan ventured.

"You sound like a senior asking me to prom," she said, giggling. "I'll drive my own car, but I'd love to meet you for a drink."

***

On the first Saturday in May, Bryan waited for Angela at the restaurant she had chosen. It had been more than two years since he had sought the affection of a cisgender woman, and Angela was the first Black woman he dated since Lawanda. He shuddered at the thought of her possibly being similar to Lawanda, but envisioned her face and reminded himself that she seemed trustworthy. She had an air of straightforwardness that was refreshing for him. It was clear she was interested, but it was also clear she wouldn't put up with drama.

She arrived, looking lovely. He gave her a hug, smelling hints of rum and tobacco, not floral or citrus, which intrigued him.

"This is a cute little restaurant," Bryan said, swiveling his head to take in the burnt-sienna walls covered with landscapes that were for sale. "I've never been here before."

The server expertly opened a bottle of red table wine. "The food is good, too," she said. "I've come a few times with friends."

He took every opportunity to make her laugh, and she did, raising a hand to cover her mouth. When a basket of steaming rolls appeared on the table, she insisted that they pray and bow their heads. She commanded the prayer like a seasoned Black Baptist preacher, making him feel a little guilty about his leaning away from his religious upbringing. Their salads, with the de rigueur giant black pepper grinder, came next.

Bryan ate his salad rather quickly. "I love your accent," he said, pushing the plate to the side. "Where did you grow up?"

She had just taken a big bite of greens, and she smiled as best she could with a closed mouth. *Nadia would never do that*, he thought, remembering how Nadia had usually picked around her salads. She'd joked that women's obsession with salads was the one aspect of femininity she would never get.

Angela took a sip of wine. "I'm from Atlanta. I came here for college."

"Atlanta. Hmm," Bryan said. "Are there as many Black people in Atlanta as I've heard there are?"

She nodded, smiling.

Bryan crossed his arms on the table and leaned on them. "Why Texas?"

"Georgia schools didn't seem to want me, whereas I was courted"—her cheeks flushed—"by every business program I applied to in Texas."

A smile stretched across his face. "That's my state."

Minutes later, plates of artfully arranged food were placed down in front of them, and they both fell silent as they began eating. For a few minutes, all they could do was eat and roll their eyes with pleasure at each other, which he realized was actually pretty sexy.

"I can't remember when you started working at—" Bryan stopped himself. "Forget it. There's nothing like shoptalk to kill a mood."

Angela's shoulders were visibly relaxed.

Bryan scooted his chair closer to the table. "We work at the same place, and that's how we met, and that's it for now. If this works out, we'll figure it out."

Her calm, open nature made talking effortless. It felt like they had been dating for years. After almost forty years, her parents were still married, which made him embarrassed that his parents had divorced. Her father was an ER surgeon, and her mother was a middle school principal. They lingered over their excellent sea bass and shared a tarte Tatin over double espressos. He tried not to think how much Nadia would love the restaurant's flavors, presentation, and decor. She would even love Angela, though not as his girlfriend. She was genuinely nice, not at all prissy. But Bryan knew the person who would truly adore Angela was Mama.

Bryan paid the tab, adding a handsome tip, and they walked together to her car. He kissed her goodnight next to her shiny new Mercedes. This girl had her life together. His mama would want to marry Angela herself.

***

Over the following weeks, Bryan was buoyant and productive, working a regular forty hours. He concentrated well on his work projects—as long as he didn't think about Jerry. He was starting to feel like his old self again. He was going to the gym and attempting to meditate more regularly.

He was beginning to feel like his life was sustainable again, and it seemed that Angela was a huge part of that equation. The only slight problem was that they worked together, but they agreed not to seek each other out during the workday and kept texting to a minimum. They sometimes bantered a bit when they ran into each other but were careful to keep it casual.

They dined together once or twice during the week and once on the weekend, met for coffee on Sundays, and went for strolls with their to-go cups. Bryan enjoyed the romance and the peace of mind that escorting a cisgender woman around town on foot or in his Porsche afforded him. By some unspoken agreement, they kissed often but hadn't yet slept together.

When it occurred to Bryan that the reason he could wait was that he did not feel as passionately toward Angela as he had with Nadia, Bryan shooed that thought away. This was how one dated a proper woman, the kind you bring home to your mama.

***

Bryan had hoped to see his mama at Lindsey's graduation in early June, and that all would be forgiven. When the day came, he slipped into the school auditorium. When scanning the rows, he was heartbroken to witness his own mama in line with Lance, Big Momma, and Lawanda. He didn't dare to approach them. Sinking into one of the worn raspberry velvet seats, tears streamed down his face long before his daughter's name was called. She practically skipped across the stage, believing the world was her oyster.

After the ceremony, Bryan stayed in the shadows until his mama and Big Momma had made a fuss over Lindsey. The plan had been for them all to go back to Mama's for a celebratory spread. When Lawanda, Big Momma, and Mama left to get the cars and bring them around to the entrance, Bryan caught his daughter's arm as she glided up the aisle, giggling with her friends. The boyfriend was nowhere to be seen.

Bryan enveloped Lindsey in a crushing hug. "So proud of you, baby girl," he choked out through tears. Lindsey raised her eyebrows as if she sensed something was off, but her words were polite.

"Thanks, Daddy. See you soon."

Bryan left and sat in his car, tears streaming down his face. He felt so betrayed by his mama as he watched her sit with the enemy. He couldn't help but wonder if she was keeping his children tethered to her for their safety, or just to be mean. *She has to know how much she's hurting me. Is she really that cruel? Would she even care if I told her I changed my ways and was dating Angela? Or am I forever ostracized?* Bryan decided he would never be able to control his mother, and in an effort to take control of himself, he called Angela.

***

On the fifth Friday of his and Angela's burgeoning relationship, Bryan waited for the restaurant valet to take possession of his Porsche. Angela's Mercedes was in front of him. The sunshine was soft, and the air was California-like. Angela stepped out of her car in a pair of jaw-dropping fitted white jeans and a red silk scoop-neck tank that showcased her polished shoulders. *Every Friday should look like this,* Bryan thought. He almost skipped toward her with a confidence he had only dreamed of before.

"I always thought most vice presidents were too big to fit inside little sports cars," Angela said, touching the lapels of his pinstripe suit.

Bryan took her small hand and enfolded it in his large one. "I'm setting a new standard."

As they waited to be seated, Bryan accidentally made eye contact with a woman sitting at the bar. She seemed familiar, but he could not place her, and he purposefully steered Angela to the other side of the bar. They snacked on bar food, casually talking about their day. A few times, he snuck glances at the brunette, who was now sitting directly opposite them across the bar. The way she applied red lipstick to her full lips seemed familiar. *Where have I seen her before?* Bryan wondered. While he racked his brain trying to solve this puzzle, he realized another part of his body was holding the key to his memory. *Oh my*

God, that's the trans woman who kissed my car. He discretely adjusted himself, embarrassed. *I thought I was over that*, he thought, *like how kids go through phases of being goth and stuff like that. I guess being into transwomen is a little different than being goth.*

"What are you thinking about?" Angela took his hand. "You seem distant."

He wrenched his gaze away from the woman and fastened his eyes on Angela's sparkling chestnut ones. "I'm sorry. Thinking about work." He finished his drink in one gulp. "I'm here."

She squeezed his fingers. "I'm glad. Would you like to finish the night at my place?"

"Yes." He kissed her, their teeth clacking together because they were both grinning. "I was hoping you would ask."

As they left the bar to enter the dining area, he smiled tightly at the brunette, and she blew him a kiss. He glanced away, his heart racing. *Did Angela see that?* he wondered. He was grateful to hear his name called by the host.

After their meal, Bryan and Angela waited for the valet to bring their cars. A Hummer swung into the parking lot, its bright lights illuminating the faint impression of the lip gloss on his windshield. He smiled because he intentionally left a small smudge to remind him of her lips. He hurriedly jumped in his car and followed Angela's taillights to her subdivision.

While they were making out on her bed, flashes of the woman who had kissed the windshield aroused him further. He and Angela copulated aggressively, but he was thinking about the brunette instead of her. While Angela seemed satisfied enough, she didn't invite him to stay the night, and he didn't want to overstay his welcome. He kissed her goodbye and drove home, deliberately steering his thoughts away from the woman at the bar. *This is right*, he tried to convince himself. *Who cares if I need to fantasize about someone else to have sex with her? It's not like she needs to know what I'm thinking. Straight sex isn't bad, it's just not great. Maybe one day, she'd be open*, he considered for a moment, then discontinued the thought. He could never tell her his innermost desires. It wouldn't help him and it would just hurt her. No, he needed to find a way to keep everything inside. He wasn't sure why it was so hard now. He had been married to Lawanda for years and had never had this hard of a time controlling his sexuality. It was as if his sexual proclivities were like extension cords neatly packaged prior to Nadia, and now they refused to go back in their original box.

He sighed, knowing the road to Mama's forgiveness was paved with a girl like Angela. Maybe if he dated Angela long enough, his mama would believe that he was going through a phase and was not like his father, whatever that meant.

30

His admin greeted him warmly on Monday morning. It was a lovely sunny June day with a lilting breeze and low humidity. Everyone in his office was in a good mood.

"Mr. Hicks, I booked your flight to Portland."

"Thank you, Laura. That's a pretty dress," he said, swiveling his new top-of-the-line chair around to smile at her. "Did you have a good weekend?"

"I did. Thank you for asking."

Bryan's impact had, so far, been positive. He had fired contractors who charged double for pipe fabrication and had placed a rash of supervisors—who had been unsuccessful at increasing production—on probation. In the past week, he visited two nearby facilities to align them with the company goals. He was busy, but not too busy to forget about Jerry's visit and a chance to make things right—with Mike's help. Bryan still wasn't sure how to broach the subject with him, but figured their upcoming business trip might be a good opportunity to have more casual conversations with him.

Thoughts of the trip reminded Bryan that he should text Angela and he pulled out his phone to text her.

Hi, babe. Wanted to remind you I'm headed to Portland with Mike and some of the other leadership.

She responded instantly. *I miss you already. Call me when you land.*

I'll call you before I land, Bryan texted back.

You're silly. And sweet, Angela responded.

Once they had boarded the plane, Bryan settled himself in first class and was already sipping a midday whiskey when a well-groomed white man indicated that he was his seat mate.

"I can only fly first class," the man said, his articulation dramatic and expressive. Up close, he looked like Tim Gunn from Project Runway.

"Me too," Bryan admitted.

"I saw you earlier, standing in the security line. You're a snappy dresser. You can't be from Texas?"

Bryan laughed. "I am, as a matter of fact." He gave the middle-aged man a more thoughtful glance. "Your orange tie contrasts beautifully against the cobalt of your suit. Working with contrasting colors demonstrates an artistic understanding of them."

The man rubbed his hands together. "Oh, this is going to be such a nutritious trip." He winked. "I'm already salivating."

Bryan laughed again. "Thank you, I think?"

They settled into a companionable silence that lasted the rest of the flight. Bryan wondered if there might be a community of trans women to meet in Portland. *Isn't Portland super progressive in that area?* Bryan wondered. When the plane landed with a shuddering thud, Bryan and his neighbor glanced at each other and chuckled at their matching grimaces. "Not the most graceful of entries," the man said.

Bryan unpeeled his hand from the armrest he'd been clutching. "Ha. No."

"Is this your first time in Portland?"

"Yes, it is."

"There is a bar I think you will enjoy. Google Aladdin."

Bryan immediately pulled out his phone and did. The banner of the bar's website showed two bare-chested men standing together, wearing rainbow-colored boy shorts. "Hey, I think—"

"Trust me," the man said, placing his hand on Bryan's. "You will thank me. I promise."

Bryan felt both at ease and exposed. How did the man deduce Bryan's leanings? Was it akin to his mama's sixth sense or the joke in popular culture about gaydar?

"I love beautiful women in all their many forms, myself," the gentleman traveler purred.

Mike's voice boomed from the row behind them. "If you're going to sit on this, then you'll miss out." Mike was standing, retrieving his luggage from the overhead bin. He was speaking into his phone, but Bryan was nonetheless startled.

Bryan tapped the button to close the screen, but he'd pressed the wrong button. Instead, the image was now in full view. The gentleman traveler grabbed the phone, smiling at Mike. Bryan's heart pounded hard.

Mike took the phone away from his ear. "Nice landing, eh, B?" He directed his gaze to Bryan's seatmate. "Hey, man."

"Hello," the gentleman said evenly.

Bryan mouthed a silent "thank you" to his seat mate, and received his phone from him.

"I'm right behind you, sir," Bryan said to Mike. Bryan gathered his things so he could catch up to Mike, who made it to the aisle first.

The man next to him leaned against his shoulder and whispered, "Who's that?"

"My boss." Bryan raised his eyebrow. He and his seatmate exchanged a quick goodbye, and Bryan rushed to catch up with Mike.

Bryan, Mike, and the three other direct reports gathered outside baggage claim to wait for their Uber. Mike's eyes widened when he saw all of Bryan's luggage. "Well, hey there, Lady Gaga."

Bryan gave a dry laugh. *This is going to be a long trip*, Bryan thought.

As the van passed through the streets of Portland, Bryan didn't see one Black person. He sent a quick text to Angela. *Here safely, but no Black people, so how safe can I really be?* She sent back a row of pink hearts and a sad emoji. Bryan replaced his phone and looked up in time to see the Aladdin nightclub, pride flags flapping in the wind.

"Every city, man," Mike said glumly. "They are everywhere."

The other direct reports tittered. 'True dat, boss," one said.

"Bryan's going to get rid of our fag problem," Mike said, twisting his head to look at Bryan in the backseat. "I'm sorry," he said, registering Bryan's dismay. "I mean gay problem." Bryan made eye contact with the Uber driver in his rearview mirror while the other men snickered under their breaths.

Bryan took in the city like a high-powered vacuum, absorbing all the modern buildings, numerous coffeehouses, and arty vibe. There were white people everywhere and very few Latinos or Asians in the mix, which was unsettling. He looked around for cops. The last thing he wanted was to stick out like a sore thumb. Turning back into the conversation around him, he saw one of the direct reports, married with three high school–age daughters, make a rude gesture with his hand.

"Oh yeah, that girl on the second floor. Blond with big titties. Every time I see her, I wish I were in my twenties again."

"Maybe she likes 'em older. Lots do," the CFO said.

"She is pretty," Bryan added. "Smart, too."

"Hey, Bryan," Mike said. "Brother, we like Angela. You guys are pretty serious, right?"

"We're having a nice time," Bryan said. It creeped him out that these men were keeping tabs on his dating life, much as he appreciated how his dating Angela diverted their attention away from his secret proclivities.

"Make sure you call her when you get to your room," Mike cautioned. "You know, women." He managed to simultaneously smile and roll his eyes heavenward.

Bryan nodded. The first thing he did when he got to his room, after hanging up all his clothes, was to calculate the distance to Aladdin's. In this moment, he only saw his interest in Aladdin's as simply taking in the city. It was only a ten-minute walk from the hotel, which made Bryan chuckle. In Texas, he would never consider walking. Aladdin's website advertised a drag show that night. In his excitement, he forgot to call Angela.

As he arrived in the lobby, he ran into his coworkers. Mike was not among them.

"Hey, Bry," the CFO called out. "We're going to a ... gentlemen's club. Wanna come?"

"No, thanks." He did his best to scrub his tone of judgment. "Just heading out for a bite. Have fun."

***

He was tempted to attend the drag show, but Bryan realized it wasn't wise knowing that his coworkers were close by and obviously keeping tabs on him. Instead, he downed a lamb gyro and a cold microbrew before dashing back to the privacy of his hotel room. The dark colors and sleek design of the room were the perfect accelerants to turn his smoldering desires into a fire. He knew he needed to call Angela, but he'd rather attend to his true desires. He could hear the moans from an adult movie through the wall behind his headboard. Shutting the blackout curtains, the light of his phone screen blared as he scrolled through pictures of phone-sex providers.

As he clicked through advertisements, one in particular caught his attention. An image of a tall trans woman with a ponytail, wearing a leather cat mask and holding a whip, stood next to a butt-naked man who was kneeling and kissing the ankle of her boot. Her ad read: *Explore Your Submissive Desires.*

He called. Her feminine and seductive voice penetrated his ears, instantly hooking him in a powerfully primal dance. She dictated how he should serve her.

"Thank you, mistress," he said, hanging up the phone forty-five minutes later. He pulled the covers over his head. *What am I doing? What about Angela? Is this only more satisfying because it feels wrong? Is it a reverse psychology thing and I need to reverse it again?* He rubbed his temples under the covers. He had no idea what to do. He enjoyed trans women, but wasn't sure he could fully commit to a life of loving them. He glanced at the clock: 12:30 am. He needed a distraction, but it was too late to call Angela.

***

"You look tired, man," Mike said, handing Bryan a mug of subpar coffee.

Bryan fought to stay focused in the meetings with the contractors, but he couldn't. Images of Aladdin's drifted in and out of his mind like clouds blocking his duties to work and to Angela. *Angela deserves better*, he thought. He thumbed through pictures of club Aladdin's during his bathroom breaks between meetings. He was too close to the women he really wanted to meet to not go to Aladdin's. There had to be some way to sneak out of the hotel without the team noticing. After a full day of meetings, he quietly exited the hotel out a side door and headed to Aladdin's. Within his first few steps, Angela crossed his mind again. *Crap, I keep forgetting to call her*, he thought. He considered taking a few minutes to call her on his walk over, but then remembered he needed his phone for directions and decided against it. *She hasn't called me yet. I can just call her later,* he thought.

Before he knew it, he arrived at the bright red entrance to Aladdin's. A pride banner draped over it like a curtain. *Or is it supposed to be a magic carpet?* Bryan wondered. He paused at the doorway, both taking in the club and trying to mentally prepare himself. He took a deep breath and sighed it out. A mixture of nervousness and excitement washed over him. He felt rooted to the pavement, as if his feet had melted into it. He felt as if he was staring into both his future and his past and he wasn't sure which one he preferred to enter. As he was gaping at the door, it unexpectedly swung toward him. He grabbed it and entered. Two women looking down at their phones almost ran into him.

"Beth," the blond poked her friend. "Girl, pinch me. Are we still in Portland?" She gestured toward Bryan. "Look at this tall dark drink of manliness here."

Beth flipped her wavy auburn hair over her shoulder. "Aren't you cute?"

Bryan toggled his head between the women, flattered but speechless.

"I want to box him up and take him home," the blond said, licking her lips.

"Too bad we have to go," Beth pouted. "I would risk lockjaw to take a bite out of that ass." They giggled and left, leaving Bryan in the wake of their lascivious giggles.

The club was small. There were a handful of small round tables, closely packed together, and the dark wooden walls were covered with black-and-white photos of drag performers and patrons. Every patron was white, and Bryan felt his palms getting damp. Being the only Black man after dark made him nervous, but he took a deep breath and ordered a drink from a waiter who was wearing a tank top to show off his pecs and lip gloss so copious it could be used as a flashlight.

Halfway through his second drink, a different server, one who wore men's jeans with a wallet chain and appeared to have bound her breasts underneath her shirt, approached Bryan's table carrying a third drink.

"The lady at the bar"—she pointed to a young woman with a sharp platinum bob—"bought you another round."

Bryan raised his glass to the blond woman in thanks, hoping she was trans. A moment later, she was at his table. Closer inspection revealed she was an attractive, very passable trans woman. Nothing special stood out—Bryan just knew.

"You don't have to sit all alone. Hi, I'm Jessica."

He gestured to her to sit. "Thank you for the drink. You didn't have to do that."

"You seem like a very capable man. I wanted to be nice."

Bryan salivated over her long legs as she gracefully sat down and crossed them, causing her short black leather skirt to ride up to her mid-thighs.

"You're different from Black guys I see on TV," she said, batting her long false eyelashes.

Bryan was both disturbed and amused by her ignorant outburst, but lust ruled out. He chuckled.

"Girl, you need to get out more."

***

After midnight, they grabbed an Uber. Bryan asked to go back to his hotel instead of her place. As far as he was concerned, closeted men end up missing by going back to stranger's places and that was the last thing he needed. As they made their way back to the hotel, Bryan took the ride there as an opportunity to make a move on Jessica, kissing in the backseat. He rubbed on her groin and realized her body felt tight. Her skin was soft and smooth. Bryan hoped his coworkers were either still out or asleep. It was late, and Bryan was alone in a new city. *I need to figure out how Angela fits into all of this,* he thought between kisses. She initiated another round of making out, and the thought faded. *That's a tomorrow problem*, he thought, trying to focus on Jessica instead of his guilt.

Inside, the lobby was empty and hushed, punctuated by the faint tinkling of bartenders washing the last-call glasses. Jessica nibbled on his ear while they watched the glass elevator make its gradual descent toward them.

The elevator doors opened, and she slapped his ass so hard he literally jumped into the elevator. She giggled. "I've wanted to do that for a while now." She stood behind him, running her hands over his chest and her crotch against his backside. He accidentally pressed the wrong button to keep the doors open before jabbing the button for the ninth floor. *I need to find out if she is a top or bottom*, Bryan thought.

"It's yours if you want it," he said submissively, pressing his buttocks into her groin.

"That's what I figured," Jessica purred in his ear. "Is that what you want? Masculine bottoms are so sexy," she said, kissing his neck. She put her tongue in his ear and whispered, "I'm going to f..," pausing, "queer ass. Do you hear me?"

Queer. That word again. Bryan nodded yes, knowing now wasn't the time to ask questions. He melted away, consumed by her lust. As they ascended, the moonlight shone through the glass and against the side of Jessica's face, highlighting her rounded cheekbones and delicate jaw. Bryan turned and pressed her body against the glass, feeling her erection. He took half a step away to take her all in, which aroused him that much more. She turned around and they began kissing sloppily and loudly. The elevator stopped, but Bryan continued kissing Jessica's neck with his back to the doors.

"Hicks. Is that you? You dirty dog."

Bryan froze.

"You must be feeling better," Mike said, taking a long pull on his Budweiser. "Obviously."

Bryan, light-headed with panic, released Jessica's hand and made room for Mike in the small space. Mike entered, eyeballing Jessica. Bryan glanced down quickly to see if she was still erect. The elevator doors closed and Bryan realized they were trapped. Bryan felt himself sweating through his good shirt and jacket. *It's like that time the elevator got stuck. Oh God, I couldn't deal with it getting stuck right now.* Bryan said a silent prayer that the elevator would keep moving and wished that Mike would forget this moment ever existed.

"Who's your friend?" Mike asked. He reached around Bryan and shook Jessica's hand. Before she had time to reply, he continued, "I'm Mike, Bryan's boss." His expression was hard to read, but he seemed confused. Jessica released his hand and scooched closer to Bryan. Her untucked semi-swollen penis brushed against Bryan through her skirt, and he willed himself not to look down. *Please look anywhere but at her crotch,* Bryan begged. But Mike did. Either discreetly or drunkenly—Bryan hoped for the latter—Mike tilted his head to the right as he looked downward. He shifted his eyes back to Bryan, though his words were intended for Jessica. "You're tall."

Bryan tried to think of anything he could say to diffuse the tension. "Hey, Mike," he said, gesturing toward the beer bottle to redirect Mike's gaze. "I didn't know you were a Bud man!" Bryan could feel his heart pounding through his chest as Jessica dropped her purse to cover herself. Mike's eyes followed her movements and were now trained on her crotch. Anger flickered over his befuddlement. Bryan prayed that he was too drunk to remember any of this scene later. "What floor, Mike?"

"Uh . . . eighth," Mike replied, still staring at Jessica. To Bryan, it felt as if the elevator were being filmed in slow motion or underwater. Every vowel sounded drawn out and ghoulish.

Mike recovered some of his swagger. "So . . . sweetheart, how are you this evening?"

"It's Jessica," she said, her voice higher than it had been all night. "And I'm fine, thank you."

"Well . . . Jessica," Mike smiled, showing all his teeth. "It was a pleasure meeting you." He reached to shake her hand again, but Jessica clutched her purse with both hands, blocking her crotch.

"Bye," she said, sweet as sugar.

"You two have a good night," Mike chuckled.

The doors closed behind him, and Jessica let out a huge exhale. She touched Bryan's chest through his shirt. "Oh, baby, you're soaked through." She brightened. "He was drunk, don't worry. He won't recall a thing about us in the morning."

"I can't breathe," Bryan gasped. Her words were heavy with logic but featherlight against the pounding of his head.

"Breathe. You're okay," Jessica said, rubbing his face. "He's gone."

"Oh my God," Bryan kept repeating.

"He was pretty drunk."

He was sick with fear, but he wanted to believe her. He placed the key card over the lock, and it clicked. He shut the door and felt himself collapse on the inside of it. His heart was pounding so fast that it was making him feel nauseous.

"Forget about him," she said, helping him stand up straight again. She led him towards the bed and kissed the back of his neck. He felt the warmth emanating from her and felt himself beginning to relax a bit. *Isn't this part of being in the moment? That's why practice meditating,* he thought.

"Let's do this," she said, sliding her hand down the front of his pants. *Screw Mike,* he thought as he felt his passion overtake him. He threw his jacket on the bed and pulled the blinds and blackout curtains tightly closed. He faced Jessica with an unbuttoned shirt.

"I love hotel sex," Jessica blushed. "It feels so dirty."

Bryan's heart was beating like an out-of-control engine again.

Jessica giggled. "Why so shy? Okay, baby. I don't mind feeling my way around." She brushed past him and reopened the curtains. "But let's not shut her out." Moonlight poured in.

"No one can see you, okay?" Jessica said. "Mama is going to take care of you." She kissed him.

He felt the warmth of her breath against his lips, her skin almost as soft as Nadia's. She unbuckled him, and they both stroked each other, feeling the warmth of each other's engorged extremities.

"The girls are going to be so jealous. I wish I had my phone to take a picture," Jessica said.

Bryan backed away.

"I didn't tell you to stop," she said. "Now be a good boy."

Bryan handed her a travel tube of Boy Butter from his suitcase. She applied the lube, stroking until the condom had a wonderful, moist shine that twinkled against the Portland moon. She bent him over the desk and he realized that he felt oddly natural in this position. He had fantasized about it for so long that the moment suddenly felt surreal. He had enjoyed imagining it the night before on the phone with the unnamed woman, but he was sober now, and this was real.

"Black men are so sexy," Jessica said, squeezing his waist. Thoughts of Nadia crowded his brain. Nadia had loved him and had wanted nothing more than a real connection.

In contrast, now he was being objectified as Jessica's fantasy to be fulfilled. It felt weird and depersonalized in this way. *It's one night,* he thought, but Nadia's face crossed his consciousness. What if he got a chance with Nadia again? How would he explain that he was not a virgin any longer?

"Just relax," she said, massaging Bryan's buttocks.

He closed his eyes and saw Nadia's face frowning at him in the scrim of curtain covering the moonlit window.

He felt Jessica's girth press against his entry and his heart began racing again.

"I'm sorry, Jessica, I can't do it," he said disappointedly, stepping away from the desk.

"What's wrong?"

"I'm still a . . ." he stammered. "An anal virgin."

Her mouth made an O. "You are?"

"I don't want to lose my virginity on an out-of-town hookup, I guess." He pulled the bedclothes off the bed to cover himself. "I thought I did, but now I'm realizing I want to do this with someone I love. Please don't be mad."

Jessica stood in silence as Bryan quickly dressed himself.

"I think you are beautiful," Bryan said, touching her shoulder, "It's nothing personal. It's me. I didn't realize how much it meant to me until it was about to happen."

"Okay, honey," Jessica said, patting his wrist. "I wish you'd been a bit more up-front, but it's okay. Unfortunately, I'm not looking for anything serious, and we live thousands of miles apart, anyway."

They sat on the couch quietly while downtown Portland's lights blinked wanly. Bryan briefly remembered the night he lost his virginity to Sarah. It had been special, and he was certain now that he wanted this time to be as well.

"I saw you when you entered the club," Jessica said, turning to face him. "I don't get to meet any African American guys."

"I can believe that," he said, gesturing to the city outside the window. "But I want to be more than just a fetish."

"That's fair. I'm sorry," she said sadly, looking for her clothes.

"Don't be," he said, leaning in to kiss her because he knew he disappointed her. She kissed him back. Her kiss was softer this time. "Stay the night. I'll make it up to you," he said, looking at her swollen girl-dick. She smiled as he placed his left hand around the base of her girl-dick and they started kissing again. He stroked her softly. Jessica gently placed her left hand on the back of Bryan's neck and lightly guided him down. Bryan slowly lowered himself, placing his mouth on the flushed red head of her girl-dick.

"There you go. Your boss will be so proud of you," She moaned.

Bryan ignored the comment and disappeared into the person he really wanted to be.

***

The next morning, Bryan awoke with the taste of joy wrapped inside feelings of guilt for his actions. Jessica had left in the dark of the morning, so as long as Mike was too drunk to remember her, she shouldn't have aroused any suspicions on her way out, but Bryan was still worried.

Bryan slowly made his way to the lobby, weighed down with dread. He heard Mike's booming voice at the front desk and took a deep breath to brace himself. The rest of the leadership team was clustered around Mike. Bryan prayed again that Mike hadn't been sober enough to remember last night. Wanting to hide but knowing he had to face his boss at some point, he took another deep breath and propelled himself as confidently as he could up to his boss. "Good morning, Mike."

"Morning, sunshine," Mike said with a frighteningly large grin. Bryan's heart sank. "Hey boys, my man had himself some fun last night." He threw his arm heavily around Bryan's shoulder and put his mouth so close to Bryan's ear, it was almost touching it. "With a special, special kind of girl." He patted Bryan on the back and walked away. *Shit*, Bryan thought, *he definitely remembers. What the hell am I going to do? Do I try to convince him he was seeing things? Does Mike seem gullible enough for that?*

Inside the stifling airport van, Mike and the other men spoke among themselves. No one talked to Bryan, but he overheard them talking in upset tones about the police officer who was indicted for shooting an unarmed Black man in the back as he attempted to run away. Bryan recalled hearing the man's name on the radio that morning: Walter Scott. *Man, they have a problem with anyone who isn't a straight white man. Good thing straight white men can't procreate together,* Bryan thought, smiling to himself. He knew that if he couldn't find humor in the situation, he risked having a nervous breakdown in front of his co-workers.

Me speaking up won't do anything to make these guys see the broader picture, he thought, resting his head against the cool glass of the passenger window. A chime alerted him to another text from Angela. He hadn't spoken to her since he sent a quick text to tell her he had landed safely in Portland. She was probably hurt and angry, but he didn't have the energy to even read her text. He was also hurting, but his pain was invisible to her.

***

He landed in Houston several hours later, desperate to talk to Nadia, and sped to Two Moons Bakery. The shop's neon sign flickered vibrantly against the dark sky. They were closed. It felt like years had passed since he had last seen Nadia and she was the one he needed the most. She was the only one who could give him the advice he needed.

It started to rain in sheets as he stood outside the lonely bakery and Bryan felt foolish for inelegantly trying to track Nadia down. Of course, the store was closed. It was well after nine o'clock.

He hadn't called Angela in two days, but it was late, and he didn't think he could keep up appearances at this point. If he called her, he might break down and tell her everything.

***

At seven o'clock on Friday morning, he awoke to a text from Angela: *I don't think we're a good fit after all. I know we can be professionals at work and treat each other well. I wish you the best, always.*

He texted back immediately. *I'm sorry I didn't treat you better. You deserve more. You are a wonderful woman. Thank you for being so gracious. All the best, Bryan.* An enormous sense of relief descended on him, soft like a mink stole.

Angela texted back only minutes later. *I'm from Atlanta. The way you acted is familiar to me, unfortunately. Also, you shouted out "Nadia" in your sleep. I didn't think much of it at the time (love is deaf as well as blind), but as a friend, it's probably something you should look into before you date again. Love, A.*

Bryan cringed at his poor dating etiquette while his heart constricted at the mention of Nadia's name. *Maybe Mama is right,* he thought, *maybe my picker is off.*

***

He turned on the TV. A CNN reporter showed scenes from a nightclub in Florida called Pulse, a now heartbreakingly ironic name. In the wee hours of the morning, a large crowd had been ecstatically dancing when a twenty-nine-year-old man had opened fire, killing forty-nine people and injuring fifty-eight before being lethally shot by police. Shuddering, Bryan moved closer to the television, horrified by all the hate and chaos which transpired while he had been dreaming of Nadia. If there was only some non-stalker-like way to determine that she was safe.

In a flash, Bryan wondered what no newscaster was even hinting at: the possibility that the shooter might have been gay himself. Hurting those people might have been covering up what was really going on in his head. This idea scared Bryan to the bone. He shuddered again. *Why is violence always the answer to fear?* Bryan wondered. CNN then flitted to a shot of Obama speaking about the tragedy, and Bryan found himself grateful that the administration's reaction to the tragedy was sober and cast no aspersions toward the LGBTQIA+ community.

Bryan remembered again why he was hiding his true self. It wasn't just about embarrassment- it was about his safety as a Black man. Nonetheless, Bryan marveled at the LGBTQ+ community's courage. They would rather express themselves truly and risk experiencing hate and violence than live a long life in the closet. *God made them stronger than me,* Bryan thought. He suddenly heard Nadia's voice in his head. *But is a life without your true self really worth living?* Nadia's words rang loud and the question deeply unsettled him. *Maybe Nadia is right,* he thought. He called in sick to work, knowing that he had a lot of work to do on himself.

31

The next week, extreme heat and humidity ratcheted up the tension, which had always been simmering on a low boil in the city and the country. His office was not immune. So far, he had successfully avoided being alone with Mike, and was beginning to think that he would need to find a way to save himself before he could save Jerry. Bryan kept his head down and produced excellent results, but he was neither praised nor overtly slighted. It was all subtle and hard to pin down, like Mike's off-kilter chumminess at the hotel reception desk in Portland. Bryan felt paranoid and sensed veiled threats, but Mike had always been a bit awkward and unreadable as a way to cement his authority.

Bryan tried his best to project confidence and pretend he wasn't walking on eggshells. He attended meetings and nodded in agreement with others, but rarely spoke. On Friday, he came across a gaggle of coworkers whispering and chortling, who, when he turned a corner and came into view, stopped abruptly and went back to their desks, barely glancing at him. *They know,* he thought, *but at least I still have my job.*

***

Two weeks after the Fourth of July holiday, the halls and meeting rooms continued to be filled with whispers of the killing of police officers in Dallas at a police brutality protest. Bryan overheard his co-workers blaming the president for tearing the country apart. Being Black at work was becoming even more tricky. He tread even more softly, his feet like feathers, approaching clusters of white males with caution. He frequently started to think to himself that sooner or later, someone was going to snap. If Black people couldn't peacefully take a knee, then violence was bound to happen. Life was always more manageable when white men did not feel threatened.

Bryan pulled himself out of his thoughts and opened the door to the large conference room. It was time for the regular leadership meeting. Everyone stopped talking when Bryan entered and Bryan quietly skittered to a nearby seat. *I guess this is my new normal,* he sighed to himself.

"Guys," Mike said archly, "let's get going. It's too hot to dillydally." Everyone else presented their reports, none of which were wholly positive. Mike said nothing. "Everyone have a great and safe day," Mike said, closing his manila folder.

"Excuse me, sir," Bryan said. "I still need to give my report."

Mike sat back down. "Please. We all want to hear," he said sarcastically.

"I successfully renegotiated our contracts. I think the contractor in Louisiana will finish only a week later than their schedule." He was nervous but plowed on. "I was able to save the company nearly a million dollars."

"So, you're still behind?"

Bryan paused. *Did they not care how much money he had just told them he saved them?* He inhaled sharply before responding, "Yes." The leadership team stared at him, expressionless. "However, I was able to get them to finish earlier than they'd estimated. After the initial delay."

Mike yawned widely, showing all of his teeth. "I promoted you to get it right, not to give excuses." Mike pushed back his seat, picking up his folder. The rest of the team did the same.

"Did I see Jerry in this building today?" Mike asked Bryan. "You told me you were ready to lead."

Jerry is back? Did I miss an email? Bryan tried to hide his shock with a tight-lipped smile. "I am," he said. He could feel his heart rate increasing again, and was beginning to wonder if he should consider seeing a cardiologist.

"Didn't I tell you to get rid of that . . . homo? Why is he still swishing his ass around here?"

"Sir," Bryan paused out of frustration. "I've been busy trying to get the contractors to catch up on late projects. Furthermore," he took a deep breath, "Jerry has been a good worker. His file has nothing but good reviews of his work. What cause do we have?"

"He's never at his desk."

Bryan opened his mouth to speak, but paused before the words came out. *Do you not remember banishing Jerry to Louisiana these past few months? Or are you trying to gaslight me?* "Sir, we are making a mistake."

"The mistake was promoting you," Mike said mildly. "If you don't take care of this today, I promise I will find someone who will." Mike was almost out the door. "I would hate for you to have to give up your new Porsche," he tossed over his shoulder.

Bryan couldn't help but jolt at the bald threat. If Mike were a different kind of boss and leader, Bryan would have rattled off behind-the-scenes work he had done in preparation for Jerry's return. The sexual harassment and racial issues inside the refineries needed to be addressed, but Bryan realized he was no longer in a position to broach the subject, much less change anything about it. Bryan wished Mike would consider sensitivity training for all contractors and employees and termination for those with complaints levied against them, but he knew Mike would never go for it. He was curious to know what Jerry thought about sensitivity training, although he would probably think it was too late for most of the problematic guys. There was still the challenge of getting individuals to speak up, report new issues, and gather more information about past behavior because so many people had quit or been fired. He had tried talking to several people he suspected were being harassed shortly after he returned from Portland, but no one wanted to risk coming forward. Bryan hoped that if Jerry did, others might be emboldened by his courage and follow suit.

He hurried back to his office, hoping that Jerry was there or had left a message, but not even his admin was around. Bryan unlocked his door, but something was dragging on the carpet when he tried to push the door open. Bryan bent down to investigate the blockage and found someone had threaded a white letter-sized piece of paper through the crack between the floor and the door. He glanced over his shoulder to see if anyone was watching, but he was alone. Someone had cut out a picture of a model in a bra and panties from Victoria's Secret catalog and glued it to the paper. Drawn over the panties in black permanent marker was a huge penis. Heart racing, Bryan crushed it in his fist and stuffed it in his bag.

He slipped into his office and hunkered into a ball behind the door. A rush of cortisol flooded him, and pins and needles prickled his skin. Was everyone laughing at him? Disgusted by him? He slammed his fist against the wall. *Why did God give me these feelings? And why won't they go away?* He canceled his meetings for the rest of the day and took the stairs to the garage. After all, what was the point in staying when he was clearly unwanted and not making a difference? When he got to his car, he found another piece of paper on his windshield.

Light-headed, he removed the message stuck underneath his wiper blade. It said "faggot" in sloppy black sharpie. He crumpled the paper up in his fist and drove off as fast as he could.

At home, he triple-locked his door and shut the blinds, as if someone could look in on the tenth floor and see his truth. He paced back and forth. *What am I going to do? Who can I talk to about this? Is this why white people go to therapy? Can Black people even go to therapy? Are there even Black therapists?* Realizing there was no one he could tell, he fixed himself a drink and tried to reassure himself that it was best to let boys be boys. He could handle their jokes. All of this would probably go away in the next few days. *This is just some middle school bullshit, right?*

***

Bryan had been tempted to call in sick, but he knew that was both not prudent as a VP and not the way to confront intimidation, especially after cancelling his meetings the day before. Unable to sleep much the night before, he had arrived close to six thirty in the morning. With only the janitorial staff at the office, he made a beeline for his office and locked the door, glad no one else had arrived early today.

At eight fifteen, there was a gentle knock. It was Jerry in the flesh, and Bryan had to do a double-take to make sure he was real. Bryan was so happy to see him he could have hugged him.

"Jerry!"

Jerry sauntered in, casual and relaxed, as though he had not been gone for months. "Did you know that your admin is out there watching cat videos? Man, did you see that new Porsche in the garage? That car is . . ."

With sickening dread, Bryan realized that Jerry being back was not good. *Jerry might try to out me,* he thought. He had been ordered to fire his old friend. His mouth was cottony. "Jerry, sit down."

"What's wrong with you?"

Bryan couldn't look at him. "I was told to let you go today."

"Let me go," Jerry intoned. "You said you wanted to help me with my harassment claim with my actual fucking harasser. You were excited to see me. We started chatting like old times." He glared at Bryan. "And this was all a setup for firing me?"

Bryan felt emotion overcome him, and managed to squeak out, "Not exactly." He looked Jerry in the eyes, then glanced down. *It's you or him,* Bryan reminded himself. He found himself thinking of Animal Planet nature documentaries and heard the phrase, "Eat or be eaten," on repeat in the back of his head. He glanced out the window and saw the vulture that had been haunting him for the past few months.

Jerry sat with a quiet eagerness for about sixty seconds as Bryan stared at the vulture. Jerry coughed, breaking the silence and Bryan snapped his attention back to Jerry.

"Bryan, what's really going on here?" Jerry asked.

Eat or be eaten, Bryan heard again. *This isn't emotional, this is practical,* he thought. *It's survival.* He glanced at the vulture again, and its eyes locked with his, startling him. He quickly looked away. He had made his decision, so he pushed his emotions down and spoke like a robot.

"I am downsizing the group. I need your badge. I will send your personal effects to your home address."

"You little Black Benedict Arnold. That's not the reason. You're lying through your teeth right now."

"Please," Bryan let the anguish flood his voice. "I have to. Please don't make this any more difficult than it already is." It was too much. Portland. Mike meeting Jessica. Losing his cover after Angela broke things off. The Pulse massacre.

"Just following orders, eh?" Jerry sneered. "You know, you sound like a Nazi. You'll get what you deserve. I promise they will find out who you really are."

They already have, he thought, *I'm probably skating on the same thin ice you are.* Unable to meet his friend's eyes, Bryan trained his gaze out the window above Jerry's head. A second vulture landed on the building ledge. The image of the Chagall print and the creepy vulture head in Mike's library flashed in Bryan's mind. Was Mike the vulture? Was Bryan? Could one be both the vulture and Tityos?

Jerry threw his badge. It skittered across the desk and fell to the floor. Bryan's heart dropped into his stomach and he almost doubled over with regret. He knew Jerry was right. They already knew about him.

32

A few minutes after nine in the morning, Bryan was at Lawanda's apartment, backing up the rented moving truck as close to the front door as he could manage. He found himself feeling a mixture of excitement and nervousness for his daughter. He imagined Lindsey when she was a baby and couldn't quite believe that today, she would be moving into her first dorm room. He slowly stepped down from the truck, feeling the sun beating down on him. *It's eight o'clock and it already feels like 85 degrees*, he thought.

Even though Lindsey was the one moving, Lance was planning on tagging along for the ride. Unfortunately, both of his kids were so scattered that Bryan was the one who ended up packing the truck as snug as a finished puzzle. Lance was so distracted that Bryan was able to toss Lance's backpack, which rarely left his son's side, in the cab without a word from his son. Bryan was hoping that the trip would help Lance visualize a college campus. So far, he hadn't expressed much interest in his studies, though he did fine in school.

Lawanda didn't come out throughout the entire packing process. Bryan assumed she didn't want to sweat her makeup off and didn't bother asking her for her help. He suddenly realized he didn't have a single woman in his life he could rely on anymore. In fact, he was shipping off the only female in his life who still deigned to answer his phone calls with more than one syllable words. He felt a pang of sadness, but pinched his nose to prevent tears from flowing.

Bryan filled the seven-hour drive to Norman, Oklahoma by talking about his college days. Lindsey was quiet and fidgety during the entire trip, drumming her fingers on the passenger door rest. It was so uncharacteristic of her not to be texting that Bryan asked her if she was okay. Lindsey admitted to being nervous about the lack of diversity at her school. Bryan heard the nervousness in her voice as they approached the campus. He parked in a campus parking lot and turned to face her. "I know you're nervous, but don't forget that you belong here," he said.

Lindsey's wide eyes continued to survey the kids milling around about campus and Bryan rubbed her shoulder to reassure her. She glanced at him, her eyes still wide with fear. He wanted to tell her everything would be okay, but he knew he couldn't guarantee that. He had to be reassuring yet realistic with her: it was hard being one of the only black kids at a predominantly white school.

"I know there are a lot of white people. It's going to be much different than Houston. But, I can assure you that it will be fine. But, that means you're going to have to get involved on campus and take advantage of all the programs available for the minority kids."

After the platitudes left his mouth, Bryan wondered if his daughter's experience really would be very different. After all, she was not only Black but a woman in engineering. He prayed silently that her primarily white male professors and peers would treat her fairly.

When the main campus came into view and they approached her residence hall, Lindsey dropped all pretenses of her cool teenage facade and stared open-mouthed at the well-groomed grass outlined by stone sidewalks. These midcentury buildings served as watchtowers over aspirations and storehouses of knowledge. The campus emitted frenetic energy as parents and kids weaved through traffic to find their way to dorms, the library, and the bookstore. Bryan quickly located Lindsey's dorm and Lindsey and Lance decided to help with the moving process this time around. As Bryan carried a load up the path, he staggered under the weight of a box and a skinny white kid held the door for them.

"Thank you," Lindsey said, surprised by his chivalry.

"Thank you, young man," Bryan echoed. As they were waiting for the service elevator with a bunch of other families, Bryan caught Lindsey's eye.

"That would not have happened in my day," he said. He noticed her phone had not appeared once in her hand since they had pulled out of Lawanda's apartment. "Have you talked to your boyfriend today?"

"He called before you got to Mom's, but I've been busy today. Did you know this university is 70 percent boys?"

Bryan laughed. "Remember, you're here to get an engineering degree. Not a husband, okay?"

After getting Lindsey settled, the three of them wandered around campus. In the Student Union building, a table with an orange banner proclaimed, "National Society of Black Engineers - NSBE". It warmed Bryan's heart to see that NSBE was still around. Lindsey practically skipped toward the sign and was soon engulfed in a bevy of young men, all vying to talk to her.

Lance tugged Bryan's arm. "Hey, Dad, I'm going to go over there." He pointed to a group of students across the pavilion.

Bryan used this opportunity to set up payment plans at the bursar's office. When he was finished, he spotted Lance at the student LGBTQIA+ table. One or two jocks were mixed in with several effeminate boys and the girls ran the gamut from butch to femme—all were laughing with one another. Lance was engrossed in conversation with the boys dressed in drag. Bryan was concerned that Lance had once again gravitated to gender-non-conforming kids. He'd hoped that the group of boys wearing wigs at the bowling alley was a fluke, but he now realized that Lance was definitely in the group that in Bryan's high school, would have been referred to as "the weirdos" if people were feeling nice or "the fags" if people wanted to be jerks. Bryan remembered that in his high school, some of the students from that group had performed magic tricks like he had. He had always been polite, but had also made it clear they weren't really friends. *Shit! I forgot his book,* Bryan remembered. As he watched Lance laughing with the other students, Bryan tried to imagine himself in his shoes again. *How does he do it?* Bryan marveled. As he watched his son from afar, he saw him talking wildly with his hands and throwing his head back with laughter. *Have I ever laughed like that?* Bryan racked his brain, trying to think of if he had ever truly unmasked with anyone. Nadia's face entered his mind, and he felt his eyes well up. He pinched his nose again. *Maybe it can be different for him,* Bryan thought. *If people know who you are, then they can't be disappointed when they find out you're really someone else.* He sighed. He knew that he wouldn't have become VP if people had known who he really was. He wouldn't have financial security, his nice clothes, or his Porsche. In fact, he might not have even finished high school if his mother had found out. She might have kicked him out of the house if he had acted like Lance had in high school. *I did what I had to do,* he thought. *But Lance deserves better.*

His heart full with empathy, Bryan tapped Lance lightly on the shoulder. "Hi, everyone. Son, are you ready?" he asked.

"This is my dad," Lance said to the group. His eyes beseeched Bryan's. "Do we really have to go already?"

"I'm sorry but we need to finish getting your sister settled. It was nice to meet you all," Bryan said, shaking each of their hands. Bryan's hand lingered on that of a tall, scrawny black student, and he briefly met his gaze before looking away. *That's me twenty years ago,* he thought. He smiled, acknowledging that he did not have the courage to seek out a LGBTQIA+ table back then. An effeminate boy wearing a wig and makeup held hands with another boy and they smiled at Bryan as he and Lance turned around. A twinge of jealousy hit his consciousness: Bryan found himself wishing he had an ounce of the courage these kids had.

***

A few hours later, it was time to go. Bryan had bought Lindsey her books for the semester, put together a hamper and a set of metal drawers for her tiny closet, and met her roommate's parents.

Bryan gripped his daughter's shoulders tightly, his eyes moist. "Aw, dad," she said. She pulled out of his grasp and dragged her hand across her face to wipe her tears. "You old softie." She even hugged Lance. "Don't let anyone . . . well, you know...stop you from being you." He smiled and kissed the side of his sister's head. *Even Lindsey knows*, he thought. His face fell as he realized his son wasn't comfortable enough with him to talk to him about who he was.

Bryan and Lance headed to the hotel in silence. They brushed their teeth together in the small bathroom, the light above their heads overly bright and buzzing. Bryan was tempted to ask Lance about the group of kids he'd met in the Student Union but decided against it, still too scared to open up a can of worms he knew he couldn't re-seal. *What if he asks about me? Or worse, Nadia? How do I have an honest conversation with him?* Bryan cycled through these same thoughts over and over, trying to figure out if honesty was really the best policy. Instead of delving into his innermost workings, he flexed in the mirror. "Show me your muscles."

Lance gave everything he had.

"Attaboy," Bryan said, impressed with his son's small yet bulging bicep.

They flopped on one of the beds, and Lance picked up the remote. He chose a house-flipping show on HGTV as Bryan checked his work email on his laptop. He had taken a few days off, and while he had prepared as much as he could before he left, he was secretly worried that he would get demoted while he was away.

"Dad, you work a lot," Lance said, his eyes glued to the screen.

"Yes," Bryan said, closing his laptop. "I'm sorry, son. But I have to. I want to provide for you and your sister."

"If you didn't work so much, we could spend more time together."

Bryan was surprised that Lance paid that much attention to his absence. He set his computer down and scooched closer to Lance so he could rub the top of Lance's head. "We're spending time together now, aren't we? Ask me anything."

Lance turned off the TV. "How do you know when you like somebody?"

Bryan had been waiting for this line of questioning for a few years. In light of his mother and sister's assessments—not to mention Nadia's—he was relieved that Lance was interested in a girl. *Wait- is it a girl?* Bryan wondered. He took a deep breath, realizing his son might be ready to open up to him. *This is a good thing,* Bryan thought. *He needs to be able to trust you.*

"Good question. I don't know. But you feel different when that person is around you. You're happy when you're with that person." Bryan found himself thinking of Nadia, and shook his head to try to shake away the image.

Lance grinned.

"Is there a girl who makes you happy when you see her?"

"I think so," Lance said. "But not a girl in the way you think of girls."

Bryan sat up. "Huh?"

Lance spoke calmly. "You are excluding so many people with your binary way of thinking."

Bryan stared at him with a mental numbness and collapsed back on the bed. "You're too young for this."

Lance sat up straighter, but his voice was gentle. "Dad, it's not the 1950's anymore. People are choosing not to be limited by old ideas."

"How old do you think I am?" Bryan asked as he noticed a smile blooming on his son's face. Bryan smiled back and sighed. "I get it, I'm an old fart. Well, does this person you like identify as a girl?"

"No. This person uses 'they' and 'them.'"

"Do they have a name?" Bryan said, suddenly feeling protective of who his son is hanging out with.

"Kasey."

Bryan did not know what else to ask. *It's not like I can ask where they work,* he thought.

"Well, I'm beat. Let's go to sleep," he said. *Why is this so complicated?* he wondered. He sighed. *At least I'm handling this better than my father would have,* he thought. Bryan's father said very few words, so Bryan had no examples of knowing how to ask questions, especially on this subject. If he did not have the words for his own desires yet, how could he begin to discuss the many shades of sexuality with Lance?

Lance's whole torso slumped. "Okay, Daddy."

Bryan's chest felt heavy again. He knew he was letting his son down, but it was easier to bail on the conversation than to risk saying the wrong thing. *Talking about my experiences with trans women is not on the docket,* he thought as he stared up at the ceiling, willing his brain to let him sleep.

***

Bryan and Lance decided that a pancake breakfast was the best way to start the road trip back home, and both father and son demolished their breakfast quickly.

As they approached the southern part of Dallas, Bryan heard a song featuring a heavy beat counterpointed with sexual moans.

"What are you listening to?" Bryan asked.

"Alaska Thunder...," Lance said happily.

"You must like that song. You know all the words, too."

"Oh yeah, and I—" Lance reached under the seat for his backpack.

"I remember you told your grandmother that she's your favorite performer. Her music sounds too adult for your ears."

"Someday, I'm going to be as good as her or Shangela Wadley," Lance said proudly. "Look," he said, unzipping his backpack. He retrieved a fistful of something that looked like aluminum foil or shiny fabric. "When I graduate from high school, I'm moving to Las Vegas to be a drag queen entertainer."

Bryan sighed deeply. He felt a real sense that Lance was limiting his opportunities to reach his full potential. *What if he goes out there and fails?* Bryan worried. *Or worse, gets killed?* Images of the Pulse nightclub shooting flashed through Bryan's mind, and he tried his best to focus instead on the road ahead. *I need to shut this down,* he thought. *For safety's sake.* Bryan pushed stop on the player.

"Son, I can't let you do this," Bryan said calmly, mustering every ounce of patience. "I don't want to hear another word about drag queens, the LGBTQIA+ whatever community, or how many different genders there are. Please stop."

Tears filled his son's big brown eyes.

Bryan pulled the car over. "Listen to me. It's my job to protect you. I know you have dreams. I had dreams once too," he said, facing Lance. "But you're a Black kid. This is already so difficult for us even when we try to present like white people. I'm scared they will punish you for wearing girl's clothes and makeup. Leave that for Harry and the white kids. That's not for us." Bryan stopped, taking a deep breath. "I know it's not what you want to hear, but it's the truth."

Lance turned away, saying nothing.

***

They still had three and half hours until they reached Lawanda's house. The tension was uncomfortable, but Bryan did not know how to fix it either. *Parents can only be supportive to a point,* he thought. *I wouldn't be doing my job as a parent if I wasn't truthful with him.* He looked over, seeing Lance's tears dripping into his lap. Lance did not raise his eyes the rest of the trip, and at a certain point, Bryan stopped looking over at him.

The second Bryan pulled into Lawanda's driveway, Lance said, "Dad, this is who I am. And you're telling me that I can't be myself," he said as he jumped out of the truck. "Why? Because you're scared. I'm not like you," he said sharply.

"Lance?"

In the doorway, Lawanda crossed her arms over her chest. "You take my daughter seven hours away from me. You know I needed her here with me. Now you bring him back crying?"

Bryan was silent.

"Nothing to say?" Lawanda mocked. "Just go. You've done enough damage." She hugged Lance, she rubbed the back of his head. "Mama's here now." Lawanda slammed the door.

Bryan felt as though the wind had been knocked out of him and he tried to stand up straight. It wasn't Lawanda's words that took his breath away though. It was the pained look in Lance's eyes as he had jumped out of the truck. Bryan recognized the look- it was the same one Nadia had given him when she was gathering her things after they broke up. *Why do I keep hurting the people I love the most?* Bryan wondered.

33

After the tumult of dropping his eldest off at college and his altercation with Lance on the way home, Bryan was halfway looking forward to work on Monday. Here, at least, he knew what to do. Numbers had always obeyed his bidding, lining up in their neat rows, never once suggesting a career as a drag queen in Vegas.

Work wasn't as uncomplicated as usual, however. Bryan became aware that his name was whispered as part of the rumor mill surrounding Jerry's firing. He hadn't realized how popular Jerry had been. People turned subtly away from him in the hallways, and in the few minutes before meetings started, groups scattered when he entered. His infamy was growing to the point that even new employees were catching wind of the rumor mill surrounding him. When Bryan called out to a new employee in the parking garage one evening, he ignored Bryan and quickened his steps. In the salad line, several women he considered good work friends only waved from a distance, their smiles grim or barely registering in their eyes. Even Angela kept her distance.

The only one who seemed not to be backing away was Mike. The day after the firing, he had descended to Bryan's office for the first time since the Jessica incident to ask him how he was doing. Bryan was bolstered by the gesture. Being welcomed as part of Mike's team felt like belonging to a family again. Coincidentally, after he'd fired Jerry, no more nasty notes had been delivered to his office or left for him under his windshield. Mike had taught him that strong leaders knew how to make hard decisions. This was the price. He was one of them now. *Is this what I thought it would feel like though?* Bryan wondered.

***

The next day, Laura was not at her desk. Bryan glanced at his watch: seven twenty-five. He was earlier than he thought.

A piece of paper was taped on his office door. There was nothing written on the side of the paper facing outward. It had been taped repeatedly and crudely to the door so that the layers of transparent adhesive had whitened, forming a vaguely cross-shaped design. Bryan stared at it for several seconds before yanking it off, tape and all.

He entered his office and closed the door. Bryan flipped the paper over to reveal a picture of a black monkey. It was drawn looking under the skirt of a muscular white man wearing a blond wig. Scrawled underneath in black permanent marker were the words "Monkeys like white she-hes." He crushed the paper into a ball, wishing he could burn it. *So much for the gesture of good will the other day*, he thought. His mind began turning like a hamster wheel. Should he ignore it or bring it up in a leadership meeting? Who could he tell? Maybe he could file a harassment claim with HR? *Is this how Jerry felt? Is this karma for me firing him?* Bryan wondered. He smoothed out the paper and folded it into a square. He decided he had to tell someone, and it may as well be HR. He hoped they would do the right thing even though they hadn't done it for Jerry. *Even though I'm a VP, am I really any different? Or am I just a black man with questionable sexuality?*

*　*　*

His bladder felt uncomfortably full from the tension, so Bryan raced to the restroom on the same floor as HR and the other executive offices. The men's restrooms were the same on every floor—two urinals, two stalls, two basins, and a large mirror. There was nothing special about the one on this hallowed floor other than the fact that it was the bathroom Mike and other executives used. He generally chose the taller urinal because there was less chance to make a mess. His entire life, the conditions had to be perfect for him to pee in public. All the stress rolling around in his head made the process take even longer and was made that much worse by the black laced shoes visible in the first stall.

The door banged open, and Mike entered the restroom, unzipping while the door was still swinging wide. He went to the urinal to Bryan's left, divided from Bryan by a metal partition.

"Just when you thought you knew somebody," Mike said, his voice soft. From the sound of liquid tinkling against metal, Mike seemed to be aiming away from the urinal toward the dividing wall. Was this gesture meant that he was pissing on Bryan?

"Yeah," Bryan agreed carefully. He wondered who had dared cross Mike.

"You gay fruitcake," Mike continued in the same congenial tone. The clash between his tone and the words was so jarring and disorienting, Bryan wondered if he'd misheard. He would have lost his balance if he hadn't let go of his member and braced himself with one hand against the metal partition.

"You know, I try to do things for you and your community. I mentored you and promoted you. I invited you to my house for dinner with my wife. Hell, I even adopted a Black kid. And you repay me by hooking up with that....that thing? I put my ass on the line for you, and this is how you pay me?"

Bryan's urine crawled back up his urethra, poisoning his bloodstream, sickening his stomach. His whole body clenched.

"You gays are sick, no exception." Mike's voice was almost a croon and far more frightening than any scream or uncontrollable yelling. He was in full possession of his facilities and knew precisely what he was saying. "I don't want any of you on my team, for sure, or anywhere in this company."

Bryan was holding his breath. There was a faint sound of something hitting the floor in his mind. He wasn't sure if it was real or in his imagination. He squinted as if he could see it if he tried. Somewhere, the metal pin holding his fear of being outed was yanked out. It was a live hand grenade that was now rolling around on the dirty bathroom floor.

Mike banged on the metal partition with a fist, which jolted Bryan so violently, it woke him from his initial paralysis. He zipped his pants, ready for whatever was coming.

Mike barked out a laugh. "I'm going to get rid of all you fruitcakes. This is what I get for a diversity hire . . . you're disgusting." He blubbered his lips in a performance of crazed revulsion.

Bryan began to breathe shallowly. Mike hadn't wanted Jerry's blood on his hands, so he'd used Bryan. Now his boss was attempting to dismantle another Black man's manhood, so he, too, would leave the company.

"Weak, weak, weak. Just look at what happened at that nightclub, full of you and your weak faggot friends. Serves y'all right."

In his reflection, Bryan observed a vague resemblance of himself, disfigured by all his own fears and lies and foolishness. He clamped his eyes shut against the vision, clenching his jaw even tighter.

"I promoted you to try to give a Black guy a chance. Black lives matter, right?" Mike's tone was high and mocking.

The grenade detonated. The bathroom had become his Alamo.

Before his brain knew what his body was doing, Bryan leaped around the metal barrier and charged at Mike like a panther, yelling, "Jessica is a person. Jerry is my friend. You son of a bitch. You're not going to abuse me or the people I care about anymore!"

He slammed Mike's face into the urinal piping, his bottom lip bleeding from the hit. Bryan jammed his foot into the back of Mike's knee, dropping him. As he went down, Mike's watch hit the urinal, shattering the clockface and stopping time.

Bryan pushed his boss's face closer to the inside of the unflushed urinal. Mike, gagging and grunting with effort, freed an arm and pushed back, using the urinal as leverage. Staggering to his feet and swinging wildly, he struck Bryan in his midsection and slammed him into the metal divider. They were breathing raggedly.

Bryan reached into the bowl and rubbed a handful of piss into Mike's face. "That's for making me fire Jerry." Mike screamed and wildly threw an elbow, distracting Bryan enough that he loosened his grip. Mike attempted to stagger to the faucet, but Bryan jumped on his back, thrashing his boss's head from side to side. Mike stumbled backward across the bathroom floor and rammed Bryan into the mirror. Glass showered the floor.

"You . . . stupid," Mike gasped, "motherfucker."

The toilet flushed from an inside stall. A middle-aged man emerged—the one with the black laced shoes.

"Bryan, Mike, stop this now," his voice boomed like a teacher scolding them. He stepped over them to get to the basin.

"What the hell is wrong with you two?" He said, briefly washing his hands at the still intact mirror and moving out of the way. "I'm not getting involved in anything that smells this foul." He sidled out just as security burst in and separated the two men.

Bryan was escorted out of the restroom, his arms restrained by security guards on each side. His coworkers popped their heads up from cubicles and clustered in small groups, bewildered by all the blood and drama. These were the people he admired and people who admired him. He cast his eyes down as he was led to the first floor. He noticed a patch of Mike's blood on his shirt—the same color and shape of the blurry kiss left on the Porsche's windshield months ago.

Bryan was placed in a room on the first floor. Alone. He sat slumped in his chair. *What have I done?* he thought. He stood up, twisting to his left, then back to his right. There was nothing in the room but the singular chair he was sitting in and the small table in front of it. He paced the length of the small room, then sat back down. *Is this where they take everyone before they get fired? Shit! Shit! Shit! I'm going to get fired.* He laid his head in his hands, trying to hold back tears. *In what world is assaulting your boss not grounds for firing?* The door opened and Bryan sat up straight, mentally preparing for the inevitable. The head of building and corporate security entered and handed Bryan something.

"Is this yours, Mr. Hicks?" The man standing in front of him was tall and unfamiliar to Bryan. He glanced down and saw the man was holding his phone.

Bryan took it, registering Nadia's picture in the cracked glass.

"Mr. Hicks, we have spoken with Mr. Mike Murphy, who claims you attacked him. Mr. Caldwell, the gentleman in the restroom at the time of the argument, corroborates Mr. Murphy's version of events. Based on these statements, it is clear that you started this altercation."

"This was not my fault."

"Mr. Hicks, look at me."

Bryan finally raised his eyes to meet the man's gaze.

"I've spoken with HR. You're terminated as of today."

Bryan was incredulous. "You're firing me? After everything Mike's done or has allowed to occur at this company?" Panicked, he rambled on. "So many good people were harassed just like me."

A man from HR entered the room. He was white and looked about twenty. Another Mike Murphy in the making. Bryan continued, "So many people have felt too unsafe to come to work. Including myself. This is bullshit."

"Mr. Hicks, did you tell anyone about any harassment going on at the company?" the guy from HR asked, his tone even.

Teary-eyed, Bryan shook his head no.

"Why not?" Mr. HR's eyes were a clear and earnest blue, with no real humanity behind them. "As you know, this company does not tolerate such treatment of its employees. Was someone harassing you?"

Bryan nodded. "Mike."

"Why didn't you tell anyone? His supervisor?"

"The CEO. Seriously. I received..." Bryan was about to reveal everything to Mr. HR. The nasty notes, the forced firing of Jerry. But his own embarrassment stopped him.

A younger man came into the room. "Excuse me, sir," he said to the head of building security. "The police are waiting outside."

Bryan was flabbergasted. "You called the police on me?"

The head of security looked at Bryan for a few beats, as if weighing something. "We're okay here." The young man left.

"Someone from HR will be in touch regarding sending your personal items back to you in a timely manner, and any property-damage claims the company chooses to file against you."

Bryan cringed.

"Mr. Hicks, if I were you, I would say my prayers that Mr. Murphy doesn't file criminal charges against you. Do you understand?"

All of his organs seemed to drop down into his legs. His feet were leaden. His breath was caught somewhere.

"Mr. Hicks?"

"Yes," Bryan said, chastened. He could seriously become yet another incarcerated Black man.

"One of my officers will escort you outside."

Squinting against the blinding midmorning sun, Bryan glimpsed his reflection in the building's glassy facade. His swollen hands dangled out of the raggedy cuffs of an untucked shirt, blotchy with blood and dirty water stains. One jacket sleeve, half-torn away, was hanging by a literal thread. His belt was missing, which caused his trousers to sag. He did not recognize himself.

A vulture flew down, landing on the Porsche's roof, while a second one fed on a squirrel carcass near the driver's-side door. Bryan waved his arms, trying to shoo the scavengers away. The bird on his car roof looked him over languidly, hissed twice, and flew off with the grace and insouciance of a teenager.

Both birds glared at Bryan over gaunt, hunched shoulders, as if watching him march toward his death. *Soon,* they threatened.

34

B ack at his high-rise, Bryan finally peed in his own clean toilet. He reeked of urine, but his own shame and embarrassment gave off a stronger, more repugnant smell. Bryan barely remembered driving home. It was probably the last trip he would take in the Porsche. There was no way he could afford it now, and he felt foolish for giving up his Jag. The shower water ran over his bruised torso and smashed ego. His body shivered from the cold temperature and the realization of his mistakes. How would he pay for Lindsey's college, Lance's child support, and support his own lifestyle?

He wrapped a towel around his waist and stumbled out of the bathroom into his living room, as if the larger room that housed his precious possessions would supply the answer. Despite the chaos swirling around him, his home was the epitome of order. His paintings were professionally framed, his furniture high quality, comfortable, and well placed in each room. Polished mahogany bookshelves contained exhibition catalogs from his favorite museums: lush art books on Degas, Dalí, and Kahlo and leather-bound classic novels chronicled alphabetically by the author. Dozens of cookbooks were organized by regional cuisine and interspersed with the corresponding sommelier and whiskey guides. One whole shelf was devoted to sartorial expertise, including *Dressing the Man: Mastering the Art of Permanent Fashion.*

The same order that had once soothed him now tormented him. Ignoring his skin color was naive. His knees buckled, and, suddenly, he was on the floor. He tilted his head back to take in his college degree and traced the edges of an old college tome on differential equations with an index finger. Resting his forehead against a book titled *Nobody Knows My Name*, he spoke to the empty room.

"Don't they see I'm more than just my race and my sexuality—whatever that means to them? I am a person."

As hard as he'd worked, as much as he'd achieved, as articulate, educated, and well-dressed as he was, and as much as he'd tried to date the right women, he was not protected by success or good taste. It was impossible for him to be above the fray or anything else.

He was so tired of playing the white man's game. He stood back up and tipped a book from the shelf, watching it tumble to the floor. The feeling of destruction felt oddly satisfying. He grabbed another book and tossed it over his head. A third book. A tenth. Sweeping his arms over every flat surface in the room, he knocked down pictures of the kids, sent knick-knacks flying in all directions.

"What was all this for?!" he screamed.

In his closet, he tore suits and shirts from their hangers and threw his shoes about like a madman. He yelled at the ceiling. "Why can't I just be who I want to be? Fuck!" He wanted to cry but couldn't.

The moonlight changed colors like a bruise. Leaden, he laid down, exhausted, wanting to die. The moon peered down at him as if looking over reading glasses, professorial and disapproving.

"I'm so damn tired. Even my mother doesn't love me anymore," he said, tears flowing freely. His eyes closed.

***

The next thing he knew, he was on the interstate doing ninety, his windshield blurred with dirty water. Taking the exit for The Yellow Brick Road, he crossed over into the strip, no longer a slave to others. He lowered his windows and turned up his music as he cruised. The voices of girls transitioning, in all of their various stages, sounded to him like a symphony tuning up. He screeched into a parking spot under a streetlamp. Strutting down the street like an uncaged lion, he walked into the trans bar, Cousins. He took in the bar, trying to place how it was different from straight bars. There were a few high tables, a well-worn pool table, and a jukebox playing nineties pop hits. He swaggered to the bar, filling a small opening between three transgender girls.

"Excuse me." He had to yell over the music. "I hate to interrupt." Bryan inclined his body toward them. "May I get you ladies a round of drinks?"

The dark-skinned one giggled. "I guess it's my lucky night!"

He pulled her close by her waist and they kissed. She tasted like the lime gimlets she had been drinking, Bryan found himself just as intoxicated as she was.

Outside, they kissed again under the streetlamp. In the Porsche, she sank into the premium leather, revealing the slit in her short skirt. He put the car in drive, though it took him a few times to work the gearshift. He silently told the sanctity of his virginity to skedaddle.

He squealed out, nearly sideswiping a Volkswagen Bug. Showing off the engine's power, Bryan floored the accelerator, only to come to a dead stop only a few hundred feet away. There was a loud growl as the bottom of the car scraped the pavement.

His passenger unclicked her seatbelt to squirm around, wiggling her back-side toward him, crossing and uncrossing her legs. "Ooh, baby, you and this car make me horny."

His voice was stern. "Put your seatbelt back on."

She ignored him. Lifting her hips, she shucked off her panties in one move-ment and tossed the wad of lace into his lap. "I love bi-curious boys. I promise, I'm going to coax you out of that iron closet," she said, laughing confidently, as she fondled herself.

"What's that supposed to mean?"

"Look at tonight as reverse-conversion therapy," she hooted. "Does your mama know you're going to be my gay boy tonight?" she asked in a faux-in-nocent manner, rubbing the inside of Bryan's thigh.

"Leave my mama out of this," Bryan ordered.

"You don't want your mama to know you like sucking off girls, do you?"

"I said, leave my mama out of this," he scowled, pressing down on the accel-erator. The dotted white lane markings on the road grew into giant snowflakes, then blown-out flowers. A dark shape, a shade darker than the midnight sky, slumped in the middle of the road. Bryan's headlights gradually illuminated two vultures with slick black heads, ravenously feeding on a large carcass. As the car approached, one bird flew off in a great flapping of wings. The other bird stood its ground, glaring at Bryan. He lowered his window and waved his hand, yelling at the bird to get out of the way. It didn't move as much as a feather.

There was no other choice but to swerve to the left into oncoming traffic. A yank of the wheel to the right would be disastrous. Jumping the median, the Porsche flipped over twice, his passenger flopping around like a rag doll. The car landed right side up, with the side and front airbags deployed and the radio hissing static.

Groggy and semiconscious, with blood running down his face, Bryan touched his forehead to make sure there wasn't a gash. His head throbbed, but he couldn't feel any cuts. Still able to move his toes and fingers, he reached around inside the car until he felt his passenger's bare leg, which was covered in blood. He wiped the blood away, and let his eyes travel up her body. He noticed her head was thrown back against the headrest, but he couldn't reach over to tell if she was breathing.

***

After what could have been hours or days later, Bryan opened his eyes and blinked. His body felt battered, and his neck was sore. Sunlight ribboned in, but he didn't know if it was sunrise or sunset. For several minutes, he was immobilized by vertigo, which caused the room to spin like a Tilt-A-Whirl. Moaning, he rolled to his right side and glanced down at his naked body. There was no blood, but every inch of his skin felt ill-used, stretched tightly over his bones. Indigo and yellow bruises resembling planets and their moons orbited his torso.

Panic seized his throat. *My passenger,* he wondered. With fumbling fingers, Bryan googled the nearest hospital and pressed the icon to call them. A curt voice asked where he wanted his call directed.

"Emergency patients . . . uh, car accident victims," he stammered.

A muffled voice answered. The nurse was finishing a bite of something.

Bryan said, "I'd like to check on the status of someone brought in last night."

There was the sound of swallowing. "Name?"

He embarrassingly admitted that he did not know her name but described her as a Black transgender woman in a car accident around one o'clock in the morning.

"Sir," the nurse interrupted him. "No one of that description has been admitted during the last twenty-four hours." In a kinder voice, she asked, "Are you sure . . . she was sent to this hospital?"

He was beginning to doubt more than just the name of the hospital. "I'll double-check," he said. "And thank you." He hoped his emphasizing that phrase conveyed his gratitude for the nurse describing his passenger by the correct pronoun.

The heaviness of his head was too much for his stiff neck, and he couldn't lift himself off the pillow. Images of the night before flashed before his eyes. The no-name woman who was cackling, taunting him about telling his mama. The vultures he'd seen in the road, and how he'd crashed the car to avoid them. The carcass upon which the birds were feeding was more apparent to him in recollection. It had been a human body. Man or woman, he hadn't seen. *We all look alike in the dark,* he thought. *On a dark road at night, we are all simply black shapes, half-formed, unfinished. Vulnerable to fantastical or nightmarish projections.* The more he thought about the previous night, the less he was sure if he really saw those birds. Or if his passenger was real. He had no true sense of what might have happened or what he'd imagined. This not-knowing shook him to his core. His body trembled violently on the bed. Overwhelmed by the crush of his thoughts, he squeezed out a solitary tear. *I can't even cry anymore*, he thought as he felt himself slip into a half sleep state.

Hours later, Bryan shot up in bed: it was a dream. He'd dreamt the woman. He hadn't left his room. Relief like a benediction forced his head low, and the enormity of his life rushed into his consciousness and coalesced into a weight he could no longer carry. He finally cried. He cried about Nadia and his mama. He cried about Jerry, and about not having a job. He cried for Lance, wishing he could be better for him. He cried for the younger version of himself who had been told that being Black meant he wasn't allowed to be anything else.

35

After a darkness that seemed interminable, during which Bryan had slept-walked through his days with the dread of a lawsuit from Mike wearing him down, he woke up one morning and felt more alive than dead.

He realized that he couldn't live as if he were under the blade of a guillotine. To Mike, a fired employee was not worth the trouble of a lawsuit. He had too many current employees to threaten, coax, thwart, mislead with false hope, and intimidate toward ever-greater productivity. Besides, having a judge peer into the company's discriminatory practices would not be pretty. These thoughts gave Bryan hope, and he realized that logically Mike would benefit more from not pursuing a lawsuit.

With relief came energy. Bryan cleaned the entire house, room by room, a rag tied over his head to stop the sweat from dripping into his eyes. Hands on hips, he surveyed his home, now recognizable. He showered, then took a stroll to the closest coffee shop for an overpriced latte. He just needed an excuse to put on real clothes for a change.

Inside the café, an ad for a week-long meditation at the Houston Zen center caught his attention. He checked the date on his watch and noticed that the retreat was starting the following day. While waiting for his latte, he called the number, spoke to an even-toned woman, and, before he knew exactly what he was doing or why, he'd signed up.

The next morning dawned fresh and clear, without a trace of Texas humidity. It was tempting to skip the retreat and take a drive, one last swan song with the Porsche. It would be returned at the end of the month, since there was no way he would be able to afford the payments. The car had been a foolish purchase, but it was the haunting of his dream that had transformed its red curves from a fiscally unwise pleasure to a horror show. He knew he needed to make a change, and spending a week somewhere else seemed to be the best way to start. So, he choked down some toast and coffee and left for the center.

Upon arriving, Bryan faltered at the gate. He had never done anything before that required focus and stamina for seven days straight. His body tingling with nerves, he pressed the buzzer and the gate swung open. Inside, a water fountain surrounded by fruit trees stood in front of a white stucco building. People of all ages and shapes milled around, every one of them white. Bryan felt his palms get sweaty and tried to swallow his nervousness upon seeing no other people of color. Remembering the reason he was there, he found his breath, which revealed the peace filling the space. He entered, smiling, with complete acceptance.

"This will be your home for the next seven days," a woman with a shaved head told him. Bryan surrendered his phone and clutched the meditation cushion given to him. He was also provided with robes and asked to change into them as they led him to his room. They felt cool and comfortable when he slipped them on. Briefly, he wondered if he looked like a cult member.

A person of indeterminate sex struck a thick wooden block, which he learned was called a han. Bryan was struck by how all the retreat workers and abbots, with shaved heads and flowing robes, presented effortlessly as unisex. Stripping gender markers such as makeup, jewelry, individuated clothing, and hairstyles also had this effect on most of the women who were attending the retreat. He remembered a biology professor lecturing about the many examples of female impersonation in nature. A stabbing pain in his solar plexus accompanied a shocking realization: he had made Nadia feel like she had to be perfect. His preference for dressing up, both for himself and his romantic interests, seemed shallow and dull. If he ever got the chance again, he wanted ardently to see Nadia waking up in his arms, barefaced.

He was the one Black person among the large group of young and middle-aged white people. Bowing respectfully to each other, they all gathered as one and moved like a wave into the meditation hall.

The han was hit again. The strikes grew closer together, signaling for all meditation practitioners to take their place on their cushion.

Carrying a pair of small, varnished Buddha bowls and a small card printed with the phrase "All of man's problems stem from his inability to sit with himself", Bryan found his spot on the floor in a bare, high-ceilinged space. Suddenly, the sound from the han faded into silence.

The presiding abbot was petite, swathed in overlapping brown robes that brushed against her pale, bare feet. In her child-sized hands, she carried a small wooden stick. Poised between good humor and gravity, she informed everyone that each day consisted of nine hours of sitting and walking meditation and three meals eaten in the Buddha bowls at one's cushion. Aside from the sermons, or dharma talks, all participants shall observe what she referred to as "noble" silence. She bowed and exited.

The first morning was relatively easy. Benefitting from a beginner's mind, *shoshin*—as well as meditating in a place other than his living room—fueled his concentration. He was able to watch the ticker tape of worries about Lance and Lindsey and various schemes for making money float by. He found his throat constricting every time the memory of firing Jerry floated through. As his mental chatter settled loudly into a groove, he lifted the needle on the record player of his mind and reset it on white noise. With eyes closed, he found his breath. Instead, he pictured a large nest. Using the fingers of his mind, he unraveled the roughly woven concavity twig by twig, a sensual exercise that opened up to the unknown again. He had seen this before, but only the mind had gotten quiet. He felt his body at peace with the darkness because his mind was starting to come to terms with it. It all took Herculean effort, and by lunch he was famished.

They were instructed to fill their bowls with water and food that was presented by the server. There were no dishwashing services, and they were expected to clean their bowls with a piece of bread, which they ate afterward. In this system, no waste was created.

Bryan piled his bowl with food, which he devoured, and refilled the vessel with an even bigger portion. Halfway through, his stomach distended, and he couldn't imagine eating another bite. But he had to finish every morsel. The abbot, noticing his distress, squatted beside him.

"Next time," she whispered kindly, "take only what you need. In all areas of life. Your discomfort is a gift to you and will serve as a reminder the next time you are tempted to overindulge."

The malaise remained with him for the rest of the week, and he consumed so little food that he was often lightheaded. Sometimes, this weightlessness helped him through the long hours of meditation, his solidity tuned to the ether that merged with the vaporous energy garlanding the globe. Other times, the strength drained from his spine, and holding himself upright on the cushion was so painful that tears leaked from his eyes. His knees, hips, shoulders, neck, lower back, and ankles throbbed. Even his wrists twinged. He moved through what seemed like hours when everything itched or prickled with pins and needles or trembled with fatigue.

The vibration of the silence also changed as the week passed. Peaceful and cozy as a lamb on the first day, it accumulated fleece and heft hour by hour until it became waxy, scratchy, suffocating. The unremitting silence felt loud. Somehow both unsubstantial and cottony, like snowflakes. A shroud settled around everything, while the drums of his heartbeat echoed in his ears.

On the third afternoon, Bryan was rewarded with a breakthrough. He remembered the accident from his dream. The silence allowed for closer inspection of the corpse in his dream and he saw his face on the corpse, his eyes devoured by vultures. Looking at the corpse, Bryan became sad. He saw his scared self, the ego self. Facing his ego, the vultures flew away. Tears streamed down his cheeks as he opened his eyes.

Though talking was still forbidden outside the main meditation room, Bryan felt more at ease milling among people in the common areas. He relished both the movements and sounds of his chores. Assigned on the third evening to one of several sous-chef positions for dinner preparation, he was happily peeling carrots for a huge vat of curried soup. For the first time in his life, he saw himself in the service of others as he worked in the kitchen.

He finished the sixth day by meditating with the rest of the participants well into the late night. The bell rang, ending the day's session, but something tugged at Bryan to keep sitting. He slid further away from his ego, hearing the sound of nothingness, which allowed his truth to be heard: I am. He felt the seeds of a new life beginning to germinate inside of him, begging him to seek out answers to questions he needed to ask. He sat until morning sun shone through the meditation hall. He continued to sit the entire day.

At the conclusion of the seven days, Bryan emerged, wobbly and squinting against the glare of sunlight. As he said goodbye to his fellow meditators and the Abbott, he was buzzing with self-acceptance, aching knees, and the power of the present moment. The stillness had swaddled him like a cocooned larva, and he felt new wings poking out of his old habits. He tilted his head back and saw the September sky as if he was seeing clouds for the first time.

Bryan embraced this new curiosity for the world around him, no longer paralyzed by shame and confusion. He wandered through the city, stopping at the front door of a rectangular white two-story building with square windows bordered in red, green, and blue. The sign read "The Montrose Center". He opened the door, his curiosity carrying him.

"Hi," Bryan said to a white lady with a very warm smile. Looking around, he asked, "What's this place?"

"We are a nonprofit to help our community—primarily lesbian, gay, bisexual, transgender individuals and their families—live healthier, more fulfilling lives," she said, smiling back at Bryan. "Are you lost?"

Bryan's heart suddenly filled with a joy that he had been missing. "For once, no. Ma'am, can you help me?"

The person at the counter tilted her head just a little, standing more erect to pay closer attention. Bryan felt something rising up in him and took a deep breath.

"I am attracted to transgender women," Bryan mumbled. The woman kindly asked him to repeat himself, and he repeated himself loudly. "Is there something wrong with me?" He lowered his head. "I am so confused about who I am."

"There is nothing wrong with you. You are perfect as God made you," she said, picking up two pamphlets: one about gender identity and gender expression, and the other about sexual attraction. "Let's start here."

***

Later that week, Bryan stopped by the same coffee shop with the overpriced coffee to apply for a full-time position as a barista. Though he had no experience, he was hired on the spot. The manager, a pimply twenty-five-year-old, had goggled his eyes at Bryan's resume and squeaked out a "Sir?" before offering Bryan the job in an almost normal voice. Everyone knew someone down on their luck. Also, Bryan was more than happy to take the daily four-thirty morning shift because it allowed him to start attending the weekly Coming Out Support Group meetings at the Montrose Center.

After three weeks of sessions, he began to feel a sense of family. He joined a group therapy session, he sat with other men who were coming to terms with their trans-amorous identities. For the first time in his life, he had a safe place to ask questions and learn about how to come out and who to tell. He was finding his family. He learned that he did not fit the traditional norms, and that the term "queer" was the most accurate descriptor for him. *Queer. Isn't that a slur*, he thought the first time he heard it. The term queer was new to him, but he was learning that words could take on whatever meaning he chose. Now he felt pride when he heard the term. This explained his attraction to trans women and his desire to be submissive which was only possible as a sexually fluid person. He started reading queer coming out biographies and memoirs from a recommended list from his counselor. He started to feel better and stronger. One morning while meditating, he opened his eyes and the universe spoke. He had found his letter in the lexicon. Q. Queer. He cried deeply. He had gained everything he needed once he embraced the unknown. He stood and said out loud to the empty room, "I am queer. I'm a straight queer man."

Now that he could afford his electricity bill without dipping into savings, Bryan knew it was time, past time, to do some relationship repairing. He found the number for Jerry in his contacts and pressed the Call button, holding his breath.

Each unanswered ring deepened Bryan's despair of Jerry taking the call. Finally, he picked up. "Yes?" The voice was acerbic.

"Hi, Jerry. It's me, Bryan," he began. "I'm calling to apologize. Again. I'm so sorry I fired you." The words tumbled faster out of his mouth. "It was weak-willed and unconscionable. I didn't want to get my hands dirty. Honestly, I didn't realize how selfish and unsupportive I was acting. I was wrong. I promise to be conscious of myself from now on, if you will still have me as a friend."

After a long pause, Jerry spoke. "I see."

"Man, you were right. I should have stood up to those guys a long time ago." Due to a brutal combination of deep shame and trauma, he was breathing quickly and speaking high up in his throat. "Long story short, I was outed by Mike. And then I started getting harassed." Bryan shuddered at the memory of the monkey picture on his door. The awful note on his windshield. "Not to center myself, but it was some seriously scary, racist shit."

Jerry whistled. "'Not to center myself'? That's some impressive ally speak."

"Oh, man, I'm sorry, I just—" Bryan stammered. "I've been trying to truly understand our community. I've been doing a lot of reading and a lot of soul-searching."

Jerry cut him off. "No, I mean it. It shows a lot of growth. You don't sound like the little mouse I used to know."

Bryan exhaled, so happy for the pamphlets and the staff at the Montrose Center.

"I'm truly sorry they did that to you. I do understand you were caught between a rock and a hard place," Jerry admitted.

"Yeah, but that's not an excuse. I could've done better. I'm a smart guy. I could've gotten another job."

"You saying that means a lot," Jerry said. "And I have to admit, before you berate yourself to the high heaven, that you firing me turned out to be the best thing for me." There was pride in his voice. "I started my own business, and it's going well."

"Really?" Bryan's relief was palpable. "That's great. What kind of business?"

"Wedding planning."

"I'm sure you're so good at that," Bryan enthused. He meant it but sensed Jerry didn't believe him unless he personalized his congratulations. He risked a joke. "You've got great taste, and you're pushy and like to be in charge. Brides must cower before you and be grateful for your bossiness on their perfectly orchestrated big day."

Jerry guffawed. It was genuine laughter, which relieved Bryan more than he had ever imagined it would.

"Man, you have no idea. I was so worried when you were out of the office in Louisiana that I hallucinated an Imaginary Jerry who haunted me." He giggled.

Jerry hooted with delight. "We should catch up again soon."

Bryan smiled, happy to be reunited with his friend. "You're right. It's been a few years since we've seen each other outside of work."

"Have you heard from Nadia lately?" Jerry asked, his tone turning serious.

Bryan stopped laughing. Hearing her name still hurt him viscerally. "No. I miss her a lot. Are you and your boyfriend still together?"

"We are, thanks for asking," Jerry said. "I hope you find a relationship like ours, I really do. Let's get drinks sooner rather than later.

"Aw, thanks, man, even though you're just saying that so I'll hire you to plan my wedding." The sound of Jerry's warm laughter was music to Bryan's ears.

***

A few weeks later, he was plowing through the morning rush at eight thirty. Whenever Bryan steamed milk or pressed the button to grind espresso beans, which smelled of sweet earth, the loud sounds were rewarding. They meant he was helping someone start their day. Surrounded by college-educated twenty-year-olds who were waiting for something better to come along, he knew he seemed goofy. A few of his coworkers had gently teased him for being in such a good mood every day without fail.

"You don't know how deep I had to go to mine this peace," he told them.

He prepared his next drink, a vanilla-flavored espresso, making it expertly and in record time, and handed the specialty java to one of his regulars with a smile. The woman who was next in line towered over everyone and was frowning at her phone. She wore a white chef's uniform top with black pants, her name stitched over her heart. Not that he wouldn't know her without it. He felt his heart flutter. Nadia. Had Jerry conjured her up?

Before she reached the counter, Bryan snatched off his barista hat and changed positions with the cashier. When Nadia looked up from her phone, he smiled with his whole face.

"Hello, what can I get for you?" Nadia blinked rapidly. "Bryan? I didn't recognize you! You're working here?"

"This one is on me," Bryan said. His hands trembled as he poured cream into her coffee. A moment later, he walked around the counter to personally deliver her order. "I'm due a break. Do you mind if I join you?" Bryan asked.

She took a sip, her gaze fastened on his left shoulder. "I only have a few minutes," she said, pulling a lock of hair behind her ear. "You've lost some weight."

Bryan removed his apron and followed her to a far corner like a lost puppy who had found his owner.

"How is that latte?" Bryan asked, leaning forward. "You know, people drive clear across town for my espresso drinks."

She laughed politely. The days were over when Bryan could win her with just charm.

"What are you doing here today?" Bryan asked.

"I'm getting my car inspected. There's a two-hour wait, so I decided to treat myself to a cup of coffee." She stared out the large window. "So, when did you become a barista?"

"A little more than a month ago," he said, waving goodbye to a regular.

"What happened to your management position?"

"Fortunately, I was fired." Her face registered shock. "At least I'm no longer contributing to the destruction of the environment."

"It seems like you're looking at things differently now."

"I see a lot of things differently now. Getting fired was one of the best things to happen to me. Next to you being in my life."

She gave him a weak smile.

"And you? I hope you're getting closer to your dream of owning a cupcake shop."

"Well remembered," she said. "I'm working on my degree. I recently started a paid internship at The Walking Zebra, in the desserts department."

Bryan put his fist out for a bump, and as she returned it, her smile warmed up considerably. "That's wonderful," Bryan said. "That restaurant is supposedly fantastic. Are they treating you well?"

"Pretty well. Why were you fired?"

Bryan chuckled. "Long story, but I can tell it in three words: top-down racism and transphobia. Maybe that's four. Add antigay, and that's the triangle of terror there."

"That sounds like quite a story." She tucked her hair behind her ear. "I'd . . . like to hear it some time. You'd need to use more than three or four words."

His heart fluttered like a dove, and she allowed him to drive her back to the mechanic's shop.

"This beat-up old Honda is yours?" Nadia said, hands on the door handle. The door didn't budge.

"You have to open it from the inside," Bryan said, hurrying around to the driver's side. Nadia squeezed herself into the car, one long leg at a time.

"What's that smell?" she asked, holding her nose.

"I believe a mouse died. I've gotten used to it."

She cracked her window. "That's better. How are the kids?" Nadia asked.

"Lindsey will be home for the holidays in a few weeks. I think she'll finish the semester with a 3.8 GPA."

"Her competitive spirit in action. Good for her."

"As for Lance," Bryan's shoulders caved toward the steering wheel. "I don't know. We're having a hard time right now," Bryan said, driving slowly because the shocks were gone. "I don't listen well," Bryan admitted. "We fell out last August, and I haven't been able to fix things. He doesn't want to talk to me. His mama doesn't help, either. Some things don't change."

"You've changed." Nadia looked him in the eye for the first time. "You seem more authentic."

"You haven't changed at all. I can't believe it's been nearly a year since we've seen each other." Bryan rolled down his window so the manual squeak would fill the silence. "Speaking of Thanksgiving, how are Stacey and Sophia doing?"

Nadia choked back a sob. "You don't know, do you? Of course, the story never made the news. She wasn't some pretty white cisgender girl." Nadia's tone was bitter. "No one cares about where she was from. What she liked. Or all the wonderful things she did in her life." She was fully crying now, and Bryan patted her hand.

"Sophia is dead," Nadia said dully.

"What?" He looked over wildly at her. "What happened? When? I'm so sorry."

"She stopped answering her phone on a Thursday night in mid-June. She went missing for a week. The police found her naked body an hour outside the city next to a field. She-she . . ."—Nadia gulped air rather than breathed—"she had been strangled."

Bryan felt his own throat constrict when imagining what had happened to Sophia. Two hands, one of fear, the other of grief, pressed against his windpipe. Or was it rope, the smell of hemp braided tightly, the strands chafing and burning his skin. Sweet Sophia, with wisdom embedded in her very name, would have never been a jerk, but even if she had been, she didn't deserve to be murdered. Bryan felt nauseated. With his hands trembling on the steering wheel, the car seemed to drag itself sideways. He knew the answer before he asked, "Do the police have any leads?"

Nadia took a tissue from her purse and wiped her eyes. "A witness said she left a restaurant with a clean-shaven guy. He had a tattoo on his upper arm. The bartender remembered them because the guy drank some kind of rare whiskey? I don't remember. They believe the person is local, not someone passing through."

Bryan shivered at the memory of Mike drinking expensive bourbon. His tattoos. Was that why Mike had never pressed charges against Bryan after the bathroom scuffle? It was too sickeningly horrible to contemplate. "Why do the police think that?"

"There have been similar murders of Black trans women," Nadia said, taking a deep breath. "We are losing so many of our trans sisters of color, and no one cares. I read that more than twenty people from the trans community have been killed in this country this year alone, and most are Black trans women."

Bryan felt sick to his stomach. "I didn't know that. We never hear about this." Outside his window, a shadow of wings passed overhead, darker than the worn asphalt of the street. "How is Stacey? She okay?"

Nadia composed herself. "Well, she's heartbroken, too, but—" she shrugged, palms up. "You know Stacey. Nothing keeps her down for too long. She got a new car."

"Clicquot?"

She laughed. It wasn't yet her real laugh, but it was close. "No, she has all-new bottoms now."

They reached the mechanic's shop. "I want to say something," Bryan said, putting the car in park.

Nadia looked at him.

Bryan paused. "I want you to know that I've been taking *coming out* classes at the Montrose Center."

Nadia raised her eyebrows in disbelief, then smiled widely. She shook her head. "Are you messing with me?"

"No, seriously. You tried to talk to me and I had my head so far up my ass that I couldn't hear anything. I didn't want to listen. I am definitely straight and sexually queer."

"Maybe more queer than straight," she joked.

He nodded with a maybe. "I'm proud to be a queer Black man," Bryan said, "If nothing else, you deserve to hear that from me. Said out loud. After everything I put you through you deserve much more. I'm proud to stand by the trans community's side."

Nadia stared at him, looking at him as she did not know him. "No straight man has ever been this honest with me before."

"You deserve it. You deserve to be properly courted like any other woman." Bryan knew he was taking a considerable risk.

He paused, and she smiled. He decided to shoot his shot. "Can I call you?" he asked, not feeling confident enough to ask her permission to apologize. A bit of the tension in the car started to escape out along with the dead animal smell.

Nadia unzipped her wallet and handed over her business card: Nadia Brooks, Pastry Chef. "You can email me," she said. "No texting for now. We'll see how things go. Thanks for the ride." She smoothed a wisp of hair behind her ear as she exited the car.

37

On Election Day, November 8, Bryan and Nadia both worked early shifts. After voting in their respective precincts, Bryan suggested a trip to the Museum of Fine Arts. Otherwise, he argued, they would have spent the rest of the day glued to their TVs, stomachs clenched, as results were tallied. Nadia agreed but emphasized that the time spent together was more a distraction than something tangential to a date.

They had emailed about three times a week since their run-in at the café. Bryan wanted to email many times a day, but Nadia's boundaries limited them to a maximum of every other day. Nadia had asked him to treat her as he would a friend until she could ascertain that she could trust him again. That meant no fancy dinners—he couldn't afford them anyway—or alcohol consumption. No dressing up. Short meetings at cafés and occasional walks were all that Nadia was currently open to. On top of wanting to rebuild their friendship first, she was busy.

Bryan had listened to her list of demands and responded truthfully.

On their first planned meeting in over a year, Nadia expressed her hesitation about jumping back into a relationship and Bryan had said, "I will respect your boundaries and gladly build a friendship with you," he said. The gravity and emotion of his own words, along with the promises embedded in them, reminded him of a swearing-in ceremony. He wanted to cry tears of joy that she was letting him back into her life. "I will hope," he continued, "for more. But I promise I won't put any pressure on you."

Nadia had nodded her head once, businesslike and unsmiling.

As they approached the museum, Bryan remembered they had a deal. Bryan eased into a parking space. Nadia's hand was already on the door handle, preparing to exit the car.

"Wait," he said. "Before we go in, there's something that I have to tell you. Mike forced me to fire Jerry."

"Bryan," she said, her voice a husky whisper.

"I didn't have a choice."

"You had a choice," she said, her voice still low and leaden with disappointment. "Have you talked to him since then? Do you know if he is okay?"

"Yes. I called him, and we talked. He's doing well. He's a wedding planner now and is much happier. But I needed you to know."

"Yes, I did need to know that," Nadia said, her voice icy.

"I told him how sorry I was. I should have said something about people's working conditions earlier. I feel horrible that I acted the way I did." Bryan's jaw began to ache.

"And, what, he forgave you?"

"Not exactly," Bryan grimaced. "But he also understood the pressure I was under and the way corporate America works, or, rather, doesn't work." Through the windshield, he watched a swarm of grackles fighting over a few dropped crumbs. They sounded like a rusty gate in a hurricane. "It's not an excuse, but people in charge set things up so that everyone below them, usually women and minorities, are forced to do their dirty work."

Nadia's posture relaxed several degrees. "I can see that, I guess." She cocked her head. "I've never had a corporate job, but I've definitely had my share of job-related issues and injustices." She looked pointedly at Bryan. "Like Jerry. But I can also understand that you were put in a shitty position."

He turned toward her with a lightness in his chest. "I appreciate that," Bryan said. "You have no idea how much."

Nadia cracked her door open. "Let's go see some great art."

Bryan was out in a flash. He ran around the car to open Nadia's door all the way. "Yes, art I love, that I'm excited to experience with you, even though these pieces were frequently created using underpaid, uncredited underlings."

"Not to mention the countless models who were assaulted," Nadia added.

The air was brisk. Women had swapped out flip-flops for leather boots. In the grand entryway, a hush came over them both. "I'm glad you're taking some time off," Bryan whispered. "And that you agreed to let me take you here instead of for coffee."

Nadia tipped her head back to take in the ornate high ceiling. "All these years I have lived in this city, and this is my first time here."

"You're going to enjoy the Degas exhibit." He handed her an exhibit ticket. They waited in a short line. Once they were let inside, Bryan went straight to *The Dance Class*. "This is one of my favorite paintings."

Nadia paused. "I have so much respect for you now that you found your place in the community. Queer. I never ever thought I'd hear you say you were queer."

"Maybe it's not true. You can teach an old dog new tricks," Bryan replied.

"I need to ask you something," she said.

"Anything."

"The past three weeks have been fun, but you destroyed my trust in you and cis men. I would rather say goodbye today than continue like before."

"That's understandable. I was confused back then, but I'm not anymore. I am happy with who I am. And I have no problem with you setting the pace."

"How's your mother with the new Bryan?"

Bryan sighed. "She's not at all happy with this. I haven't talked to her since last Thanksgiving," he said.

"Oh, my goodness," she said, her eyes reddening with unshed tears. "I had no idea your mother could be that closed-minded." She reached for his hand, simultaneously comforting him and sending sparks up his spine. "No wonder you were so scared to tell her. I'm scared of her now."

"You shouldn't be."

"Why do you say that?"

"You stood up to her and her friends when you walked through that room like a Paris runway supermodel. They were scared of you."

"You really thought so?"

"Yes, because they don't understand you. All they know is what they see on TV. Their only reference is Flip Wilson dressed as Geraldine from the early seventies," he said.

"I don't know who Flip Wilson is."

"I'll show you," Bryan said, taking out his phone. He typed in the fictional character Geraldine in his browser.

Nadia leaned over to see the screen. The ends of her hair brushed against Bryan's arm, causing his skin to prickle delightfully. "This just shows we need more depictions in the media," she said. "So that one person or a few people are not representing an entire community."

"Nadia, can we sit down?" Bryan asked, slowly guiding her to a nearby bench. She nodded and sat down next to him.

"I want to apologize for my mistakes. Can I formally apologize?" Bryan asked. He wanted to signify the seriousness of his apology by asking her for permission.

Nadia tilted her head, making eye contact with him. "Apologize." Her demeanor turned serious. "I'm loving this," she said.

Bryan stood, pulling out a carefully folded piece of paper from his front pocket. He looked at Nadia, then began to unfold it. He cleared his throat, sitting back down.

"I know I hurt you, and I regret I did that," Bryan said, looking up, making eye contact with Nadia. "My pride and image were so important to me that my actions were nothing less than transphobic because I focused on you passing. That was wrong. You shouldn't have the pressure of passing forced on you," he said, loosening the tension in his shoulders. "That's my problem. Not yours. Secondly, I've learned to detach gender identity from sexual attraction. That is where my confusion grew from. I can be sexually queer, I can love being a bottom and still be a straight man who is attracted to women. In all of my confusion, I treated you horribly, as if loving you was a sin or something shameful. I was wrong and regret my actions because I hurt you. Thirdly, I fetishized you as a trans woman, and that was wrong. I never treated you like a full and complete woman, and I will never make that mistake again." He looked up, making eye contact again.

Nadia blinked.

"I spent more time exoticizing you than getting to know you," he admitted. "I liked that you desired me. Honestly, I loved it, but I can't just look at trans women and only think of sex just as I, or anyone, shouldn't with any woman."

Nadia nodded. "Yes. I am—we are—more than our genitals." She paused, seeming to gather her thoughts. She continued, "We want deep connections just like anybody else."

"I am sorry that I hurt you," Bryan said, folding up his paper. "But I also don't feel that saying 'I'm sorry' is enough. I want to make up for what I've done, if you'll allow me. What do you think is appropriate?"

Nadia folded her arms. After a pause, she said, "I have an idea."

"Okay, what do you have?" Bryan asked.

"Well, two things. First, can you tell me more about your mother's view?" she asked. "Like, do you know why this bothers her so much?"

"I don't fully understand it myself. She said something about what my father put her through and how she will not let me do the same thing to her," Bryan said, hesitating, "I have no idea what that means."

Nadia looked up, thinking. "You said that your father was very hard on you as a kid. Using gay slurs."

Bryan nodded yes.

"Do you think your father was on the DL? You know the down low, and she found out?" she asked, shrugging her shoulders.

Bryan stared at her in shock.

"I'm just saying," Nadia said, trying to fill the silence.

"Who? My father?" Bryan coughed as if he could clear the conversation out of the air.

"A closeted gay man? No way," Bryan said, laughing, "You can let that go. Okay, what's the next one because for the first time, I'm happy with who I am, and I'm not changing for nobody. So, Mama will just have to be mad." He smiled.

"Well, I'm going to wait to tell you the second one," she said.

"I can live with that," Bryan agreed. "I've enjoyed the past few weeks, just talking, getting to know you. I've learned things about you that I never knew."

"Like what?"

He counted off his fingers. "Your favorite color is green, and your celebrity crush is Chris Hemsworth.

"I will admit, I'm surprised that your celebrity crush is Kate Beckinsale." She pursed her lips. "I always thought you liked tall girls."

"I do." He chuckled at the hint of jealousy she had revealed. It was a positive sign. "But, oh man, watching her in Underworld in that tight black leather . . ." he trailed off. "Hey, you ready to go see some more exhibits?"

After wandering the museum for two hours, they walked to the car, holding hands. This was another first since they came back into each other's lives. He opened the car door for her.

"You want to come over for Christmas?" Nadia asked.

His heart flew out of his chest, ruby red as the Degas birds. "Seriously?"

"Yes. My parents are coming into town. There is no reason for you to be at home alone."

He flapped his arms, strutting like a peacock.

"What are you doing?"

"I'm dancing."

Nadia grinned. "You fool. Is that a yes?"

Bryan stopped dancing. "I don't want to spend another holiday without my best friend."

Nadia folded her long body into the car. "You mean Reggie?"

"No. You."

Bryan revved the engine. "I spent so much time focused on outside appearances that I neglected everything else."

The two of them looked at each other silently for a full minute—something Bryan could not have done before the Buddhist retreat. Nadia broke eye contact first. "That warms my heart to know," she said. "I missed your friendship, too." She glanced down at her phone. "This election better swing our way, or we'll be needing friends more than ever."

***

On Christmas morning, Bryan paused before knocking on Nadia's apartment door, partly because he was nervous about meeting her parents, though less so than he had been a year ago. He could hear the sounds of clattering dishes and murmured conversation, punctuated with booming laughter from outside the door. The raucous enjoyment of a family at ease made him jealous. Even when things were not as acutely fraught, his family had been more stilted, hewing closely to decorum, even within the walls of their own house.

Nadia answered his knock. She was wearing a natural wash of makeup and an old pair of jeans. Her hair was in a frizzy, loose ponytail. Pecking his cheek, she said, "Welcome, come in."

Two middle-aged white people got up from the couch and joined them in the entryway. "Mom and Dad, this is Bryan. Bryan, my parents, Lisa and Greg." Taller than his daughter, Nadia's dad had brown hair streaked with gray and beetle-browed, which added to his formidability. In heels, her mother was taller than Bryan. He felt a bit like a shrub among redwoods.

Bryan handed Nadia her Christmas gift, a Danez Smith poem cut into puzzle pieces, and a good bottle of wine for her parents, which they accepted graciously. As soon as they all sat down, Bryan felt more at ease. Her father's name was perfect for his gregarious personality, and her mother radiated warmth. They welcomed Bryan into their circle of conviviality, easily jumping from one topic to another.

Greg leaned in. "You know, my daughter loves taking care of animals, including strays."

"Yes." Bryan grinned, thinking of Brad Kitt.

In a stage whisper, Greg added, "Like her mother, who took this mutt in"—at this, he gestured at himself—"and I've been grateful every day since."

They all laughed.

"Anyway, Nadia was about ten, and she had spent hours making a cake as a surprise for her mother's birthday. This stray dog we'd taken in at her pleading—we called him Bubba—ate most of that cake while we were blindfolding her mother in the other room for the surprise! I'm talking mere seconds. Nadia cried for two days."

Nadia called from the kitchen good-naturedly. "All right, Dad, that's enough." She emerged, bearing steaming platters. "And dinner's ready." Bryan marveled at the precise, elaborate manner in which Nadia had cooked and laid out an entire Christmas meal in her limited space.

For a while, there was no sound except forks scraping against plates and the clack of tongs around deliciously roasted meat.

Her mother licked her spoon. "Mmm, honey, I just love this cranberry sauce. Is that apricot and allspice I taste?"

"Yes, Mama. I experimented."

Her father crossed his fork over his knife on his nearly dishwasher-clean plate and folded his napkin. "So, Bryan, where do you stand on politics, young man?"

"Greg, we're enjoying ourselves," Nadia's mother said, swatting his arm. "Bryan, you don't have to answer any of his questions."

Undeterred, Nadia's dad leaned back and crossed his arms. "I'm glad that woman lost. She was going to ruin our country. Trump's going to make a great law-and-order president." He laced his hands behind his head. "So we can get our country back from people like my daughter. These bleeding-heart liberals."

In Bryan's peripheral vision, Nadia rolled her eyes. He sensed her father was testing him.

"Oh yes, Sir. Isn't that what Make America Great Again is all about? You know, so good white folks feel safe from all the immigrants, Blacks, Jews, and gays they've been redlining, locking up, disenfranchising, and legislating against? Not to mention killing? I concur completely. Otherwise, who would we blame when things go wrong?"

"Wow," her father said, beaming at Nadia.

"I told you, Daddy."

"Young man, I had to see what you were made of. Any man serious about my daughter needs to be able to articulate where he stands." He slapped Bryan on the shoulder.

Bryan took a big swallow of water. "White people," he muttered, and all four of them laughed.

"Lisa and I are, or were, Republicans, but we voted for Hillary. Trump is a dangerous cretin." Her father grimaced. "That much has been obvious from the beginning to anyone with two brain cells to rub together."

"I'm still in shock over the election," Bryan admitted. The other three murmured their agreement.

"I hope and pray he's not as awful as I think he is," Nadia's mother said wistfully. She tucked a lock of hair behind her ear in the same gesture as her daughter, though she wore hers in a bob instead of down her back. "But I'll be damned if he ruins this Christmas."

Lisa swore just as she spoke in her sweet Hill Country accent. Bryan couldn't help comparing her to his mama, who would never risk her status by cursing but was strong and steady in her way. The two women would get along like a house on fire—if his mama could come around to accept his identity.

The men cleared the plates. Bryan was about to wash the dishes when Greg tapped him on the shoulder. "Leave it, son. I appreciate it, but I'll do it later. Let's rejoin our women."

When the sun started to set, Bryan got up to leave. He and Greg shared a warm handshake, and Lisa hugged him. "Bryan, thank you for spending Christmas with us," she said. "Nadia told us that you and your family are going through a rough patch. Things will get better over time, I promise."

Bryan was filled with gratitude and sadness in equal measure. He didn't have the heart to tell Lisa that he and his own mother would never reconcile. "Thank you."

Propelling him toward the door, Nadia said, "I'm walking Bryan to his car."

Once outside, she kissed him quickly on the mouth. Their first kiss in over a year. Bryan thought he'd be disappointed at the lack of fanfare, not making it into a "moment," but he was too happy to care.

"They love you. I can tell."

"They're wonderful people, and I had a good time. I wish my mother was as nice and accepting as yours," Bryan said, hugging her closer.

Nadia broke their embrace. "I feel like a teenager, worried about getting in trouble for making out with my parents nearby," she giggled. "Oh, I almost forgot. A friend of mine is getting married on New Year's night. The wedding is in Eureka Springs, Arkansas, for a cute lesbian couple. I would love for you to go with me. Sophia was supposed to be my plus one," she said, her face falling. Bryan thought he saw a tear forming in the corner of one of her eyes, but she quickly brushed it away. She inhaled sharply before responding. "Now I'm all alone traveling by myself."

He put his hand on her shoulder to comfort her. "I would love to," he said somberly.

As he went to leave, he discovered his decrepit car wouldn't start. Nadia turned around and began toward her apartment. "Wait, Nadia, where are you going?"

"To get my dad," Nadia tossed over her shoulder. "He likes to feel useful."

Bryan tried a few more times to start his car. He was worried that his broken-down car might change Greg's impression of him.

A few minutes later, Nadia's father was beside him, holding jumper cables. "My daughter told me that you fixed her toilet last week," her father said as he clipped on the cables.

"It just needed a new valve and gasket. It wasn't worth calling the property manager."

"It feels good not to have to worry about her."

Bryan thought about his mama, who no longer worried about him, as far as he knew. "She is lucky to have you as a father. Thank you, sir."

"I'm glad I could help." He successfully jump-started the car and closed the hood after removing the cables. "I'm not going to tell you to be a good man. When it comes to her, I need you to be a good partner and her rock because this is no cakewalk. I don't care how you identify but realize this is your community now too if you're going to date my daughter. As her father, the LGBTQ community has my total support because I support my daughter. The whole idea of 'separate but equal' is flawed, whether in terms of gender roles or anything else. One of many things Nadia has taught me."

What Greg said stayed with Bryan on the way home, the weight of his words occupying the space in the passenger seat. Bryan's father never gave him the freedom to simply be. He always had to be a man (however "man" was defined at the moment) and rarely, if ever, considered the feelings of a romantic partner. After spending the afternoon with Greg and Lisa, his perspective underwent a seismic shift. He now felt sorry for both of his parents, instead of being sorry about how they felt. He wanted to be completely transparent with Nadia. The question was, could he be?

38

After six hours of driving, Bryan and Nadia were in Arkansas. Nadia's car drove like his Porsche compared to his beat-up old car. The landscape had morphed into long stretches of fenced land and sporadic gas stations. As the buildings and houses dwindled, the number of Confederate symbols exponentially increased. Practically every vehicle boasted flags, Trump 2016 bumper stickers, and white men with fully or partially buzzed haircuts. A red truck kept pace with them in the next lane. Bryan continued driving, keeping the truck in his sights, an episode of This American Life filling the car. He chose to reflect on his friendship with Nadia.

Nadia turned, facing him. Bryan got nervous because this meant they needed to talk. I hope I'm not in trouble.

"You seem so much more comfortable being in the community," Nadia said.

"Actually, I am," Bryan said. "I feel like I've finally learned who I am. And I'm no longer ashamed to acknowledge every part of myself."

Nadia replied, "Too much responsibility is put on the trans community to explain itself to the cis community. We grow when we do the work ourselves."

"Yeah, that's true. Most people have never met a trans person, so there is little interest on their part to understand."

Nadia nodded. "My problems don't affect them."

"I never realized how difficult transitioning is and how it is different for everyone."

Nadia smiled. "Look at you."

"I've been trying to do my research," Bryan said.

"Transitioning is a journey," Nadia said, taking a deep breath. "Thank you for taking an interest in me. In my community."

Bryan slowed down. He was too close to an F-250 truck. "They think that isn't gay," Nadia said, pointing to the tailgate of the truck, "I've never seen that before."

"Yeah, those are truck nuts," Bryan said, laughing at the golden pair of testicles hanging from the tailgate. "They are everywhere."

Nadia laughed. "These are the same macho guys who are so convinced my genitalia is offensive. Who wants to look at their low-hanging balls? That's offensive."

Bryan noticed Nadia wriggling in her seat. "I need to use the restroom. You, too, right?"

She nodded.

"When you get quiet, I can tell that you're trying to figure out where you're going to go to the bathroom." Bryan was freshly conscious about how little he had to strategize to simply pee. It was harder for any woman, but exponentially harder for a trans woman. He took the next exit for the rest stop toward Hindsville. The red truck followed them and screeched to a stop next to them at the gas pump. Two bearded guys with potbellies lurched out of their vehicle and slammed the doors. The slams seemed extra hard to Bryan, as if they were peacocking their strength, but no looks were exchanged, to his relief. The men hiked up their jeans, adjusted themselves, and stiffly half-strode, half-waddled toward the men's room.

One of them was whistling, and Bryan strained to hear the song. Was it "Dude (Looks Like a Lady)"? If so, they were leaving now, no matter how full their bladders were.

Nadia, coiled like a spring, was ready to leap out of the car. Trying not to panic, Bryan grabbed her other hand. "Wait."

The guy was now singing, loud enough that the words were unmistakable: "I've got jungle fever, she's got jungle fever. We've got jungle fever, we're in love."

Oh great, Bryan thought, *the other one*. The only good thing was that if this one stayed away from Nadia, she'd be safer. Either way, it was dangerous for him, and they'd both be alone in the separate bathrooms, which were on opposite sides of the long, low building. "Hear that?" He tried to keep the panic out of his voice.

"Some guy with truck nuts serenading us?" Nadia said jokingly. She appeared shocked when Bryan met her gaze with serious eyes.

"He's singing 'Jungle Fever,'" Bryan said. Nadia nodded slowly, and fell quiet. Bryan drove quickly toward the building and parked as close to the entrance as possible. *Did they follow us here?*

"Make sure you're extra careful. And stay away from me, okay, honey? Be quick, and we'll meet back at the car. You take the keys," Bryan instructed.

Taking the key ring, Nadia spoke through clenched teeth. "I hear you, and I will, but if I don't go now, I'm going to have an accident." She lopped toward the nearest restroom door. A third guy, whom Bryan hadn't seen due to his incredibly short height, jumped down from the rear cab of the truck and veered toward the side of the building where the women's restrooms were located—where Nadia had gone.

With his bladder uncomfortably pressing against his five-button fly, he jumped out and made a beeline in the direction of the restrooms, a security officer's shadow convincing him to keep moving. He looked around for the men from the truck but didn't see them. Slipping quietly into the bathroom, he listened. The only sound he could discern was water dripping from one of the sinks. Bryan tightened the faucet, and the sound ceased. He closed the door to the first stall, locked it, and finally relieved himself.

The beige ceramic tiles reminded him of his altercation with Mike in the slightly cleaner office restroom. He tried to take his mind off that incident by focusing on the writing on the walls. Scrawled all over the stalls was evidence of the lowest common denominator: Obama is a monkey. Niggers aren't welcome. White power. The words were written by different authors and dated, but as Bryan read them all, they ran together as one voice, impacting him like a rod through his spine. *Why hasn't management erased all of this*, he thought.

Finished, he ran out of the bathroom and past the security officer, who thankfully, didn't stop him as he headed toward the women's room. *What should I do?* He knew he couldn't go in. He idled outside the restroom door for a few minutes but felt conspicuous. The short white man from the red truck appeared, and he and Bryan accidentally made eye contact. The man gave him a creepy, knowing smile, showing all of his teeth, which were tiny and yellow, like a rodent's.

"Where is she?" Bryan whispered under his breath. He was more afraid than he'd been in a long time. His heart was in his throat. He bolted for his car and glimpsed a dark shape in the passenger's side. Flinging open his door, he gasped, "Nadia. Thank God. Are you okay?"

"I'm okay. A short guy said some scary, misogynist stuff to me when I came out of the bathroom, but I just kept my head down and focused on getting to the car."

Bryan searched for the red truck, but it was gone. He laid his head back against the seat.

"What did he say?"

"He called me 'sugar tits,' that Mel Gibson garbage, which I guess I should take as a compliment." She waved her hands as if she was swatting a mosquito away. "Made some rude gesture. That sort of thing. I enjoy being a woman, but some . . . men make it so difficult some days."

Bryan groaned in disgust. "Nothing about being with a Black man?"

Her voice was blithe, but there was a small tremor in it. "I think he wasn't smart enough to remember that I was with you since you weren't with me at that second. You were smart to make sure we separated, which the building made easy, I guess. What would a mother with a ten-year-old son do in this situation? They're too old to go into the restroom with them at that age, but I'd hate to be that far from my kid. Same situation if it were a father with a ten-year-old daughter." She puffed out her cheeks. "Whew, I hate this. So much stress, just to perform a universal human function."

Starting the car, Bryan said, "I hate that you were alone over there, but as unpleasant as that was, it was probably the lesser of several evils." At this moment, Bryan realized that the power of perceived threats can be worse than actual threats on one's psyche. Being a lone Black man at a rural rest stop had been nerve-racking, not to mention the additional worries about her. He'd never thought about how simply being a human doing human things like relieving one's bladder was somehow a luxury.

"I want to say something," Nadia said, turning down the radio.

Bryan turned, concerned something was wrong.

"I never considered my white privilege until I met you. When I pass as a cis white woman, I generally get what I need. I will try to be more conscious of your feelings, but first, I have to acknowledge the issue of my white privilege."

In his anxiety, Bryan hadn't noticed that they were almost out of gas. He exhaled loudly and exited at the next rest stop. No truck followed them in, and they were the lone vehicle at the gas pumps. The pump counter changed numbers faster than a slot machine. Annoyed, Bryan forced a smile to his lips.

"What are you smiling about?" Nadia said, tearing open a travel package of Oreos. "Besides the name of the towns around here." She winked. "Hindsville."

"You're lucky you're cute. You didn't fill your tank before we left." He raised his brows at her. "As usual."

She shrugged. "I have to have one irritating quality, or else I'd be too perfect."

He laughed, a genuine joy bubbling up from his abdomen. He felt the vacation vibe creeping back into his veins. "You're beautiful."

"Oh, that." She stuffed a cookie into her mouth. "Tell me something I didn't know."

***

Eureka Springs was a quiet community of Craftsman houses half-hidden by unclaimed forest, the Ozarks blue in the distance. Rows of pride flags saluted them from awnings on Main Street.

Bryan had rented a cottage for two nights. The pictures of it online had featured a bed covered with a double quilt with a wedding-ring pattern; a claw-foot tub, ornamented with antique fixtures, which took up most of the tiny bathroom; and a breakfast nook located within a screened-in porch. While Nadia was exclaiming over its cuteness, he anxiously checked his bank balance to make sure the charge would go through. He wanted to show her he could still provide and romance her, but it was bleeding his savings to prove his case.

They noted that everything was clean and cute but smaller than they'd appeared on the site. Propped up in one corner, a mirror served as an attempt to make the room seem larger. Bryan carefully hung up his suit and shirt and folded his casual clothes into the drawers.

Unpacking her stuff more haphazardly, Nadia said, "The walls are pa-per-thin. I can hear the girls next door talking."

They dressed quickly and drove to the ceremony.

The wedding was held in a meadow circled with birch, oak, and hawthorn trees. Hurricane lamps with votives lined the makeshift aisle. The wedding party included the two brides, family, friends, and a handful of drag queens. Bryan and Nadia had learned that there was a huge LGBTQIA+ community in the northern part of Arkansas.

Two fiddlers, a banjo player, and a cellist struck up the "Wedding March." A man, clearly the father of the flower girl, nudged his daughter, and she emptied her basket of petals in one heap as soon as she noticed that all eyes were on her. Everyone laughed, and she hid her head in her dad's shoulder. The crowd hushed as the first bride, wearing an ankle-length white lace dress with a beaded headband, stepped nimbly over the hill of petals and floated down the aisle. The second bride wore a white dress as well, but hers had a large train, and her face was covered with a veil. After the brief but moving ceremony, the brides tossed their bouquets into the air, and everyone clapped and hooted.

The reception was held at a 134-year-old hotel, a beautiful white mansion on a hill overlooking the town. White Christmas lights garlanded pillars, railings, and awnings, and the chairbacks were wrapped with white satin. There were no place cards, which lent an air of joyous informality to the ornate ambiance.

After everyone feasted on bucketfuls of buttery crawdads, tangy brisket, and delicately fried catfish, servers wheeled out a giant cake, surrounded by four ringed tiers of mini cupcakes, each one as beautifully iced as the cake.

Nadia poked Bryan. "I know how to spin sugar and butter into lace like that."

"Amazing. That will come in handy when you open your own bakery," Bryan shot back.

"Believe me, I'm thinking about it all the time. I just don't know how . . ." she trailed off, a crinkle of worry between her brows.

"Let's talk about it seriously," Bryan said. "But for now, let's eat some of that sugar lace before everyone else gobbles it up."

They each had a slice of cake and a cupcake and danced a few slow songs before finding a pillar to lean against. Bryan wasn't tired as much as he was contemplative. As far as his eye could see, stars popped against the dark sky and the moon glowed fuzzily, like a lantern through rain.

"There is something about weddings," Nadia mused.

"I know. I got all warm watching them say their vows." He held her hands, rubbing her knuckles gently. "There is something that I want to tell you."

"I'm listening."

"In the beginning, I did not trust anyone. That was where all my problems began," Bryan said. "I know I can only have a real friendship, a real relationship with you when I am ready to be truly vulnerable. I am ready." He reached into his pocket.

Nadia watched him digging into his pocket.

"Do you remember the time I wanted to be submissive?" Bryan asked, smiling from within, holding up a device to the light. He was giving his vulnerability as his ultimate gift.

Nadia took the device. "Is this what I think it is?"

"Press the button."

Nadia looked to her left. She hesitantly pressed the button.

A moment later, an inaudible buzz shot through Bryan's spine. "Ahh." She pressed again. Bryan's eyes closed, and he fell into Nadia's embrace. "Ohh."

Nadia gushed. She held him close to protect his vulnerability, spinning him away from the crowd. She flashed a big grin. "Did you buy this online?"

"No, I bought it in person. I'm not scared anymore to be myself."

"You have changed," she whispered.

Both brides appeared nearby, and they were surrounded by a flurry of congratulations and hugging. The brides moved on to the next group, and Bryan took Nadia in his arms. He whispered in her ear, "Take me to the B and B."

***

The night air was crisp. Sounds of animals rustling in the dense black trees surrounded them. An owl hooted overhead. Bryan cuddled Nadia close. "It's like the Arkansian Serengeti."

Inside their room, they kissed. Nadia dotingly untied his necktie as if he were a young bride on his wedding night, her eyes glued to his. She ran one hand slowly over his chest and, with her other, undid his belt.

Bryan reached into his bag and handed her a bottle of Elbow Grease. "I got the good stuff," he whispered.

Kissing his neck, she unbuttoned and unzipped his pants, tugging his underwear down until it hit the floor. "I want to make love tonight." She pushed the remote once more, and as his legs became soft, she wasted no time carrying him to the bed. He felt like an antelope felled by a hungry lioness. She stripped off every bit of clothing, revealing her absolute beauty. Bryan had not seen her naked in more than a year, and her erotic body was even more electrifying than he remembered.

Climbing onto the bed, she touched the inside of his right thigh, spreading open his legs. Her hands were warm, calming, and inviting. Offering his unwavering eye contact as his implicit consent, he opened like a book, no longer interested in divisions, past caring about the dictates of masculine or feminine roles, only fearing that he could not be the partner she deserved.

"Honey, I remember my first time," she said. "I'll make it wonderful for you. Do you trust me?"

"Yes," he said. He did, utterly and completely. Her girl-dick was dripping with lube. Nadia ran her nails softly over his chest down to his navel, patient and intentional, letting his anticipation build. As she played with his curly pubic hair, she lightly touched his entry.

"Look who's awake now," she said, stroking him with her free hand.

Streams of pleasure pooled in his abdomen. He clenched the mattress' edge. Nadia slid in, and he moaned in discomfort, balling the bed sheet in his fists. She pushed in deeper, and he yelped. She paused, waiting for his sign.

"Don't stop. I'm okay," he eked out, his body too tense to facilitate the experience. As Bryan focused on the pulse of her inside his body, his discomfort gradually eased, and once Nadia was completely within him, he began to feel real pleasure. Not being in control was euphoric. Through the long golden strands of hair curtaining Nadia's face, Bryan caught glimpses of her eyes and lips above him, which made her thrusts leave an even more indelible mark on his psyche. His back arched to meet her. The switch to a strong feminine force, taking pleasure while he received it, was erotic, intense, and powerful. His soul expanded under her and he let go of the bed sheets completely. He was hers now.

He tried to pull her hair back to see her face, but she put his wrist behind his head as she plowed forward, unwilling to give him any control. The more submission she demanded, the more he felt like himself. For the first time in their relationship, he was finally giving all of himself to her. Bryan wanted to please her as she positioned him in front of the mirror, forcing him to look at himself. Sweat blurred his vision, but he could make out her form, poised above him like a jungle cat.

"Keep looking in the mirror," Nadia commanded.

Bryan looked back at this reflection, seeing the woman he always wanted but was too scared to face until now.

"Say my name again. Scream it."

"Nadia. Nadia!"

"Are you my man?" She slapped his ass hard.

"Yes," he screamed.

Finding the flow, he moaned as she claimed more of him with each thrust. He saw an impression of her smile. He squinted to see further into his reflection: love in all its glorious forms reflected as one undifferentiated whole. Like a star hurtling through space, he felt himself moving toward a truth buried within, unbarred by hang-ups, oppositions, or reluctance to intimacy in all its forms.

As the moment of ultimate vulnerability drew closer, he happily shut the door on his old self. He was grateful to it for getting him here, but it no longer served him. Nadia's wild mane was sweaty and wet, streaming down to her shoulders and shadowing her eyes as she clasped his hips. She pushed herself deeper where his truth existed and began thrusting faster, causing the headboard to knock against the wall. He reached out for the headboard and held on tightly to stabilize them both. Like a maestro, Nadia conducted the orchestra—the steady tempo of the headboard against the wall balanced with his wild moans and her thundering grunts counterpointed by the high pitch of the squeaky bed frame. When she released her love into him, the quietness was tangible. She lay next to him. His body lay tensed up on the bed, and he mumbled something inaudible.

"What, honey?" She kissed his chest, holding his manhood.

"I'm close. Don't stop." He pushed the words out in between big gasps for air. "You are so handsome," she said. Her breath was ragged, too.

"Please, Nadia, don't stop." She continued stroking him. She pulled her hair back away from her face, and he was finally able to look into her eyes, darkened to malachite. It felt like he was reaching the end of a long journey. He blasted a loud, wild, uncontrolled orgasmic sound of pure release.

***

The Serengeti was quiet now. As his chest heaved, a profound sensation of pleasure and love flushed through his entire body.

"I love you, Nadia Brooks. Also, I can't move my legs," he said with a breathless chuckle.

There were only a few minutes until midnight. They gathered blankets, wine, and two glasses and picked their way through their strewn clothes to the porch. They sat naked on the porch, bundled together. Bryan was experiencing happiness in its truest form as he looked into her eyes.

"Stacey was right about being a bottom," he said. "Wow," he laughed, "there's lube everywhere."

Nadia winked.

Everything was different. She looked practically angelic, her skin glowing from within, aided by the moonlight. "You know I always loved you, right?"

"Yeah, I knew." Nadia nestled into his chest. "I needed you to love yourself before you could love me."

The owl hooted again. Bryan said, "I know how to make money, show up to the kids' volleyball games and performances. I thought I was a good partner by washing the dishes. But there's so much more to it." Fireworks popped in the distance. "Happy New Year, love," Bryan said before kissing her deeply.

Nadia smiled into his mouth. "I think it's going to be a great one."

Her words hit him just as the sky crackled with the firework finale. His heart exploded into iridescent shards, petals, and rockets. Unable to contain himself, he sprinted outside naked, jumping around in the cover of the night.

"I feel so free!" He swooped his arms wide and ran in place with his knees high, the cool dark air drying his sweat. "I'm queer. It feels good to be a queer man," he screamed.

Nadia's head poked out the screen door. "Bryan, Bryan," she whispered, "Get back in here, goober, before somebody sees you. They will lock your Black ass up."

***

The next morning, Bryan slipped outside and watched the mist rising like a window shade. Nadia, wearing a TRANS IS BEAUTIFUL T-shirt and jeans, came out to the porch with mugs of steaming coffee for them both.

"I like your shirt," Bryan asked. He turned to face her, wearing his own shirt. QUEER LIVES MATTER.

"Awwh. Look at you," Nadia said, "You are just too much. See, this is why I love you." She handed him his coffee.

"I love it out here. It's so beautiful and quiet. No one would bother us if we moved out here."

"Girl, we can't live here."

"Why not?" she asked.

"Have you seen any Black people?" He sipped his coffee, and she gave him an understanding nod. "Exactly. We are going back to Texas." Finishing his coffee, he put the mug on the railing and made for the car. "We can't be the only Black couple living here."

"I'm not Black," Nadia said, with her hands on her hips.

"When you're with me, you are," Bryan quipped.

Nadia chuckled, appearing as if she had never thought about it before. "Wait, you feel so strongly about not living here that you're leaving this instant?"

"I noticed the tire was low," Bryan called over his shoulder. "I'm going to check it and change it if necessary." Sure enough, there was a tear. He blew Nadia a kiss as he retrieved his jack and lug wrench from the trunk.

"I could do that, you know." Nadia tripped gracefully down the porch stairs and was soon by his side. "But I appreciate you noticing something and fixing it on your own initiative." She pressed her body against his and bit his ear.

Nadia's dad was right, Bryan thought. It was the initiative that counted, not the particular faux-gendered labor that one did for one's partner. The lesbian couple next door emerged from their room, each dragging a small suitcase. One of the women called out to Bryan and Nadia.

"You crazy kids at it again?" she snickered.

"Hi, bye," the taller woman said cheerfully. "Happy first day of 2017, even if Trump is our president." She shuddered.

"How was your New Year's Eve?" the other women asked. Her curly hair haloed her head.

Bryan couldn't look at Nadia. "It was nice." He shrugged. "Kind of quiet."

The two women burst out laughing. "That's what you call quiet?"

Bryan blushed.

"I wished she screamed like that," the tall woman said. The other woman hit her on the shoulder, and all four of them cracked up.

Bryan expertly packed their car, and he and Nadia jumped in. As he maneuvered onto the main road, he said, "I feel like a new man. I love you."

Nadia squeezed the inside of his thigh. "I love you too," she said.

39

It was a Friday in April when Bryan picked up some beer before heading to Nadia's. Since they had returned from Arkansas, Bryan had given his two weeks' notice at the café and had trained two teenagers to take over his shifts. His manager had accepted his resignation graciously. It was not the same young man who had hired him, but a carbon copy, who had transferred from another location soon after Bryan had been hired.

"No one expected you to be here this long, but you were cool to be around," this version of the manager had said, smiling through a mouth full of braces. "That is, after we stopped thinking you were doing some kind of undercover exposé on us."

In between reading up on financial details of owning a food establishment and dipping his toe into the enormous morass of regulations and ordinances, Bryan had reached out to an old boss, Fred.

"I won't say 'I told you so,'" Fred had said after Bryan had relayed some of the details of Mike's microaggressions, which had resulted in the bathroom brawl. "I knew something was up. Word gets around, you know, but I didn't want to call you or give voice to the crazy things I heard. I figured you would reach out at some point, and here you are."

"Here I am," Bryan had repeated. "Fred, I'd like to do some consulting, and I figured you were the man to talk to about that. Do you have any leads? Not in oil and gas. Just regular building projects."

"Bridges slated for burning?" Fred had chuckled at his own joke. "I'll funnel some stuff to you," Fred had said. "You do good work. I know how hard it was to work for that SOB and what a difficult process the postmortem, so to speak, can be."

Fred was as good as his word and quickly sent several things Bryan's way. He hadn't drawn anything else from his savings since early February, and his high-rise was in escrow. If all went smoothly, he could be completely out of his high-rise and fully moved into Nadia's by the end of June.

When he arrived at Nadia's, he found that she had made her version of street tacos, and he dug in.

"Scrumptious," he said when he came up for air. "Okay, let's talk cupcake business."

Nadia tossed her hair over her shoulder. "I've written pages of ideas in my notes app."

"Girl, you're unstoppable."

She grinned.

"I'd love to be your first investor," Bryan said. "Once the hi-rise is sold, I'll rent someplace more modest. I'll have money from the sale to pay for Lindsey's college and my child support for Lance and still have a nice amount left over to give to you."

Nadia scoffed. "You wouldn't do that. Luxury is everything to you."

"Was," Bryan said emphatically. "You are everything to me now. Let's be honest, up until recently, things were financially easy for me. After I was fired, I started to understand your struggles and developed an appreciation for how you make it work. I wonder what we can accomplish together if we join forces."

Nadia didn't say anything but returned her taco to her plate untouched. Bryan reached for his backpack, unzipped it, and pulled out a folder bursting with tabbed papers.

"I've started working on this since we got back from Arkansas."

Nadia scooted her chair closer. "What is all of this?"

"Once I sell everything," he said, "I think I can give you fifty thousand dollars to start your business." He was momentarily pained by speaking that intention aloud. He was going to miss his beautiful clothes. It was damn expensive to outfit himself the way he had, and he almost cringed at the thought of selling his suits. *It's worth it though*, he thought. *She's worth it.*

"Bryan, are you serious?" She pressed her hands to the sides of her face.

"We are a team. I love you. We can do this."

"Yes! Yes! Yes!" She jumped up and into his lap, almost toppling their beers and knocking over the bottles of hot sauce on the table. "I know you said you wanted to rent someplace, but why don't you move in with me? It's the least I can do if you're willing to front me that kind of money."

Bryan felt as if his heart was soaring, and smiled broadly. "I would be honored," he said, kissing her.

***

Moving in was a little more challenging than Bryan expected, as Nadia inspected every box he carried. He never considered all the stuff she didn't have space for, but this was good for him because he realized that in order to get what he wanted in life it was worth giving up what was no longer necessary. Those items, like his books and his expensive clothing that once defined him, were no longer important.

They began to merge routines, and also create new ones in the process. He maintained his weekly Skype calls with Lindsey, but in the chaos of moving, had forgotten to mention the change to his children. Once he had finally finished moving and turned his keys in, he logged on for a call with Lindsey in his new home. Bryan never considered Lindsey would notice the background was different.

"Where are you, Daddy?" Lindsey asked suspiciously.

Bryan, completely caught off guard, said, "I'm at a friend's house." He suddenly realized that not only had he failed to mention that he was moving to his kids, he had also neglected to tell them Nadia was back in his life. He had been so focused on helping Lindsey through questions on homework and navigating college in general on their weekly calls that he hadn't told her much about his own life in the past few months. *Man, I need to figure out a way to work this in at some point. Let's see how stressed she is about physics before I get into that,* he thought. He was also not convinced she was ready to accept he had gotten serious with someone other than Lawanda. *She doesn't need to know everything,* he thought.

"I see," she said in a way that expertly mimicked a lawyer casting doubt on a witness testimony.

"You sure you don't want to be a lawyer?" he said, smirking.

Lindsey smiled back. "Maybe. Are the guys in law school still jerks though?"

Bryan adjusted his camera and saw frustration on her face. "What's wrong honey?"

Lindsey went on to say that many boys in her science classes were not treating her as an equal. Her basic engineering classes had three other girls in a huge auditorium full of white boys. And just as in her first semester, she was sometimes the only Black person, or one of a small handful, in her core classes.

Bryan knew how she felt, except he'd at least had gender on his side. It was almost a sour taste in the back of your throat, the feeling that you did not belong. He needed her to be strong and ready for whatever these guys threw at her. He tried to listen, and hoped he advised her as well as he could. He reminded his daughter that the most important person she had a responsibility to was herself —her goals and her promises to herself. Staying true to that, no matter what, would see her through almost anything.

"If you weren't capable of doing the work, then you wouldn't be there, right? Your math scores are as good as any boy in your classes." He hoped she wouldn't doubt herself. "Don't let a bunch of coddled guys threatened by your intelligence get you off your game."

"Okay," she sniffled.

He felt good advocating for his daughter. "So, what else is going on?"

In the next breath, she said, "Daddy, I need money to go shopping," she said.

Bryan hadn't often said no to his daughter, but he had to start now. Not only was Bryan currently financially strained, but Lindsey was getting old enough to make her own spending money.

"Lindsey, if you want to go shopping, I think you should get yourself a part-time job on campus," he replied, hearing Nadia enter the house.

"Sugar Bear. Where are you?" she said excitedly.

"Lindsey, I'm going to get off now. Let's talk about this more later. I can help you with your resume if you need it. Bye-bye," he said hurriedly. He clicked off the video. He walked out to the entryway and she threw her purse onto the couch.

"I did it!" Nadia exclaimed, beaming with enthusiasm. She jumped into his arms and kissed him.

"You did what?"

"I met with the landlord to lease a space for the cupcake shop!"

"Slow down, girl. Are you serious? Tell me where?" His body buzzed with excitement from the news.

"In the gayborhood, closer to Midtown, not too far from the Rothko Chapel. You will love the space. I can't wait to show you. But I gotta pee first," she said, running into the bathroom.

Wow, he thought, *she's not messing around*. Once she exited the bathroom, they sat on the couch so Nadia showed him pictures of the space on her phone. Nadia outlined her vision, explaining where the front counter, the chairs, and tables would go. She insisted on having a large portrait of Sophia for everyone to see. The house buzzed with the possibilities of achieving their dream and Nadia began sketching her interior design vision.

***

Bryan created a little spot in the corner of the bedroom to meditate. His meditation practice was becoming stronger as sitting became more a part of his morning routine. He continued attending a few weekly Zen Buddhism classes and occasionally sat with other practitioners at the Zen Center. One evening, Bryan sat on his knees and gradually found his breath. The *in* breath and the *out* breath was a single count. At the fifth count, his mind grabbed hold of a vision of muted blues and pinks. He felt a sense of being an out and proud queer man who saw the beauty and humanity of trans women and allowed a soft smile to appear on his lips. His body relaxed as he found his breath and he started the count over again. After five minutes, the timer chimed ending the session. He was not scared anymore because he was starting to find his deepest self through mediation.

They continued to settle into their routine and the following Thursday's video call with Lindsey came around. "Nadia, I really want you to join me on the video call if Lindsey is okay with it," Bryan said, moving a chair next to himself, "I feel like you need to start being a part of my weekly video calls with Lindsey. We're family now, and it's time you two get to know each other."

Nadia smiled.

The video started and Lindsey appeared on camera flashing a huge smile.

"Hey Babygirl," Bryan said.

"Hey dad," she said cheerfully.

"Hey, I need to tell you something. Well, actually two things."

"Okay…" she started.

Bryan took a deep inhale and Nadia squeezed his hand off camera.

"Does this have something to do with why you were acting weird last week?"

"Umm, well yes." Bryan said. Lindsey's face became inquisitive and Bryan knew he was about to be interrogated by his daughter. He only hoped she would take it better than his mother would have.

"Did you move?"

"Yes," Bryan said, finding his breath again. "That's one of the things I wanted to share."

"Okay, that's not bad. Geez dad, you were scaring me for a second there. I thought you were about to tell me you were sick or something."

"Nope, I am perfectly healthy. Knock on wood," he said, knocking on his head as a joke.

"Where did you move to?"

"That's the other piece of news…I wanted to tell you sooner, but I knew how stressed you were about school and was trying to find the right way and time to tell you…" Bryan trailed off.

"Dad, did you move in with someone?"

"I did," he said. "You have great deductive skills. You sure you don't want to be a lawyer?"

"Dad, I'm not stupid. I can see a cupcake clock hanging in the background and I'm 90% sure that it doesn't belong to you. Plus you were all weird when I asked about where you were last week and before you abruptly ended our call, I thought I heard a woman's voice."

"You're right, those are the two pieces of news," Bryan said, gathering his thoughts.

"You know I want you to be happy, right Dad? Did you not want to tell me because you thought I'd be mad?"

"That's right, Babygirl. I guess I just didn't know how to tell you. You know, life can be a funny thing," Bryan said, trailing off again.

"So, who is she?" Lindsey asked eagerly.

"You actually have already met her," Bryan said.

Lindsey's expression turned from happy to shocked.

"It's not Mom, is it?" she asked.

"No, it's not," Bryan said. He took another sharp inhale. "It's Nadia."

"Nadia," Lindsey said, her face transforming from disappointment to confusion. "The girl from last year you were seeing? The real tall one."

"Yes," he said, pausing, "I'm bringing this up because I want you to feel comfortable with her being on the call sometimes."

"I don't know. This is supposed to be our time," she said. "Mama told me that you and Lance haven't been the same since you dropped me off to college. Does this have something to do with that?"

"No, the two are completely unrelated," Bryan said, "But it's true that we haven't talked. I've tried to reach out to him, but he doesn't want to talk to me."

"Mama said you don't support him, and she's the only parent who knows how to care for him," Lindsey said.

Bryan twisted his head to the side at her statement. "What are you talking about? It's your mother who isn't caring for him. I'm not the one with a problem with who he is," Bryan said, feeling a heatwave of deep truth building up inside his belly. "I worry about Lance but I'm the last one in this family with a problem." He paused, realizing that he crossed a boundary. But, he was tired of everyone always having an opinion.

Lindsey stared back at the screen.

"You need to know who I really am and how I identify," he said, rubbing his hands together. He took another deep breath. He was ready. "Lindsey, you need to know that Nadia is transgender, and I identify as a queer." He grinned into the camera and sat up straighter.

Lindsey scoffed. Then she laughed. "I should have known. Wow," Lindsey said rudely, "I knew something was up with her."

"I thought it was time to finally tell you. I'm tired of hiding," he said, "Me and Nadia would love your support."

There was silence.

"I need time to process this. You're queer. Gay. Whatever," she said, "And this is why you and Mama can't get back together again. Because you're gay?"

"Queer."

"Whatever. You'd rather be with *her*?" Lindsey said with the inflection on the word *her*.

I'd rather be with anyone but your mama, he thought.

"I love her," Bryan said confidently.

Lindsey shook her head. "I never thought we'd be having this conversation but you're old enough to be her father."

"Are you done?" Bryan said sarcastically.

"I'm so disappointed in you. There's so many single Black women out there, including mama," Lindsey said, "There is much wrong about this on so many levels," her voice sounded deep with malice and her mouth twisted with disgust.

"I guess you got that off your chest. Do you want to talk about anything else?" he asked.

"No, I don't think I want to," Lindsey said quietly, and hung up. Bryan sighed deeply, knowing this was not going to be easy for Lindsey.

***

A week later, Bryan opened the front door. Nadia walked in solemnly and practically slumped onto the couch. She buried her head in her arms and said, "I didn't think anything of it at first, but when I told the landlord that I was trans, he became distant." Her voice was muffled. "He hasn't gotten in touch and won't return my calls."

Bryan calculated that it had been more than a week since she found a place—and she had been so excited about it. He'd forgotten to check in about it because he had been consumed with a deadline for a consulting project. He sat next to her and put his arm over her shoulder. The whole situation felt weird, and Bryan realized that he needed to state the obvious. "You're being discriminated against."

She raised her head.

"They don't want to lease it to you because they want only customers that look like them to patronize the place. Think about it. All your clubs are gone now, replaced with high-rises. I would know. I bought a place in one of them, so I was a part of it." He paced several times from the front door to the kitchen. "This is bullshit." He picked up the phone. He knew exactly who to call.

"Who are you calling?"

He hadn't talked to Reggie in a year and a half. Would Reggie throw a tantrum? Bryan's temples throbbed as he dialed Reggie's number.

His college buddy answered before the phone had finished ringing once. "Man, where have you been? I called. I went to your place. They said you'd moved. I've been worried about you."

"I apologize broham," Bryan said, "So much has happened since I talked to you last."

"Same here, player," Reggie replied. "I started my own law firm focusing on social justice cases. I know I'm not going to make a lot of money, but as long as I pay my child support and mortgage then that is all I need," Reggie said happily, "Things are good. Kids are good. I'm seeing them nearly every weekend and I stopped fighting with Katrina."

"Shit, man, I'm proud of you. Things have really changed for you," Bryan said. "My news is just as good. I don't work in oil and gas anymore. I was a barista at the coffee shop on Westheimer and Post Oak for a while. Now, I'm consulting. Engineering projects, but not oil and gas."

"How much does that pay?"

"Not as much, that's for sure." Bryan laughed. "I thought you were going to give me some props for not killing the planet."

Reggie chuckled. "I don't know, man. A barista, wow. All those damn to-go cups. You know they bond plastic to paper to make those. A recycling nightmare."

Bryan waited for the right time to break in with his other found an opening after a lull in their recycling tangent.

"Nadia and I are back together. We moved in together."

"Wow! Sounds serious."

"She's a godsend. She makes me a better man every day. Look, we really need your help."

"You sound happy," Reggie said. "How can I help?"

There was silence again. Bryan knew that the much larger truth he needed to tell was best handled in person.

***

The next evening, Bryan and Nadia found Reggie at the bar at Larry's. When Reggie met Nadia, he gave Bryan the look of approval that guys give each other.

"What are you drinking?" Reggie asked, eying their glasses of water.

"Just water for now," Bryan said. "Okay, here's the deal. Nadia just got her certificate from culinary school, and we are looking to lease a space to open a cupcake bakery." His heart raced as he prepared himself to open up about his private life. "She's being denied the lease."

"Why?" Reggie asked, with apparent confusion. "Her credit is fine, right? No felonies?"

"No issues there." Bryan hesitated. He took a deep breath as if he had reached the top of a roller coaster ride. 'She's being denied because she's a transgender woman." He squeezed Nadia's hand hard, and she applied the same pressure back.

"Who's a transgender?" Reggie swiveled his head back and forth between his friend and Nadia.

"It's not a transgender," Nadia snapped.

"Transgender is an adjective. Not a noun," Bryan explained, wincing at how similar Reggie sounded to himself from a few short months ago. "She is a transgender woman."

The silence was frosty.

"She," Reggie blurted loudly, "is a he?" The nearby table looked over.

"Nope," Bryan said evenly, trying not to grit his teeth. He was unconcerned about the adjacent table eavesdropping. "Nadia identifies as a woman."

"Why didn't you tell me?"

"Man, it's really nobody's business."

"I'm sick and tired of people treating us like we lied to them whenever they find out. He hasn't lied to you about anything," Nadia said.

"It's our choice to disclose what we want, when, and to whom," Bryan added.

"Does she still have a . . . you know . . .?"

They sidestepped this question, much like someone who does not want to deal with cat vomit on the floor.

Reggie snickered. It was out of nervousness, Bryan knew, but it came out mean. Tilting his head to the right, he peered at Nadia, then cast a wavering glance at Bryan. "Man, you're shittin' me, right?"

"No, he's not shittin' you. Man." Nadia's voice was icy.

"You're trying to tell me this person is a dude. Damn," Reggie tittered. "You must really like white girls because you go for them even if they only look like girls."

"I'm sitting right here," Nadia spat out.

Bryan placed his hand on Nadia's arm. "Reggie, don't do this."

Reggie shook his head, not making eye contact with either Bryan or Nadia. "My best friend likes she-males."

Bryan's blood boiled, but he tried to keep his anger out of his voice. "Reggie, I ask that you not use hurtful language. You disagree with my relationship choice. I get that."

"This is your friend?" Nadia asked indignantly.

"We don't have much money. I really need your help, but I'm not going to put up with disrespect and unkindness. Especially from my oldest friend."

There was silence.

"So, how does this work for you two?"

Bryan got up and reached out his hand to Nadia.

"You're a fudge packer," Reggie said, giggling like an idiot.

"Reggie, grow up. Everything is a joke to you," Bryan said. "But people's lives are not a joke. What goes in our bedroom is our business. Not yours. Not anyone else's business. Period." He was no longer going to be embarrassed or put up with this kind of treatment.

"Look, man, just be honest with me," Reggie said, getting in Bryan's face. "Are you gay?"

Bryan maintained eye contact with Reggie, never looking at Nadia, "Reggie, I don't need to give you an explanation of who I am or who I love. No, I'm not. I'm queer," Bryan said, smiling, "I'm a proud straight queer man."

Nadia is worth it, Bryan thought as he stood tall.

Reggie held a confused look.

"So, that's your answer. Whatever that means," Reggie replied.

"Yep. It is. You know, I've known you for more than twenty years now. I'm the same person that I always was. She's the person that I love. The world tries to pull us apart mostly because of their perceived notions. Here is the part that saddens me. You know me. If there's anybody who should be able to accept my truth, it's you. We're simply trying to live our lives. We're not hurting anyone. I hate that I don't have your support." Bryan reached for Nadia's hand. She grasped his hand, smiling.

"I don't know, man," Reggie said, standing. He turned to exit. "I don't know man."

They watched Reggie walk away. *Whatever, man,* he thought, knowing he was tired of being scared of losing the people who should be the most on his side. He turned to look at Nadia and gave her a passionate kiss. She kissed him back.

"We have each other," he said, "Screw anyone who doesn't believe in us."

"You're right. Screw them," she said.

***

The following Thursday, Bryan looked at his phone to see a text from Lindsey. They hadn't talked since their call last week, and Bryan held his breath as he opened her text.

Dad, I disagree with your decisions. Lindsey texted.

That's fine. Do you want to talk tonight? Bryan texted back.

No. I need my space to continue processing. I love you dad. Take care.

Bryan reacted with a heart emoji.

He walked into the kitchen with a heavy heart. Lindsey wasn't his biggest fan and Lance hadn't spoken to him in over a year. *I'm really not winning father of the year this year,* he thought.

Nadia washed another dish. Bryan stood next to her, ready to dry the next plate.

"Everything okay?" she asked.

"Where do I start?" Bryan tried to wrap his head around his emotions. Lindsey wouldn't accept him, and Lance wouldn't talk to him because he hadn't accepted Lance. It felt like a vicious cycle he couldn't break through.

"Nadia, I'm lost," he said.

"About what?" she said, trying to search his eyes.

"I'm struggling with how to talk to Lance," Bryan said, turning around to face away from her. "My son loves to entertain in women's clothing. What if he's gay?"

Nadia stopped washing dishes and turned off the water. "Come sit down," she said, motioning to the kitchen table.

Bryan held his head down. "I'm scared I'm going to lose him."

Nadia held his hand, "First of all, he needs to know that you accept him, no matter what."

"Yeah, I know. But look at my mother. It's not like I have any barometer for what acceptance looks like. How do I show him that?" Bryan sighed loudly.

"In this family, there will be no shaming or name-calling. You need to be open to listening to him talk about his sexual orientation or gender identity when the time comes—"

Bryan opened his mouth.

"Without interrupting or arguing," Nadia continued. "You are so affectionate with me. And I love that about you. I want you to be more affectionate with your kids. Especially Lance. This is a difficult time for him right now. Show him how much he's loved. Most people are tossing us away."

Bryan smiled. He hugged Nadia.

"You should try to reach out to him again," Nadia said, rubbing his shoulder, then kissing his cheek. "Start there."

***

That night, Bryan lay in bed, looking at the ceiling, with Nadia's head on his chest. His mind rewound the years, the good times with Reggie. He was surprised that what bubbled to the surface was not anger but peace.

Since returning from Arkansas, even his dreams were free of their metaphorical deaths and terrifying prison imagery. He realized he hadn't seen a vulture anywhere since he'd shooed one off his Porsche the day he'd been fired. He hadn't thought of anyone from work other than Jerry in ages, and he thanked the universe again that Mike hadn't pressed charges. Forget nighttime dreams- that would have been a nightmare. Thoughts of work reminded him that he needed to follow up with Jerry about that drink they'd been meaning to get and he put a reminder in his phone.

Nadia rustled in the sheets, making herself more comfortable.

"Would you like to meditate with me tomorrow morning?"

"Why not?" she mumbled.

***

They had about two hours between her shifts at The Walking Zebra. After a quick lunch, Bryan led Nadia to his meditation cushion. He sat on his knees.

Nadia's knees butterflied out to the side. "I guess I'm just a natural at this."

"Find your breath," he whispered.

His phone rang. It was Reggie. Bryan was scared to answer but pressed Accept. That's what meditation teaches, after all—acceptance with what is.

"Hey, Reggie," he said nervously.

"Bryan, what you do with your personal life is your business. However, discrimination is another issue entirely. I will do my part." Reggie's tone was brisk and businesslike as if Bryan were simply a client. "I want to be clear. I totally disagree with your choice of partner. I can't believe you would lie to me all these years. You were gay our whole friendship. Who are you?"

Bryan had been holding his breath. He let it out in a whoosh that was probably audible to Reggie. Find your breath—always the challenge. "Okay, Reggie, I hear you. I'm grateful you'll help us."

"I'll call the landlord and tell him that a discrimination lawsuit would be filed against him unless he has a legitimate reason to deny her the lease. Send over all of the information and I'll take it from here."

Bryan thanked him again, and the call ended. "He'll help," he told Nadia.

"Are you okay?" Nadia was still in the lotus position.

"Yeah." A text came through. "Wow, okay. Reggie wants us to consider meeting with a television reporter in front of the lease location. We need to be ready to plead our case."

Nadia winced. "Maybe we should just find another place."

"You know that this place is the ideal location. And remember," he said as he bent to kiss her forehead, "You're doing this for your future and for everybody else who comes after you."

***

On the spring equinox, which Bryan took for an excellent sign, they met with the television reporter not far from Bryan's former high-rise complex. It was a bright morning, with a hint of the heat to come lurking in the caressing breeze and buoyant, dry air. The sky matched the light-blue couch in Helen and Mike's house and Bryan shuddered at the memory.

A cameraperson accompanied the street reporter as they set up their equipment on the sidewalk. High-rise luxury condominiums soared overhead, and eateries fanned out on both sides of the building where Nadia had hoped to open up her cupcake shop. Bryan and Nadia voiced hope that maybe the interview could spark a resurgence of LGBTQIA+-owned businesses and clubs. The reporter set up the story and introduced Nadia, who described her dream of owning a bakery in the city.

"I want my bakery to be a place where everyone feels welcome." Her voice broke a bit, but that added heart and authenticity. "Since there are places where not everyone is accepted." A crowd began to form.

"Sir? And you are?" the reporter asked Bryan, holding the microphone perilously close to his chin.

He cleared his throat. "Her boyfriend and co-owner," he said, speaking softly until he was prompted by the cameraperson to speak up. "We aren't asking for special treatment, only equal treatment and equal opportunity. What makes America great is that our dreams are possible when there is equal access to the opportunities. We also have reason to believe that this is not the first time this particular landlord has discriminated against an applicant. Please"—he appealed to the camera—"don't let Nadia's dream die here."

The reporter encouraged people to find Nadia on all the various social media platforms at the end of the piece.

There was an outpouring of support after the piece aired the following day, and only a few bad apples who trolled Nadia on social media. Some people wanted to donate money, so Bryan set up a crowdfunding account.

***

Three days later, Bryan was sitting in his car when his phone buzzed.

"The landlord will probably cave." Reggie's voice was dull, monotone. "My guess is he has a backlog of dirty dealings that he doesn't want to come to light. Plus, he's aware of the response to the TV spot."

Bryan grinned, glad that the court of public opinion was powerful and on their side for once.

"Oh wow, that's great." Bryan knew there was a lot of work ahead, but this was the first step, and he wished he could celebrate with his oldest friend. "We . . . I can't thank you enough."

Reggie barely grunted in response.

Bryan sighed into the silence. "I was tired of hiding. I don't know what else to say."

"Not much else to say," Reggie said thoughtfully, his voice brittle. "I thought we were good enough friends not to hide things from each other."

"You always had such a transphobic position that I didn't know what to say. Or how to say it."

"You should've trusted me enough," Reggie countered.

"So, you feel like I lied to you. And you can't sympathize with how I might be feeling?" Bryan watched his college friend rubbing a hand over his face.

"I didn't know who I was, so how could I even begin to explain to you who I truly was? I didn't know, man. Wow. Can't you see that?" Bryan pleaded.

"You only came out to me because you needed my help," Reggie said. "I wish you hadn't lied, and I wish you hadn't told me. I guess that's the whole of it." He hung up.

"I thought I would lose your friendship if I admitted who I was seeing," Bryan offered.

"Man, you are my boy. I don't understand what the attraction is but maybe you can teach me," Reggie said, changing his tone. "Don't worry about us. We can figure it out but it'll take some time."

Bryan looked up at the sky and realized that self-acceptance also meant being strong enough to live with the chapter of the story no one talked about, the part when your oldest friends might not want to know you anymore.

***

A couple of nights after the segment aired, Nadia was scrolling through Facebook. "A lot of people on here mention what you said on TV."

"Is that bad? I was the supporting role. That's my Oscar category. Everyone knows that, right?"

"I don't know. It bothers me that my cisgender boyfriend's voice counts for more than mine," Nadia said.

"I'm sorry, honey. I was only trying to help. Most people see me properly, as the helper, not the . . . pioneer."

"Yeah, I just wonder," Nadia's voice was plaintive. "When will my voice be equal to yours?"

Bryan's heart dropped. He didn't know the answer, but that was the question he and the rest of the world needed to answer, and soon. Bryan turned off the light, but he couldn't get comfortable. Drawn to the window by the streetlight, he got out of bed. He passed his palms over the plastic slats of the blinds to flatten them, smoothing them over and over, as if petting the raised hackles of an animal.

Did Mama see us on TV? he wondered.

"I don't know," Bryan spoke into the dark room, answering both Nadia's question and his silent one. Nadia didn't reply. She was already asleep, dreaming of a new day.

40

May passed in a flurry of activity. Lindsey finished the year with a 3.9 GPA and opted to stay in Oklahoma for the summer, working for one of her professors. Lance had rejected Bryan's olive branches so far, but Bryan learned from Lawanda that he, too, had finished his school year in good standing. Nadia graduated from her culinary program, which meant her internship at The Walking Zebra was over. Bryan was making decent money consulting, plus they had some crowdfunding money to fall back on, so they were stable enough to proceed with the next steps of Nadia's bakery and they signed the lease on June 3. Nights, which were formally spent watching TV, now consisted of Bryan pricing ovens and restaurant-sized refrigeration units while Nadia flipped through recipe books. Most evenings, they had cupcakes for dessert. Nadia focused on producing the same flavor combinations three ways: regular flour, gluten-free, and vegan yet Bryan never tired of her cupcakes.

***

On the Friday before Pride Week, Bryan found himself feeling proud of his most recent life decisions. It had taken some time, but he was finally feeling like he was officially part of the community and for the first time ever, considered going to the Pride parade. Nadia quickly reminded him of how much they needed to accomplish that weekend, but promised him they could attend the following year. Bryan had begrudgingly agreed. He knew they had a lot to do in preparation for opening the bakery. On top of that, he had several boxes, plus his couches and two mattresses to move out before closing at the end of the month.

After dinner, Bryan opened his laptop to clock in another hour of work, though he mainly read reviews of large-scale appliances. Nadia had made chocolate cupcakes with rainbow frosting. As Bryan was licking a smear of bright red frosting off his wrist, he was briefly reminded of the woman who had left an imprint of her lips on his windshield so long ago. Part of him wished he could find her and thank her for nudging him towards his true self. But he knew that realistically, it was better to pay it forward by loving Nadia with passion and constancy. "What do you think?" Nadia asked. "Too sweet, maybe?"

Bryan maneuvered her onto his lap. "Well, how could they not be, with you baking them?" He kissed her deeply, and she responded by softening into his arms. Just as he was about to ease their bodies down to the floor, his phone vibrated. "Unknown Caller." He put the phone on silent and continued kissing Nadia.

The phone buzzed again.

Nadia pulled away. "You better answer that. It might be important."

He pressed *Accept* and put the caller on speaker.

"Bryan, it's Joe, one of Harry's parents," Joe said hurriedly. "Are you there?" he asked frantically.

"Yes, I'm here. What's wrong?"

"The boys ran away!" he said.

"What? How do you know they're together? What happened?" Bryan asked, jolting upright. He began pacing the length of his living room.

"I don't know, but they're okay. I just got a phone call from a place called Covenant House. They ended up there I guess."

The blood that was aggressively pounding in Bryan's ears slowed to a throb with the knowledge that his son was safe. "I'm glad they're okay. What are the boys doing there?" Bryan asked.

"I'm a little fuzzy on the details right now, but we can go pick them up. They might be calling you soon, so don't get alarmed if they do. I think they might have just called Lance's mom first."

"Of course," Bryan sighed, hoping he wouldn't run into Lawanda at Covenant House. That was the last thing he needed.

"We need to go, honey," Steve said in the background. "Meet us there, okay," Joe said.

Bryan agreed and hung up. "Nadia, we need to go. It seems that Harry and Lance ran away. They're at this place called Covenant House." Bryan said calmly, knowing they were safe. "Any idea where that is?"

Nadia thought for a second. "I think it's maybe ten minutes away. It's a good place. They helped Stacey get on her feet." She picked up her mobile phone and looked up the shelter. As Nadia and Bryan hurriedly shrugged coats and shoes on, she dialed the number for Covenant House and handed the phone to

Bryan. They quickly left the high-rise, and Nadia tore down the road as Bryan confirmed that Lance was in fact with Harry and that Lance himself wanted Bryan, not Lawanda, to pick him up.

"Nadia..." Bryan began, "what do I say? Something clearly happened with him and Lawanda if he wants me there. The kid hasn't spoken to me in almost a year."

"I don't know if you need to say anything right now. I think he just needs to know that you're there for him," she said softly, caressing his hand with her non-driving hand.

"God, I wish there was a handbook for this. We need 'Coming out for dummies' or something like that, and a chapter for how to help your kid through it."

"That would be helpful," she chuckled. "Don't be too hard on yourself though. They say it takes a village to raise kids and you're a one man show right now."

"I guess. I need a village."

"I got you," Nadia said with a smile as they pulled into Covenant House. Scraggly trees covered with Christmas lights did their best to stretch their spindly, bare limbs over the front of the modern brick building. Bryan sighed deeply.

"It's been eleven months since I've seen him," he said.

"Then maybe I should give you a head start so you have some alone time with him. I'll go in in a few minutes," she said as Bryan exited the car.

Bryan stepped inside to see Steve and Joe talking to Harry and Lance as a young blonde woman supervised. Lance swung his head around when he heard Bryan shut the door and looked at his father with a mixture of fear and shame on his face. Bryan smiled with relief and bent down slightly, offering a hug. Lance trepidly walked over, and Bryan straightened, sensing his son didn't want to be touched.

"I'm sorry, Dad," Lance began, "I shouldn't have run away. I just didn't know where else to go. Mama's new boyfriend found my wigs and makeup and started calling me all these names. No one else was home, so I called Harry, and he said we could go here."

Bryan cringed, knowing his father would have reacted the same way. Bryan handed Lance last year's Christmas present, the book Drama. Lance held the book against his chest.

"Daddy, thanks," he said, flipping through the pages.

"It's okay, Lance. I know I haven't been the most supportive in the past. I thought I knew what was best for you. But I recently realized that it's not my place to make those decisions anymore. You're growing up, and while things like running away should be off-limits, wearing wigs and make up shouldn't be.

Can we start over?"

Lance's face lightened. "You really mean it? You'll let me dress up and come to my drag performances?"

Bryan felt his jaw reflexively twitch and tighten, then remembered how he wished his own parents would treat him and made a conscious effort to soften his face. "Yes," he said, smiling, "I'd love to see you perform." They embraced, and Bryan felt a newfound warmth in his heart for his son. He wasn't sure, but maybe this was what people meant when they used the term "unconditional love".

"We all would," Nadia interrupted. Bryan swiveled his head around to see Nadia flanked by Jerry and Stacey on each side. He had been so focused on his son that he hadn't heard the door open or shut.

Bryan beamed and hugged Nadia.

"You're the best," he whispered in her ear.

"You said you needed a village," she replied.

The mood of Covenant House quickly turned from somber to upbeat and social as Bryan profusely thanked everyone and slipped the blonde receptionist a cash donation.

"Daddy, this is not going away," Lance said as he and Bryan walked to Nadia's car, Nadia trailing behind her.

"Sometimes, we don't know how much we hurt those closest to us," Nadia said. "Your mom might not understand, but she loves you."

Bryan placed a hand on Lance's shoulder, and Lance didn't brush it off. "Just because her boyfriend said those things doesn't mean she feels that way," Bryan said. "And when she finds out, well...she might be . . . shocked. But she'll come around." He sighed. "No one is the perfect parent that we all hope to be when our babies are born, myself included. I'm sorry for not acknowledging how you want to express yourself. I love you the way you are. I was wrong to act the way I did before."

Lance nodded, sniffling.

"Daddy, I'm not going back to my mama's house."

"You don't have to, at least for tonight. But I do need to call your mother to let her know you're okay." Bryan excused himself to make the call, which ended with him leaving a voicemail.

"Your mama is relieved," Bryan said as he approached his village, who were all waiting in the parking lot. "I told her that you are staying with us."

"Okay," Lance said.

Bryan changed the subject. "You wouldn't know this, but Nadia is a transgender woman. I was trying to hide that from . . . everyone. Myself, included, when it didn't suit me."

"I knew that." Lance pointed a long skinny finger at Stacey. "So is she."

"It's always the kids who clock you first," Stacey said, shaking her head in disbelief.

Bryan gulped. "You knew she was trans?"

"We didn't," Joe said. "This is your girlfriend?"

Bryan smiled at Nadia. "Yes, she is."

"We saw you as a straight ally, but we had no idea you were part of the community," Steve said. "We're glad you're out of the closet."

"I am, too," Bryan said to Steve and Joe. Then he turned to address his son.

"Lance, I did not want to admit I was in love with a transgender woman. I believed there was something wrong with me, and I took it out on you. I'm sorry." Bryan hugged his son close. "Let's go get you boys fed."

41

The boys scarfed down two orders each of chicken nuggets. Lance wiped his mouth and looked beseechingly at Bryan. It was nearly ten thirty at night.

"These boys were hungry," Jerry said, looking at Stacey.

"I remember the feeling," Stacey replied.

Harry sat between his parents, looking up at them both. Joe stroked Steve's face lovingly.

"Daddy, there's something else." Bryan's face must have shown alarm because Lance quickly added, "I was practicing my routine for a junior drag competition when Mama's boyfriend came in my room." Bryan felt his jaw drop. Lance plowed on. He hadn't taken a breath since he had begun talking. "It's on Saturday."

Bryan almost spit out his cola. "Saturday, as in tomorrow?"

"Yes," Lance said, his expression halfway between resolute and hopeful. "We have to be there at two thirty tomorrow in the afternoon." Lance's chin dropped. "I'm not ready yet," he whispered.

Bryan glanced at Steve and Joe with a confused look.

"He was going to carpool with us," Joe said trepidly.

Bryan's heart fell into his stomach. His own son had felt so isolated from his parents that he had tried to find substitute parents. *I have so much to make up for,* Bryan thought as he patted his son's back. "We'll pull together and get it done. You're not going to miss your competition."

"Daddy, I only have one costume." From his backpack, Lance pulled out a wrinkled silver jumpsuit, a matching pair of silver go-go boots, an incomplete makeup kit, and a brown Afro wig. "But I have to lip-synch two songs."

It then hit Bryan why his son had been inseparable from his backpack. It held his true identity.

"We'll figure something out," he told his son.

"What do you know about drag?" Jerry asked.

"Nothing," Bryan admitted.

"Well lucky for you, I know a thing or two," Jerry said with a sassy wink. "And thankfully I've got my makeup bags in Stacey's car."

Bryan wanted to hug him, but he could tell Jerry was there for Lance, not him—not yet. "I didn't know you did drag," Bryan said admiringly.

"I'm more than just a pretty face," Jerry said, standing up. He struck a pose and pouted.

Bryan glanced at his watch. It was nearing 11. "Stacey, what are you, about a size two?"

She didn't shift her gaze from the young man she'd been eyeing at the restaurant. "Yeah, what about it?"

"We need one of your dresses for Lance," Jerry spelled out. "Stop staring at that guy and get with the program. And try not to bring something slutty for the boy to wear."

Steve chimed in, "We want to help, too."

"Okay, guys, come with us. Stacey and Jerry, we will see you at my place later tonight," Bryan instructed.

Bryan's space was an orderly mess. He had sold much of his artwork, which made the rooms appear smaller and shoddier. The only evidence of the paintings was slightly darker rectangles on the wall where they had once hung. Most of the clothes and other sundries that he was keeping were boxed up.

"This is your place?" Jerry asked, looking around. "Is this how VPs live?"

"In my defense, I'm in the process of moving," Bryan said. "Be grateful there's still furniture."

"Bryan, I will take it from here," Nadia said once they walked through the door. "Lance, let me see your outfit." She held the jumpsuit up to the light. "Did you design this? And you did the sewing?"

"Yes."

"The back seam looks like it was cut with a knife, but you did good."

"I ripped it running away from the house."

"Honey, don't worry about it. When I was your age, I taught myself to make my own clothes to look fabulous," Nadia said. "Let me take care of it."

"I'll get my sewing kit," Bryan said.

"Steve and Joe, please grab the iron from in there," Nadia said, pointing to a closet.

From behind the ironing table he was carrying, Steve said, "Neither of us knows how to iron."

Joe unrolled the cord from around the iron. "That's what cleaners are for."

"Oh, good lord," Jerry said. "What can you two do?"

"We can cook," they responded in unison.

"That's no help. We just ate," Bryan replied.

"Do you already have your routine?" Jerry asked Lance.

Lance broke out into a huge smile, scrolling through his phone and firing up the songs he'd chosen.

Bryan opened his sewing kit, a giant envelope made of quilted fabric.

"Your father has a sewing kit and he still thinks he's straight?" Jerry said, nudging Lance's shoulder.

Lance grinned.

"First thing," Bryan snapped. "Every good magician worth his salt knows how to sew."

Nadia and Lance spoke at the same time. "I didn't know you performed magic shows!"

Bryan addressed Lance. "I quit when your sister was born. Life became serious. Secondly"—he directed his words mainly to Jerry—"do you see this beautiful woman standing right here? I may be in a queer relationship, but I know I'm not gay. She's who I come home to every night. If she sees herself as a woman, think of how it makes her feel when you call me gay."

Nadia fanned herself. "Oh, Lordy, I love this man."

Jerry saluted. "Okay. I'll be honest. Some days, I don't understand the trans community. I never thought about it from a trans woman's perspective. I apologize. I guess I have some work to do myself."

Bryan walked past the kitchen to get more material, feeling like a major breakthrough had been made. Bryan laid out material for Lance, glad that he had saved a handful of fancy scarves.

Bryan was consumed with happiness by watching everyone do their part. This was his chosen family. He sent Sophia a kiss skyward.

"Are you sure you want to use these two songs?" Jerry asked Lance, shaking his head at the R-rated lyrics. "We need to go more family-friendly. There are a bunch of songs every diva should know."

"Put your hips into it," Jerry said, demonstrating. "You've got to own the audience, or they will own you. You gotta say to yourself, I'm the baddest bitch here."

Bryan took Joe and Steve aside. "Can you do me a favor?" He handed them some scissors, a plastic toy hoop, and a large piece of black velour material. He instructed them how to encase the hoop inside the velour material at the top.

Luckily, everyone else was so busy, no one asked what they were making or why.

Jerry grabbed Lance's shoulders and shook him slightly to rouse him. "You can rest later. Do you know anything about your competition?"

Lance pulled up YouTube. He clicked on a video of a teen queen named Origina'l de ArtWork.

Bryan whistled. "She's good."

"She's won the regional competition for the past two years," Lance said, "but she lost nationals, so maybe she has a weakness?"

Jerry high-fived Lance. "That's the spirit."

Ms. Origina'l de ArtWork was a bouncy petite fifteen-year-old from the Texas panhandle. She could dance, sing, and do the splits. Her costumes looked professionally commissioned, and her makeup was flawless. Most of all, her charisma and command of the stage gave her a preternatural It Factor.

"Daddy, I can't beat her," Lance said gloomily.

"Yes you can!" Harry chimed in.

Bryan hugged his son to his side. "This is show business, son. Keep working with Jerry. When I was performing magic shows, I had to stay with it until it was perfect." Bryan enjoyed giving this pep talk, though he had never imagined pumping up his son for a drag competition.

By the time two A.M. rolled around, Jerry felt Lance's performance was satisfactory and Lance had chosen a second ensemble from Stacey's provided wardrobe. The rag-tag group found themselves drifting off, and slept until eleven.

After Steve and Joe assembled a quick breakfast for the group, everyone rallied around Lance to help him get ready. Nadia teased up the Afro wig and pulled it down over Lance's head, tucking in his edges. Jerry glued on another row of false lashes and fluffed a brush full of glitter over the boy's brow. Jerry, Nadia, and Stacey leaned back to appreciate their handiwork.

"Wow . . . incredible." Bryan was startled by the vision of his child. Lance looked radiant and somehow more fully himself than Bryan had ever seen. Jerry unearthed a full-length mirror from a closet and positioned Lance in front of it. A dawning joy of his own fabulousness crept over the boy's face until he was grinning from ear to ear. Bryan quickly crossed the few feet between them and pressed Lance's head against his heart. Bryan felt the fractures from his own father's narrow judgment begin to heal, as if the warmth of his son's cheek had dove below Bryan's skin, had mended the fissures, and had softened the scars.

The tug of the metaphorical sutures threading towards wholeness almost hurt, but it was a good pain.

Nadia kissed Bryan on the forehead. "You know, he is such a good kid. And you're going to be a better father now."

"I have my second request now," Nadia said.

"What are you talking about?" Bryan asked.

"You asked what you could do to support your apology when we started dating again," she said.

"Oh, yea."

"I want you to ride on the cis-trans float with me at the PRIDE parade on Sunday," Nadia asked.

A big grin formed on Bryan's face. "I thought you said we were too busy?"

"We can pick out curtains and blinds for the bakery next weekend," she said. "Seeing you rally for Lance like this reminded me how important making time for each other is."

"It would be an honor to ride front and center on the cis-trans float with you," Bryan said. They started kissing.

"Oh, my. Look at you two queer love birds. I love this," Stacey said, snapping her fingers. "He's ready."

Bryan gave Lance a big squeeze and released him. "Let's go, everyone. It's almost showtime. We're running late." Bryan, Nadia, Lance, Stacey, and Jerry piled into Nadia's car. Joe, Steve, and Harry would meet them at the competition.

***

Due to construction, the freeway was a sea of idling cars, but Bryan did his best to keep the car moving. Jerry spread glue over Lance's eyebrows with a tiny spatula.

"You need to slow down," Jerry said, trying to position the brow piece, "or this boy is going to look like he's on crack by the time I'm finished."

"Ouch!"

Jerry clicked his tongue. "You young queens are such divas."

"Drive!" Bryan yelled at the car in front of him, honking the horn frantically. Bryan exited the freeway, turning left at the light. The club was about a mile away.

"I don't like to rush," Jerry sighed. "I need to blend, blend, blend."

Nadia's car started sputtering. A minute later, it stalled.

"Daddy, why are we stopping?"

"We're out of gas." Shit! He didn't look at Nadia. He was about to lose his composure and didn't want to glare at her. He knew that contempt killed relationships.

Nadia clicked her tongue. "Shit."

"What do we do now?" Lance wailed.

"We gotta run for it," Bryan said, getting out of the car and pulling Nadia and Lance along with him. "C'mon, we gotta go. Move your butts. Jerry can do the final touches there."

Stacey folded her arms and shook her head. "I can't run in these heels."

"Girl, get your narrow white ass out the car," Jerry pushed her out the door. They all ran along the sidewalk. Drivers honked. The car horns made Bryan stop to check that his chosen family was safe. He realized they didn't look like a traditional family is any sense of the word: a drag-queen teenager with an incomplete makeup job wearing a shiny silver jumpsuit, matching go-go boots and a stocking over his head; a lanky trans girlfriend, who was nearly a foot taller than the queer son; an effeminate man wearing a scarf, wide-brimmed purple hat, white silk shirt, tiger-print pants, and purple boots; and a petite trans woman with green streaks in her hair, a garment bag containing a se-quined minidress and black pumps for the queer son's second act slung over her shoulder, posing for men honking their horns.

"Stacey!" Bryan shouted.

"I'm only saying hello to my admirers," Stacey said, showing a little bit more thigh for a guy in a BMW.

They stopped short in front of the club to take in the regional junior drag competition written on the marquee, then busted through the door. The club was packed with young queens and their parents.

"What took you guys so long?" Joe asked, sitting with Steve and Harry at a small round table. Each of them was sipping a fruity drink in a tall curvy glass.

"I'll tell you later," Bryan replied, breathing heavily.

"I haven't run that hard since I played hide-and-go-seek with a male stripper in Vegas," Jerry said, fanning himself.

"Did he catch you?" Stacey asked.

Jerry winked. "I was breathing too hard for him to miss me."

Lance found the sign-up sheet and was about to write his name in the fourth spot when Bryan stopped him. "You always want to go last. Going last gives you a chance to see all your competition, and the judges will remember you first because you went last."

Jerry rushed to finish Lance's brows and lips after Lance signed up for the last spot. Just as he was powdering over everything so it would stay on under the hot stage lights, Origina'l de ArtWork strutted in with her well-groomed parents. This young queen was captivating and confident, and her parents walked with the same swagger. The father looked around with a look of mild amusement on his face, but the mother did not smile. She was battle-ready.

"I think I hear theme music," Jerry said, clutching his chest. "I honestly hear the theme song to Shaft."

"Oops, that's my phone," Stacey giggled.

Nadia rubbed Lance's back. "Don't look at her. Don't let them get in your head."

"She reminds me of my younger self," Stacey's voice was wistful. "I like her."

"Whose side are you on?" Jerry admonished.

"Will you two focus?" Bryan asked while motioning them to go sit down. "Son, you got this. I'm proud of you. Let's go kick some butt."

An announcer asked all contestants to line up. The club, converted from an old theatre, was packed with parents, families, young queers, and trans youth.

Nadia took Stacey's arm. "This is the future. Look at all these queer kids."

The lights went off, and the mistress of ceremonies walked out to center stage. After revving the crowd up, her voice turned serious. "First up, all the way from Lubbock. Put your hands together for Orgina'l de Artwork!"

Orgina'l de ArtWork was as impressive as expected, finishing with flourish after flourish until the finale of all finales: she jumped high, side-split her legs in the air, and landed gently, somehow in a perfect front split. Bryan bit his nails.

"Good Lord, this girl is good," Stacey said, accidentally clapping.

Jerry shoved her.

"Lance will be just fine," Bryan said, crossing his fingers.

There were nine more acts to go. Each contestant was spirited and often brilliant, but none had the wattage of Origina'l.

The mistress of ceremonies strutted onto the stage. "Our last performer is a new queen, and she has it all. Put your hands together for Lady Degas!"

"Lady Degas?" Jerry's eyes were wide. "I thought Lance was next."

Nadia smiled smugly. "That's him. I helped him with his stage name."

Bryan was too nervous to smile back. His leg bounced frantically until Nadia put her hand on his knee.

Lady Degas was a vision in a shiny silver jumpsuit and go-go boots. Her mahogany face was contoured into sharp planes, and she wore an Afro wig so high and large, it could have weighed as much as she did. Her lids were highlighted with silver eyeshadow under swooping dark brows and her lashes dripped with mascara. She cooed at the crowd, which roared in appreciation. Lady Degas's waist, accentuated by a tightly cinched belt and the jumpsuit's wide bell-bottoms, appeared girlishly tiny. She sparkled under the spotlight, from the rhinestone clips on top of her wig to her glittery shoes. Her eyes, dancing with excitement before the music even began, were the sparkliest part of her entire ensemble.

The first beats of the song rang out over the stage. Lady Degas wobbled at first, but she got herself together and finished strong. When the first song ended, Lady Degas leaned into the velour curtain and bent down to grab the curtain by its hoop part. The audience was silent and stone-still. Lady Degas straightened and pulled the curtain over her head in one motion. It took longer than anticipated, and there was more rustling than Bryan had hoped for, but soon enough, the curtain dropped, and Lady Degas was revealed once more, wearing the emerald-green party dress and a blond wig that fell past her shoulders.

The audience erupted, clapping and calling out, "Brava!"

Bryan reached for Nadia's hand. "Damn, that's my boy. That's what I'm talking about!" he shouted, tears drenching his cheeks.

Lady Degas finished, sliding on pantyhose-covered knees to the edge of the stage. Falling backward, shoulders to the floor, she spread her arms as wide as possible. The music stopped.

Jerry jumped to his feet, stomping up and down, hugging Stacey. Bryan fell into Nadia's shoulder, too caught up to show his face, while she rubbed his back. The entire audience rose to a standing ovation. Lady Degas sauntered off the stage like a seasoned entertainer.

The judges asked all the queens to line up onstage. The emcee for the night named Origina'l de Artwork as the first runner-up. Lady Degas held hands with another contestant, looking out at her family, bouncing a little on her tiptoes.

The emcee told everyone how special they were. "I am so inspired by the courage of such young people to be themselves," she said. "And without further ado, the winner of tonight's competition is . . . Lady Degas!"

Lady Degas dropped to her knees.

"He did it!" Bryan exclaimed, turning to Nadia. "He did it!" They jumped around like contestants chosen to play The Price Is Right. Nadia wiped the tears from Bryan's face.

Everybody ran backstage to congratulate Lance. Origina'l de Artwork's parents came over to shake Lance's hand, asking where he learned to do the clothes-changing trick.

Lance snaked his arms around Bryan's waist. "My dad taught me."

"Mr. Hicks, you've got a real star there," Origina'l de Artwork's mother said, shaking Bryan's hand and beaming at both kids.

"Son, even if you never became a famous drag queen like Alaska or RuPaul, I will be proud of you and love you. Even if you only become an engineer or doctor." Father and son shared a giggle. Bryan looked directly into Lance's chocolate brown eyes. "Today is fun, full of laughter and triumph, but believe me when I say that I will be here even on the sad days, the angry or lonely or stormy days. No matter what." Bryan hugged his son tightly. He realized he wasn't just hugging Lance, but his own inner child. *He'll be okay, because I'm okay*, Bryan thought.

***

They took their party to the Pride celebration that was still happening in the streets. He knew the pride parade had started at 4:30 and he was glad he was able to catch the tail end of it now that Lance's competition was over.

Look at all these people, he thought as he weaved his way through the crowd.

Lance held his father's hand, leading him deeper into the community that he was very much a part of already.

Bryan felt his heart soar alongside the banners, its beats harmonizing with the chants and songs belted out by people of every color and shape. Their message was, "love is in every incarnation that exists." Nadia pointed out the floats rumbling down the avenues, each more joyful, silly, winking, and baroque than the decorated platforms preceding it.

Since day one, Bryan had questioned what letter in the LGBTQIA+ lexicon he represented. Standing there, Bryan looked around, realizing he was queer to the LGBTQIA+ community, or maybe he was just queer+ in his own way. If nothing else, he was simply happy.

Before the rest of them knew what she was doing, Stacey had gotten a leg up on a half–pirate ship, half–Capitol Building. The float was replete with people of every persuasion wearing little else than white sailor hot pants and tricorn hats. Hanging from makeshift masts, a banner proclaimed the name hamil-femme, while streamers covered with old-timey writing fluttered behind it. In a flash, Stacey nabbed a hat off the head of a sailor and stripped down to her skivvies. She waved and blew kisses to them as she passed.

Jerry caught a fistful of colorful bead necklaces and draped one over Lance, another over himself, and a bunch over Bryan and Nadia, linking them together. They kissed on the mouth before Nadia unshackled them.

As Nadia broke away from the kiss, she waved to friends on a nearby float. "C'mon," Nadia said, making her way to the front and leading Bryan by the hand. The float banner read: Cis-Trans Love is Love.

Jerry put his hand on Bryan's shoulder and squeezed. "You're okay, go! I can keep an eye on Lance," he said, tears glinting in his eyes. Bryan embraced him. "Thank you."

He turned to Lance, grabbing him and holding him tight. "I'm going to go with Nadia okay. You're with Uncle Jerry and the rest of our family," Bryan said, looking around, "I love you." The police let Bryan cross the crowd line with Nadia and they got on the float. Bryan looked out over the crowd and started dancing on the float. Nadia was standing behind him and grabbed him from behind. He turned around to face her and looked up into her emerald eyes that were glistening. *Is she crying tears of joy?* Bryan wondered briefly. The soft smile on her face told him that they were exactly where they were supposed to be and they started kissing passionately on the float in front of the television cameras. He hoped Mama and Rebecca saw them on television. They deserved to see that he was truly happy. The crowd started yelling and screaming as the five other cis-trans couples on the float started kissing too. Bryan held Nadia as he looked at the other couples on the float. He finally had a community and a found family who accepted him. They waved back to the crowd. "I just thought of something," Bryan yelled into Nadia's ear.

"What?"

"You know they probably are towing our car right now," he yelled.

"Let them have it. Who cares?" she said. They started kissing again.

THE END

Afterword

Cakewalk

The cakewalk was originally a nineteenth-century dance, invented by African Americans in the antebellum South. It was intended to satirize the stiff ballroom promenades of white plantation owners, who favored the rigidly formal dances of European high society. Cakewalking slaves lampooned these stuffy moves by overaccentuating their high kicks, bows, and imaginary act of doffing hats, mixing the cartoonish gestures with traditional African steps. Likely unaware of the dance's derisive roots, the whites often invited their slaves to participate in Sunday contests to determine which dancers were most elegant and inventive. The winners would receive cake slices, a prize which gave birth to the dance's eponymous name.

After emancipation, the contest tradition continued in Black communities. The *Oxford English Dictionary* dates the widespread adoption of *cakewalk* to the late 1870s. It was around this time that the cakewalk came to mean "easy"—not because the dance was particularly simple to do but because of its languid pace and association with weekend leisure.

Acknowledgements

Where do I begin?

I want to start with my friends: Sophia, Tomas, Dana, Greg, Adrian, Michael Piana, Meg Booth, and Christina Lyons all of whom were surprised that I'd taken on this creative endeavor but never killed my dream. Thank you.

A special thanks to the trans women—Lucy, Jordan, and Jesse—in my life who have been so inspirational to me with their courage, strength, and never-give-up attitude. This novel is my attempt to say thank you to the LGBTQIA+ community—more specifically, the trans community—for being who you are. This novel hopefully gives trans amorous cisgender men the courage to openly love and support the transgender women in their lives in the way they want and deserve to be loved.

I must acknowledge the books and media that broadened my understanding of the transgender experience: ***Real Queer America*** by Samantha Allen, ***The Argonauts*** by Maggie Nelson, genderbread.org, and the Netflix original documentary ***Disclosure.***

I want to thank my editor, Rachelle McKeown. Rachelle's impact is immeasurable as she challenged me to dig deeper in this second edition to find my true voice. I could not have reached this level without her help.

And thank you to Christina, the most wonderful wife, partner, and friend in the world. I never could have gotten this story out into the world without your support.

***

If *Cake Walk* moved you—if it made you pause, reflect, or see yourself or someone else more clearly—I invite you to take one small step that makes a big difference.

Leave a review.

Your words don't have to be long or perfect. Just honest. Just real.

Reviews help this story reach readers who may be struggling with identity, love, or the courage to live authentically. They help amplify voices and experiences that are too often unseen—especially stories centered on queer love, self-discovery, and what it means to belong.

If this book stayed with you, let someone else know why.

Leave your review on Amazon, Goodreads, or wherever you found *Cake Walk*—and help ring the bell for stories that matter. **https://mybook.to/5y9F6**

About the author

Douglas Bell is a Black fiction author, former magician, and LGBTQ+ ally based in Houston, Texas. With a unique blend of lived experience, meditation, and Buddhist practice, Bell's writing seeks to uplift marginalized voices and inspire authenticity, resilience, and social justice. His work, including the *Cake Walk* series, explores the concept of living authentically by challenging society's white/masculine/cisgender/heteronormative labels. Bell believes that through meditation and self-reflection, individuals can discover their true selves, free from societal expectations and attachments.

Informed by Buddhist teachings, Bell's storytelling encourages readers to embrace the idea that rejection stems from our attachment to false beliefs, labels, and societal delusions. He posits that when we let go of the need to define ourselves as either good or bad, we open ourselves to patience, understanding, and the resilience needed to navigate life's complexities. Bell's work invites readers to question whether they can transcend these labels and simply *be*, offering a path toward deeper self-awareness and peace in an often challenging world.

He and his wife, Christina, are empty nesters living in Texas, where Bell continues to write stories that inspire transformation and illuminate the power of being true to oneself.

"Consider signing up for my newsletter at the bottom of my website to receive updates on my latest projects, YouTube conversations, and a touch of spiritual wisdom to carry with you." https://www.douglasbellbooks.com/

Douglas Bell Website

Love Cake Chapter 28

December 12, 2019

Cold Houston weather: the high was in the mid-fifties, which was coat-wearing weather for native Houstonians like Bryan, but shorts-wearing weather for everybody else. He had received another late notice for Lindsey's fall bursar bill. She still had not called Bryan to say when she was coming home. The holidays were here, and Bryan decided not to worry about Lindsey. He rushed inside the bakery excited about the surprise for tonight's cis-trans couples holiday program tonight. Bryan had planned an unforgettable night. Everybody came out. The bakery was decorated with handmade ornaments and holiday music played as everybody enjoyed fruit punch flavored with sprite. Bryan watched Stacey secretly pouring vodka into her punch. He approached her and Posh. Posh pulled Bryan to the side. Bryan just knew he was in trouble.

"Hey, you know. You're okay in my book," Posh said.

Bryan smiled. "Thank you." Bryan put his open arms out looking for a hug. He hugged Posh, looking over her shoulder at Stacey. Stacey gave a wink and smiled back.

Cody arrived optimistic and at peace. She had finally updated all her vital records—driver's license, birth certificate, passport, and bank accounts—with not just her name but also her gender. Fortunately, she had found a lawyer willing to do pro bono work to help her navigate this unfair system. She held up her new library card as if it were a trophy inscribed with her full name: Cody Russell.

Bryan started arranging the chairs so that there was a middle aisle, and he moved the tables to the storage area. He erected a portable black velvet curtain from his magic show. He asked everybody to sit and darted away to change into his costume. Hiding behind the curtain he started the music: the *Soul Train* theme song.

Bryan stepped out wearing a 1970s vintage baby blue tuxedo, a ruffled tuxedo shirt, and a giant afro wig; he looked like Don Cornelius from *Soul Train*. The group burst into a loud roar upon seeing him. He lowered the music.

He brought a thin fake microphone close to his mouth, lowering his voice to let his natural Black swagger take them back in time. "Welcome to the Soul Train. This is the hippest trip in Houston running across the tracks of your mind. I'm your host, Don Cornelius." Bryan gave a quick little shimmy with his hips to get the crowd excited. "The excitement begins with the coolest queen you've ever seen. Put your hands together for Lady Degas," Bryan said, projecting every bit of Don Cornelius coolness.

He stepped to the side as the next track started, and Lance, in drag as Lady Degas, stepped out wearing a red satin gown, a feathered red robe, and six-inch platform pumps. As he lip-synced in a sultry voice to "Ain't No Mountain High Enough," the audience swayed from side to side, clapping in rhythm. Lauren stood up to sing the final chorus with Lady Degas. The song ended and Lady Degas took her bow. Lady Degas strutted behind the velvet curtain.

"I needed that," Lauren said, sitting back down. "That felt good."

Bryan again stepped forward, smiling at Jerry. Bryan continued his impersonation, entertaining the small audience with a bit of comedy while the queens prepared near the bathrooms. When he got the cue from Lance, Bryan said, "We ain't done yet. Let the groove hit you in the ass and funk split you from the rooter to the tooter. Put your hands together for Lady Degas and the Rhythm Nation!"

Five queens marched out dressed alike in all-black body suits, black ball caps, black combat boots, and long ponytails. The music started. Bryan was impressed at how the queens had learned the entire Janet Jackson "Rhythm Nation" routine in only a few days. Each queen did a solo routine with Lady Degas, voguing ballroom style and finishing with an earth-shattering death drop. The audience rose to their feet, and the queens took their bow.

Bryan asked everyone to move their chairs to the wall. He changed the music to Sister Sledge's "We Are Family." Everyone formed a soul train line. Bryan grabbed Jerry by the hand, pulling him to the front of the curtain.

"This is Soul Train," he belted out extending the "o" and the "a", he continued, "And we always end the night with the soul train line," Bryan belted out. Bryan stepped forward first, dropping to the floor and popping back up, and then he did the Rerun dance. He looked back at Nadia and winked, giving her a *come join me* look.

Nadia looked lost but she quickly gathered her bearings, put on her sunglasses, strutted out with a serious look, and started waving her arms widely in front of her body. Then she flung her long right leg out, rotated her shoulders, and put the tip of her index finger first on her tongue and then on the side of her butt. She and Bryan finished the line together.

Jerry pulled the brim down on his large yellow hat, hiding his face, and he took that cue to start vogueing: duck walking, dipping, cat walking, spinning, and executing his own slower, mature death drop. Then he popped back up like a young man.

In five-inch high heels, Cody did a cartwheel at Jerry's side. Through some mental telepathy, Jerry and Cody started dancing as if their moves were choreographed. Two lines naturally formed, giving the next dancers their chance to go.

Stacey and Posh started with a true retro disco '70s vibe, really throwing their bodies around. They both hopped two hops forward at the same time; they moved to the right and then the left. Stacey spun around several times as Posh shimmied forward on her left leg while holding up her right leg parallel to the floor with her right hand. As they threw their bodies down the soul train line, Stacey jumped into Posh's arms, and they exited with Posh carrying Stacey away.

Mark started doing the robot, and Amber started twerking. Lauren started spinning, doing the sprinkler dance, while her wife, Violet, tried to do a split. They had to help Violet's old self get up. The queens flowed down the soul train line one by one. Bryan and Nadia swayed back and forth together, clapping and smiling. Love was abundant. There was a loud noise, a crashing sound like glass breaking. Everybody stopped, and Bryan cut the music immediately. By the window, he saw a brick lying on the sidewalk. A second brick hit the glass, and Bryan jumped in front of Nadia.

"I'm scared," Nadia said in a high-pitched voice.

Bryan ran outside, where he saw a familiar face. Trevor, the manager who had quit earlier, was running away. He picked up the brick; he read a transphobic slur written on it. He looked at the cracked window and he picked up the second brick: another slur. He walked back inside, locked the door, and pulled off his afro wig. Everybody was shaken. Bryan held Nadia as she laid her head on his shoulder and cried.

"It's not supposed to be like this," Nadia agonized.

Bryan pulled back and looked into her eyes. "I'll protect you, I promise," he said. He grabbed Lance and huddled his family together. Then he made sure everyone got to their cars safely. He turned on the alarm after the others went home.

Bryan sighed deeply at the amount of hate required to throw such a heavy brick. He put the bricks into the trunk of his car. He questioned his decision to not install security cameras covering the front. He decided against calling the police because when the state got involved, minority communities always somehow ended up on the losing end.

At home, Nadia stayed revved up all night. She couldn't sleep. Bryan stayed awake, too, looking out his bedroom window for this lone wolf to show up at their home. Tonight's attack validated Bryan's feelings that the broader society would not care because white male society always condemned this behavior as individualistic, not a unified threat. He was starting to care less about society's doxa that Black and Brown men's natural tendencies for villainous things—rob, threaten, and destroy property—and more about protecting his family from the patriots who strayed called lone wolves.

*Love Cake: A Nov-
el, 2nd Edition*